Annie Randall White

The Blue and the Gray

Or, the Civil War as seen by a boy. A story of patriotism and adventure in our war

for the Union

Annie Randall White

The Blue and the Gray
Or, the Civil War as seen by a boy. A story of patriotism and adventure in our war for the Union

ISBN/EAN: 9783337308964

Printed in Europe, USA, Canada, Australia, Japan

Cover: Foto ©Andreas Hilbeck / pixelio.de

More available books at **www.hansebooks.com**

THE BLUE AND THE GRAY

OR,

THE CIVIL WAR

AS SEEN BY A BOY

A Story of Patriotism and Adventure in Our War for the Union

" We live for freedom; let us clasp each other by the hand;
In love and unity abide, a firm, unbroken band;
We cannot live divided—the Union is secure!
God grant that while men live and love, this nation may endure."
                                                    —DR. FRED A. PALMER.

BY

A. R. WHITE

ILLUSTRATED WITH
OVER 150 WAR PHOTOGRAPHS AND ORIGINAL DRAWINGS

TO THE
SONS AND
THE DAUGH-
TERS OF THE VETER-
ANS OF THE CIVIL WAR;
TO THOSE WHO FOUGHT ITS
BATTLES AND LIVED TO INSTIL ITS
LESSONS OF PATRIOTISM IN THE HEARTS
OF THEIR CHILDREN; TO THOSE OF ALL CLIMES
WHO LOVE LIBERTY AND THE NOBLE LAND WHERE
FREEDOM HAD HER BIRTH; TO THE MEMORY OF
THE HEROES OF NORTH AND SOUTH WHO FELL
IN BATTLE; TO ONE UNITED COUNTRY,
BOTH NORTH AND SOUTH, FOREVER ONE
IN ALL NOBLE AND LOFTY PUR-
POSES AND AIMS; TO THE
HOMES OF AMERICA; THIS
BOOK IS LOVINGLY
DEDICATED BY
YOURS SIN-
CERELY

THE AUTHOR.

WILLIAM H. SEWARD,
Secretary of State.

SIMON P. CHASE,
Secretary of Treasury.

EDWIN M. STANTON,
Secretary of War.

GIDEON WELLES,
Secretary of Navy.

PRESIDENT LINCOLN AND HIS CABINET.

EDWARD BATES,
Attorney-General.

CALEB B. SMITH,
Secretary of Interior.

MONTGOMERY BLAIR,
Postmaster-General.

JUDAH P. BENJAMIN,
Attorney-General, War, State.

ROBERT TOOMBS,
Secretary of State.

CHRISTOPHER G. MEMMINGER,
Secretary of Treasury.

JEFFERSON DAVIS AND HIS CABINET.

LEROY P. WALKER,
Secretary of War.

STEPHEN R. MALLORY,
Secretary of the Navy.

JOHN H. REAGAN,
Postmaster-General.

PREFACE.

HE scenes of the war, related by a boy who followed the flag from the beginning to the end of the war, must carry with them a sense of accuracy, for they are the recollections of actual service. Those books which have been written upon the war have, with very few exceptions, been penned from the standpoint of mature opinions and experiences. In this work the views and struggles of a boy who went into the army, from an honest desire to do right, are portrayed. To fight was abhorrent to his nature, but there was a call for men who were willing to defend the institutions of his beloved land. And that defense was only possible through bloodshed and conflict. Tenderly instructed by a loving and gentle mother, whose early home was in the South, it was almost a wrenching of her cherished opinions, to give him up to fight against her kindred. But her boy did not enter the contest with a thought of conquering his fellow-beings, but as a duty which, though painful, must be performed. How that dear mother gave him to his country, how he marched, and fought, and endured hardships, are here set forth in the colors of truth, for it is a true story.

And that the boys and girls of to-day and their fathers and mothers may follow the varying fortunes of the boy of our story, thus ushered into the conflict, with pleasure and profit, is the heartfelt hope of

THE AUTHOR.

TABLE OF CONTENTS.

PART I.

THE CIVIL WAR.

	PAGE		PAGE
A Biography—General Robert E. Lee	294	Old Bill Dies	138
A Biography—Robert Anderson	291	Ordered to Washington	38
A Bootblack of Tennessee	300	Ralph at Headquarters	63
After the Battle	297	Ralph at Home	169
An Incident of the War	269	Ralph Does Picket Duty	58
Another Battle	75	Ralph is Sent Home	156
A Reminiscence	265	Ralph Re-enlists	179
A War Story	278	Ralph's First Battle	49
Camp Fun	116	South Mountain	122
Confederate Cemeteries	305	The Army in Winter Quarters	103
Crossing the River	195	The Beginning of War	17
Fair Oaks	111	The Disaster at Ball's Bluff	90
Fredericksburg	144	The Proclamation	205
His Northern Brother	264	The Surrender	234
More Fighting	130	Two Voices	263

PART II.

EVENTS FROM THE CLOSE OF THE CIVIL WAR DOWN TO OUR WAR WITH SPAIN.

	PAGE		PAGE
A Biography—James Abram Garfield	313	Our Noble, Heroic and Self-Sacrificing Women—Emory A. Storrs	363
A Biography—Ulysses S. Grant	308	Presidential Campaign of 1896	355
Alaska	320	The Atlantic Cable	318
Antietam	364	The Johnstown Flood	331
Battle of Wounded Knee Creek	349	The Swords of Grant and Lee	365
Centennial Exposition	323	The Telephone and Phonograph	331
Chicago Fire	327	The Union Soldier—Robert G. Ingersoll	361
Edison, the Genius of the Age	324	The World's Columbian Exposition	352
George A. Custer	344	Under Both Flags	307
Home Sweet Home—Frances E. Willard	359	War and Peace—The Rev. O. H. Tiffany, D. D.	360
Indian Wars	336		

OUR WAR WITH SPAIN.

	PAGE		PAGE
Annexation of Hawaii	392	Dewey's Victory at Manila	376
Biography—Acting Rear-Admiral Sampson	406	Hobson Made Famous	384
		Puerto Rico	394
Biography—Admiral George Dewey	402	Roosevelt's Rough Riders	382
		Surrender of Manila	390
Biography—General Fitzhugh Lee	398	Surrender of Santiago	387
		The First Gun Fired	368
Destruction of Cervera's Fleet	387	The Maine Disaster	367

LIST OF ILLUSTRATIONS.

PAGE

Abraham Lincoln and His Cabinet...................... 8
A Business Street in Manila.... 389
A Cuban Home................ 371
Allan Pinkerton and Secret Service Officers.................. 73
An Alexandria Anti-bellum Relic. 69
Appomattox Court House...... 227
Artillery Going to the Front..... 126
Asking for Furlough........... 95
A Southern Mansion........... 86
A Stolen Child................ 338
A Sugar Factory in Manila..... 377
Attack on Fredericksburg...... 145
Attack on the Mail........... 337
A Typical Colored Boy........ 80
Battle of Bull Run...........50, 51
Battle of Chancellorsville....... 298
Battle of Malvern Hill—Lee's Attack 76
Battle of Phillipi.............. 46
Battle of Shiloh.............. 194
Bearing Dispatches........... 106
Burning of Chicago........... 328
Burnside Bridge.............. 135
Burying Old Bill.............. 142
Camp Douglas................ 159
Camp Fire Songs.............. 117
Camp Life—In the Kitchen..... 71
Camp Life on Monday........ 77
Camp of the Army of the Potomac...................... 104
Capitol at Richmond.......... 65
Captain John L. Worden Commanding the Monitor......... 175
Capture of a White Child....... 340
Caring for the Dead........... 55
Charge of a Confederate Cavalry at Trevalian Station, Va..... 221
Colonel John S. Mosby and Group of His Raiders.............. 211
Confederate Soldiers' Monument —Richmond, Va........... 259
Crossing Big Black River...... 191
Custer's Last Charge......... 347

PAGE

Death of Sitting Bull.......... 343
Decoration Day—Gettysburg... 262
Destruction of Cervera's Fleet.. 385
Devil's Den................... 208
Dewey's Victorious Battle...... 375
Diamond Joe and Aunt Judah When Young............... 82
"Do Any of You Know Peter Hall?"...................... 123
Drinking from the Same Canteen. 245
Earthquake at Charleston...... 334
Episcopal Church at Alexandria, Va...................... 88
Fairfax Court House........... 27
Fall of General James B. McPherson near Atlanta........ 215
Federal Gunboat.............. 164
Foraging..................... 72
Foraging..................... 197
Fort Donelson................ 161
Fortress Monroe.............. 22
Fort Sumter.................. 19
Franklin Buchanan Commanding the Merrimac.............. 172
Fremont's Body Guard........ 101
Fun in Camp................. 119
Garfield Lying in State........ 314
Garfield's Struggle with Death.. 316
General Grant's Birthplace..... 309
General Hancock and Friends.. 153
General Lee on His Favorite Horse...................... 295
General Longstreet Wounded by His Own Men.............. 213
General Meade's Headquarters.. 208
General Miles................. 393
Gettysburg Cemetery Gate..... 212
Grant's Tomb—New York...... 258
Grant Breaking a Horse........ 311
Grant Plowing at the Age of 11. 310
Hailing the Troops............ 64
Harper's Ferry............... 40
Horticultural Hall, Philadelphia. 323
House Where Lee Surrendered.. 242
Indian Chief................. 349

xii

PAGE

Indian Dance.................. 339
Indian Schools of To-day....... 341
Indian Scout.................. 350
Interior of Hospital............ 249
In Winter Quarters............ 105
Jefferson Davis and His Cabinet. 10
Joe Hiding in the Woods....... 83
John Brown's Capture......... 42
Location of the Union Troops—
  Henry House............... 53
Making a Military Road Through
  a Swamp.................. 198
Map—Battlefields of the Great
  Civil War................. 147
Map—Loyal and Seceding States. 52
Map—Showing the Seat of War
  from Harper's Ferry to Suf-
  folk, Va.................. 132
Map—The Shenandoah Valley.. 121
McLean House............... 232
National Cemetery at Richmond,
  Va........................ 217
Negro Village in Georgia....... 36
Off for the War.............. 18
Old Aunt Judah.............. 81
Old City Hall—New Orleans.... 113
On Board the Hartford—Battle
  of Mobile Bay.............. 168
On the March................ 39
Picket Off Duty Forever........ 59
Proposed Monument to Jefferson
  Davis..................... 260
Portrait—Alexander H. Stephens 24
Portrait—Abraham Lincoln..... 236
Portrait—Admiral Cervera..... 381
Portrait—Benjamin F. Butler... 43
Portrait—Brigadier-General Neal
  Dow...................... 222
Portrait—Buffalo Bill, a Foe of
  the Indians................ 342
Portrait—Belle Boyd.......... 257
Portrait—Charles A. Dana..... 133
Portrait—Captain Charles Wilke 203
Portrait—Capt. Raphael Semmes 218
Portrait—Commander David D.
  Porter.................... 186
Portrait—Christopher Carson... 351
Portrait—Colonel Charles W. Le
  Gendre................... 214

PAGE

Portrait—Florence Nightingale.. 255
Portrait—Frances Willard...... 358
Portrait—General Ambrose E.
  Burnside.................. 125
Portrait—General Custer....... 218
Portrait—General George B. Mc-
  Clellan................... 47
Portrait—General George E.
  Meade.................... 151
Portrait—General Grant....... 163
Portrait—General Grant....... 231
Portrait—General Hooker...... 154
Portrait—General John A. Dix.. 25
Portrait—General James Long-
  street, C. S. A.............. 62
Portrait—General Joseph E.
  Johnston.................. 91
Portrait—General John C. Fre-
  mont..................... 100
Portrait—General John A. Logan 190
Portrait—General James B. Mc-
  Pherson.................. 196
Portrait—James Abram Garfield. 315
Portrait—General Lee......... 399
Portrait—General Lew Wallace. 127
Portrait—General Oliver O.
  Howard................... 220
Portrait—General P. T. G. Beau-
  regard.................... 45
Portrait—General Phil. Kearney. 139
Portrait—General Pickett...... 209
Portrait—General Rosecrans.... 136
Portrait—General Stonewall
  Jackson................... 182
Portrait—General Winfield Scott 30
Portrait—General Winfield Han-
  cock..................... 152
Portrait—General William Te-
  cumseh Sherman........... 189
Portrait—General Wade Hamp-
  ton...................... 205
Portrait—General Robert Ander-
  son...................... 292
Portrait—Harriet B. Stowe..... 206
Portrait—Henry Ward Beecher. 21
Portrait—Hobson............. 383
Portrait—Honorable Charles
  Sumner................... 87
Portrait—Horace Greeley...... 204

PAGE

Portrait—James Murray Mason.   20
Portrait—John Slidell.........   20
Portrait—John Brown.........   41
Portrait—Jennie Wade........ 209
Portraits (from War Photo-
    graphs)—John M. Morgan and
    Wife...................... 216
Portrait—John A. Winslow..... 219
Portrait—John B. Gordon.... .. 229
Portrait—Jefferson Davis...... 230
Portrait—John Wilkes Booth... 237
Portrait—Lee's Surrender...... 239
Portrait—General Montgomery
    Meigs.....................   26
Portrait—Major-General Philip
    H. Sheridan............... 226
Portrait—Miss Nellie M. Taylor. 251
Portrait—Miss Hattie A. Dana.. 252
Portrait—Mrs. Mary D. Wade.. 252
Portrait—Miss Clara Barton.... 253
Portrait—Major-General Fitz-
    hugh Lee, C. S. A. (From a
    War Photo.)...............   94
Portrait—Miss Louisa M. Alcott. 256
Portrait—Mrs. Mary Livermore. 254
Portrait—Miss Margaret Breck-
    enridge.................... 256
Portrait—Robert E. Lee.......   78
Portrait—Rear Admiral David G.
    Farragut................... 186
Portrait—Thomas A. Edison.... 325
Portrait—Walter Q. Gresham.. 223
Portrait—William H. Seward... 320
Portrait—William McKinley.... 356
Portrait—William J. Bryan..... 356
Pickets Examining Passes...... 175

PAGE

Prayer in Stonewall Jackson's
    Camp...................... 183
Prayer at the Funeral of the
    Maine's Victims............ 369
Punishment in the Army....... 207
Ralph and the Officer..........   29
Ralph's Good-Bye.............   32
Recruiting Office, New York City
    Hall Park.................. 181
Rejoicing.....................   66
Review of Soldiers—Washington 241
Ruins of the House............   85
Sharp Shooters................ 107
Sheridan Reconnoitering at Five
    Forks...................... 224
Siege Gun.....................   20
Soldiers Near Santiago......... 395
The Art Palace, World's Fair... 353
The Battle of Atlanta, Ga......   97
Stand of Flags................. 170
The Death of Ellsworth........   43
The Frigate Cumberland Rammed
    by the Merrimac............ 173
The Sister's Farewell.......... 277
Thomas A. Edison and His Talk-
    ing Machine................ 326
The Soldier's Farewell......... 180
Troops Going to Manila........ 373
Uncle Ned.................... 149
United States Military Wagon..   35
Warning the Inhabitants....... 332
Wesley Merritt and His Staff... 199
West Point.................... 293
What Caused the War--The Ne-
    gro and Cotton.............   57
Wounding of General Stonewall
    Jackson.................... 178

INTRODUCTION.

OOKS without number have been written upon the Civil War. There will probably be many more, for it is a fruitful theme. Many of them are faithful and accurate presentations of the great deeds done in that war. But whether large or small, they are all imbued with a desire to perpetuate that love of our country which should become one of the absorbing passions of the soul. It is a truth worth remembering—that the man who is a traitor to his country will be a traitor to all the relations of life.

Our land, young as it is, has received an awful baptism of fire and blood. It sprang into being amid the anguish of the Revolution, and before it had achieved a century of freedom, it was plunged into one of the saddest conflicts which ever desolated a nation—the conflict between brothers, speaking the same tongue, living under the same government, and enjoying the same great privileges. But from that terrible ordeal it has emerged, and we are once more one in aim and purpose, and have taken our stand among the proudest nations of the earth, their equal in intelligent achievements, religion and progress.

The little book we offer our young readers is the simple story, told in plain language, of a boy who was really in the army—one who left a pleasant home, as did thousands of others, a mere lad, loving his native land, knowing her need of strong hands and willing hearts to defend her. His purpose was noble, his mind fresh and ready for impressions; the scenes of those days are as ineffaceable as though written on marble, and not even the corroding touch of time can eat them away. So the present volume has been penned, that the boys and girls who read its pages may know of the hardships and self-sacrifice of the boys of those days—how cheerfully they enlisted to uphold the "starry flag," whose folds shall ever "float o'er the land of the free, and the home of the brave."

There are other lessons to be taught, as well as that of courage alone; the lessons of patriotism, of sacrifice, of respect for a government that offers to all its protection so long as they obey its just and equitable laws. No one doubts the courage of our boys, but they must remember that there is a higher quality than mere bravery—regard for human life, that it be not destroyed wantonly, a respect for others' rights and opinions, a readiness to submit to discipline, a willingness to yield up life when honor and duty demand it. All these thoughts were impressed upon the boy of our story, and made him a grander man for their lessons, when the pursuits of peace claimed him.

To the boys and girls whose fathers and friends fought that a great principle should live, to those whose dear ones fell in battle, or died of wounds, to all who read this true history of one boy's life in the army, we send forth this picture, the type of a true soldier, who did not love war for its noise and glitter, but who conscientiously fought the battles of his country because he revered her beneficent institutions. It was there that he was taught what true freedom meant, and through all his trials, his privations, he kept his faith in God and humanity undimmed.

Such was our boy, and of such material heroes are made.

THE PUBLISHERS

THE CIVIL WAR

AS SEEN BY A BOY.

CHAPTER I.

THE BEGINNING OF WAR.

THE early spring days of 1861 were dreams of beauty. The skies smiled blandly upon the earth, and every heart was glad that the long winter was over, and the charms of outdoor life could be enjoyed once more. Surely nature had done her part in making men happy.

A spirit of unrest and uncertainty, however, brooded in the air. The long conflict between opposing ideas, which had waged so long and bitterly in politics and churches, and through the columns of the press, had come to a focus, and dread murmurs were abroad, of an impending war, and its attendant horrors. Men looked in each other's faces, and asked, with sad forebodings—"What is coming next?"

The South made ample preparations to seize two South Carolina forts, Moultrie and Sumter, as early as December, 1860.

SEIZING THE FORTS. Lieutenant-Colonel Gardner was the commander of Fort Moultrie, and, loyal to the government, he sent to Washington asking for reinforcements to help him hold that fort. This request offended the Southern members of Congress, who construed it into an insult, and demanded his removal. This demand was acceded to by Secretary of War Floyd, and Major Robert Anderson of Kentucky was appointed to supersede Colonel Gardner.

2   17

Major Anderson, faithful to the trust reposed in him by the government, soon decided that Fort Moultrie could not be held against a vigorous assault, and he moved his garrison secretly to Sumter, a fortress across the harbor. This fort could not be approached by land, and, consequently, from this fact, was deemed more secure against any opposing force. The undertaking was a dangerous one. The harbor was full of guard boats, vigilant and watchful, and only their supposition that the little rowboats containing Major Anderson and his men were laborers going to the other fort to work on it, prevented their detection and arrest.

OFF FOR THE WAR.

Moultrie's guns had been trained to protect this transfer in case the Major's intention was discovered, and the fort, whose defense rendered the gallant Anderson immortal, was occupied by his troops at only twenty minutes' notice! We think that was the quickest "moving time" on record.

A siege gun which was turned upon Fort Sumter is shown on page 20. Its carriage is broken, and it was thus rendered useless by the Confederates, when they abandoned the fort in 1864.

France and England would not acknowledge the South as an independent nation, but the Confederate government did all possible to bring this about by sending Messrs. James M. Mason of Virginia and John Slidell of Louisiana **THE SOUTH ENDEAVORS** as ministers to London and Paris, with **TO SECURE RECOGNITION.** the hope that their claims would be recognized. Henry Ward Beecher, when in the height of his fame, afterward went to England, addressing immense audiences, and setting forth the true condition of American affairs.

FORT SUMTER.

The hope of the Southerners was that the government would allow a peaceable withdrawal of the dissatisfied States, and that no bloodshed would be necessary, but as time went by and the most active preparations for keeping them in the Union were made by the general government, they commenced hostilities, and the first gun of the war was fired by the Confederates under General Beauregard on the morning of April 12, and while the officers and men within the fort were eating their breakfast, a perpetual bursting of shells and shot kept them awake to the fact that the peace had been broken, and war had begun.

SIEGE GUN.

After breakfast the force was divided up into firing parties and the first reply on the part of the Union was made by Captain

FIRING ON
THE FORT.
Abner Doubleday. But their guns were of very light
metal. A fierce bombardment followed, and on the
14th of April, 1861, General Robert Anderson evacuated the fort.

Blockade running was so common it became necessary to fit
out an expedition to close the most valuable of the openings,

Hatteras Inlet. The
first expedition pro-
jected for this pur-
pose was fitted out
near Fortress Mon-
roe . and was under
command of Flag-
Officer Silas H.
Stringham. The en-
gagement lasted
three hours, with a
complete victory for
Stringham, and sev-
eral blockade runners
entered the inlet and
were captured.

The news fell like
a pall upon the North.
It was impossible, so
many an old man
urged, that Ameri-
cans, our own people,

HENRY WARD BEECHER.

could be so disloyal. Why had they done it? What did it mean?
And when, in consequence of this act, President Lincoln ordered
them to disperse within twenty days, and called for
75,000 men from the various States, to enlist to **RECRUITS TO THE FRONT.**
"suppress this combination against the laws," the
response came swiftly.

In every town and village the patriotic fires were kindled, and
boys and old men pressed on, side by side, willing to give their
lives, if need be, to uphold their country's flag.

FORTRESS MONROE.

Many a smooth-cheeked lad, loved dearly and tenderly reared, went forth from his home, never again to enter its portal. Alas, for those sad days! Recruiting went swiftly on. Speech-making and passionate appeals to the people were heard in every quarter of the North. Women could not fight, but they could organize sewing societies, and work untiringly for those who had gone to the front. Many an article found its way to the army that was useful, and when blood had been spilled, these same patient and tearful women sent lint, and bandages, and medicines, for the sick and wounded.

As the call for soldiers awoke the boys and men of the North, so did a like summons from their leaders arouse the spirit of the South. They had orators in their midst, whose tones swayed them, and they, too, enlisted to form an army which should repel the "encroachments" of those whom they deemed their enemies.

GENERAL DIX'S FAMOUS DISPATCH.

Boys went forth from luxurious homes, and stood shoulder to shoulder with the humblest, clad in the gray, all equally ready to sacrifice life and home to their idea of duty.

THE BLUE AND THE GRAY LEAVE HOME.

One lad, in his Western home, a dreamer thus far, the light of his widowed mother's life, heard the war cry, and the blood tingled in

ALEXANDER H. STEPHENS, VICE-PRESIDENT OF THE CONFEDERACY.

his veins as he listened to stirring arguments day by day, and saw one after another of his companions leave their homes to join the forces that were being hurried forward to headquarters.

He felt that he must go with them. Why not? His eye was
as keen, his brain as clear, his arm as strong to do whatever
his country required of him, as were theirs.

GENERAL JOHN A. DIX.

This longing haunted him by day and night, until it became
unbearable. He went to his mother, and with earnest words
begged her to send him. Alas, that mother was not equal to the

task. She was loving, gentle and shrinking, and when he urged her to let him go, her answer was—

"Ralph, you know not what you ask. Do you forget that I am a Southern woman, whose childhood's days were spent in that beautiful country? All my people are there. Would you have me send my boy away to fight those I love, and whose feelings I must share? You are asking too great a sacrifice at my hands."

"Mother, it is true that you were born and educated there. But did you not love my father so dearly that you left your home and all your friends to come to the North with **RALPH'S MOTHER HESITATES.** him, where I was born?"

A tender smile flitted across her still beautiful face. "Yes, I did love him," she said softly to herself, "and I honor his memory. What shall I do?—I cannot forget my dear childhood's home. It is too hard a question for me to decide."

GEN. MONTGOMERY MEIGS, QUARTERMASTER-GENERAL.

"Let me decide for you, mother. You surely love your Northern home and friends. The people of the South have fired upon our forts in Charleston harbor, and driven the garrison away. I, too, am a Southerner in many ways. Are you not my mother, and do you not know I honor every thought or wish of yours?"

"There must be some other way to bring them back, rather than by fighting. War is a cruel and unnatural alternative. Why, they will be firing upon their own people—like brothers in one family falling out, and seeking to do each other deadly harm."

FAIRFAX COURT HOUSE.

Ralph was silent. His heart burned with patriotic fire, and it seemed to him that it was his duty to help swell the numbers of those who were ready to respond to the President's call. But he also knew that his mother loved her early home, and that it seemed to her unnatural for him to be so ready to take up arms against "her people," and he respected her too deeply to wound her willingly. That mother had been gently born, and when she met the young Northern lawyer, she had loved him from the first, and cheerfully shared his humble but peaceful home. She was now left alone in the world, with her three girls and this boy, the youngest. The fortunes of war were too varying. She might never see him again, and how could she live without him?

To Ralph was presented a problem that he was called unexpectedly to solve. He pondered over it in the silence of night, and in the busy hours of day. Was it right to fly in the face of his beloved mother's prejudices by joining the Federal forces? On **RALPH'S STRUGGLES.** the one hand he felt that he, too, was Southern in feeling and in birth. His father was a Northern man, and he would uphold the old flag; but which side it was his duty to join, he could not determine. He was resolved to go into one of the two armies. In the crisis that had come, it was clearly every one's duty to come to the front.

The boy talked with every one whom he could interest. He was not able to study out the problem alone. One of his schoolmates had the proud distinction of having an uncle who was a commissioned officer, and he took the bold step of meeting him one day when he was walking past his home.

"Sir," he said timidly, "may I speak to you?"

"Certainly," the officer replied. And then and there he poured forth his doubts, his desire to do what was right, his mother's objections—all, he told the waiting gentleman whose opinion he so desired.

The officer laid his hand kindly on the boy's shoulder.

"Your wish does you credit. The fortunes of war are too varying for me to decide for you. Try and work out the proper answer yourself, and may you be helped to make a wise decision."

Alas, the question was too hard for a boy like him to answer. He was humbly trying to see where his duty lay, and then he was ready to enlist on whichever side called him. On one hand was his mother and her early teachings, on the other his dead father, with all his views. "What side would *he* choose were he here?" was the ever-recurring thought in his anxious brain.

But after weeks of this long, weary struggle, he decided to join the Union army. His mother saw that he believed he was shirking a duty, and that he longed for action. She thought she would make one more effort to change his purpose. She said to

RALPH AND THE OFFICER.

him suddenly one day, when she saw his troubled face: "Ralph, you are only seventeen. You have never been away from your home, and know nothing about hardships and privations. Do you think you could face a cannon, and know that its deadly mouth might lay you low on the field, mangled and torn?"

"Oh, mother, I never think of such things. If I enlist, I must take my chances with the rest. I want to go with the other boys. Eddie Downing and George Martin have enlisted, and are going into camp to-morrow, at Readville."

RALPH'S FRIENDS ENLIST.

"But will the government accept you? Eddie and George are three or four years older than you. There are plenty of men, without taking a boy who is his mother's chief comfort."

GENERAL WINFIELD SCOTT.

"I am strong and well. When I come back, you will be the proudest mother in the land, to think you sent your boy away. I may go with your blessing, may I not? That will protect me."

The boy's eyes were moist with emotion. His mother, with a sigh, gave her reluctant consent, and though many a bitter tear was shed in the loneliness of her room, she bravely hid them from the boy she loved.

Now that the decision was final, she made every preparation for the comfort of the boy who was to leave them so soon. His sisters wept continually—not a very cheerful parting, but Ralph was the idol of his home.

"Mother," he said to her a day or two after she had given her consent, "do not worry about me. I shall do my duty. This war *can't* last long. Then I'll come back to you, and stay at home as long as I live, depend on that."

His beaming face half reassured her, and she began to share his enthusiasm. He was enrolled as a soldier. Although his youth was at first objected to, his earnestness carried the day, and he was told to report at Camp Hale at once.

He was a real soldier at last! A genuine soldier, who must fight. He did not belong to the would-be soldiers, such as they used to call the "militia," who simply paraded on the open green, or turned out on dress occasions, with the curious for an audience, who would watch and be astonished at their evolutions and their showy uniforms, when the Fourth of July or kindred days made their demands upon them.

In his neat-fitting suit of blue, the cap setting jauntily upon his head, his musket in hand, and his belt with its bayonet buckled around him, he looked so manly that a thrill of pride flashed o'er his mother's face, as she looked at her boy, her Ralph, in his "soldier clothes."

But when the day came for him to leave the only home he had ever known, and he turned to take a last look at its plain walls, his heart almost failed him. His beloved mother stood in the doorway, her hands pressed over her face, while she strove to keep back the choking sobs, as she bade her boy—"Good-bye, and may God bless and protect you." Those solemn words came back to Ralph in many a lonely hour, and brought him consolation and support.

Thus, in many homes, both North and South, were the heart-strings torn, as mothers and sisters bade farewell to the boys in blue and gray, who went to the front, to lay down their lives for duty's sake.

HER BOY SAYS GOOD-BYE.

Ralph was a proud boy when he joined his companions in camp, wearing the blue uniform, with its shining buttons bearing the U. S. stamp upon them. He was naturally

RALPH'S GOOD-BYE.

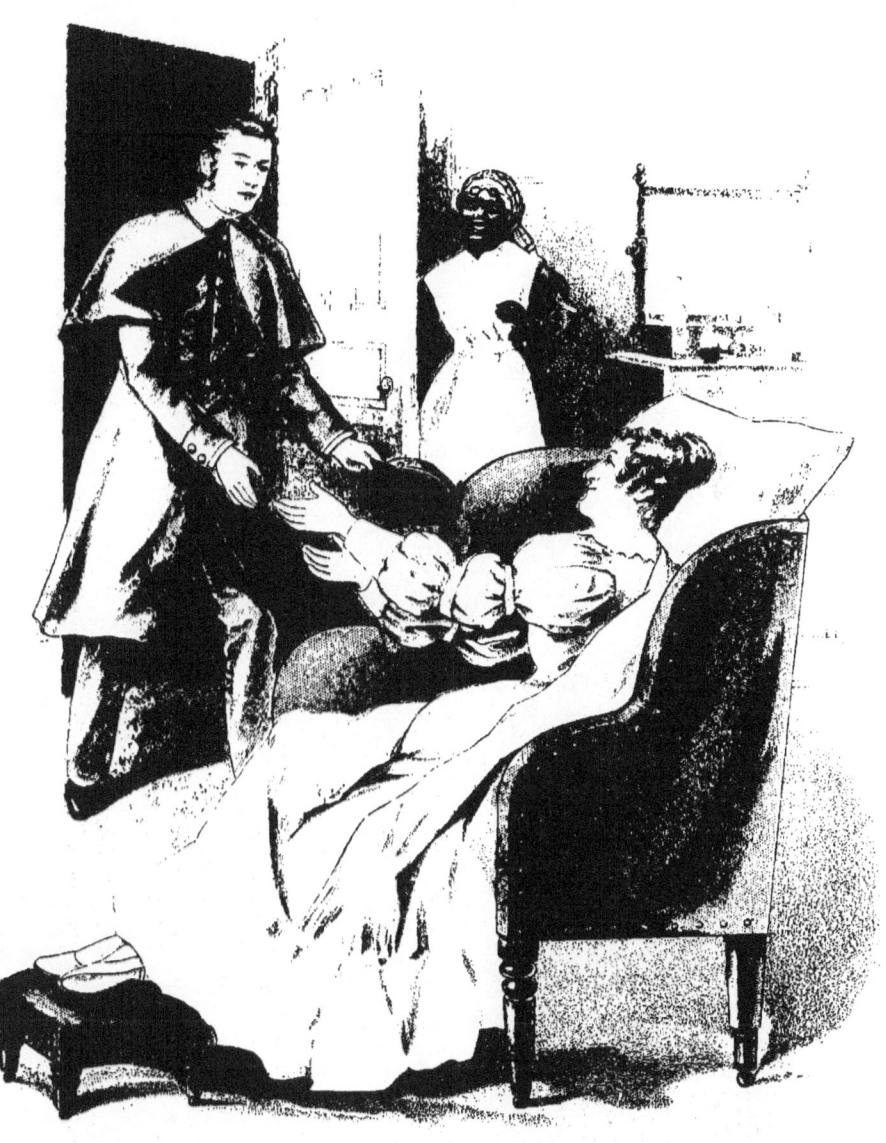

retiring, but now he felt as if the eyes of the world were upon him. He had taken an important step, and he would show his friends and that great big world that he knew exactly what he was doing.

Camp life was one continual drill—so it seemed to him. Readville was a quiet little town, but its people were ablaze with patriotism, and the "boys in blue" were the recipients of perpetual admiration. Every move they made was noticed and approved, and it is not to be wondered at if some of them did greedily swallow considerable flattery, which led them to assume quite lofty airs.

The sameness of life in camp soon wearied, and Ralph longed for something more stirring. When the bugle call rang out, every man sprang up, and, after a hasty ablution, at a second call they made a charge upon their breakfast with vehemence, and tin cups and plates rattled in a most discordant fashion. Then the drill began: first with musket and rifle, and then with the bayonet. A bayonet charge was a fierce reminder of the real thing. When men meet the enemy with fixed bayonets, a dreadful slaughter may always be counted on. This drilling was kept up at intervals, all through the day; first in squads and companies, and then the entire regiment would take part in the use of these weapons, and the various evolutions that the drill-master taught.

Ralph was very anxious to become proficient in their use, and while many of the older men grumbled at this work, he kept on, learning at each repetition something more of their

RALPH LIKES DRILLING. actual value.

"You'll have to know all about this," said Lieutenant Hopkins to them, "or you'll be in a nice hole when you're caught out in the field. "We don't know how soon we may be sent to the front, and then there won't be much time for this sort of practice. It'll be march and fight then."

Way down in his heart this quiet stripling, hitherto jealously guarded from a knowledge of the world by a fond mother and sisters, had his own dreams of fame burning brightly and steadily. What if he could plan or assist in some grand sortie, and be men-

3

tioned in the dispatches as "the gallant private of Company K ——
Mass. Volunteers, whose valor turned the tide and carried the
day?" Then probably he would be summoned before the commanding officer, and honors would be thrust upon him. Perhaps,
if he kept on, he might be a general! What would the dear ones
at home say then? The picture was too brilliant; his head fairly
grew dizzy at the prospect.

"I'll tell you," he said to a comrade, "we are in no danger of
starving here in camp, at any rate, if we don't have much variety."

"That's so. What's the matter with pork, beans, soup,
bread, molasses (here he made a wry face), rice and hard tack?
If we get enough of these, we'll pull through all right," his companion responded cheerfully.

"And we sleep as sound as kittens in our wooden bunks, with
plenty of straw for a bed, and our big army blankets over us,"
continued Ralph.

"The pillows might be a little softer," said Harvey Phillips.
"Overcoats doubled up ain't quite as easy shook up as feathers."

"No, but our captain tells me that we are living in clover just
at present. Wait till we go into a battle. Perhaps we'll come
out without any heads, then we won't need any pillows," laughed
Ralph.

"That's true. Your easy times are right here just now," said
a "vet," who had been in many a battle in the far West with the
red men, and had "smelt powder" to his heart's content. "War
looks very pretty on paper, with the big fellows at Washington
moving the men like they're at a chessboard, but wait till the guns
speak up on the field, and men to men are hurled against each
other, to fight like demons. The real thing ain't so romantic, let
me tell you youngsters."

"You can't frighten us," said Harvey. "We are no three
months' men. We enlisted for the war and we propose to see the
war out."

"Boys, I tell you war aren't no pastime. It means
work, and hardest kind of work, at that. It's a great thing to
organize an army, and keep its various parts in trim. We don't

usually go out to fight the enemy with only a flask of powder,
and a knapsack filled with soda crackers. There are men and
horses and ammunition to carry along."

"Who takes care of all these matters?" asked Ralph.

"The quartermaster. He looks after the rations, the
ammunition, in fact, all the supplies—blankets for the men,

U. S. MILITARY WAGON.

medicines for the sick and transportation for the baggage. He is
usually a captain or a lieutenant. The government appoints him."

"Does he fight?"

"Oh, no. He's got no time for that. He has to look
after the fellows who do the fighting. The quartermasters have
excitement and danger enough, however, in protecting their stores.
They ain't like the sutlers."

NEGRO VILLAGE IN GEORGIA.

"What is a sutler?"

"He's a chap that gets permission from the government to carry things to sell to the soldiers. He furnishes them at his own expense, and then trades and sells them to the boys."

RALPH ASKS QUESTIONS.

"Is he a soldier?"

"Not much. You don't see him in the battlefield. He takes good care not to interfere in any skirmishes going on. Somehow, the smell of powder don't agree with him."

"Then he goes to war to make money?"

"That's just what he does. He oftener loses it, though, and then his friends don't cry nor take up a collection for him. Still, he's generally a good sort of a fellow. He's obliging and always willing to trust a man. Often the boys help themselves to his goods without his leave, and then he's out that much. He has his ups and downs like the rest of us."

CHAPTER II.

ORDERED TO WASHINGTON.

AMP life was pleasant, aside from the perpetual drilling, marching and countermarching. Friends had access to the boys at stated times, little gifts and pledges were exchanged, and the time passed swiftly. One day there was great excitement. Coffee was swallowed hastily, knapsacks were packed in a hurry, arms were brightened up, ammunition was dealt out, and the word ran through the camp—"We are ordered to report at Washington."

"Now I shall know something of what is going on. Poor mother, she will grieve over her absent boy, and fancy me in a thousand dangers. But I will write to her often,
WAR IS NOT FAR OFF. and that will cheer her up."

And he did. Many a line he scribbled on his knee with a bit of pencil or a blackened stick, telling her of his safety and health. These short but welcome missives were read over and over, and fondly kissed, the dear little messengers of love and hope.

The war cloud was growing darker. The government arsenal at Harper's Ferry had been burned by Lieutenant Jones, who knew it would lessen its value to the Southern forces, who were marching upon the town. The latter, however, saved considerable of the government property, and next seized the bridge at Point of Rocks, thus circumventing General Butler, who was near Baltimore. They also took possession of several trains, which they side-tracked into Strasburg, a measure which helped the Confederate train service in Virginia very perceptibly.

The ride of the boys in blue to Washington lay through the mountains of West Virginia, where nature revels in grand surprises. Many a little cabin perched far up the hillside was

the home of those who had shed tears when old John Brown
was led forth to die. Poor and scanty though their daily fare
was, they were loyal and true, and the spirit of defiance to the
old flag found no echoes in their breasts.

ON THE MARCH.

To Ralph the scenery appealed with deep solemnity. He
was born in the West, where the green seas of the prairies seemed

to know no limit. To him hills and valleys, with their somber
shadows, were objects of awe. He noted the
**RALPH IS CHARMED
WITH NOVELTY.** beautiful homes of wealth and taste as he was
whirled swiftly by on the train. He saw the
black faces of slaves working in garden or field, and heard
their voices as they talked.

HARPER'S FERRY.

"Fore de Lawd!" he heard a grizzled old darkey say, as
they drew into a small station for water, "'pears like dey look
jess like de white folks do down here!"

"You 'spected dey had horns, didn't you? Well, I knowed
better. I'se been Norf wid Massa too many times to take in
dat *idee.*"

Washington, the capital of the nation, was reached. As

they steamed into the depot, and began to unload, Ralph, for the
first time since leaving home, felt lonely. He saw throngs of
people, but all was strange and new to him, and his heart sank.
The city was full of soldiers waiting for orders, so full that it

JOHN BROWN.

was a puzzle where
to quarter t h e m.
The Government
buildings were full
to overflowing, they
"b u n k e d" every-
where, a n d w i l d
pranks these boys
played, their love of
fun leading them in-
to many a mad
frolic. The city
was too small for
their mischievous
natures, and it was
no uncommon thing
to make a trip into
the surrounding ter-
ritory, bent on ex-
torting all the sport
they might out of
what most of them
regarded as a sort
of a gala time.
"But we are
ready whenever we

are called upon," was their unanimous cry. The shooting of Colonel Ellsworth at Alexandria, because he tore down a secession
flag, so short a time previous, and his prompt avenging, as you
remember, had roused them to a sense of the hostility which
was felt by those who sought to divide the North and South.
Then the attack of the mob of Baltimore upon the Sixth Massa-

chusetts, while being transported from one depot to another, was another proof that their brothers of the South had trampled friendly feelings beneath their feet, and that the fires of sectional jealousy were burning fiercely.

Their journey lay through a hostile State, and sober faces succeeded the jokes and laughter of the past few weeks. The

JOHN BROWN'S CAPTURE.

South was plainly up in arms, and that "rebellion," which the whole North at first thought but the task of a few weeks to crush, began to assume the appearance and proportions of a long and cruel conflict.

General Butler was in command of the military department of Virginia.

"Wonder if that means fight?" soliloquized Ralph. "The lads say he is a smart lawyer, but I don't know as that proves him to be a good fighter."

Ralph wrote often to that dear mother who was praying for her boy. "We move to the front

SIGNS OF WAR. to-morrow,"

so his letter ran. "I know how fond you are of your boy. I am going to do my duty, I believe. But is it not an awful

THE DEATH OF ELLSWORTH.

thought that it is no foreign foe we shall meet, but our own people?—that is the sting in it to me."

The night before the battle the boys slept as calmly as if they were at home. At dawn they were called to march, and

BENJAMIN F. BUTLER.

after an attack upon their rations, they began the advance into Virginia. Raw and undisciplined, they did not accept the gravity of the situation. They marched along, light-hearted and gay, enjoying the change from quiet camp life with all the zest of school boys. Many of them fell out of the ranks and picked the luscious berries growing thickly by the wayside, while others wastefully tossed out the water in their canteens and filled them with fresh every time they came to one of the springs which abounded in that beautiful and fertile region.

"This isn't hard work," Ralph thought. "We are having more fun than ever."

A halt had been called for a few moments' rest. A few rods from the road a dark stream ran slowly by, whose depths no one knew. A swim in its cool waters was proposed at any hazard, and, quickly disrobing, some of the younger ones plunged in, and were having a merry time, when the roll of the drum was heard and the marching was resumed. Here was a fix! The army began to move, and a dozen soldiers were still in the stream, who snatched up the first garments they saw and hastened to dress. In their confusion they had almost to a man seized the wrong clothes, and the fit of some of them was ludicrous. But changes were quickly made, and after much good-natured "chaffing" they fell into line, and were as sedate and soldier-like as any "vet" among them.

The cry, "On to Richmond!" sounded throughout the land. Officers and soldiers had been massed near Washington long enough, and the people, as well as the boys **"ON TO RICHMOND."** in blue, were impatient for some results, now that an army had been called into being. The soldiers pined for action; the people were anxious to know what would be the outcome.

"Who commands the Southerners?" Ralph asked old "Bill" Elliott, a soldier who had taken quite a fancy to the boy, and was ready to answer his questions at all times.

"Beauregard, the same chap who opened fire on Fort Sumter."

"And what does he propose doing now?"

"Well, as I am not in his confidence, I can't just tell you, but I 'low we're not going to be in the dark long, neither are we likely to be the gainers by any move he makes if he can help it. He's got some thirty thousand men with him, and we'll have a lively time soon, you bet."

"The men want a brush, I think, from what they say. They're becoming tired of waiting."

"And so does the country; but they don't know how much easier it is to talk war than to be in it. What does the man

GENERAL P. T. G. BEAUREGARD.

who stays at home know about the dangers and trials of a soldier's life? How is he capable of judging whether it is time to fight or where it is best to strike, or how many odds a general of an army has against him? We'll have war enough before long—they needn't fear."

BATTLE OF PHILIPPI

"Well, I suppose we'll some of us be in it soon, and who knows how many of us will come out?"

GENERAL GEORGE B. McCLELLAN

"Why, boy, you're not showing the white feather, I hope!" and Bill peered anxiously into the lad's troubled face.

"No, sir, I am not, but I can't help thinking of my poor mother, and, besides, you know I am going to fight her people. My mother is a Virginian."

"Is that so? I know, then, she must feel bad

RALPH AND HIS MOTHER. to have you in our army. I can't blame her, nuther."

"But she's loyal to our flag, Bill," the boy hastened to add. "It would break her heart, though, if anything should happen to me."

"Cheer up! You'll get through all right. I can feel it in my bones."

Ralph laughed. "Why, of course I shall. It seems to me this war won't be a very long one."

"Perhaps not—you can't tell. But McClellan taught the Johnnies a lesson at the 'races' the other day."

"The 'races?'" Ralph's eyes opened wide.

"Yes, the 'Philippi races,'" Bill went on. "The Confeds ran so fast from our boys at that battle that they dubbed their retreat the 'Philippi races,' in honor of the speed they showed. He has been made a general, and given the Ohio troops to command. He crossed the Ohio with four regiments and banged after the enemy. He found it hard work, for they say Colonel Porterfield burned all the bridges. He wasn't long in putting them in order, though, and getting over some big reinforcements. He routed them at Philippi and at Rich Mountain. Government ought to remember him, I tell you."

And it did, for "Little Mac," as he was called, was made commander-in-chief of the Army of the Potomac.

CHAPTER III.

RALPH'S FIRST BATTLE.

T Washington all sorts of rumors were plenty. It was generally known, however, that General Beauregard was making for Bull Run, where the stream presented a natural barrier. General McDowell left Washington with a force, whose accompaniments of civilians, following the marching columns on foot, reporters, congressmen and idle sight-seers in carriages, was a motley and curious sight. Everyone declared this to be the battle which was to close out the rebellion, and all were jubilant at the prospect.

McDOWELL'S ADVANCE. On the army pressed under the brave McDowell, who was planning to execute a flank movement upon the Confederates' left. A two hours' engagement routed the Rebels, who fled before the Union charge.

The victory seemed to the Federal troops an easy one, but Generals Johnston and Beauregard took the field in person, and, planting their artillery in a piece of woods, they held the open plateau across which the Federals were advancing, wholly at their mercy. General McDowell could see nothing of this, owing to the shape of the ground, only by mounting to the top of the Henry House, where they took their stand, and where the attack was resumed in the afternoon.

The men on both sides were raw troops; they had not become the machines that after fighting made them. This was to most of them their first encounter, and as shot and shell flew rapidly by them, as the Union men advanced over the open ground upon the enemy, who were concealed within the woods, only to be picked off, one by one, by the Confederate sharpshooters, who took the gunners at their batteries, they became disheartened.

4   49

BATTLE OF BULL RUN.

50

SECOND BATTLE OF BULL RUN.
From a War-time Sketch.

The fight in the forenoon had exhausted them, and they were unprepared for the work still to be done.

The battle was fierce; men were falling like hail, in all the agonies of death. Here a drummer boy was lying face downward, his stiff hand clutching the stick whose strokes would never wake the echoes again. There an officer, his uniform dyed with blood, lay prostrate on the ground, his horse half across his stiffening body, while at every turn the wounded were huddled together, in the positions in which they fell.

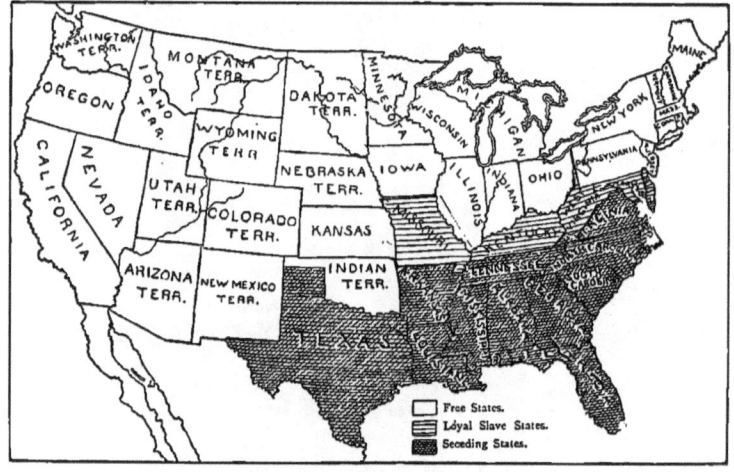

MAP OF LOYAL AND SECEDING STATES.

Ralph's heart turned sick, as he saw the brave fellows who manned the batteries tumbling over each other, many of them shot through the heart, as the Confederates, tempted by their success, stole nearer to the guns.

Captain Griffin, who made the sad mistake of thinking the troops were his own men coming to his aid, permitted the nearer approach of the Confederates. He discovered his error when a volley of musketry took nearly every gunner and stretched Lieutenant Ramsay low in death, as the rebels rushed in and seized the guns.

STAND OF THE UNION TROOPS AT THE HENRY HOUSE.

The fighting went pluckily on; both sides were in deadly earnest. The batteries seemed to be the coveted prize, and they were taken and retaken, first by one army, and then the other.

Worn and harassed, in the confusion that ensued, regiments and companies became mixed, and thousands of men lost track of their companies and wandered about, not knowing where they belonged.

In the dense smoke that covered the battle ground, Ralph became lost, and, making a short turn, found a clump of trees with a thick growth of underbrush. He heard voices, and threw himself flat upon the ground, determined not to be taken prisoner.

DISCUSSING THE SITUATION. "Wonder what General Beauregard's next move will be?" The tones were low and even.

"Well, Lieutenant, we cannot know at present, but it is certain we have taught the Yanks a lesson this day. They'll never forget Johnston's brigade. They were so sure of whipping us. It was a hot battle, and three or four times I thought we had lost. Those fellows fight well, but they're no match for the South. What's the matter over there? See, our men are retreating. Don't they know we've won the day?"

It was true. So many times had the victory changed hands, that it was hard to tell who had won finally and it looked as if the Confederate line was breaking.

Jeff Davis' heart sank as he came up from Manassas and found that hundreds of Confederates, under the impulse of fear, were fleeing to the rear. He kept on, only to find that the Northern army was in full retreat, and the battle of Bull Run was a bitter defeat for the Federals.

Ralph lay there in ambush, pale with dread. He feared capture more than death. He rose quickly as the two officers galloped away, to stay their men, and looked upon the scene. Lines of men in blue and gray stretched away in the distance, while the noise of the guns, the neighing of wounded horses, the huzzas of the victors, drowning the groans of the wounded, made him faint with horror, and his cheeks grew white as he saw men lying on their backs, their glassy eyes staring up to the sky, their faces ghastly and white, and peaceful, or else distorted with pain. Here a wounded soldier would half raise himself on one arm, and beg for water, while others, bleeding and dying, lay uncomplainingly, their eyes fixed on the blue sky, which nevermore would greet their waking vision.

In the dim light he saw all this, and knew not where to

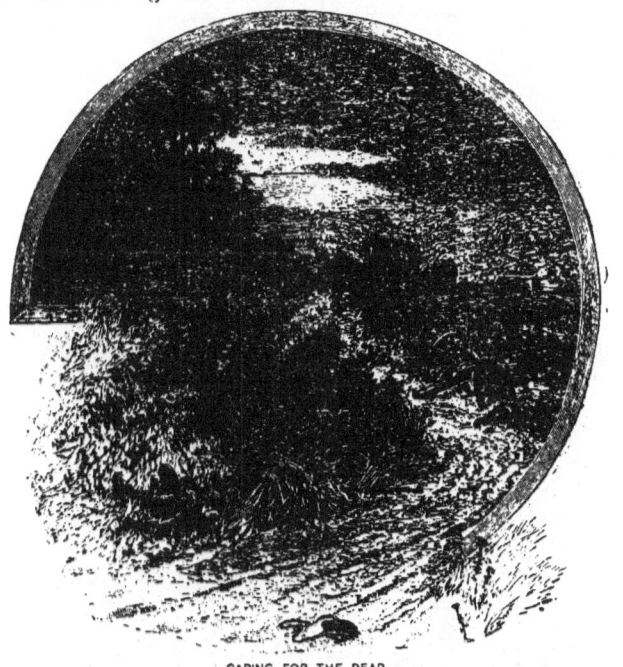

CARING FOR THE DEAD.

go. The terrible sights and hideous silence which succeeded the noise of conflict sickened him, and Ralph, the brave soldier boy, actually fainted.

RALPH FAINTS. "What's this? Why, it's Ralph! Is he killed?"

The tones sounded, to the boy's benumbed senses, far away,

as a heavily bearded man knelt down and placed his hand upon
his heart. He saw it was Bill, and the flush of mortification
mounted to his brow, as he tried to rise.

"I was weak—dizzy—and I—"

"I know all about it!" good-humoredly laughed Bill Elliott,
for he it was. "This is your first appearance, and you had a
sort of a stage fright."

Ralph bit his lips with vexation.

"Oh, that's nothing. You'll make a better showing next
time. You'll live to be a brigadier-general. But I was kinder
rattled myself when I saw you so still. I didn't know but some
fellow had tuk good aim at you!"

"I'm not hurt in the least, Bill."

"Well, boy, come on. We've been whipped bad, and are
most unpleasantly nigh those fellows with the guns over thar,
and as I'm pretty tall, they might choose me for a mark, just
to keep their hands in."

The Federal army, broken and defeated, straggled back to
Washington, footsore, dirty and hungry. No battle during the
war was fought with more desperation, and bravery was shown
by both sides—the Union and the Confederate.

And though the defeat of General McDowell's forces was
a blow to the pride of the North, it carried a valuable lesson;
that the South would not be persuaded back to its old allegiance.

To the boys of this generation slavery is almost a myth.
But when the Civil War broke out the blacks were held in bondage to masters who had acquired them by purchase or inheri-
tance, and thus they represented property or wealth.

The South bitterly resented any interference with an institution which many of them honestly regarded as divine. In the
North opinion was divided, some believing slavery to be wrong,
but that it would gradually die out. All classes were unwilling
that it should be extended into new territory.

This difference of opinion led to the conflict which caused
brave men to take up arms and arrayed brother against brother,
in defense of what each believed to be just and fair.

WHAT CAUSED THE WAR THE NEGRO AND COTTON.

CHAPTER IV.

RALPH DOES PICKET DUTY.

LD Bill was a little fearful, spite of Ralph's pro-
testations, lest his boy, as he dubbed him, was
going to show the white feather, after all, and so
he kept him well under his eye.

"I don't want the tarnal little rascal skipping,
for it 'ud go hard with him to be caught. They'd
shoot him sure."

But he didn't know the true mettle of the boy. He was no
coward, if he did turn sick at the scenes of his first battle, and
he was a lad of honor, and would have died before he would
leave his post.

So he felt a little down-hearted when orders came for a
detail from Company K to turn out for picket duty. The men
themselves felt rather blue at this news, for they were worn out
and disheartened by their late tussle, but they didn't expect
their wishes would be considered in the matter. Ralph's eyes
gleamed with joy, for he longed for adventure.

"Bill, I believe you think I am cowardly. You'll change
your mind soon, I know."

That individual grimly responded:

"Picket duty is a very cheerful way of passing one's time,
but I guess you'll do."

The picket line was twelve miles distant, and as the men
got into line, the air and the excitement infused courage into
Ralph's breast. They had been ordered out to relieve a regiment
which had seen some hard work, and who were anxious to get
into shelter.

The newcomers were told what spots needed the most
watching, and as soon as they were stationed at their posts and

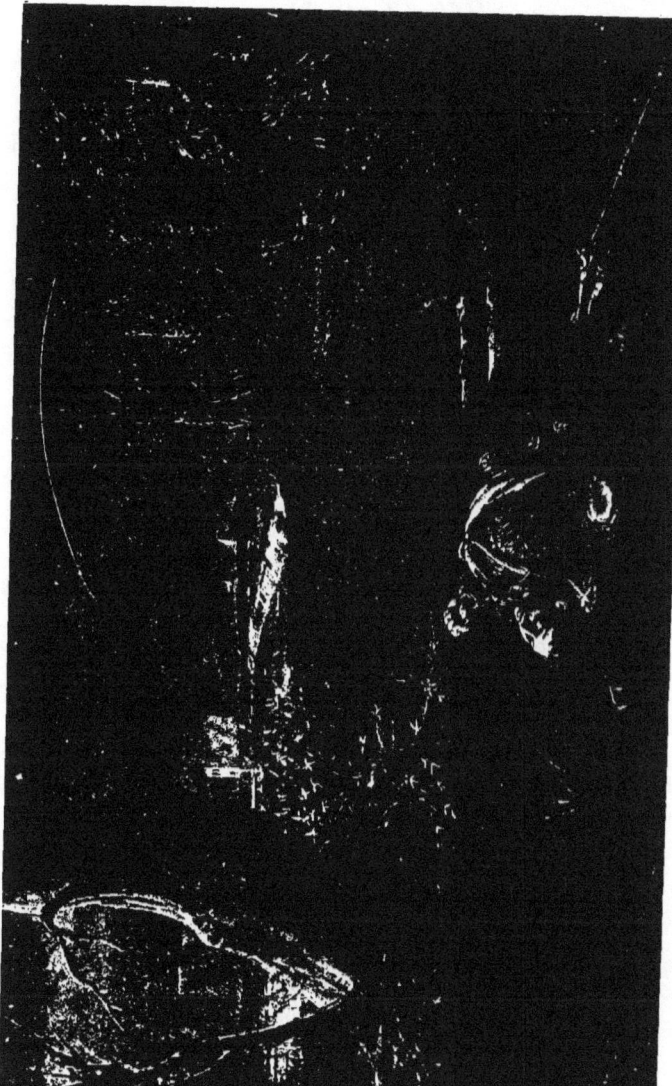

PICKET OFF DUTY FOREVER.

59

received the necessary instructions, they settled down to the importance of the duty assigned them.

The woods lay behind them, and each picket sought their friendly shelter, well aware that any "change of base" on their part would be an invitation to the enemy to pick them off.

Memories of home filled Ralph's breast. The night was dark and starless. A strong wind blew at intervals, now howling dismally through the trees, and then shifting its course, rushing down the bank, as if it would rend the earth and the tall grass in its anger.

"I wonder if mother thinks of her soldier boy," he pondered.

When does a mother ever cease to think of and pray for her children?

The night wore on. Perfect quiet reigned, and Ralph began to consider picket duty not half so risky as Old Bill called it, after all. But as he kept his eyes on the opposite bank, where the "Johnnies" were, he fancied he saw a small dark object creeping through the grass down to the river, where it seemed to be looking up and down its shore. His heart beat fiercely. What was it? he asked himself. Was it a man or some animal hiding in the grass? If it were a reb, he would be shot dead, at the least move on his part—that he well knew.

I am afraid you will not think my boy was much of a hero, but the truth is, he was very much in love with life, as all young people should be, and, though willing to do his whole duty, he could not help feeling a trifle nervous about his surroundings, so he stooped quickly down behind a tall bush that appeared to be growing there just for his benefit.

The object on which his gaze was fixed seemed so small that he almost laughed aloud at his own fears.

"Why, it's only a dog that's strayed into camp," he said. "Wonder if they fatten him on hard tack."

A STRANGER COMES ON THE SCENE. His gaze was riveted upon the dark mass, and his surprise nearly found vent in a low whistle, which he speedily checked, as he saw a man or a boy steal noiselessly along the bank, till he came to a place where the grass was tangled and thick, and stooping down he pulled a wide board from its hiding-place, and picking up a long piece of wood which lay there, he stepped on the plank and commenced to paddle across the stream.

Ralph lay in the grass behind the bush, breathlessly watching the approaching figure. Suddenly a dog began to bark on the opposite shore, and the man on the plank gave utterance to a low, angry exclamation. The dog stopped barking, and the stranger came slowly on, till his novel craft touched the shore within five feet of Ralph.

He saw to his amazement that it was a boy, even younger than himself, it seemed in the dim light, and he waited breathlessly till he came closer, and was halted by Ralph's gun, which he brought sharply against the other's breast, while his own was on fire with excitement, as he cried aloud—" Halt—you are my prisoner!"

For a moment these two boys faced each other; then the stranger threw his head proudly back, and, with a gesture of impatience, replied:

"I will not be made a prisoner—I am merely going about my own business."

"And that business is to spy upon our lines!" Ralph said hotly.

"Take me to your superior officer. I can soon convince him that I am doing no harm," answered the boy.

A stir ran through the picket lines, as the news was passed on that a rebel spy had been captured, and soon the lad, whose **IS HE A SPY?** proud carriage and haughty face involuntarily commanded attention, was at headquarters, where to all questioning he remained dumb, after telling an apparently truthful story that he was crossing the river to visit an old uncle, and knew nothing of the movements of either army.

"This 'old uncle' is one I fancy we'd better try to unearth," said Colonel Tuttle. "His acquaintance would be worth cultivating."

The boy would give no further account of himself. His frank, boyish face and manly bearing impressed the officer of the

GENERAL JAMES LONGSTREET, C. S. A.

day favorably, and he muttered to himself—"Wonder if he is a spy. If all the Johnnies are as brave and resolute as this youth we'll have to work hard to conquer them."

An opinion which he found cause to verify often.

CHAPTER V.

"OU'RE in luck, my boy," and Bill Elliott's face showed genuine pleasure as he shook hands with Ralph. "You are to show yourself at headquarters and receive your reward, as the good boys in story books always do."

An orderly came up to Ralph, and said:—"You are wanted at headquarters."

Ralph proceeded to the officers' tent. For the first time he stood in the presence of his commanding officers, and as he saluted respectfully, a tall, kindly-faced man looked at him with some surprise.

"How old are you?" was the abrupt query, as the officer looked in the beardless face of the boy.

"Nearly eighteen, sir."

"Have you seen any service yet?"

"I was at Bull Run."

The fine face clouded with sadness. "That was hard and tedious fighting. You brought in a prisoner last night, whom we have strong reasons to believe is a rebel **RALPH IS PROMOTED.** spy. You have shown two qualities befitting a soldier—pluck and forgetfulness of self. Your captain commends you to me, and I have thought proper to make you a corporal."

Ralph's heart beat loud and fast. What had he done to deserve this honor?

"Your warrant will be handed to you, and you are expected to attend strictly to all its requirements."

To a general or a colonel the promotion would not seem very exalted; but to this boy, who could not realize why he had been selected, it was as if he had suddenly been lifted into the seventh heaven To be sure, it only meant two stripes on his jacket sleeve, and a trifle of authority, but it also meant encouragement and notice from his superiors. He could not answer, but, bowing low, he left the tent.

"A board of inquiry must be appointed at once, and we'll see what this lad whom Corporal Gregory brought in is doing within our lines."

The boy was marched before them, but he parried all their questions, and maintained a resolute and fearless mien.

"I have told you the truth," he said proudly. "I was going to make a visit when I was seized. You see I have no weapons."

HAILING THE TROOPS.

"Spies do not always carry arms. Papers are more to their taste. You say you came to see an uncle. Where does he live? Why did you visit him at night?"

"I knew that the enemy lay near us, and I didn't want to be taken prisoner."

"Where is this uncle?"

"He lives back of the bluff, on the right hand side of the road."

"We'll invite him into our camp, and see if he'll own the relationship."

CAPITOL AT RICHMOND.

The boy's face flushed with wounded pride, as he answered scornfully:

"We call our old servants uncle and aunt. He is an old colored man, and lives on this side of the river—one of our old slaves, whom my father freed."

"We'll send you to the guard-house until more is known about you," was the stern retort.

The boy was removed to the guard-house. To Ralph he

5

was an object of much interest. His sympathies went out to
him and he longed to say something comfort-
**THE "UNCLE" IS
INVITED TO CAMP.** ing. And so when it came his turn to act as
corporal of the guard, with the abrupt frank-
ness of youth, he blurted out:

"What were you doing over here the other night?"

REJOICING.

"I have given an account of myself to your superiors."

"Don't be so lofty. I don't mean to be inquisitive, but I
thought you might like to know that I am awful sorry I brought
you into this trouble."

The boy's face softened.

"I don't know as you could do anything else under the

circumstances. I suppose, in fact, I know, I'd have done just as you did. Perhaps worse," he muttered. "I might have shot you."

"Then you don't hold any grudge against me?"

"Well, I can't pretend that I'm grateful to you for my detention in this hole, but I can't blame you, either."

"Were you really going to see the old slave you told the colonel about?"

An indescribable expression flitted across the boy's features. "I said so once. My word is usually taken, where I am known. Why do you ask?"

"Oh, from curiosity, I suppose. You look too young to be very dangerous."

"I'm as old as you are. You look too young to be carrying arms against your countrymen."

"Oh, I'm going to help put down this rebellion."

"A hard job you've selected. It is not a rebellion; it's an uprising against meddlesome Yankee interference."

Ralph's eyes flashed fire. "You don't mean to say that you justify the South, do you?"

"I not only justify it, but am proud to belong to a people who can never be subdued. Your people are trying to force us to give up our rights, but we won't be driven. We have thousands of men in the field, who do not know how to fear. And when their places are vacant, more are waiting to fill them. We despise the North, and want to be a separate people."

"You despise a government that has always protected you in all your rights. You have no cause for wishing to be disunited. How dare you talk so to me?"

"'Dare?' Am I not your equal? Why should I not speak when I am insulted?"

"Don't talk treason to me again, then."

"I am a prisoner," the boy said, sadly, "innocent of any crime, surrounded by foes and powerless. Were it not so you would not give me a defiance."

Ralph's conscience smote him. It did appear as if the odds

were on his side, and with the quick generosity of youth he
said—

"I am sorry for you. We will not quarrel."

Not to be outdone in generosity, the other replied—"I
believe you; but we had better not talk about it any more, for
we can never agree, and we are both hot-headed. You see affairs
in a different light from what I do, that is all."

The next day the youth was rigidly examined. He gave
his name as Charles Arlington, stated that he was merely crossing the river to look after the old slave; that he had chosen the
night-time as he heard the Union pickets were thrown out, and
he did not think, with his knowledge of the stream, that he
would be captured in the darkness. Meantime, the soldiers had
been searching, and had found an old half imbecile negro in a little
cabin half a mile back from the river, whom they brought into
camp, shaking with fear.

THE OLD SLAVE. "Old man," one of the soldiers said, "do
you know this boy?"

"Yas, honey. I knows him well. I'se old Marsa Thomas'
boy. I bin on his old plantation since he was a baby. His mudder was one of de —"

"Say, we don't care who his mother was. What do you
know about the boy standing there?"

"Yas, yas, I knows lots. Why, he was de littlest pickaninny
of de hull lot, and his father he say to me, 'Jim'—I was young and
strong den—'Jim, dis yere boy's gwine to be your young mastah
some day, if he ebber grows big enuff.' And I tole him de sweetest
posies were always small, like de vi'lets and lilies ob de valley,
and--"

"You black rascal, we don't want a dissertation on flowers.
Tell us about the young man standing there."

"Yas, marsa, but you tole me to tell you all 'bout him, and
doan't I hab to begin at the beginning?"

"Well, go on," the Colonel interposed.

"Dat ar chile dere was de idle of Massa Thomas' heart. My
old woman, Easter, who's dun been dead dese free years, nussed

AN ALEXANDRIA ANTE-BELLUM RELIC.

him. And when she died she cried mo' for leabing him alone in dis cold world dan she did fer me. You see de boy's mudder was put under de roses when he was only a few days in de world, and Easter she lubbed him mo' fer dat. Oh, de old times kaint come back no mo'. Marsa Thomas is in de war wid Gineral Johnston, and 'fore he went he say to me—'Jim, you'se been a faiful old servant, and I gibs you yo freedom.' 'I doan't want it, Marsa,' I say. 'Let me lib and die wid you.' 'Yo neber shall want,' he kep' on, 'go lib in de little cabin toder side ob de ribber.' You know he owns bof sides ob dis yere big plantation. 'Go lib dar, and de chilluns will look arter you.' An' bress dere hearts, dey all does care for po' old Jim. But I fell sick wid some sort ob a feber, and de rest ob 'em got a little scared like, all but dis yere chile. He neber left me till I done got well and able to hoe my leetle truck patch. And now he's tuk a prisoner, fer being kind to de po' ole man, who won't lib many years longer, to git him into trubble."

The old man's withered features shone with a light that was beautiful; his utterance was choked, and the tears rolled down his black cheeks as his simple eloquence found its way to the hearts of those who heard him.

"Sergeant, release the boy and let him go home. And while we stay here, see that the old man is not molested."

"Praise de Lawd! Bress you for yore kindness."

The boy bowed courteously to the Colonel, and with a look of gratitude he passed out of the officer's tent, with the old man hobbling after him. As he approached Ralph he said, "Good-bye. We may meet again."

It was not all danger and dread with the boys in the army. Weeks passed swiftly, and fun reigned in camp. The gypsy life held charms for them such as no indoor employment could offer. The men were hardy and strong, and with light hearts talked of the battles yet in store for them. And when jests **CAMP LIFE.** were exchanged, often after having come from a scene of carnage, it would be hard to believe that these same men were ready to respond at any moment if summoned by the long roll of the drum into action.

In the early part of the war many little conveniences were provided for the rank and file, among them being tents for shelter, which did not keep out the cold, however, and many a man died from disease who would have lived to fight, had he been properly housed. The second winter, however, many huts were put up, rough enough, but better calculated to withstand the cold than canvas. Each company had a "cook tent" and a cook, generally

CAMP LIFE—IN THE KITCHEN.

selected from the men, the officers boasting a "cullered individual" who was always, according to his own account, a "perfeshunal." The culinary department was ever a point of interest to the men, whose appetites were never so dainty that they failed to enjoy their daily rations. No soldier, no matter from what part of the North he came, ever turned up his nose at the beans, which were cooked in holes dug in the earth, and filled with hot embers, in which the iron pot containing them was buried and kept there all night.

To Bill Elliott fell the task of ministering to the hungry ones of his company, and many were the compliments he received.

"You can broil a chicken as good as any French cook," a man would coaxingly declare.

FORAGING.

"Not a boughten one," Bill replied; "somehow those kind of chickens the sutler has on hand don't have the genooine flavor."

The hint was always taken, and alas, for the poor farmer who had a nice hen-roost, or a young porker in the sty. They had no regard for property rights, and **HELPING THEMSELVES TO CHICKENS.** although they were not supposed to forage, except under orders, yet the temptation was too strong to be resisted.

At such times the cackling of the fowls, whose quiet was disturbed, the melodious grunting of the pigs, who often led them a hard chase, and the laughter and shouting of the pursuing soldiers, made a scene of wild merriment never forgotten.

But Ralph could not see the funny side of these depredations. To him it was a clear wrong to take what did not belong

ALLAN PINKERTON AND SECRET SERVICE OFFICERS.

to them. He never would join them in these expeditions, a course which exposed him to much ridicule for his "pious notions," but which had no effect upon him.

Often their zeal in this direction brought its own punishment. On one of these forays a long-legged, awkward fellow, who could outrun the fastest chicken, chased an anxious hen into a thicket, where the grass was long and rank. As he peered round for his game he spied a dozen or so eggs shining in the sun. "Ah," he said, "my lady hen is stealing a nest. Well, they look white and fresh, and I'll just confiscate them." His pockets

ZACH'S MISHAP.

were full of sweet potatoes, he had a brace of chickens slung over his shoulders, he had lost his handkerchief, if he ever owned one, and the problem was how to hold possession of the coveted prize.

"I know how I'll fix it. I'll put them in my cap. I can carry them all right."

The eggs were tenderly deposited therein, and he started for camp. He heard the boys who were still engaged in the chase laughing boisterously, and saw Rob Douglass, one of the new recruits, with a rope tied to one of the hind legs of a monstrous pig, who was jerking him right and left, in quite an unmilitary fashion. Now he was nearly on the animal's back, and next he was measuring his length on the ground, but he never once released the rope, while the shouts and cheers of the boys who were watching the contest made Rob more determined than ever to land his prize at the cook's tent.

Zach Smith joined in the merriment and began to chaff Rob, whose face was grimy with perspiration, while his dust-covered clothes looked as though a good brushing and a few stitches would improve them materially.

Seeing Zach he called to him to help haul in the "critter." The latter started toward him, but Mrs. Piggie was of the same mind, for she turned quickly and ran between his legs. Zach lost his balance and fell, and as he instinctively shot out his hands to save his eggs his head struck them squarely, while the liquid streaming down his face and neck sent forth such an odor that the men, who had inhaled many strange ones since leaving home, voted unanimously that that particular one "beat anything on record."

Zach made his way back to his tent, followed by the jibes of his comrades, as he bade Rob, in very strong language, to settle the pig as best he could while he attended to disinfecting himself.

CHAPTER VI.

ANOTHER BATTLE.

"OYS," said Lieutenant Graves, "we have our orders to turn out and show what we are made of. You know General McClellan has command of the Army of Virginia, and he thinks we've been rusting here long enough; so we're to help General Stone in drawing out the enemy. They've so far kept in hiding, and we've got to force them out into a square and open fight."

"The General thinks we're spoiling for a battle, doesn't he?"

"I suppose so. Anyway, we are to cross the Potomac at Conrad's Ferry and wake 'em up. General McCall has his hands full watching the river crossings, and we must help him do it."

This was good news to most of the men, who had grown tired of inaction. The long summer had worn away, and Ralph had often slipped away from camp and run into the negro cabins near by, where he was sure of a nice piece of hoe cake, baked on the hearth. The garrulous darkeys liked to see Ralph coming, and many a question they put to him which he could scarcely answer, so little did he know of the true state of affairs.

There are few idle moments in camp, for the duties of the soldier are too numerous to afford him that leisure which permits of homesickness. He has letters to write home, old ones to read; then, too, his spare time is occupied in looking for something to eat which his knapsack doesn't hold—not because his rations are scanty, or he is hungry, but he grows tired of the regular diet. He is always doing duty, police or fatigue, and the perpetual drilling, all keep him busy. Mending clothes became quite an art among the soldiers, and the manner in which some of them darned their stockings would reflect credit

75

BATTLE OF MALVERN HILL—LEE'S ATTACK.

76

upon many a housewife who has the reputation of being an ex-
pert seamstress.

Wash day in camp was as important an occasion as it is
at home, and preparations were made with as much regard to
convenience as the surroundings would permit.

Ralph was very fond of running into old "Aunt Judah's"
cabin, for her "pones" were especially toothsome. The old

CAMP LIFE ON MONDAY.

negress was not handsome—her black skin was shriveled and
seamed with age, she was nearly blind, but she was an admira-
ble cook.

"Massa," she said to Ralph one day, when she had filled his
knapsack with smoking hot pone and luscious sweet potatoes, whose
pulp was as golden as the sunflower's petals,—"I'se been ponder-
ing in my own min' and I kaint see what you all is fighting
'bout. Clar to goodness I kaint."

GENERAL ROBERT E. LEE.

"We are fighting to make the Southerners come back into the Union."

"De Union? What you mean by dat?"

"The Union—the States. There are thirty-five States, and one man governs the whole of them. Your old masters didn't like the man who was chosen, and so they said they wouldn't stay in the Union to be governed by him."

RALPH'S TALK WITH OLD NEGRESS.

"Is dat man a big man? Does he b'long to a good family? How many slabes does he own?"

"None at all. We don't have slaves up North."

"Don't hab slabes? Who totes your water and picks de cotton and hoes de fields?"

"We don't grow any cotton, and all our work is done by people whom we hire and pay money to."

The old slave's eyes opened wide with curiosity.

"And when dey gets sassy, does de oberseer whip 'em?"

Ralph laughed heartily as he thought of the suit for assault and battery whipping a servant up North would bring about. Here was an old colored woman as ignorant of her relationship to the great tide of humanity as a child, and how could he explain to her the difference between servants North and South? To him slavery was a mere name. He knew nothing of its blighting influence. Born in the West in a little village where no negroes were to be found, he had seldom met one, and could not understand how dreary and hopeless the life of a "chattel" could be.

RALPH IS QUESTIONED NOW.

The old woman seemed to be talking to herself.

"It pears to me dey must be dissbedient and sassy sumtimes. All niggers are. Wonder how dey makes dem mind. When dey runs across a right smart uppish cullered pusson how do dey settle wid him? Did you say, massa, dey neber whip dem?"

"No, auntie, they never do."

Aunt Judah shook her head doubtingly. "Massa," she

broke out suddenly, "dey flogs dem down here; dey has to,
sumtimes. I neber was struck a blow. I was a house servant,
but my man worked on de plantation. 'Diamond Joe,' dey
called him; he was lashed ebery now and den, and I tink it
made him ugly. He was a likely boy. Wy, massa used to
clar if he wan't so stubbon, jess like one of our plantation mules,
he wouldn't take de price of two boys for him, for he could
hoe and pick mo' cotton dan any 'mount of boys. His skin was

as shiny as de
satin in Missus'
dress, and dark,
and he was tall
like de poplar
trees, and strong
and big. Joe
lubbed me in
dose days."

Ralph looked
at her wonder-
ingly. Here was
a new thought.
Did those un-
couth black folks
care for each
other as white

A TYPICAL COLORED BOY.

people did? Were they capable of attachments? She was
almost hideous—had she ever been young?

A tear rolled down Aunt Judah's withered cheek, and she
seemed to be looking far away. She was silent so long that
Ralph began to be impatient to get back to camp with his knapsack full of good things.

"Well, auntie, where is Joe now? He must be pretty old
by this time."

A solemn look stole over her features, and looking up to
where the blue sky showed through the chinks in the little cabin
roof, she said—

"In Heben, I b'leeve. Oh, honey, it makes my heart heaby eben now, and offen and offen de tears dey makes my old eyes burn. Many a day I'se asked my hebenly Fader whar on dis big yarth my Joe was, but it must hab been wicked fur me to ask de Great King anyting 'bout a po' cullered boy, fur I neber had any answer. But Joe was a powerful hansum boy, de best one on de plantation."

"How did he die?"

"Die? I didn't 'spress my 'pinion dat he *was* dead. I has looked long for Joe, and I 'mos knows he must be gone up above, for he lubbed me and he lubbed de little missie—de little daisy, Missie Flossie. She was de only one who could bring him out of his tantarums, fer po' Joe did hab spells, when he was ugly.

"Massa Steve— he owned us bof— I'members dat day

OLD AUNT JUDAH.

well; it was a sunshiny day, de yarth was all carpeted wid de short, green grass, and de flowers filled de whole land wid deir sweetness. It was so bright my heart was singing a song, and Missus Flora wanted to be druv to town to buy some nice tings for de little missie's birfday party.

6

JOE DISAPPEARS. Massa say 'Joe, Dick's got a sick hoss to 'tend to. You hitch up de big black team, and take your mistress to town.' Joe, he whispered to me—I had tuk de little lady out on de lawn—dat he cudn't dribe dem speerited critters, fur he had burnt his hands roasting corn in de ashes de night afore. 'Don't stan' dar, you brack rascal,' massa said, fur he seed him talking to me. 'Massa, I'se dead anxious to go, but I hab a bery bad hand—caint Dick go dis time wid de missus?'

"Then massa, he got as white as a sheet wif temper, and his voice was like funder—'No! go as I told you. Do you want anoder flogging?'

"I felt way down all fru me, sumfing was gwine to happen, for Joe he looked so wicked, and he kep' muttering and muttering, and I was scared, fur I

DIAMOND JOE AND AUNT JUDAH WHEN YOUNG.

knowed sumfing was about to break, when Joe 'muned wid hisself. But oh, massa, I shall neber forget de awful night dat fell, and no Joe, nor no missus, nor no carridge and hosses cumd home. Massa was wild. He tore up and down de lawn, running here and shouting dar, and sending fust one nigger, den anudder, to the neighbors' plantations to see if missie had dun gone visiting at any ob dem. Den he called fur Dick and his white hoss, and was jess jumping on his back when de hans' set up a holler·

ing and de carridge cum taring onto de lawn, and fust dey 'lowed

Missus Flora was dead, fur she was cuddled up in a heap, as white as snow. Wen dey got her to cum to she tole Massa Steve how Joe had dun gone to town wid her and den wen she wanted to cum home he had rode 'em off, way off inter de woods, and way inter de midst of de fick trees, and gibing de hosses a terrible lashing he started dem, heads toward home; den dey runned all de way ober sticks

JOE HIDING IN THE WOODS.

and limbs of trees till dey foun' de open road, wen dey went so fas' Missus lost her breff and cudn't see any mo'.

"You should have seen massa den! He swore so loud it made my ears ache, and all de time he was looking right at me. He said Joe had run away and he'd hab de young black debil's hide off when he kotched him, and if he was shore any ob de slabes knew he was going it ud be wuss for dem; he'd sell 'em to de very next trader dat cumd along, and dey'd be toted down Souf, whar dey'd be showed how to work. He swore he had nuffing but a pack of lazy niggers roun' him, who didn't desarve to hab a good master. And, honey, fore de Lawd, Massa Steve was a kind master, only he wud swar and cuss at us once in awhile."

"What became of Joe? Did they catch him?" asked Ralph, who was so deeply interested in her story that he had forgotten all about the boys in camp who were waiting for that hot corn bread.

"Yes, massa, I seen him dragged in de next day, after dey had hunted all night wid de dogs. Dey had torn his clothes in tatters, and his han's and face was all red wid de blood whar he fought wid dem. De master he was so mad he made de slaves all come outen deir cabins, to see how dey sarbed a runaway. I can see it now"—and she covered her eyes with her wrinkled black hands—"I can see it all. Oh, Joe, I neber forgits dat day. And when de cruel 'black snake' cut his back ebery time it hit him he neber said a word, but he kind o' shibered all over and set his teeth hard, but I screamed out 'Po' Joe! Will nobody pity po' Joe?' and fell down on de grass all cold as a stone. My breff was gone, and I fought de angel ob de Lord had done called me home and jess den Massa Steve say—'Go to your quarters, Joe.' My Joe, he walk off as proud as a king. Missus she was bery sorry for me, and was allus bery kind to me, but Joe neber sing in de field any mo'. He would fix his eyes on me so terrible I was almos'. afraid of him, and he would mutter dat de avenger was on de white man's track. 'I'm gwine to be free. Neber no more will dey lash Joe.' I used to tink de walls would hear him and tell de massa. But dey didn't, and one night wen ebery libing soul 'cept de watch dogs were in deir beds, de hosses 'gan to stamp and kick in deir boxes, and de dogs were howling, and den we heard de white folks screaming, louder and louder, and fas' as we could, we ran outen our cabins, and dar up on de little knoll whar de house stood, we saw de black smoke pouring out ob de windows and rolling up to de sky, and den turning redder and redder, and we could 'stinguish Massa Steve and Missus Flora out on de lawn jess as dey jumped from deir beds.

"De oberseer was fighting de flames and he tole us to get all de buckets we could, and fotch de water from de well in dem, and he jumped on a hoss and galloped to de nearest plantation for help, and dey all turned out, white people and slabes, and brought water, and soon

FIRE IN THE HOME.

de fire wasn't red no mo', but de house—you can see de walls now ober dar, whar dey stand to 'min' me ebery day ob de dear massa and missie and de little lamb, Flossie—was no house any more, all de insides gone, and de black outside standing up in de summer air."

She paused to wipe away the hot tears that blinded her.

"What became of your master and his family?"

RUINS OF THE HOUSE.

"Massa and missus were presarbed, but de little white blossom, whose birfday had been so bright, dey didn't know whar to look for her, and her mudder was screeching 'My baby—my baby!' and going out o' one faint into anoder, and her pa trying to rush inter de smoking house and calling for his Flossie— oh, it was enuff to make de har turn gray!

"She muss hab been frightened so when de smoke got in her pretty blue eyes dat she didn't know how to fin' de way out, fer she was crouched down behind de front stairs, and dat's de spot whar Dick found her, wid her night-dress all on fire, but de light tole him whar to look.

"When he put de little precious chile in my arms she put

her baby fingers on my black face and she said, 'Judah, tell mamma—I am not hurt—but I caint see!' Honey, de nex' day she shut dem po' little eyes on dis world, and missie, whose heart broke den, followed her lamb to de hebenly pastures whar de good Lawd 'tends to all deir wants."

"What became of your master?"

"Massa Steve?   He went ober de sea, and he died in anoder country.   De plantation and all de slabes went to his **THE NEW** brudder, who had de big house yo' sees ober dar on **HOUSE.** de road put up.   No one eber goes near de old place, ' fer dey say it's hanted."

A SOUTHERN MANSION.

"But the old home and Joe?   You don't think he had anything to do with setting it on fire?"

"Massa, de good Book tells de po' creatures dat dey musn't form no 'pinion to hurt deir neighbors.   It goes agin me to say dat he did, but yo' didn't know Joe, and I did."

"Did they suspect him?"

"I neber could look dem in de face to know, but Joe neber was seen after de house was burned, and dat's many years in de past."

Ralph drew a long breath, and bidding the old negress good-bye, he went back to camp with a sad heart. When he entered the camp he found the men gathered in knots, discussing the news they had just received of a coming engagement.

"What are we going out for?" asked a new man.

"So as to give the rebs a chance to lay us out, or be laid out themselves. What do you suppose we go to war for?"

Old Bill's gruff tones nettled the man.

HON. CHARLES SUMNER.

"It don't hurt you to answer a civil question, does it?"

"Well, not exactly. You see General Mc-Call has had an advance guard out reconnoitering, but he can't persuade the boys over on the Virginia side to show up on open ground. They say there's a big force of Confeds at Leesburg, five miles or so back from the river."

"This will be my first battle," the new recruit said, with a sigh, "but I don't expect it'll be my last."

"That's right— never say die. The man who is a little chicken-hearted at first, often turns out to be the most courageous soldier."

"I remember reading once," Ralph interposed, "that at some charge on a battery in one of the battles Napoleon fought when the odds were greatly against him, his attention was called by one of his officers to the cowardice of one poor fellow who was pressing on, up to the cannon's mouth. His knees were shaking, his eyes bulged out, and he gave every evidence of being terror-stricken. But his gaze was fixed on the coveted point, his teeth were set hard, and he kept resolutely on. **NOT ALWAYS COWARDICE.** 'That man is not a coward,' said the great general; 'he sees that his life is in danger, and still he does not shrink from his duty, but faces death like a man. He will be shot before he yields.'

EPISCOPAL CHURCH AT ALEXANDRIA, VA.
Generals Washington and Lee were Communicants at this Church.

"But the soldier was not wounded. He lived to become an officer in the very regiment which one would have expected to see disgraced by his cowardice, and won great fame through his heroic bravery in after engagements."

"Boys," said Old Bill, who was always the spokesman for

the party, "the 'Little Corporal'—that's Napoleon Bonaparte," he continued in an aside to the new man, who made a wry face at being singled out for an explanation—"was right. It's agin human nature not to feel a little shaky when you are going into your first battle. It's how you do your duty that settles your standing. If you attend to that no one can blame you for having a leetle private fear of your own."

CHAPTER VII.

THE DISASTER AT BALL'S BLUFF.

HASTY breakfast, with a rigid inspection of their muskets, and a hurried packing of knapsacks, preceded the long role of the drum, the signal to be up and doing. The sight of a body of soldiers with their glittering arms and tasty uniforms is inspiriting, and dull and cold must be the bosom that does not leap quicker at the thought that he belongs to this grand whole. Ralph felt a thrill of exultation as he realized that he was a part and parcel of the men who were massed on the bank of the Potomac that bright October day. There were Ralph's regiment of Massachusetts men, the Forty-second New York, Seventy-first Pennsylvania and a Rhode Island battery, counting, in all, some 2,000 men, watching for a chance to cross at an island which lay there.

The day was beautiful—the sun poured down his warm beams, for in that region the winter is late. Many were the openly spoken murmurs of impatience, however, on the part of the men.

"We shall never get across till doomsday," Bill Elliott said to Ralph. "Look at our men, over 2,000 of them, and we've only got two or three old boats to carry us over. With all due respect to General McClellan, I think he's made a great big mistake, as General Stone will find to his cost before we're over. The Johnnies can see all we're doing and get all ready for us. Why, it'll be dead easy for them to receive us in fine shape."

"They are having hard work with that battery, getting it up the bluff. See how they slip at every step."

And as Ralph watched the battery being dragged up with prodigious exertion his heart felt heavy, and he, too, began to fear there was an oversight somewhere.

At the top of the bluff lay a broad field of about ten acres, hemmed in on all sides by thick woods, so dense that neither infantry nor artillery could penetrate them in line. Colonel Baker was given entire command of all the troops. Then began a

GENERAL JOSEPH E. JOHNSTON.

desperate and gallant attempt, which the Confederates met, dashing out from the timber, and though the Federals fired round after round from their battery, it was a hopeless conflict, for the rebel sharpshooters picked off their gunners, one after another, and the pieces were left useless.

Still on the Union forces pressed, to be met by a heavy body of infantry, whose hot fire cut them down. For two hours they stood their ground gallantly, and returned the fire with spirit. Suddenly an officer riding a splendid horse, whose snowy sides were covered with foam, dashed out of the woods, and coming toward them, waving his sword over his head, he beckoned the Union forces forward.

Colonel Baker took new courage; he thought he recognized General Johnston in the horseman, and wildly cheering to his command to follow, he pressed forward, hoping at last he should meet the enemy in an open fight. But he was met by a fierce onset of the Confederates, who came on with tremendous force. Like a solid wall they met the Federals, and as part of the latter's columns charged, Colonel Baker received the whole contents of a revolver in the hands of one of the rebels, and fell dead.

His body was rescued through the bravery of Captain Beiral and his company, who fought their way back through the thickest of the opposing force, and with desperate courage rescued the body of their dead commander, and conveyed it to the island. At once the rout began, and the Union forces were driven back, down the steep clay bluffs, one hundred feet high, falling, jumping down, pushed by the Confederates, who followed at their heels, killing and taking prisoners.

It was an awful spectacle. Men whose courage could not be doubted, were panic-stricken, and throwing away coats, muskets, and everything that could impede them, plunged into the river, whose rapid current overwhelmed them, and **THE ROUT AT BALL'S BLUFF.** to their shrieks as they drowned, was added the rapid firing of the Confederates on the cliff above, the roar of the artillery, the cries of the wounded, making a scene of horror which cannot be described. The imagination alone can fill in the picture.

Among the incidents of this day may be mentioned a desertion of one of the regiments by its colonel, who swam the river on horseback, thus making his escape. Many took to a boat, which was quickly filled, and as quickly sunk with every soul. A captain in the Fifteenth Massachusetts came to the rescue of the fleeing Federals, with two companies, and charged up the hill, only to see how little help he could give, and a few moments decided him to wave his handkerchief, and surrender to the Confederates.

Dispirited and weary, the remnant of the troops moved back to camp. Their loss had been heavy. Over five hundred soldiers had been captured by the Confederates, Colonel Baker had been shot, and they had lost arms, ammunition and clothing.

Corporal Ralph Gregory had shown coolness and clear-headed courage, equal to the oldest and bravest. When the battle began, the color-sergeant had received a ball in the breast, and had fallen dead. Seizing the flag from his **RALPH SAVES THE COLORS.** stiffening fingers, Ralph rushed to the front, and held it manfully, through the storm of bullets that riddled its folds, and clinging desperately to it, he carried it proudly and safely, soiled and torn, but not disgraced.

But his strength was not equal to his courage, and handing it to a stalwart comrade whose arm was more powerful, he bade him to "protect it from capture." The colors went back to camp, and with them, went the story of the boy's bravery.

Ralph was weak, his nerves were unstrung. His ears still echoed the noise and confusion of the battle that had not yet died away. Still the Union men were fleeing, pursued closely by their enemy, who wounded them with muskets and swords, as they ran. The agonized shrieks of those who met their death in the swift-flowing stream rang in his ears with fearful distinctness, and he vaguely wondered if he would ever cease to hear them.

He was unnerved. It was not cowardice, but the reaction that so often follows times of great excitement. Exhaustion, complete and unavoidable, had taken possession of him. He reeled like a drunken man. Making a frantic effort to recover himself, he sank on the earth amid a clump of leaves and brush, that half hid him from observation. How long he lay in this stupor he could not tell, but when he became conscious of the dreadful place he was in, he slowly struggled to his feet, half-dazed and bewildered. His first thought was to wonder where Bill was. He recollected that he had fled in hot haste with the others, and the last glimpse of him which he had, was when the plucky Massachusetts captain made his stand, but was compelled to surrender. He was sure that he had been wounded, for he saw blood streaming down Bill's face, as he ran.

"Could he have escaped, or is he among the dead lying here?" he thought. "I must search for him."

And as he threaded his way among the dead and wounded as best he could in the twilight, he stumbled over the body of a boy. Kneeling down, he turned the lad's face upward, and in the dim light he knew him.

"It is Charlie Arlington! —he is surely dead!"

The boy opened his eyes, and seeing Ralph, he assured him that he was not wounded, but he feared his ankle was sprained. "I told you," he said, with a smile, "that we should meet again."

MAJOR-GENERAL FITZ HUGH LEE, C. S. A.

"You did, but I did not think it would be so soon. Are you injured?"

"Only by my horse, who stumbled and threw me with such force against that old stump that I fainted with pain. Do you think my leg is broken?"

"Let me examine it. No, I don't think it is. How are you going to ride, however? Where is your horse?"

"Oh, he ran away after serving me that mean trick. But

why are you here? Don't you know you are my prisoner now?"
he continued, smiling broadly.

"How's that?" Ralph spoke sharp and loud.

"Hush!" the other cautioned. "You'll have a dozen soldiers after you. They're coming back to bury the dead. Of
course you're my prisoner. You're on our field—were you not
routed?"

This fact rather staggered Ralph. It had not come home
to him till then; he looked anxiously toward the river's bank.

The boy divined his thought.

"It's no use to try to swim that stream here. The current's too strong."

"It seems I'm your prisoner, then." Ralph's sad tones spoke
volumes. The
horrors of cap-
tivity stared him
in the face. He
thought at that
instant, of his
mother, sisters
and the dear old
home, and his
heart was heavy
as lead.

Charlie ap-
peared to be
enjoying the ad-
vantage he had
over Ralph, for
he never re-
moved his gaze.
"I've but to
raise my voice

ASKING FOR FURLOUGH.

and you'd be surrounded in an instant."

"But how is it you are here now; I thought you knew
nothing about the army," said Ralph.

"I didn't when I last saw you, but I joined the Southern army the next week. I am in the cavalry service."

Ralph's curiosity would never be silenced. "Do you like it?" he asked.

"Yes, and no. I have been in several engagements, but the hardest blow I had was when they carried my father home dead, and I asked for a furlough, to go home to see him once more, and was refused."

Here the boy nearly broke down. Ralph's sympathies were aroused at once. He knew not what to say. But Charlie recovered himself soon, and continued—

"You see how I'm placed now. I shall *have* to take you into our camp."

"I wish Bill were here!" Ralph blurted out. "He wouldn't see me taken prisoner so easily."

To him Bill represented the sum total of all knowledge, and he felt confident of his ability to rescue him, even in the face of the danger that now menaced him.

A low whistle startled both boys. A few feet from them, stretched lengthwise of a fallen tree, lay Bill, who raised his head, which was bleeding freely.

"I've a good mind to take you both prisoners!" he said, jocosely. "What are you exchanging courtesies for? The boy's right. Unless we can get away in a very big hurry, he can land us both in the rebel camp, and then it'll be all over with us. You'd better be planning each other's escape, and then you'll both be likely to be court-martialed!"

"It's my luck, isn't it? I can't blame Charlie if he does take me. But I haven't got anything against him."

"Neither has any of us got anything against any of the Johnnies. This is not a personal affair, at all. But just the same we've got to fight 'em because they're agin the government."

Ralph looked closer at Bill. "You're wounded, and will be carried to prison, too! Oh, Bill, what will become of you?"

"It's nothing but a scratch. I lay here awhile till those

THE BATTLE OF ATLANTA, GA., JULY 22, 1864.

97

fellows' guns gave out, for I felt a little dizzy, and didn't care to
get up till the smoke cleared away, and I could make out my
bearings."

A groan from their companion recalled them to their position. Ralph was in a fever of anxiety. War was a brutalizing
affair, he pondered. "You mustn't have any feelings at all, Bill,
if you want to be a good soldier."

"Nary a feeling. Humanity don't cut no figger in a battle.
Why, boy, I've stood in the ranks and seen father on one side,
and son on the other, blazing away with hate and bitterness in
their eyes. And all on account of a mere difference of opinion."

Ralph shuddered. "It is dreadful; but war shall never
make me so hardened and indifferent to suffering that I will not
do all I can in honor to relieve it. I intend to fulfill all my
duties as a soldier, but do not see why I should hesitate to
show mercy to an injured foe."

"He's the right sort," Bill chuckled to himself.

With that thought in his mind, Ralph went nearer to Charlie,
and said—"Give me your handkerchief, and I will bandage your
ankle." In a few moments he had finished binding it on, tightly
and skillfully, while the boy looked his gratitude.

"It feels a little easier," he said, "the pain was intense."

Bill watched them both narrowly. In his heart he admired
"the little rebel cuss," but he wished him a thousand miles
away, for he saw that it was impossible to make their escape,
as Charlie had only to raise his voice as he had suggested, and
the enemy would be upon them.

It was a moment of anxiety for the man and his companion.
Charlie was the most indifferent of the three. "I'd rather have
been killed than have to go to their prison, for who knows
how long it may be before I am exchanged?" thought Bill.

The firing had ceased, and darkness had settled o'er the earth.
Suddenly Charlie seemed to recollect something, for he whispered—

"Go—you must go, at once. The detail will soon be here,
to bury our poor boys, and they will have you, sure. Go down
the bluff as still as you can; don't loosen a pebble even, for

7

RALPH AND BILL ESCAPE CAPTURE. there are sharp ears near. Keep close to the river bank, and about half a mile down you'll see an old tree standing that has been struck by lightning. Two rods north of the tree a little skiff is hid in the tall weeds. Take it and row across. Go quick, and, above all, make no noise. My life, as well as yours, is in danger. They'd shoot me in a minute, if they knew I helped you escape."

"You're a brick—you are!" broke out Bill, admiringly.

Ralph wrung his hand. "What will you do? You can't lie here all night."

"They'll find me all right and carry me off to the hospital. I can talk, if I can't walk, and I'll soon let them know where I am. But you haven't a second to waste. Go!"

The hint, so urgently given, was acted upon, and none too speedily, for a moment after, the men appeared, and Charlie was suddenly seized with a violent fit of coughing, so loud and boisterous, it was well calculated to cover any noise which Ralph and Bill might unintentionally make. He was placed on a litter and borne away.

Bill scarce drew a breath until his feet touched the bottom of the boat. Charlie's violent cough had served them well, for though they stole noiselessly down the bluff, the night was so still that a breath almost could be detected. They were soon across the noble river, and their hearts beat tumultuously when they found themselves safe within the Union lines.

Bill's wound was not serious, so he declared. He even objected to the few days in the hospital which the surgeon prescribed. His good nature never left him.

OLD BILL ISN'T ALARMED. "Sick men may go and lay up, but you cain't kill Old Bill. I'm presarved for something better than to stop a bullet. I've been through too many hard sieges to give in for a little blow like that was."

"You've got another invite to see the Colonel," a grizzled old soldier said to Ralph a day or two after the engagement. "He desires the pleasure of your company in his tent. Leastwise, that's what it amounts to, though that ain't the language he made use of. Wonder why I don't be asked once in awhile? He don't know what he's losing by not consulting me. But hurry up—'tain't perlite to keep him waiting."

Ralph trembled visibly, and every drop of blood turned to ice. He knew something must be wrong. Perhaps he ought not to have helped Charlie, but what else could he do? He walked briskly toward the tent of the officer.

Colonel Hopkins was a stern, battle-scarred old soldier, who wasted no words. His keen vision could discover merit, however, and as he looked steadily at Ralph, he took his measure at once.

"Your captain tells me you saved the colors of the regiment, in the late engagement?"

"I did, Colonel."

"And you risked your life in so doing."

"Why should I not? I am a soldier, sir!" and the boy's proud look met a corresponding gleam in his superior's eye.

"You are beginning young to do good service. You are not of age yet?"

"I am eighteen."

The officers standing near, looked their admiration of the manly lad, who made his replies with modesty and becoming deference.

RALPH IS MADE SERGEANT.

GENERAL JOHN C. FREMONT.

"You are a sergeant from this day. See that you always uphold your colors."

"I will, with the help of Heaven!" was Ralph's fervent utterance, as he followed the orderly from the Colonel's tent.

One of the most brilliant affairs of the war was the charge of a body of cavalry under Fremont. This was a fine and

CHARGE OF FREMONT'S BODY GUARD UNDER MAJOR ZAGONYI, NEAR SPRINGFIELD, MO

MAJOR CHARLES ZAGONYI.

choice array of cavalry, known as "Fremont's Body Guard," whose exploits were famous. It was commanded by Major Charles Zagonyi, a Hungarian, whose military record had been made in Europe. This dashing and fiery soldier, with a band of 160 men, charged upon a Confederate force of 2,000, who were drawn up in a hollow square. He rode across the field, unheeding the firing of the skirmishers, but charged into the midst of the Confederates, and with pistols and sabers, scattered them like dry leaves in the autumn wind. Not content with this, the daring Major chased them into the streets of Springfield, and fought them hand to hand.

After this daring and unequaled achievement, he hoisted the National flag upon the courthouse at Springfield, sent a guard to care for the wounded, and then went quietly back to Bolivar.

CHAPTER VIII.

THE ARMY IN WINTER QUARTERS.

INTER so far had brought them much suffering and privation. To Ralph it was peculiarly dreary. With the prospect of a period of inactivity, it was strange that so little provision was made to protect them from the cold, raw winds that were so frequent. Many of the soldiers put up rude huts, made from the fine timber which grew so plentiful in that region, and those who were independent and enterprising enough to build for themselves, often fashioned a very snug, cozy little house. The rough stone fireplace, put together with Virginia mud, was never wanting. What though it was neither symmetrical nor artistic? The warmth and cheer compensated for the absence of both these features.

In some of these huts—they surely deserved a better title—the men threw themselves down at night on the ground, which was covered with blankets, rubber coats, and any material the jovial occupants could find to keep out the dampness. Some, more pretentious, constructed bunks or boxes

PREPARING FOR COLD WEATHER. round the sides, which were as comfortable as a spring bed would be at home. It was quite common to find home-made chairs, benches and tables, round which they gathered when off duty, and told stories or discussed the situation. The walls were papered with illustrations cut from newspapers, which added to the charms of the dwelling.

But the greater number shivered under canvas tents, feeling keenly the light snows and rains, followed by days of thaw and sunshine, which were so frequent. To add to the dreariness of their surroundings, the funeral dirge was often heard, as the dead were carried out from hospital, who had succumbed to that ap-

CAMP OF THE ARMY OF THE POTOMAC AT CUMBERLAND LANDING.

parently simple disease, the measles, but which leaves its victim feeble, exhausted, and unable to rally.

To a new recruit, or to one who is full of sensibility, as Ralph was, these sights were particularly depressing.

A snowstorm during the day had been succeeded by a windy, cold night. Ralph had been writing to his mother, and while he took care to make every word as cheerful as he could, and never to mention his discomforts, yet the mother heart

IN WINTER QUARTERS.

read between the lines, and knew her boy was homesick, pining for her, as she, alas! was longing for the loving caress and the sound of his voice.

As he pushed back the stool which had answered for a writing desk, the wind gave a sudden whirl and lifted the canvas, sending a shower of sleet over him which made him shiver.

"The winter here is full as cold and disagreeable as up North!" he said. "I thought this was a land of perpetual sunshine and flowers!"

He peered out at the sentry, who hugged his great coat closer, as he paced to and fro. He fancied he saw in the gloom a man and horse, and heard the sharp challenge—

"Halt! Who goes there?"

The horseman drew up, and replied promptly—

"A messenger from General Shields, with dispatches for Colonel Hopkins. I must deliver them at once."

BEARING DISPATCHES.

The sentinel called—"Sergeant of the guard—post number five—a message from headquarters!"

The words were passed along the line of guards, until it reached the sergeant, who came instantly.

He carried the papers to his colonel, who read them hastily, and signed each one, handing them back to the orderly, who rode swiftly away.

Ralph was by this time outside his tent, unmindful of the

sleet which tore his flesh like sharp-pointed arrows. He longed to know what those dispatches signified, but his curiosity had to remain unsatisfied, and he went back to his tent to try to sleep, as well as he could, for the biting wind that forced its way into every crevice.

He seated himself on the side of his bed, and tried to think. He wondered when General McClellan was going to take Rich-

SHARPSHOOTERS.

mond. The cry "All Quiet on the Potomac" was heard continually, and weary men and weeping women **RALPH MEDITATES ON THE WAR.** all over the land were longing for the dawn of peace which should bring back to them fathers, husbands and sons. But ah, that peace was far distant. The boy reasoned that he had no right to criticise the men who held trusted positions in the army. But surely the boys in camp and field were doing all they could, under orders, to hasten the end of these troublous times. Would the conflict ever cease?

Perplexed and worn out in trying to solve the problem agitating so many of the most patriotic and the most far-seeing, all over the land, Ralph at last fell asleep, to be roused by the reveille. He sprang up, sure that he must be dreaming, for he had just been sleeping but a moment—a mere "cat nap," and this couldn't be a summons to leave his comfortable bed. He had neither time nor right to object, however; his sole duty was to obey orders, and he hastened to dress. Outside, the soldiers were hurrying about, most of those who were called on glad of any break in the monotony of their first winter in camp.

"Breakfast at two, march at half-past," was the captain's peremptory order.

"What an unearthly hour," was Ralph's comment. "Where are we bound? And why march at night?"

"Can't say," a comrade ventured, "unless it's so we won't have to march by day!"

They were not long in suspense.

A portion of their regiment was ordered to assist a force of Ohio and Indiana men under Colonel Dunning, in routing a body of Confederates who were posted near Romney, Va., at a point called Blue Gap.

The wind had died away, the stars were out, and the moon shone brilliantly. The cutting sleet had turned to snow, and the soft carpet lay white and pure, muffling the sound of their footsteps. It was a weird sight—that mass of men tramping along with steady steps, while their shadows falling on the ground danced and flickered in the moonbeams with startling vividness.

Blue Gap was a natural opening between hills, and was well defended by howitzers and rifle pits. As they approached the Gap, Ralph's keen eye detected a dozen men piling up limbs, straw, and other inflammable material, against the bridge that spanned a stream running through the Gap.

"Captain," he said, "some of those fellows have left the lines, and are fixing things nice to burn that bridge."

"We'll block that game, instanter. We need that bridge more than they do."

A dash was made for the bridge, led by the captain, who opened fire upon them, and thus ended that attempt. On the hills the entrenchments were held manfully, but the Confederates had scarce time to pour forth their fire, before the two Ohio regiments dashed upon them, and captured two pieces of artillery. The surprise was so complete and the attack so overwhelming, that defense was vain.

The hills were swarming with Federals, fighting hand to hand, and forcing their opponents back. The houses on the other shore were filled with sharpshooters, whose constant firing harassed the Federals, and brought down a soldier at nearly every shot.

A score of men sprang into a large boat lying at the bank, and with a storm of bullets hissing and rattling about them, they crossed to the shore where the sharpshooters were hidden. Death menaced them, but with a huzza that would have put life into a stone, they rowed fast, and sprang out of the boat. Dashing up the hill, to the houses which the enemy had used for vantage ground, they found them vacated.

"They didn't wait to make our acquaintance," Ralph said.

"No, but those sharpshooters introduced themselves to us in fine style. Why, a man went down at nearly every shot."

Bill said not a word, but leaned heavily over the side of the boat. No one paid him attention, for their hearts were filled with a longing for revenge.

"Boys, we have missed the rebs ensconced in these houses, but we can prevent their using them again. We will burn them to the ground, and take good care that not a timber stands, after we have done with them. They have picked off some of our best men, and we won't leave a roof to shelter them."

A dozen pairs of willing hands were at work in an instant gathering wood and brush, which they piled around the dwellings. With faces grimy and soiled, these resolute men touched the pile with a match, while they stood ready to shoot the first man who dared to show himself to protest, and soon the flames leaped upward, crackling, sputtering and curling round doors

BURNING THE HOUSES. and windows, licking up every object within reach, till naught but the charred and blackened timbers stood to mark the spot where the sharpshooters had dealt their deadly work.

The skirmish was brief. It was an easy victory, and no loss had been sustained by the Federals, save those who were shot in the boats. But the Confederate loss was greater. Forty soldiers were lying dead in the grass and weeds, and as many more were carried back to camp, prisoners.

Even while the houses were being consumed, Ralph went back to assist those who had received the bullets of the sharpshooters. Some had fallen overboard, and sunk in the stream. Others were lying as they had fallen, their cold hands still grasping their weapons, which they would never use again. One poor fellow was kneeling in the bottom of the boat, his finger on the trigger of his musket, and his staring eyes fixed on the shore. Ralph shuddered. Could he ever become inured to these dreadful sights?

Bill Elliott was leaning over the side of the boat, in a half-stupor. The wound in his head had opened afresh, and the red stream was running down his face, staining its ghastly whiteness crimson. His arm hung useless by his side, shattered by a bullet. Opening his eyes at the sound of Ralph's voice, he whispered faintly:

"I thought you'd come arter me. They've fixed me this time, sure," and he relapsed into unconsciousness.

A litter was soon hurried together, and Old Bill was placed in hospital.

CHAPTER IX.

FAIR OAKS.

"THE Johnnies are busy these times, aren't they?"

"And so are we, chasing them up. I don't see that we are any nearer Richmond than we were a month or so ago."

"Nor we won't be," broke in another man, "if General McClellan repeats his Yorktown tactics. Perhaps, by the time we get to Richmond, we'll find some 'Quaker guns' there."

"It must have been kind of disheartening to the boys after lying 'round a place a month to have the rebs move out just as they were getting ready to go in, and find they had left a lot of wooden guns behind."

All the next day the soldiers were working on the redoubts, and wholly unaware of the surprise in store for them. May 31st dawned, and while they were still fortifying their position, a tremor ran through the line. "The Confederates are upon us!" was the cry, and as they tossed aside the shovels, the Confederates charged upon them with their well-known "yell" that so often echoed and re-echoed on the battle-field.

But they found brave men ready to repel their assault. The Chickahominy had swollen to such a height that bridges were carried away in its mad rush. General McClellan had thrown the left wing of his forces across the stream, but it was impossible to get reinforcements to their help.

Both sides showed unexampled bravery. General Johnston moved on toward Richmond, six miles away, where he halted, for the purpose of striking the detached wing of the Union forces. The rise of the river had hampered the movements of the latter, and it seemed as if capture was certain.

The half-finished redoubts had been occupied by General

Casey's division of Keys' corps, and although they rallied several times, it was in vain. The rebels made a detour, and stole upon their rear, and they could no longer hold them. Their line was in danger.

Meanwhile General Johnston's evident intention was to bring up a heavy flanking force between General Casey and the river whose banks had risen so unluckily for the Federals, cutting off all hopes of reinforcements.

And now a magnificent exhibition of courage was shown by Sumner. He expected orders to go to the rescue, and his men were drawn up in line ready for the summons. One bridge alone remained with which to cross the river, and its approaches were under water. Some of its supports were gone, and as the soldiers stepped upon it, the frail structure swayed to and fro, mid the rushing waters, but they passed over as speedily and safely as though it were a solid piece of masonry.

General Sumner's appearance was most opportune. He met the flank attack, and was victorious. The slaughter was fearful. In this battle 12,000 men gave up their lives—5,000 Northern men, and 7,000 Southern.

General Johnston fell, a Federal shot having taken effect. He was carried off the field, and at first it was feared by the Confederates that his wound was mortal, but after some months of suffering and enforced retirement he recovered, and a year after assumed command of the Confederate forces of the Mississippi.

Ralph was sent with one of the details to bury the dead and bring in the wounded. Trenches were dug, and the dead piled in them. Many were left where the last shot had struck them down, and earth was heaped upon them. The ground was literally blood-soaked. The dead were everywhere—the battle-field was one vast graveyard, with its tenants left unburied.

Ralph entered a little log house in a pasture near the railroad, and seated himself on a bench for a moment's rest. Just outside the door, he found the dead and the wounded packed so close that he could scarcely avoid stepping on them. To distinguish them was a hard task, for the wounded lay there so quiet and motionless, fast in that silent resignation born of despair, that, save for the dull blackness that covered the faces of those from whom life had fled, it would be easy to mistake the living for the dead.

All sorts and ages were there, in one mass—the boy, who had gone from home, ardent and hopeful, the old man who had left the record of an honorable life behind him; officers who had cheered their commands on to victory, privates who had fought fearlessly—all lay there, while horses had fallen dead across their riders, or were struggling in agony. The picture was horrible!

He was reminded of his duty by the voice

OLD CITY HALL, NEW ORLEANS, WHERE THE SURRENDER OF THE CITY WAS DEMANDED.

of an old man, who came into the room where he was musing.

"This is a cruel war, sir!" he said to Ralph. "I've been

RALPH MEETS A PROPHET. raised here, man and boy, nigh onto seventy years, and I never thought, when I played in these fields, that I should ever live to see them desecrated with human blood."

Ralph raised his head, and looked at him earnestly.

"No," the old man continued, "I have looked for the coming of the Lord·these many years, but I never thought He would come in blood and smoke, and the noise of battle."

"What do you mean?" the boy asked, breathlessly. "How has the Lord come?"

"Has He not come to set human beings free? Is not the black man's bondage nearly over? Is not slavery doomed? Then the only blot upon the fair name of America will be wiped out. The North and South will become brothers again, and go hand in hand in all worthy undertakings. Thus, as one family again, they will march on, to a grand and glorious destiny."

"If my mother could hear him talk!" his listener thought. "What does he mean by the blacks being set free?" For the Proclamation of Emancipation had not yet been given to the world, and the position of the slaves during hostilities had not been settled.

"Are you a Northerner?" he asked the old man.

"No, I am a Southerner," with a tinge of pride in his tones.

"How do you dare say such things?"

"I am an old man, and they call me childish and silly. But I love my country, and I want to see her truly great."

"Have you always talked in this way?" queried Ralph, puzzled at the old man's language and manners.

"Always. Oh, I have paid dearly for my opinions. I have had my house torn down over my head, I have suffered in my young days; but I have lost all I ever loved, and they pity me now. I know I shall live to see my prayer answered—that we may become a free and united country. Then I shall be ready to die. Yes, it comes to that with old and young. We must all be ready to die at any moment."

With a courteous nod to Ralph, he passed out of the door, and the boy was left alone.

"We must be ready to die at any moment!" The words sounded like a knell to Ralph. Was *he* ready to die? He had been carefully nurtured by that blessing to a child, a praying mother, and his boyish days were spent in the Sabbath school. Like all in the springtime of life, death seemed afar off, something that would not approach him for many years. Death was the expected portion of the old, but he had always resolutely put aside all thoughts of a future that did not belong to this life.

Now these words came home like a shock. Was he ready? He had never been a bad boy, in any sense, but still he was not ready or willing to die. At that possibility his courage forsook him; memory went swiftly back to many a childish piece of wrong-doing, which, under the fear of death, he magnified into black and unpardonable sins. Filled with sorrow and repentance he fell on his knees on the hard floor of that little cabin, with the dead so near him, and cried—"Help, O Lord, or I perish!"

A wave of tender feeling swept over his soul, and his mother's favorite psalm, the 118th, **RALPH COMMUNES WITH HIS SOUL.** which she had read to him so often, came to his remembrance, and one verse was as music to him,—"The Lord is on my side; I will not fear. What can man do unto me?" He rose to his feet, refreshed and made strong.

CHAPTER X.

CAMP FUN.

THAT time should not hang heavy on their hands, much inventive genius was brought into play, and no schoolboys, famous for their ability in making up games, could equal these grown men in originating sports to fill in the hours that otherwise would have been exceedingly dull. Some such safety-valve was necessary, or else many would have broken down with memories of the dear ones at home, and the depressing sights of war, and its hardships.

The camp echoed often with the songs so dear to all who can be moved by tender thoughts. Many of the men were the possessors of rich, melodious voices, that brought many a thrill of delight to their listeners, in their tones.

Ralph had a fine voice, and to please his comrades he often sang the sweet old songs of childhood, while they listened with an enthusiasm and rounds of applause that many a prima donna could not have inspired. Throwing themselves around the blazing camp fire whose ruddy sparks flew heavenward, the whole company would join him in singing the melodies with hearty goodwill, and at those moments care and danger were forgotten. Now he would give them a plaintive, gentle ditty that would make the eyes of those brown-faced soldiers moist with emotion, as home pictures started into life before them, and then a stirring song of patriotism and victory would ring out, until the blood would leap in their veins, and each man there was ready to attack any foe single-handed.

But the boy's heart was heavy, even while his humble efforts in the musical line were giving pleasure to his comrades. His constant prayer was that some decisive move might be made, by which the war might be brought to a speedy close. He was lonely, too, for "Old Bill," as he always called himself, had been in the hospital for some time, and he missed his cheery ways.

One afternoon as he sat in his tent reading, he heard peals of boisterous laughter ringing out upon the air. Going to the

CAMP FIRE SONGS.

opening, he saw a group of soldiers gathered round some object, and heard them chaffing some one whom he could not see.

"What is the excitement, Harry?" he asked a companion who had evidently come from the scene of action.

"I just came for you to pile out and see the fun. They've

got one of our boys, and are amusing themselves at his expense. Come on, or you'll be too late. The performance will be over."

Ralph hurried after Harry, who was off like a deer, and going straight up to the group, he saw a crowd of men tossing another one up in the air, and letting him fall into a blanket, amid screams of laughter, and cries of "Send him up higher!" "Pickle him in his own salt!" "Head him up in a barrel, and send him to the cook!" "We'll make a high private in the rear rank of him!"

"Gently, boys," the victim panted. "You don't want to be too hard on a poor fellow for having a little joke of his own."

"Who is it—what has he done?" inquired Ralph, who didn't enjoy such rough sport, and was really concerned lest they might carry it so far as to injure the man.

"It's Corporal Fred Greene, the funny fellow of Co. H,"
THE BIRTHDAY FEAST. Tim Mackey responded. "It's his birthday, and we're celebrating it. Ain't he having a high time?"

Fred was a mischievous young fellow, who had just seen his twenty-third birthday. If there was any chance for a joke on any member of the company, he never lost the opportunity of making the most he could out of it.

In order to impress the fact that he had a birthday, he had invited a score of his comrades to a "small spread" in his tent. The colored cook was in the secret, and through his connivance, and the help of a few cracker boxes draped with bunting, and some tin cans, he had succeeded in making quite a tasty looking table. Before the banquet began, he made a short speech of welcome, which was responded to in good faith by Franklin Field, who was deputed to do the speaking on all occasions, as he had quite a gift of extempore oratory.

Without further ceremony, Fred cordially pressed all of them to "fall to." Just at this interesting moment, the cook, a loose-jointed, wrinkled old darkey, whose huge mouth looked as if it was always ready to utter a guffaw, entered the tent, and scraping and bowing to the "gemmens," broke out with— "Sorry to put back your 'joyment, Massa Fred, but youse wanted outside, bad."

Fred rose, and with a graceful salute to his guests, begged them, in a most elaborate manner, to attack the food, which was entirely at their service. It was unfortunate that he should be disturbed at such a moment, but duty called him, and he would return at the earliest opportunity.

"This black rascal is bound I shan't have my share, but fall to, friends." Once outside, he hunted a safe hiding place behind the hedge, and waited.

FUN IN CAMP.

Those left behind sat a moment lost in wonder as to where the good things sprang from. They did look inviting to these devourers of hard tack and bacon. The table had for a center-piece a fine-looking chicken, flanked on both wings by oranges, potatoes roasted in the ashes, canned fruit, and—two huge cakes!

"Where did Fred get these dainties? He's too lazy to forage, and I don't believe he could buy them at the sutler's

tent. His credit ain't good enough," was the comment made by
one of his "friends."

" Never mind where he got 'em," a gaunt, hungry-looking
fellow answered. " Let's try 'em fust, and investigate afterwards."

No further urging was necessary. They all "fell to," as
they had been ordered, but the wry faces, choking, gasping
breath, and muttered expletives, as one after another bit into some
tempting morsel to find a mouth filled with salt, pepper or sand,
would have been a subject for a painter. The chicken was a sham;
its unusual plumpness was due to a liberal stuffing of cotton
batting, the oranges were well sanded, while the cake was plenti-
fully seasoned with salt and pepper—two condiments that are
very well in proper proportions, but rather nauseating when taken
in large doses.

They rose in a body—all were of one mind when they
rushed out after their host, who was making for the woods at
the other end of camp. A dozen fleet-footed men soon overtook him, and, bringing him back, proceeded to inflict sum-
mary punishment, amid roars of laughter, for he was liked by
every man of the company.

Fred didn't play any more jokes upon those boys, and after
his undesired elevation, he was quite subdued. But they all
forgave him, and " Fred's birthday party" passed into a byword,
when some illustration was needed to indicate a good time.

Ralph was homesick. It was useless to disguise the fact,
for it began to tell upon his health. Malaria had fastened its
strong hand upon him, and he grew more listless every day.
He did not waver in his duties, however, and when marching
orders came, he was among the first to pack his knapsack and
shoulder his musket.

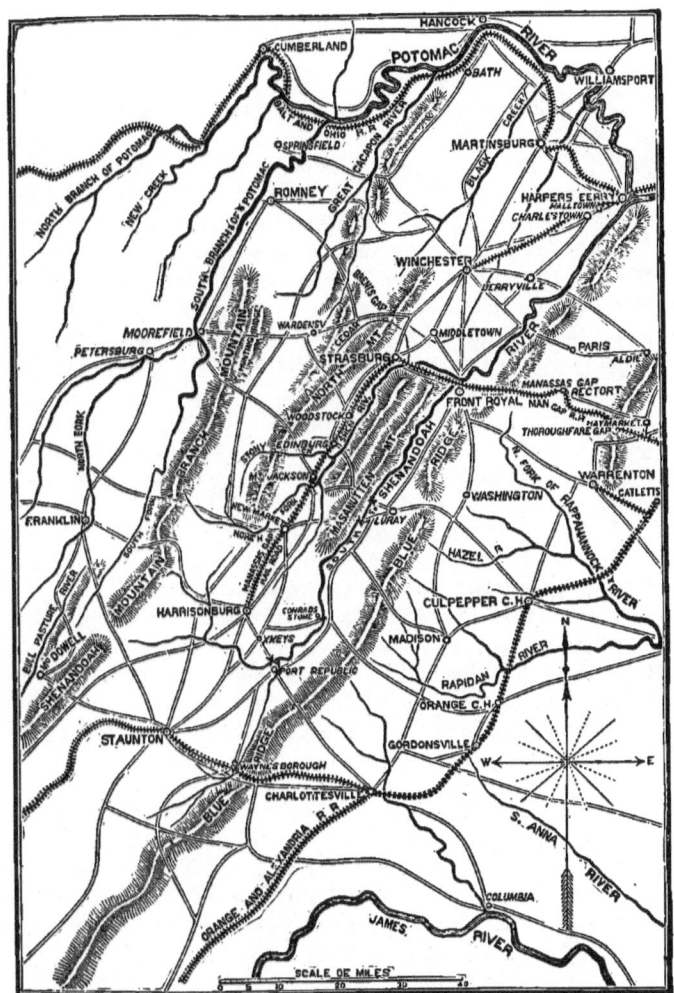

THE SHENANDOAH VALLEY.

CHAPTER XI.

SOUTH MOUNTAIN.

THE summer of 1862 was hot and dry. Streams were parched, the grass was brown and burned. The army trailed through the dust, and lay down at night footsore, weary and sick. Often the only water they had to drink was supplied by "brackish" ponds, whose surface was covered with greenish slime. Fevers and malaria broke out among the regiments, and dissatisfaction was loud and outspoken. Now and then a brush would take place, or a skirmishing party would sally out, surprise a party of Confederates, bringing some of them into camp prisoners.

MARCHING ORDERS. "Knapsacks and rations ready by seven in the morning!" Fred Greene said, one September afternoon as they were watching eagerly and impatiently for some move to be made.

"Sure it's not another of your jokes, corporal?"

"No joke this time, as you'll find to your sorrow, perhaps."

"How many days' rations are we to carry along?"

"Can't say. We're going out to interview General Lee. His victory at Manassas the other day has given him the idea that he can bring the whole State of Maryland into his army. He's traveling in that direction. He has a poster out inviting the Marylanders to enlist, but by all we hear, it won't bring many valuable accessions to his ranks."

"Why not?"

"For two reasons. If they want to enlist, they'll do so, without his starting recruiting offices. Most of the able-bodied men who wanted to go to war did so long since. Then again, most of the Marylanders are fond of the old flag. The State has never left the Union. General Lee is a fine military man, but he surely don't understand the people he's trying to interest. Hallo! what's a woman doing here? She's coming this way."

A woman, dressed in cheap, but neat and tidy-looking clothing, and holding the hands of two sad-eyed, poorly attired children, was making her way toward them. A soldier stepped up to her, and with a pleasant smile asked her if she was looking for any one.

The woman looked earnestly into his face, as she said—

"You'uns all look kind. Can you show me whar to find Peter Hall?"

The man looked puzzled, and uncertain as to how to answer her.

"Don't know him, ma'am. What regiment is he in?"

"I can't tell you, sir. He is my man, and he 'lowed he wouldn't go against the old flag, for any one. The neighbors said he

was a traitor to the cause, and wouldn't give him any work. So he went off in the night, and told me he'd make his way into the Union army, and as soon as he could he'd send me word whar he was. He 'lowed I could take care of the babies somehow, but I've found it mighty hard work to get bread for 'em often. They're good children, though, no better nowhar, and they don't complain, not even when they're hungry. I

"DO ANY OF YOU KNOW PETER HALL?"

heard you'uns were in the neighborhood, and I thought as perhaps you'd know whar my Peter is."

"Boys!" the soldier cried to a group who were listening at a little distance. "Do any of you know Pete Hall?"

"*Peter* Hall," the woman corrected, with great dignity.

"Excuse me, ma'am; *Peter* Hall, I meant to say."

"Why, certain, I know him," a man answered. "He's in the Second Maryland, and they're over there, on the brow of that hill. Go right over, ma'am. You'll find him, I hope," he added in a lower tone. "Don't be afraid. No one will harm you."

"Me and the children have walked twelve miles since yesterday noon, and we want to see Peter bad. He'd have come out and met us, I know he would, if he'd have thought we were so near," she added, with refreshing simplicity. The idea of Peter's leaving his company, even for so important a matter as meeting her, caused a general laugh, which she did not seem to observe, but continued—

"You see, we have moved since Peter went away, and he doesn't know where we live now."

"God bless the woman and her Peter," was the honest invocation sent after her, as she hurried away in the direction pointed out, and they were rewarded a few moments later, by seeing a soldier spring up from the grass where he had been lounging, and hasten forward to receive the greeting of his wife, who sobbed for joy upon his breast, while the little ones could only jump and shout in the fullness of their pleasure at seeing "Pa."

Many a man stood there, and silently wished some of their loved ones could meet and greet them also.

FLATTERING RECEPTION IN MARYLAND. The entrance of the boys in blue into Frederick was a perfect ovation. General Lee had retired from the town only two days before.

This welcome thrilled their hearts. From every door and window the national flag fluttered, and the stores were decorated with the colors. Banners were strung across the streets, from house to house, while crowds of happy men and women with radiant faces, spoke words of welcome.

Good luck seemed to be showered upon them, for General McClellan here captured a copy of the orders of General Lee, which gave him a key to the whole situation. It was of very recent date, and the Confederate commander had mapped out his campaign. The information contained in these explicit instructions to his generals, enabled General McClellan to see plainly how to thwart General Lee. So he proceeded to send two corps through the two Gaps of South Mountain, with the prospect of being able to cut the enemy's forces to pieces.

Dividing his command, General McClellan ordered Franklin to Crampton's Gap, while Reno and Hooker, with Burnside at their head, were sent to Turner's Gap.

It was a toilsome task for even those sturdy men to ascend the sides of the Gaps. South Mountain towered a thousand feet above them, while the most accessible points were the two Gaps, each nearly 400 feet high.

"We've got to reach the top of those hills somehow," Ralph said. "But it's one step forward, and three back-

GENERAL AMBROSE E. BURNSIDE.

ward. Our men are gaining a little. They show splendid pluck."

Clambering, toiling up the rocky hillsides, the Union forces made their painful way. From behind ledges and trees, the rebel riflemen marked their slow progress, and sent many a man to his death. The company to which Ralph belonged was under Reno, and assaulted the southern crest of Turner's Gap. On the northern crest of the mountain General Hooker, with splendid courage, kept on.

Ralph now realized how desperately men will fight. He even felt that hot hatred which two foes ever feel, when pitted against each other. He saw the Federal army, scratched and bruised from forcing their way through the brush and over rocks, while the Confederate riflemen poured bullets into their midst

ARTILLERY GOING TO THE FRONT

like rain. Hot, and panting with their efforts, still they never wavered. Gibbon, with his brigade, was trying to force a passage through the turnpike in the Gap, and here also the enemy did terrible execution. The heat was blistering. The fervid rays of the September sun burned into their very blood, and the dust

GENERAL LEW WALLACE.

which rose in clouds mixed with the smoke of the powder, and choked and blinded them.

They had fought continu ously the entire day. Their canteens were empty—their mouths parched and dry. Ralph saw a tall officer spur his horse forward, and fire at General Reno. That gallant soldier reeled in his saddle, and fell, but as he was borne to the rear to die, his eyes were fixed on the men he had so gallantly led, with a last look of farewell.

The contest was long. Each side fought to the death. As Ralph turned to speak to a companion he heard a wild shout:

"Forward! One more such charge, and we'll have the Gap.

TWO GENERALS KILLED.

It was the colonel's voice, and as he rose in his saddle and cheered them on, they took fresh courage. Wild responses answered his appeal, and new strength was given them.

"We are sure of victory," Ralph said to himself, At that instant a horse dashed madly by. He bore General Garland, of the Confederate force, who was lying half across his back, as he was vainly striving to raise himself in the saddle. His hat rolled down the hill as he came to the ground with a shock; his fine features were distorted with pain, and his long, dark hair was dabbled with blood. He made one frantic effort to

recover his sword, which had slid from his grasp, and then he
sank half on his knees, a livid corpse. Ralph was so near he
could almost have touched him, and to his dying day, he never
forgot the look of agony on the wan face, as the eyes fast glazed
in death.

Darkness settled down upon the earth, before the battle was
won, by the Confederates withdrawing and leaving the Union
forces masters of the field. But what a sacrifice of human life!—
three thousand human beings sent into eternity, as the result of
one day's conflict.

The loss of life was felt equally by the two opposing forces;
but the boys in gray suffered a loss of fifteen hundred, who were
taken prisoners.

The night was warm. The stars looked down with kindly
gleams upon thousands of worn-out soldiers sleeping as quietly
as little children, while the wounded were groaning with pain, as
the life-blood slowly trickled over the grass which the hot sun
and the trampling of feet and stamping of horses had matted
into a tangled and brown mass.

Ralph's captain threw himself down by the side of the boy,
as he was trying to shut out the dreadful pictures which were
burned upon his brain.

"Is the victory ours?" he asked.

"It is, and a dear one to us," the captain replied. "We
have left over a thousand dead upon the field; but the Johnnies
have moved off, and we have orders to push on to the western
side of the mountain. They raked us down in terrible fashion,
but the men stood their fire like statues. There was some heavy
firing over at the other Gap a while back, but it has stopped
now. Hallo!" he called to a man in the uniform of an officer,
"where are you going in such a hurry? Has anything happened
—any new move ahead?"

The man stopped suddenly, and coming up close to them,
with features convulsed and pallid, with either pain or fear, he
made answer:

"Oh, captain, I'm sure I'll die, I'm in such misery. I'm all doubled up, and can't sleep. I'm in perfect **A COWARDLY** agony. There—-there goes that twinge again. I **OFFICER.** must try and find my regiment, and hunt up the doctor right away."

Ralph looked incredulous at the man's apparent suffering. He felt sure it was a pretense. "It's strange that he's so far away from his command, and going in an exactly opposite direction. Can it be that he's going to skip?" This was a painful thought, and brought an angry flush to his brow, for he held nothing in such scorn, amounting to abhorrence, as he did cowardice or dishonesty.

"Are you going in the right direction to join your company? If you keep on the way you are faced, you'll be more than likely to find some friendly boy in gray to snap you up."

The officer looked steadily at him a moment, while his face turned scarlet.

"Your advice is not required, sir. I shall remember your incivility at a more fitting time." And he stalked away, quite oblivious of the anguish that had racked him so short a time before.

"That fellow must be a mind-reader," laughed the captain. "He plainly knew what you thought about him. But seriously, your opinion was rather harsh; he's probably shamming to get excused from duty. For the honor of our cause I should hope no officer would be guilty of such dastardly conduct. Nor a private, either," he added, a moment after, "for the boys who carry the muskets have true grit, and don't run, only after the enemy."

"I know that's so, but when I saw him making such haste to get away, the suspicion would come into my mind. To me it seems a shame for a man with a spark of cowardice to wear a uniform."

9

CHAPTER XII.

MORE FIGHTING.

ALPH arose from the heap of leaves and brush which had served him for a bed the night through, with his bones aching and sore. The army was already stirring, for although the Passes were won, there was promise of another engagement at once. Word was passed along the line that General Lee had withdrawn his forces and crossed the Antietam, where he took up his position on a high bluff near Sharpsburg, and was thus able to command a view of the whole country. But he had met with great losses, from the dead in battle, and from stragglers. He realized the injury the latter had done him; indeed, he complained openly and bitterly, saying that his army was "ruined by straggling." But the best men of his army were still left with him—picked men, of splendid courage and vast endurance. He was determined that the coming battle should decide the campaign, and he waited calmly its issue.

"Lee has the choice of positions," the men said. "He has both flanks resting on the streams. He has the whole four bridges across the creek well guarded; that is, all but one, and that's the point we have to take. We intend to call the attention of the Johnnies to our point of attack, and throw our entire strength against the bridge that is left unguarded, and then cross. They say Lee hasn't much over 40,000 men, but they are a body we shall be proud to meet, and whip."

The artillery practice on both sides was sharp all day, but not much execution was done. At nearly five in the afternoon General Hooker's corps made a dash across the upper bridge, and advancing through the woods, fell upon General Hood's brigade, and a fierce skirmish followed, but the darkness brought it to a close for that night, and both armies rested, eager for the morning light, that they might rush at each other again.

Before sunrise General McClellan hurried Mansfield's corps to Hooker's aid, while Sumner was ready to follow.

The renewal of hostilities began early. As the sun rose, his beams lighted up the two armies, angry and threatening. General Hooker threw his forces with vigor against General Jackson's, and pressed him so hard he fell back. The batteries came promptly to the front, and raked the Confederates with shot the entire length of their line, breaking their ranks in wild haste.

Crowding and forcing them back, General Mansfield came to the Unionists' aid, when a shot struck him, and he fell dead, but his command kept on, and entering the woods, got their position and held it, against immense odds. General Hooker here received a serious wound, and was carried away, just as General Sumner crossed the stream, drove the boys in gray before him, and entrenched his men near the little church of Dunker. Here the fighting raged so madly, and the artil- **HEAVY ARTIL-** lery fire was so heavy, that a historian relates **LERY FIRE.** that years after, when the trees were cut down and sent to a sawmill to be made into logs, the saws were torn to pieces by the quantity of metal that had pierced the trees, and been hidden there by the growth of the wood. But in spite of this vigorous fire, no irresolution was shown, and as fast as men were shot down at the guns, others were ready to take their places, with undismayed zeal.

A lull occurred, and as the sounds of firing seemed to die away, there was great rejoicing, for to the Federal army a victory was apparently assured, when the hope was suddenly dispelled by the arrival of two divisions of the enemy, who, with a loud yell, threw themselves into a gap in Sumner's line, forcing him from his position, and across the meadows and cornfields, where he made a stand, but the foe retired again to its own position.

"Harry, see those regiments," Ralph said to a fellow sol-

MAP SHOWING THE SEAT OF WAR FROM HARPER'S FERRY TO SUFFOLK, VA.

dier—"look at the race. Which will come out ahead, I wonder?
They are pretty well matched—both are fleet-footed."

**A RACE BETWEEN
TWO REGIMENTS.**
It was a race, indeed. A New Hampshire
regiment was marching parallel with a Confederate regiment, and each were intent on reaching a certain high piece of ground. As they ran, the bullets

whizzed back and forth, from both sides, and these pleasantries were kept up.

"The Johnnies are ahead—no, they have fallen back a little. The New Hampshire boys are in the lead now. They've reached the ground. Hurrah!" shouted Harry, and in his excitement he threw up his cap, and caught it on the point of his bayonet. As soon as the winners gained the coveted point, they poured shot into their late rivals' ranks.

The artillery was heaviest near the church, and the dead lay so thick that they could have formed a foot bridge the entire length of the line.

"Wonder why Porter and Burnside keep so still?" This question was asked again and again. "See the rebs mowing down our men like ripe grass! Why don't they come to our assistance?"

CHARLES A. DANA, ASSISTANT SECRETARY OF WAR.

"They are keeping their troops as reserves. The Confeds don't hold any of their men back, but launch every one of them at us."

"That don't seem to me to be the right policy," said Ralph. "But look—Franklin has come up from Crampton's Gap just in the nick of time. He is very welcome, for there are fresh troops advancing, from the right flank of the boys in gray."

Franklin's opportune coming infused new hope, and the

boys' eyes brightened, cheery words went round, and muskets were handled with a will.

"General Burnside's orders are to take that bridge. We've got to do it; it won't be very much work, and then we'll soon be over to see our friends on the other side."

"You think that's easy, do you? Wait and see. We're on low ground here, but the land over the other side is higher, and the road runs alongside the stream. Those fellows have their guns well placed, and can damage us bad."

The bridge they were expected to take, was of stone, and rather narrow. The first brigade to attempt to cross was General Crook's.

"Hark! he's gone the wrong way. The rebels are pouring shot into him. He'll be cut all to pieces."

The General had struck the wrong road, and was being subjected to a heavy fire. A Maryland regi-
REINFORCEMENTS.
ment and a New Hampshire followed him on the double quick, but retreated, as they could not stand the fire!

"There is help for us now," said Ralph, "for they are bringing up some guns that will speak loud for our side."

Two heavy guns were soon thundering over the ground, and commanding the boys in gray who were guarding the bridge. Their persuasive tones opened the passage, and triumphantly the Union men crossed the bridge, and secured the position.

Four hours had been consumed, and thus General Lee improved his chance to bring fresh troops to his aid, who drove Burnside from the heights, and retook a battery which he had captured.

The battle was over. When the rattle of musketry is heard, the smoke of battle, and the wild plunging of the frightened horses, and the shouts and fierce onset of a maddened mass of human beings is felt, there is an excitement, a fever in the blood that strengthens the arm, and hardens the muscles— thoughts of self are forgotten. But when those accompaniments are missing—when the awful stillness of a deserted battle-ground succeeds them, then the heart grows faint and cold.

BURNSIDE BRIDGE.

Both armies were glad to rest; both sides had been rent and dismembered. Many regiments in both lines had been slaughtered unmercifully. The victory belonged to McClellan, but the sorrow and anguish belonged to those who loved the fallen ones—to the friends alike of the blue and the gray, in cottage and mansion, all over this broad land of ours.

Daily papers were a luxury, and the boys in the army were always glad to purchase them at a good round price. The newsboy is ubiquitous. He is the product of the century, and will never be shelved as are so many useful things. Their cries were welcome to those men, who were anxious to know what each day was bringing forth, and when one galloped into camp, two days after the battle of the Antietam with a bag heavily freighted with New York dailies, he was surrounded at once, and his stock rapidly melted away.

GENERAL ROSECRANS.

"Good news!" flashed through the ranks as they eagerly devoured the news of the battle of Iuka, with Rosecrans at the head.

"It was a daring attempt," Ralph read aloud to the eager group; "the account says that the Union forces attacked Price's men in a narrow front, with ravines filled with undergrowth, where it was difficult to maintain a foothold, with but one battery, and with hosts against them, three to one. Yet they swept down the enemy, and fought till darkness overtook them, and in the night the Confederates beat a hasty retreat."

This news cheered the hearts of the boys in blue, and while they were giving vent to their joy in different ways, Ralph's heart was filled with a solemn thankfulness, for to him it seemed as if One above surely ruled their destinies.

CHAPTER XIII.

OLD BILL DIES.

HE beautiful autumn days grew shorter. November's blasts were keenly felt, even in that sunny clime, and the boys looked forward with dismay to a winter passed in inaction.

"Why, we'll have to fight to keep warm," jolly Fred Greene said to the comrades gathered round.

Old Bill had been in hospital for many months. Ralph visited him often, and the sick man's face would brighten, and his voice grow stronger, whenever the boy came to his bedside. But he seemed to have lost interest in everything pertaining to this life. Ralph tried earnestly to induce him to talk of the events passing around them, but without success.

One morning early in November, when he went to pay his usual visit, the boy said:

"Bill, this is my first experience as a soldier. But you have seen plenty of service before?"

The sick man shook his head slowly, but made no reply. Ralph waited a few moments, and began to think his question had not been considered worthy of an answer, when Bill suddenly spoke:

"Yes, I have been out on the border fighting Indians, for years. How I detest the redskins. They seldom come out and give a man a fair show, but they just go on the warpath, and then it's skulk and lie in ambush, and burn sleeping villages, massacring women and children. Their mode of warfare don't suit me." And the disdainful curl of the lip showed what he thought of them. After a long pause, he resumed:

"Then I was in the Mexican War. I was quite a stripling then, and I fought under General Phil Kearney. He was a

138

fighter, brave as a lion, and when he lost his arm not a man
under him but would rather it had been his own
arm shot away. He's one of General McClellan's most trusty officers. His experience is
worth millions to younger men. How I'd like to see noble

BILL EULOGIZES GEN. KEARNEY.

GENERAL PHIL KEARNEY.

Phil Kearney!"

"Why, Bill, didn't
you know that he was
killed at the battle of
Groveton, Va., in Sep-
tember?"

"Kearney killed
—and I've been lying
here, and knew noth-
ing about it! It's too
hard. Let's hear all
you know, Ralph."

"I can only tell
you what we heard.
You know we wasn't
there to see it, but he
was sent to Hooker's
support, when the lat-
ter's men charged Jack-
son with bayonets.
They had an awful
battle, but General
Kearney had been sent
to their assistance too
late, and he was forced
back. Hooker almost
broke the enemy's line,

but fresh bodies of Confederates hastening up, changed the
outlook, and so the Union boys were repulsed. At six in the
afternoon General Pope ordered another attack, and Kearney
came up in fine style, seizing a railroad cut on the Warrenton

turnpike where Jackson was nicely entrenched, and holding it for awhile. One of the Confederate regiments who ran short of ammunition, hurled great stones and fragments of the rocks at our men, killing many. General Kearney still maintained his position, but was overpowered by numbers, and driven out of the cut."

Ralph paused, but Bill's eyes were gleaming with excitement. "Go on," he said, earnestly—"is that all?"

"The two armies rested till the next day, when a still fiercer attempt was made to rout the rebels, but in spite of the most stubborn fighting, our army was withdrawn from the field, and fell back to Fairfax Court House; but the next evening, September 1st, Stonewall Jackson made another attack upon General Pope's flank, which was resisted hotly, and again General Kearney, with Hooker, Reno, McDowell and Stevens, were there to help, but General Stevens fell dead at their fire, and as all their ammunition had been used up, his men retired at once. General Kearney started forward to reconnoiter, and was confronted by a Confederate band; he put spurs to his horse, hoping to escape, but they shot him dead."

RALPH AROUSES BILL'S ATTENTION.

Bill shook his head solemnly, and leaning back on his pillow, he closed his eyes, as if he had fallen asleep. Glad to have awakened even so slight attention as he had succeeded in doing, the boy continued:

"Bill, we have a new commander now. The President has relieved General McClellan, and we are to have General Burnside. What do you think of that?"

A look of the old time came into Bill's face, as he answered:

"Yes, I have a new commander—one whose call will soon be heard!"

Ralph shuddered. He knew too well the meaning of Bill's words.

"I mean our army commander, Bill; General McClellan has been relieved of his command, and General Burnside has been appointed in his place."

"General McClellan—yes, he's too slow. It needs some one with a little push. But it's all the same to me, now."

And that was all he said about the change. He lay on his cot, looking intently at Ralph, and suddenly he broke out with—

OLD BILL'S STORY. "I don't know why I'm so fond of you, boy, unless it's 'cause you mind me of Eddie. He was just such a little plucky, fair-faced lad as you are, and I can't help mixing you up with him."

Ralph wondered who Eddie was, but he waited patiently. Bill's eyes burned with a luster the boy had never seen there before. The sick man's face was very thin. The brown tint that outdoor life always gives had faded, and the sharp features looked more pinched and wan from their pallor. He went on in a weak and trembling voice:

"She was a beauty, and I was powerful fond of her. Her eyes were like a young fawn's, and her hair was brown as the chestnuts when they ripen in the sun. She liked Frank better nor me, and she told me so. Then when they were married, I hated him bitterly. But when the little fellow come, and they sent for me, somehow from the first time I took the little tot in my arms, and he smiled up into my face, all my anger died out. After that I would have died sooner than harm his daddy. They were happy with each other. But he died when the lad was ten or so, and left the poor wife alone. I didn't know how to comfort her, and she grieved continooally. One day, when he was quite a lad, nearly sixteen, and needed his mother most, they found her dead on her husband's grave. Ah, that is the way some women love!

"That nigh killed me, but I meant to be a good friend to the boy. They took even that comfort from me, for they carried him away down South to his father's folks, and I never seed him again."

The man's face was fever-flushed now, and his words came almost in a whisper. He tossed uneasily from side to side.

"Ralph, my head bothers me—it aches so strangely. I wish—"

But the wish was never told. A wild look came over his face, his words became incoherent. A delirium had seized him, and kindly as he was tended by the nurses and his comrades, he never regained his senses. A few days of apparent suffering, and Bill Elliott's kindly heart ceased to beat. The uncouth, rugged, but brave soldier had passed on to the Great Beyond.

BURYING OLD BILL.

It was late in the afternoon of a raw November day, while the winds shrieked mournfully, when they carried him to a little valley in which they had dug a grave, into whose depth they lowered the body of a brave and true soldier, who never shirked a duty. The chaplain, a plain and tender man, read impressively that beautiful Psalm:

"Hear my cry, O God; attend unto my prayer.

"From the end of the earth will I cry unto Thee, when my heart is over-whelmed; lead me to the rock that is higher than I.

"For Thou hast been a shelter for me, and a strong tower from the enemy.

"I will abide in Thy tabernacle forever. I will trust in the covert of Thy wings. Selah."

In a clear and ringing voice he read the solemn burial service, and the comrades of the dead soldier listened reverently. When he had concluded, some one suggested that they sing, and a clear, sweet voice broke plaintively into that exquisite hymn,

> "Abide with me, fast falls the eventide;
> The darkness deepens—Lord, with me abide;
> When other helpers fail, and comforts flee,
> Help of the helpless, O abide with me."

RALPH'S SORROW. The voice suddenly broke into a passion of tears, and Ralph threw himself on the grave, which was fast being filled up, and cried—"Bill, Bill, you were my best friend—I cannot let you go."

There were many looks of sympathy for the boy, but death was, after all, nothing but a passing incident to men who faced it every hour, and as Ralph went back to his tent, his heart rebelled at the levity which allowed the merry jest to pass around, as to whose turn it would be next.

To him it was a new experience. He had seen hundreds of men shot down in battle, but no one had died whom he had cared for, and it came home to him. He had become deeply attached to Bill, whose cheerful, off-hand manners had enlivened the homesick boy. He had lost his comrade, but his memory was cherished, and he was missed for a long time.

CHAPTER XIV.

FREDERICKSBURG.

T was with many forebodings and some outspoken prophecies of failure that many of the Union officers learned that they were to move at once upon Fredericksburg.

"It looks to me like a mad freak to send us out to assault such fortifications as are thrown up on the hills south and west of the town. It isn't right for a soldier to grumble, but when he sees a man perpetrating a piece of folly, that is going to cause a needless sacrifice of life, why, he can't help expressing himself as opposed to the scheme."

The plaint of the captain found a ready echo in the hearts of his fellow officers, but a soldier must obey instructions unquestioningly.

Early morning hours came, the camp was astir, and all preparations were made for a speedy move upon the fortifications.

DISSATISFACTION OVER THE ORDERS. "Lee has thrown up forts for five miles that will stand any attack that General Burnside can make. We are going to our death."

A two o'clock breakfast, eaten in haste in the fog of early morning, was all that the men were allowed. The outlook was gloomy. The river must be crossed, but while Burnside was trying to lay pontoon bridges, the engineers were terribly harassed by the continuous fire of the rebel sharpshooters, who were using the houses skirting the river bank as places of refuge.

General Burnside determined to try the effect of shelling the town. The men who were detailed to lay the pontoon bridges were falling at their posts by the rifles in the hands of a Mississippi detachment which was hidden securely in cellars, behind walls and fences, and in every corner where it was possible

ATTACK ON FREDERICKSBURG

145

to conceal a man. Crack! crack! their rifles were heard, and many a boy in blue was tumbled into the water with a bullet in his brain, to be carried away by the current. It was a fruitless endeavor to keep on with the work, the loss of life was so great. The Federals had better luck at the lower bridges, being able to dislodge the sharpshooters from their rifle-pits.

"What are the prospects for crossing?" asked Sergeant Gregory of an officer who passed at that moment.

"We'll be over somewhere about doomsday, judging from the outlook. The three bridges we need the **LAYING THE PONTOON BRIDGES.** most can't be laid under the present régime. We've got to evict those sharpshooters from the houses along the river bank, for it's worse than murder to post our men there to be picked off in that cruel fashion—all to no purpose, for bridges can never be built when men are shot down as fast as they show their heads."

The country was hilly, now and then dotted with clumps of trees, while barns, fences, and everything that was combustible, had been converted to use by the two armies, as each in turn had passed over the land. All was dreary and desolate. The sky was leaden-hued, save when a burst of flame from the cannonading would lighten it for a short space, and then it would die down, leaving it almost a pitchy blackness.

General Burnside's resolve to bombard the place had no power to oust the sharpshooters, even when tons of shells were thrown into its streets, setting fire to many of the buildings. When, after a brief rest, the engineers resumed the construction of the bridges, the same result followed—destruction of their numbers.

The town itself was almost impregnable, being completely encircled by hills, save on the river side. These **BOMBARDING USELESS.** heights were bristling with forts, entrenchments seamed them in every direction, and batteries were planted in such profusion that no opening presented itself for attack.

How long this slaughter would have continued it is hard to

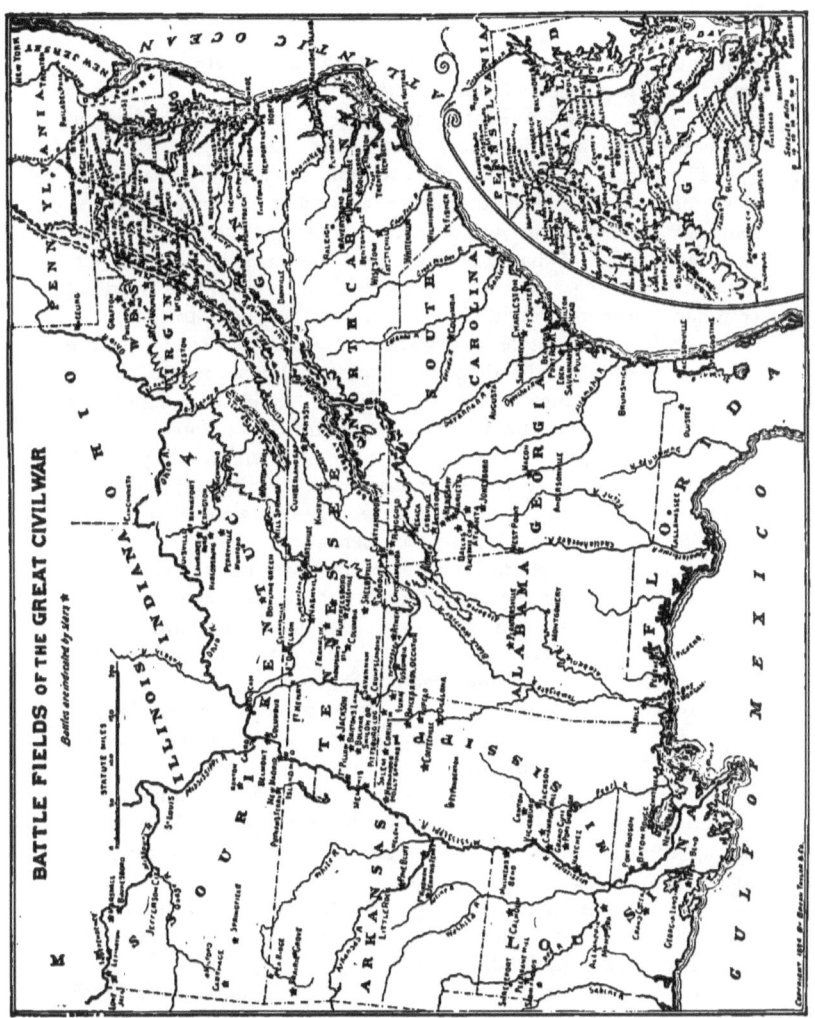

BATTLE FIELDS OF THE GREAT CIVILWAR

Battles are indicated by stars ★

tell, but a happy inspiration came to General Hunt, chief of artillery. He suggested that a body of men could make a dash for the river, cross in boats, and besiege the sharpshooters in the houses, driving them out, and taking possession.

The daring of the plan almost took away one's breath, but it seemed the only way to silence the enemy's murderous fire, and it was quickly put in execution. The pontoon boats lay at the river bank. A band of tried men was selected for the perilous undertaking, who at a sign, without a sound or word of command, rushed from their concealment, leaped into the boats, shot out from the shore, and were half across the stream before the Confederates realized their intention. Then came a shower of bullets from their rifles, rattling like hailstones about the heads of the brave men, who held boards up before them for protection, dodging the murderous fire as well as they could, while those who were rowing pulled with a will, and the boats were across the stream in swift time. A few were shot, falling into the river, but the largest number went over safely.

Reaching the shore, the regiments ran up the hills, and succeeded in forcing the sharpshooters from their lairs, capturing over a hundred of them, while the rest fled to the hills.

The way was now clear for the completion of the bridges. A pontoon bridge is a fine piece of ingenuity.

Heavy boats, perfectly flat, often twenty feet in length, **THEY CROSS AT LAST.** are anchored at equal distances from each other, lengthwise of the current, and beams are placed upon them to unite them; then strong, thick planks are laid across the beams, thus making a steady, wide roadway, strong enough to endure the weight of horses, heavy pieces of artillery, and the tramp of thousands of men.

While the bridge was being made, the enemy did not remain quiet, but dropped shells at various points along the river, which exploded, but happily did little injury.

The smoke of the artillery, the flames bursting from the houses, and the struggling army of the Union exposed to a pitiless fire made a picture which was never effaced from Ralph's mind,

UNCLE NED WAS GLOOMY OVER RALPH'S LAST LETTER.

149

and years after, when he saw the panorama of "The Battle of
Gettysburg," in Chicago, the memory of that day at Fredericksburg came back with vivid force. He was once more a stripling,
in the midst of the noise and shock of battle, with comrades
falling about him, torn and mangled out of all semblance of human
beings, while he was miraculously preserved.

That night the Union forces rested on the ground, in the
mud and frost, not far away from the pontoon bridge; and though
they knew the morning would plunge them into further conflict,
yet tired limbs and aching heads found the refreshing slumber
which they needed. Early next morning, after a hasty breakfast, they were ready for any events which the day might
bring forth.

A heavy fog hid the other shore, while the air was cold and
raw. Long before the sun scattered the mists, cannonading
began at the bridge, the main point of attack, but the firing
became so severe that orders were issued for them to retire behind
the bluffs.

At last the bridges were finished, and the army crossed to the
other side of the river, under the continuous shells of the enemy.
Now began a terrific struggle. General Franklin had advanced
against the troops on the hill, but they had repulsed him, with
much loss. General Meade's division was chosen to lead the
attack. Down across the railroad they dashed, under heavy fire,
their skirmishers having been sent forward, while the well-
directed batteries hurled against the hills did some execution.

A HARD FOUGHT ENGAGEMENT. But the Confederates from their elevated positions poured destruction into their ranks, mow-
ing them down. The Union forces were not
daunted, but made an entering wedge between two rebel divisions,
turned back their flanks, and captured prisoners and battle flags.
Scaling the heights, they were met by the second line, which drove
them back in confusion, and they were only saved from utter
rout by General Birney, who threw his command in front of the
enemy, who were pursuing them.

The sounds of battle grew louder, and as the divisions of

French and Hancock moved in columns through the town, the
Confederate batteries burst upon them, but they charged across

GENERAL GEORGE G. MEADE.

the open ground, to be met by a veritable sheet of flame, which
swept into their faces, and literally consumed them.   No bravery,
no determination, could withstand that awful fire of the enemy,

who had taken advantage of an ambush which nature had seemed to furnish them, from whence they sent forth their deadly aim.

GENERAL WINFIELD HANCOCK.

A road ran at the foot of Marye's Hill, which had sunken so much as almost to be unobserved, at a little distance. This road was bounded at its outside edge by a stone wall, where were hidden two brigades of Confederates, who had sent forth this sheet of flame and death. Their numbers were so great, that every man at the wall was assisted by several behind him, who loaded muskets as fast as they could, and passed them to him, while he discharged them as rapidly, leaving only his head exposed for an instant, as he raised it to take aim.

In the face of these fearful odds, the Union soldiers were undismayed. No disorganization, no wavering in their ranks, but they kept on, only to meet certain death.

And now General Hancock, he whose presence was an inspiration, led the charge with 5,000 men, whose intrepid daring carried them within twenty yards of the fatal wall, only to be beaten back, leaving 2,000 dead **DEATH AT THE STONE WALL.** to tell the tale of the slaughter at Marye's Hill.

General Burnside was beside him self with rage. In the face of these defeats, he de manded that Gen-

GENERAL HANCOCK AND FRIENDS.

eral Hooker make a bayonet charge, and those doomed men rushed forward, with a valor never surpassed, rallying again and again, until nearly half their number lay dead on the road, or torn with fearful wounds.

The rebel artillery was not idle, but as the Federals retreated, sent shells after them, still plowing their numbers with deadly effect.

A heavy storm of rain came on in the night, and under cover of its inclemency, the Union troops withdrew to the north bank of the Rappahannock, although it had been General Burnside's determination to renew the assault the next day, and lead it in person. This was a step which needed a vast deal of dissuasion on the part of his generals ere he relinquished his mad attempt.

GENERAL HOOKER.

EVACUATING FREDERICKSBURG. Mud was over the shoe-tops, and the rain was falling fast, when the Union army received orders to evacuate the town, and no time was lost in obeying. The pontoon bridges carried them safely across from the scene of disaster, and left the army in a sorry plight.

Decimated in numbers, the dead alone counting 12,000, disappointed, hospitals full to overflowing, the dead to bury, the predictions of defeat had been bitterly realized. It is said that the brave and dashing General Meagher went into that battle with the Irish brigade, over 1,200 strong, and came out with a little over 200.

It was plain that the men had been sacrificed through incompetency and stubbornness. Murmurs and discontent were abundant, as the army prepared to settle down in its winter quarters.

CHAPTER XV.

RALPH IS SENT HOME.

AFTER the slaughter at Fredericksburg, Ralph rapidly failed in strength. The excitement of that scene of carnage and his increasing exhaustion told upon his frame. He fulfilled his duty as well as he could; he was cheerful and alert; he wrote more often to his dear mother without ever alluding to his health.

"I can't understand what ails me," he thought. "I have never received a wound, while some of the boys who have **RALPH GROWS WEAKER.** been badly cut up are well again, and seem as strong as ever. I do believe I miss Old Bill more every day. I never felt sad or lonely when I had him to cheer me up."

He grew daily worse. Often when on duty he would halt, with weak and failing breath. He lost all desire for food, and his lusterless eyes and pale skin told how he suffered.

"What seems to be the matter, sergeant?" one of his comrades asked, anxiously. "You don't 'pear to have any vim about you. Why, if you hadn't shown such pluck—fact is, if it was any one but you, I mout 'cuse you of playing off."

"I'm all right, Hank. I feel a little weak and have hard chills sometimes—but I'll be better soon. I'm a little sick, that's all."

"That's enough. You ain't been yerself since we fit at Fair Oaks I've seen it a long time. That malary from the swamps has finished many a strong man."

At last Ralph had to succumb. His condition was observed **RALPH IS DESPONDENT.** by the doctor, who called the attention of his captain to the fact that he was no longer fit for duty. And when one morning he was not able to report at early roll call, it was with gloomy forebodings that he heard the order that he be removed to the hospital at once.

"Is this the end of my ambitious hopes?" he queried. "Am I going to die when I am willing to serve my country? I would not mind being killed in battle, as a soldier should be, but to die in hospital, far from my mother. It is hard!" And he buried his face in his pillow to hide the hot tears that he could not keep back.

When weeks passed, and Ralph grew no better, the Colonel's attention was directed to his case. He was a severe disciplinarian, but he had a kindly heart, and he speedily forwarded a recommendation to the war department that Sergeant Gregory, Company K, ——Massachusetts Volunteers, be honorably discharged from the service of the United States. A document granting the request came back in due time, to the Colonel, who passed it to the captain, and he handed it to Ralph, who could not repress his emotion.

RALPH RECEIVES HIS DISCHARGE.

"I enlisted to the end of the war. I do not want a discharge. Could you not have obtained me a sick leave? I know I shall be strong soon."

The doctor shook his head solemnly.

"You are not fit to march, or do active duty—perhaps never will be. The hardships incident to a campaign have broken you down. You were very young to have undertaken them. I do not wish to wound your pride, but the government does not want sick men on its rolls."

So Ralph was given his papers, and after writing his mother a few lines, saying that he was quite sick, lest his sudden coming should alarm her, he was sent home by the same route by which he came. It was a painful journey, not alone from his physical suffering, but his heart bled as he noted the ruin that had been wrought in the land—the deserted houses, neglected fields, miserable-looking people, mostly women and children, whose woe-begone faces told of the privations they were daily enduring, uncom-

RALPH'S JOURNEY HOMEWARD.

plainingly. The contrast between the early days of the war and the present was bitter, and he felt how terribly real that war was to these people. Their farms had been overrun by the tramping of two armies, and each had equally despoiled them of their possessions—both were alike unmindful and indifferent to their sorrow.

But brighter thoughts succeeded these gloomy musings, as he drew nearer to his home, and already saw his beloved mother's sweet face, and felt her warm kiss upon his cheek. But even in the Western country, as the train stopped at the various stations, he noted careworn faces, and anxious glances, as the murmured "God bless you!" was sent after the boys in blue. There were several soldiers on the train, some going home on furlough, and some on the same errand as Ralph—going home to recuperate, or, perchance, to die.

When Ralph reached Chicago, he was glad to lie down on one of the benches in the depot. He found he had to wait three hours for the train that would convey him to his prairie home. The rest was welcome, and after a nap, and a strong cup of coffee, he felt a little better; so much so that he thought he would take a short walk of a block or so. The city was, so to speak, in holiday attire. The streets were teeming with an excited yet happy-looking people, and an unusual bustle pervaded them. He wondered why every one was crowding to the edge of the sidewalks, and as he was about to ask a by-stander, he heard the tramp of many feet. How familiar the sound of the steps was to his ear. The boys in blue were coming, he thought, and again a wave of wounded pride came over him, as he realized that he was shut out from the ranks, by reason of an illness which he could not understand or conquer.

THE CONFEDERATE PRISONERS.   But no—these were not his comrades, he saw, as he looked curiously at the long procession filing past him, closely guarded by the boys in blue, who kept step, while the men they hurried along were the subjects of ridicule from the thoughtless crowd. They were prisoners—

CAMP DOUGLAS.

159

these men, some clad in the well-known gray, some wearing
butternut suits, some of them without coats or hats, their pants
frayed and torn clear up to the knees. Here would proudly
march a clean-shaven, erect young fellow, with a suit of gray,
scarcely soiled, while at his side a mere shadow of a man,
ragged and dirty, would shamble along, barefooted and wild-eyed.

Nearly all of them were emaciated, while the expression
upon their faces was one of sullen despair. Men were there
who were the flower and chivalry of the South, who had staked
their lives and fame upon the success of their cause, and there
were men who scarce knew for what or who they were fighting.
To the former defeat was bitter humiliation—to the latter capture
meant something to eat, and beyond that, they did not look.

But to the careless crowd who watched them pass, they
were merely rebel prisoners. No sympathy
**PRISONERS FOR
CAMP DOUGLAS.** with their anguish and shame was felt; no pity
for their long months of captivity, when heart
and brain would chafe restlessly, moved the crowd, who jeered
and exulted. It was so, we know, the country over. The boys
in blue were hooted at and mocked, when the fortunes of war
threw them into the hands of the enemy. They all forgot that
those who wore the blue and those who wore the gray were
alike animated by a love of country, and that all were brothers--
equally brave, equally earnest, equally true-hearted.

Thoughts like these passed through Ralph's mind as he saw
the wretched men on their way to Camp Douglas, the military
prison at Chicago. To him they were objects of sympathy, and
he shuddered as he asked himself what would have been his
feelings had he been taken prisoner. He was startled by a
smart blow upon the shoulder, under whose force he almost staggered. He turned in astonishment, and saw Alfred Boneel, a
merry French boy, who had been a schoolmate of his.

              "Why, Alph, is it possible—you are look-
**RALPH MEETS AN
OLD SCHOOLMATE.** ing well. You're as brown as a nut, and say,
              where *did* you get those whiskers?"

"In the service, of course. There's nothing like army life

FORT DONELSON.

to bring out a man's good qualities. But say, Ralph, I'm sorry I can't return compliments. You are neither brown nor rugged looking. What's up?"

"They are sending me home as unfit to serve any longer," Ralph replied, dejectedly. "I don't know why they should single me out for such a distinction."

"Oh, you'll come out all right. I see you've done some thing besides get sick, judging by your sergeant's stripes."

"Yes, I won them, and was hoping for something better. But tell me all about yourself, Al."

"I haven't got much to tell, but I've seen some fighting, too. I was at the Fort Donelson scrimmage, and it was the coldest time I ever saw—snowing and blowing, and afterward turning out clear, but bitter cold. The storm of rain and snow had been pretty severe, and the fellows who were in the trenches must have been frost-bitten. I know we had no shelter and were hungry besides, as rations had given out, and had nobody round to ask us in to take dinner with 'em. We had pulled up stakes at Cairo, and had to go up the Ohio to Smithland, and then up the Cumberland River. Cavalry was no good in . that country, for there was too much big timber, and the ground was too rough. We were kept busy trying to plant a battery, for those fellows in gray have some sharpshooters worthy of their name, and though not one of them showed himself, it was whiz! pang! every few minutes, and some one was sure to go down. We lost Eddie Downing that way."

Al paused a moment to brush an imaginary fly from before his eyes.

"Eddie Downing was shot? He was a noble boy. So he's dead!"

Al nodded assent.

"Where's George Martin? Do you know what regiment he joined?"

"Oh, sure. He was in the gunboat service. Poor fellow, he fared worse than Eddie. He was on the Cumberland and had his right arm shot away."

GENERAL GRANT.
163

"Is he at home?"

"He was sent home as soon as the stump healed, and his only regret is, so his father says, that it wasn't the left arm, for he declares he'd try it again. But of course they wouldn't have him in any branch of the service."

"Of course not. But George always had grit. But how did you come out at Fort Donelson?"

"We had taken Fort Henry, but didn't feel so certain about Donelson. General Buckner had swelled the Confederate numbers there by about ten thousand men. Then the fort stood on high ground, and had a fine battery on the river front, as well as several lines of strong fortifications on **AL DESCRIBES** the land side, such as immense logs, bags of sand, **THE FORT DON-** and bunches of brush and sharp sticks. They **ELSON FIGHT.** were well protected, and their riflemen were in little pits dug in the side of a hill. All the time the weather staid stinging cold, and we suffered terribly. But it was inter-

FEDERAL GUNBOAT.

esting when the gunboats came to the front. Their gunners looked death right in the face every instant, but the way they made the shells fly was lively. Commodore Foote is a hero, and he bombarded them in gallant style. He had six boats, and the sight was worth seeing, as they would come up toward the fort, getting nearer, one by one, and then each delivering its fire, and circling round to give the other boats a shot at the rebs. And the fort was giving them trouble, too, for they were sending solid shot over the decks, which were doing damage.

"When a bomb from the enemy struck the iron plates a terrible racket would be heard, as they crashed into them, wrecking smoke pipes, and tearing down the rigging, and wounding the crews. The Commodore kept his flagship, the St. Louis, in the front. But he received a bad wound in the ankle, which did not make him give up, though, but when his boat and the Louisville began to fall behind, and they could not be managed, it was seen something was wrong. It seems they had their machinery hurt, and their steering gear gave out. So he had to stop, for the guns of Fort Donelson were making sad havoc with his disabled fleet, and it was found that the fort could not be captured by an attack on its water side. The flagship had been hit fifty-nine times and the others twenty or thirty times apiece, before it became clear that Fort Donelson must be assaulted by the land forces.

BOATS ARE DISABLED.

"That night kept us all well occupied, in making preparations for the next day's fight. That day was an awful one, and hundreds went down before the desperate fire of the butternut boys, but we drove them back into their entrenchments. Sunday didn't see us ready for church, for we had other engagements. The boys in blue had just enough taste of the excitement to make them want more, and General Grant had us all up in line of battle early in the morning, and we were waiting impatiently for the order to attack, when the word flashed along our ranks that an officer carrying a white flag had come to visit the General. We knew what that meant—some sort of an understanding, and we were not very sorry after all, for we had lost many a gallant soldier, and didn't know who'd be called away next. Still, we were ready, if it had to be.

"Ralph, I tell you, when we heard that the distinguished

looking gentleman on the black horse had come to ask that the
battle might be stopped for a time, so that they could argue it
out on some terms, every man amongst us felt like throwing up
his hat and hurrahing for the plain, unassuming little man who
commanded us, when he sent his answer—'No terms other than
an unconditional and immediate surrender can be
accepted. I propose to move immediately upon your
works.' That speech is as grand as any you'll ever
find in history. It will be repeated through all the ages. Why,
it's good enough to have been uttered by the great Napoleon."

A FLAG OF TRUCE.

Alph's eyes glistened, as he unconsciously expanded his chest,
and took on a more dignified air, as he walked proudly by the
side of his friend, who was trembling with the effort to keep up
with his robust companion.

"The whole world knows what his firm answer did. General
Buckner sent another flag of truce, with the acceptance of
General Grant's terms, and the Union troops moved in to Fort
Donelson."

"You must have been glad."

"Glad! Indeed we were. You should have heard us shout
and yell. We pulled the Confederate colors down in a hurry,
and ran up the Union flag. The very earth almost shook with
the cheering of the boys, while the band played 'Star Spangled
Banner,' 'Red, White and Blue,' and a dozen other patriotic
airs. We almost felt like having that bright little ditty 'In
Dixie's Land' served up to us, we all felt so jubilant. Before
an hour had gone by, we were on the most friendly terms with
them all. We were trading off our greenbacks for tobacco, and
they were getting bacon and biscuits from us. They didn't have
any hard feelings against us, and I know we didn't have any,
for they showed themselves brave and worthy foes wherever we
met the Confederates in battle."

Ralph had listened with delight to his description of the
taking of Fort Donelson. But he suddenly recollected that the
train must be due, and he reminded Al of the fact.

"That's so, and here I am, going home on a furlough, and

forgot all about it, while I was spouting. We'll hurry a little; we are only a block or so from the depot. You're all out of breath!" he said, half alarmed, as he observed Ralph's short, quick breathing, and the pallor of his face. "We'll be there in a jiffy, and you can rest. **AL AND HIS FRIEND.** It's a good thing I'm going to be on the same train, for when we reach Marion, I can take you to your own place. Pa's expecting me, and we'll drop you down at your own door."

This was pleasant news to Ralph, for his home was over a mile from the station, and he sighed as he recalled how little that distance affected him when he was leaving home, but now that he was returning, alas! he knew that he could not walk so far.

ON BOARD THE "HARTFORD," BATTLE OF MOBILE BAY.

CHAPTER XVI

RALPH AT HOME.

OME at last! And when that longing mother took her boy in her arms once more, and looked long and earnestly into his weary face, she saw only the boyish Ralph, whom sickness could not change; he was to her the same lad who had left his home with strong hopes and sunny smile. True, he was older and more care worn looking, but the honest look of his childhood shone from his eyes, and the same truthful, frank expression was on his features.

Ralph, as he rode up from the depot, with his friends, the Boneels, looked around at the old familiar place with eagerness. He expected to find everything changed—he had been absent so long, that to him it seemed as though the landscape, even, must have taken on new features, or at least changed its old. But there was the same gentle slope in front of the door, the same trees in the fields beyond, the same sunny knoll where he had played when a little boy. Oh, how long ago that seemed to him, now, when he reviewed the experiences of the past four years! Al and his father would not enter the house, though cordially invited to do so; they did not wish to intrude upon the sacredness of the first meeting with his mother.

She could scarcely speak for joy. At last she broke forth with words of greeting:

"Oh, my boy, my boy, you are home once more; you have come home to me, and you shall never go away again."

"I am glad to be with you, dear mother; as glad as a little child, who needs a good petting. But it was a bitter disappointment when I found that I could not stay with the brave boys who are offering up their lives for their country."

"Never mind, dear boy. You could not help getting sick. I will bring you back both health and strength, and then—"

"And then they will take me back in the army, again. Oh, mother, do you think it possible?"

Her face grew sad. She had not thought of that, and her heart experienced a bitter pang, for she felt that not even her

STAND OF FLAGS.

love and care were to him so sweet and dear as was his country and her cause. It wounded her deeply when she saw that even in the flush of his delight at being home again, he could not help clouding her joy by expressing a wish that in her bosom found no response.

She sighed deeply, and made him no answer, but he was so absorbed in greeting his sisters and friends who had met to welcome him, that he did not notice her silence.

Ralph could not endure patiently having to play the part of an invalid, but the home doctor's peremptory orders were that he should keep his bed, and visitors were to be admitted only when he felt as if he were able to talk with them. **RALPH IS ILL.** There were many long days when his voice was so faint and his strength so nearly exhausted that he was forbidden the excitement caused by their presence. But as the winter passed, under the tender ministrations of his mother and sisters, hope again sprung up in his breast, that health might return to him, and with health would come a return to the service.

The medical man was using every effort to restore him to health. He was wise, keen-sighted and skillful, and he fathomed the secret of Ralph's low vitality. His diligence and care were at length rewarded, and he had the satisfaction of seeing the elastic, springing step return, the bright color come back to his cheek, and the luster to his eyes, as he grew stronger daily, and to those who had come to greet his home-coming, and had mentally felt they were taking a last farewell, his recovery seemed almost a miracle.

Soon he could walk long distances, and even spring on the back of a horse for a ride. Al Boncel had returned to his regiment, but the young man's father had sent Ralph a horse, with a suggestion that he should ride every day when he was able, a privilege which brought the boy more healing than even the doctor's careful attentions.

He had instinctively shrank from visiting George Martin, although that young man had been to his home three or four times during his illness. It was a fine afternoon, and he knew he was able to ride over to George's father's farm, over three miles distant. He longed to talk over the war with him, and yet he had a feeling of delicacy lest George might be sensitive about any reference to his own misfortune. But he could not help going, and he found **RALPH VISITS AN OLD SCHOOLMATE.** George sitting on a bench in the orchard, where the green buds were just beginning to shoot forth their promise for future abundance.

"I'm glad indeed to see you able to come down here, Ralph,' was George's cordial greeting. "I've been wishing all day for some one to talk over old times with."

"Old times! Yes, we were happy, good-for-nothing lads in those days, I know, and gave our teachers lots of uneasiness."

"So we did, but I don't refer to those days; I mean the days in the army."

Ralph was all attention at once. "How did you like the service?" he ventured.

"Liked it clear through—way down to the bottom. You know how I lost my arm?" he said, pointing to the empty sleeve.

COMMANDER FRANKLIN BUCHANAN, COMMANDING THE MERRIMAC.

Ralph nodded. He longed to know more of the particulars, but would not ask.

"That was a great day. You should have been there, and seen a real fight. Not that a fight on land ain't all right, but there's a dash and inspiration about a battle on board ship that I enjoy! You feel as if the boat were your castle—you can't get away from it, and you're bound no one else shall get into it. Then the waves rocking beneath your feet, the shells screaming and dancing over the water, and the thought that your boat is almost a living thing, lends you a desperation nothing else can equal."

Ralph smiled faintly. To his way of thinking those sensations were common to all who went into battle, whether on land or water.

"You know when I went into the service I made my way

THE FRIGATE CUMBERLAND RAMMED BY THE MERRIMAC.

to Washington at once. I didn't wait to be enlisted here, but
I knew Uncle Dick, who lived there, could
get me onto a war-ship, and he did. Through **GEORGE RELATES**
his influence I went on the Cumberland. **A SEA FIGHT.**
She was a wooden vessel, but stanch and tr'm, with a good

commander, Lieutenant Morris, whom we all liked. He was brave, resolute and determined. The Merrimac, under Commander Franklin Buchanan, was trying to raise the blockade, and do us all the harm she could. She was steaming round Hampton Roads, waiting to sink any of the boats that were maintaining that blockade. Commodore Buchanan evidently fancied he had an easy job on hand, but as soon as we sighted the ungainly-looking craft, our hearts were made glad with orders to pour a broadside into her, which we lost no time in doing. We tried our best to destroy her, but her heavy iron plates withstood the assault. Had she been made of wood, we would have made a sieve of her with our charge. We did her some damage, though, for our shot went clear into her open ports, and killed some of her crew. I heard some one say when a man's hit he don't cry out, but I know better, for the shrieks of the wounded on both sides that day, mingled with the roaring of the shells, the crashing of shot against the iron-sheeted monster, and the confusion of voices as orders rang out, sound in my ears yet.

"Lieutenant Morris would not say die, and when the rifled shot from the big house, for that's what it looked like, tore our decks fore and aft, the Merrimac's commander followed it up by turning his boat so that he rammed into our gay little vessel's side, and left a huge gash. Our commander's blood was up. We felt the frigate slowly settling beneath our feet, but not a man dreamed of forsaking his gun, but steadily poured fire into the Merrimac. We were willing to die, rather than surrender, and even though the breath came quick and hard, and we may have quailed a little as we looked at our watery grave, yet we waited calmly to hear our leader's orders, while the enemy was dealing us terrible blows with shot and shell.

GEORGE RECEIVES A WOUND. "I felt a sharp pang, a numbness followed. The whole world was growing black, and for a second I thought the night had suddenly settled over us, and I knew no more, until one day I woke up in hospital, and found my right arm and shoulder had parted company. A messmate told me what happened after I fell to the deck. Our brave commander would not surrender; the water rose steadily, or, rather, the Cumberland sank steadily, until the waves washed across her gun deck, when the crew sprang overboard, and the ship's boats carried them ashore.

PICKETS EXAMINING PASSES.

Tom said it was a sickening sight—they had done us great havoc, but all of our wounded who could be dragged into the boats were saved, myself among the number. Tom said it was a gloomy sight when the trusty frigate keeled over, and sank to the bottom, but she went down game, for her top-masts stood above the water, with her flag flapping in the face of the Merrimac and her commander."

George paused. A sparkle was in his eyes, and he laughed aloud at his own idea. He continued: "But I had my revenge when I heard about the Monitor giving it to the Merrimac. You know Ericsson invented that queer boat. It's a curious affair. You never saw it? It looks for all the world like a big cheese box, with a round chimney or turret on it. This turret carries two

GEORGE DESCRIBES THE MONITOR.

CAPTAIN JOHN L. WORDEN, COMMANDING THE
MONITOR.

monstrous guns, and it can be turned round so that they can be pointed in any direction. The mischief she did was something worth talking about. Lieutenant John L. Worden commanded her, but he met with a mishap at the start. He was looking through the sight hole, taking observations, when a shell struck it, and hurt him badly, making him blind for a time, and he had to turn over the command to Lieutenant Sam Greene. The two boats kept on fighting wildly, each trying to ram the other. Why, they came so close once in the fight, that both guns went off together, causing such a shock that the crew at the after guns were knocked down, and some of them bled at the nose and ears. They fought four hours, so the paper stated, and the Merrimac went back to Norfolk, badly used up, for they put her in dry dock."

George would have talked on all night, it seemed, but Ralph, who had enjoyed the brief story of the sea-fight, said he must go, as the sun would soon be down. But that visit was but one of many which he made to George, and each one increased his anxiety to return to the army. He was gaining health under his mother's care and the long rest he was having, and he often laughingly declared that if the regimental doctor could see him now, he'd never believe in his own predictions again.

Grateful as his mother was for his restoration to health, yet it saddened her, for she saw it was useless to keep him back, for he talked of nothing else but returning to the army. She felt that he had done his duty, and she could not see why that did not content him. But she realized that it did not; she saw that he was determined to go, and her heart sank like lead in her bosom at the thought.

The day for parting came, and as Ralph, with a few other soldiers who were returning to their regiments, started for the great city beyond, from which **RALPH LEAVES HOME AGAIN.** they were to proceed to the front, she thought her heart would break at this second leave-taking. Her boy loved her more dearly than she knew; but he honestly thought his duty to his country was above any private considerations, and that he should be guilty of a great sin if he did not return to that duty.

The news from the front was most inspiring. Each day the "war news" was of more absorbing interest. Ralph wanted to be back with the army. He had no longer any ambition to win any especial distinction, but he was content to do his part as one of the vast army of great heroes of whom the world will never hear, but whose whole duty was done, quietly and unobtrusively.

How many sublime acts of self-sacrifice, of generous comradeship, were performed, on the field of battle, in camp and hospital, and even in prison life, will never be known. But a record has been kept in a higher ledger than a worldly one, and when that is revealed these deeds will come to the knowledge of all men.

WOUNDING OF GENERAL STONEWALL JACKSON.

178

CHAPTER XVII.

RALPH RE-ENLISTS.

NCE again our hero was in Chicago. The city had put on its spring dress, and well was it named the Garden City, for the streets at that time were nearly all bordered with trees, and their green foliage gave it, at a little distance, the appearance of a wooded plain, for the city is built on level ground —indeed, it was once a swamp, and it has cost the labor of years and an outlay of millions of dollars to reclaim it from its original state, and fill in and grade and elevate its highways.

The terrible battle of Chancellorsville had been fought, under General Hooker ("Fighting Joe," as the soldiers loved to call him), and a victory had resulted for the Union army. The news electrified the North, and great results were predicted. General Hooker had been given the command after the utter failure of General Burnside at Fredericksburg, and his soldiers were ready to follow him to the death, for he was intrepid and fearless. This memorable engagement had been fought with Hooker on the Federal forces, and Stonewall Jackson, the brave Confederate leader on the Confederate side. He was General Lee's right hand man, the ablest and best Lieutenant he ever had. Close upon this victory came the news that General Jackson had been shot by his own men. When the shades of evening began to fall, he rode to the front to see what could be learned of the movements of the Federals, and as he rode back to his own lines, surrounded by his staff, some of his own followers, watchful and faithful to their duty, not recognizing him in the dim twilight, but mistaking the mounted men for cavalry belonging to the Union side, fired a volley at

GENERAL JACKSON FALLS AT THE HANDS OF HIS OWN MEN.

them, killing several of the horsemen, and wounding others. This was, of course, supposed to be an attack from some of the Union soldiers, and to them was imputed the firing. The Confederate loss in the day's encounter had been severe, and they smarted at their defeat. They had been met by such a storm of grape and canister as no mortal power could withstand. The charge of Major Peter Keenan, which had been ordered by General Pleasanton, had been so brilliant that it had surprised the Confederates, who could not believe that Keenan, with four hundred men, would dare oppose ten thousand of their infantry, and they concluded that tremendous numbers must be behind them. The Major, with his little band, was slain, but his charge stopped the onset of the Confederates.

The stories of individual bravery which are furnished by the annals of the conflict, are alone enough to fill a volume, but will probably never be written. The heroic Major knew that he was inviting death, but he never faltered. Indeed, his own words were to that effect, for he said to his officers, "It is the same as saying we must be killed, but we'll do it." And his words proved prophetic, for he fell, and but few came out of that engagement alive.

The twilight was falling, veiling every object in its uncertain light, the trees cast their dark shadows over the path which General Jackson had chosen. As his men, ever watchful, saw the result of their first volley, they became exultant at their success, and again they loaded their guns, discharging them at the form of the leader of the approaching party, who had thus singularly fallen into their hands. They knew that they had wounded an officer, and as he fell from his seat, they rushed forward to learn his rank and name, if possible. Alas, to their consternation, they discovered that their beloved commander, General Jackson, had received three wounds. His steed, mad with fright, plunged wildly forward, and dashed into the depths of the thicket, tossing him against the limbs of the trees in his path, and bruising him most severely. While his men were sorrowfully conveying him to the rear, a Union battery belched forth

185

RECRUITING OFFICE, NEW YORK CITY HALL PARK.

From an engraving published in "Frank Leslie's Weekly," during the war.

its fire down the road after them; one man was wounded, and
the General fell to the ground.   He was borne to an hospital

GENERAL STONEWALL JACKSON.

but lived only one week, after having endured amputation of
his arm.

Bounties had been offered in all the Northern States.   New
York was offering liberal sums to recruits.   The new levy for
300,000 men ordered in April had not been filled,
CHICAGO.   and trouble was anticipated, as a draft had been threatened.   But in Chicago no such fears disturbed her people.

PRAYER IN "STONEWALL" JACKSON'S CAMP.

187

Ralph found that city full of activity. Groups were gathered on every street corner discussing the war and their hopes of its probable early ending. The South had suffered severely in loss of men and means, and so had the North. Many a family could point to the "vacant chair" and lament the dear one who had gone, never to return. Death had been busy at every fireside and the cruel war had wrought the havoc.

But the spirit of patriotism was not dead, but burned more brightly than ever, and those who had lain down their lives were embalmed in the hearts of a grateful people. They fell in a sacred cause, and their memories will live forever.

Ralph walked through the streets with a hopeful step. He had won his mother's free consent to go to the front, but little **THE DEAD NOT** did he dream how far from willing the consent **FORGOTTEN.** she had spoken was. He knew, too, that her blessing accompanied him everywhere, and he wished he could see her now, and tell her how happy he was. Turning down a street near the river, he saw a crowd standing round an office, on whose front was a big poster, with the words —"Recruits wanted—Enlist here!" Stepping in at the door, he saw a motley crowd of men pushing and jostling each other in their desire to be among the earliest to be enrolled. A military man sat at a desk, with a huge book open before him, and two officers sat near at desks, writing busily.

Ralph made known his business as soon as he could engage the officer's attention. He was questioned as to his age, occupation, and many other particulars.

"You say you've been in the army already?" the officer queried, while he looked earnestly into the boy's face. "How is it that you are here now, trying to re-enlist? Why did you not serve your time?"

"I got sick, really sick, sir," as he saw a smile flit over the other's face. "I did not want to come home, but the doctor said I would surely die if I remained. I received a discharge and went home to mother, and she cured me all up, and I am well—well, and stronger than ever. And now I want to go back

to the boys in the army, and help them finish this contract they
have taken, to bring the South back into the Union. Yes, I
want to enlist 'for the war.' "

As the boy concluded, his eye grew bright, his cheeks were
flushed, and his form seemed to expand with the strength of his
emotions.

The officer seemed to enjoy his earnestness, and writing
down his name, age, and place of birth, passed him over to the
doctor for examination. He passed satisfactorily, and thankfully
he heard the verdict of the doctor. He was sent to military
headquarters, and then he was assigned to the Seventy-second
Illinois Infantry. That regiment was the first one organized by
the Board of Trade of Chicago. It was then at Milliken's Bend,
after having tried in vain to make the Yazoo Pass. A canal
had been ordered dug by General Sherman in a bend opposite
Vicksburg, into which he was confident he could divert the river,
but this plan was checked by the sudden rising of the river, and
it was only by a miracle that entire regiments escaped drowning.

The attempt afterward made by Geneal Grant to enter this
Pass had proved equally disappointing, even though an embankment which the Confederates had thrown up had been as
promptly blown up by him. His boats entered the streams, whose
banks had heavy growths of timber, only to find TRYING TO MAKE
that the Confederates had cut down trees of THE YAZOO PASS.
immense bulk, and thrown them across the
channel. But General Grant kept on, removing the fallen trees
that blocked the way, but he at once discovered that he was
placing himself in a trap, for the rebels were felling trees and
throwing them across the channel behind him, so that he could
not get out again. They had also raised earthworks at a point
where two rivers met, and they were well guarded.

There was one forlorn chance left, yet untried, and that was
to go up the Yazoo a short distance, in boats, and pass into Big
Sunflower River, and then descend that stream into the Yazoo
again. This hazardous expedition was intrusted to Generals
Sherman and Porter, to carry forward.

The situation was desperate.   The channels were narrow,
there was no solid ground on which to plant troops, the cane-
brake was dense and nearly impassable, and they actually had
GRANT TRIES THE to pick their way through the dark and un-
YAZOO PASS. canny swamp by the aid of candles.   It was
inviting death too openly to proceed, for, added
to nature's horrors, the whole region swarmed with sharpshooters
to whom every step of the way was familiar, and whose unerring

COMMANDER DAVID D. PORTER.   REAR-ADMIRAL DAVID G. FARRAGUT.

aim told heavily all along the lines of the Federals, who were
glad to escape from the narrow pass.

Commodore Farragut, with one gunboat and his flagship, had
shot by the batteries at Port Hudson, and several boats had
passed Vicksburg.   On the night of April 16 Commodore Porter
ran by the batteries, but the watchful enemy had provided for
this move, and suddenly setting fire to huge heaps of wood on
the bank, a brilliant flame darted up to the heavens, and by its
light for an hour and a half they sent a heavy fire into the fleet,
which as industriously returned the courtesy as it steamed past

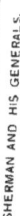

SHERMAN AND HIS GENERALS.

its adversary. But the Federal fleet met with no loss save the sinking of one transport.

This was some of the history of the campaign which the regiment to which Ralph was sent had taken part in, and the thought of joining it gave him unbounded delight.

"I was not contented, dear mother," he wrote to her a few days later, "until I was back with the boys in blue. This is a lovely country. When this war is over, I'll bring you down here, and we'll spend our days where nature has done so much for her creatures."

Down the river they steamed. When they reached Milliken's Bend, Louisiana, their corps united with Grant's army in its memorable march on Vicksburg. Ralph was on the alert to see all that he could of the country. But there were no signs of aught but desolation. Fences had been torn down, and consumed to cook the camp fare on marches; here a pile of charred timber told where a house had once reared its stately head; a few half-starved animals roamed round an old, deserted place, in search of the food they needed. Poverty, devastation and ruin were evident everywhere, and spoke plainly of the blight that followed in the wake of the armies that had tramped over and destroyed the beautiful homes of former days.

The morning of May 16, they reached Champion's Hill, where they found severe work. General Sherman had been left

DESOLATED HOMES. at Jackson to destroy the railroad, and the factories which were making goods for the Confederate soldiers. He performed this task with thoroughness. He now received orders from General Grant to send forward an ammunition train, so as to be ready for the battle that must take place soon. He was not disappointed. At Champion's Hill, on rising ground, he found General Pemberton waiting to receive him, with 23,000 men drawn up in line. His force held the vantage, as they were stationed on high ground, commanding three roads, and thus it was admirably calculated for a defensive point.

For hours the fighting went on. The Union forces made a

GENERAL WILLIAM TECUMSEH SHERMAN.

189

overwhelming charge, and the rebel lines wavered, but speedily regained their position. It was a desperate duel, and fought to the death. General Pemberton had a splendid army of well-disciplined men, and when the two lines met with impetuosity, the day seemed lost to the Federals. General

GENERAL LOGAN COMES TO THE RESCUE. Logan saw the danger threatening them, and pushing forward on the right with his magnificent division, he passed the rebel General's left flank, and secured the only road by which the latter could make his retreat.

The enemy were dismayed. Cut off from escape, they knew defeat was inevitable. The movement of Logan had been so sudden and brilliant that there was not a moment of grace given them. But that General was not conscious that he held the road in his grasp, and when General Hovey, who was besieged vigorously by the Confederates, a few moments later, shouted for aid,

GENERAL JOHN A. LOGAN, FOUNDER OF THE GRAND ARMY OF THE REPUBLIC.

Logan fell back to his assistance.

Now was their chance, for the road was left unguarded, and a dash was made by General Pemberton, whose flying columns

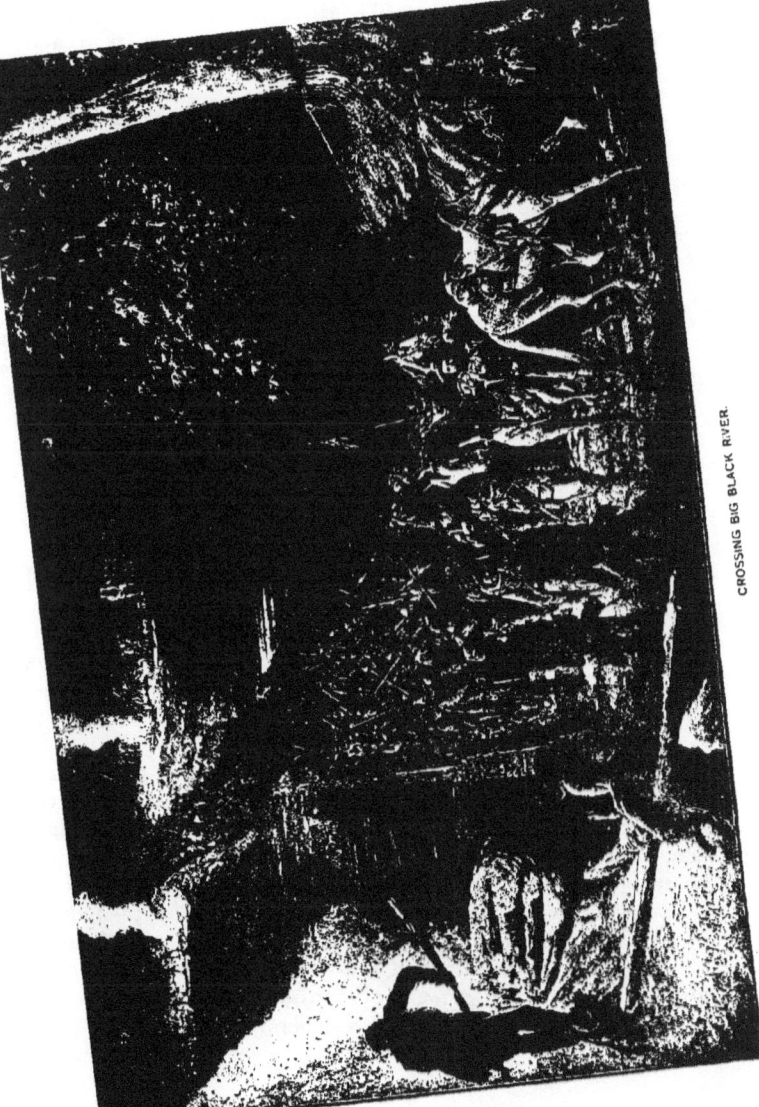

CROSSING BIG BLACK RIVER.

were in full retreat, without giving a thought to his dead and wounded, left uncared for on the field.   He also abandoned thirty guns, and crossed the Big Black River.

The battle was over, and to the opportune move of the brave Logan was due the hard-won success of the day.   Four hours of hard fighting had been followed by the usual harvest of dead and maimed.   Nurses and hospital stewards succored all whom they could find, but wounded men were lying between the lines and in every corner, groaning with the anguish of uncared for injuries.   Among those lost on the Confederate side was General Tilghman, who fell early in the day.

The soldiers found a brief rest in sleep.   Ralph had thrown himself on the ground in a state of perfect exhaustion.   He would not confess, even to himself, that he had overrated his strength.   But when the stars came out, and the silence of night succeeded, nature asserted her rights, and he slept undisturbed by dreams of carnage and bloodshed, but his visions were of home and its charms.

RALPH SLEEPS CALMLY.

"Wake up, young fellow!"

He sprang to his feet, while a man of about forty, who had been shaking him violently, said, with a hearty laugh:

"You're something of a sleeper.   Rip Van Winkle is nowhere.   Reveille has sounded, the regiments are ready to move as soon as we get a cup of coffee, and you've been sleeping through it all, as sweetly as if you were in your little bed at home.   It's a mighty fine thing to have a clear conscience."

And the pleasant-faced soldier gave Ralph a gentle push as he gathered himself up, and made a jump for one of the fires that were burning in different spots, kindled by the hungry men to boil their coffee, or cook a bit, before they took up the march again.   The other followed closely at his heels, and sitting on a fallen log they were soon busy "fortifying their inner man," amid much laughing and chaffing going on around them.

That is a marked trait of the American soldier, be he from North or South.   No amount of hardship, no deprivations, can destroy that love of fun which is inborn.   He is always ready to see the comic side of all situations, as he merrily laughs at danger, and jokes almost in the very presence of death.

That day General Pemberton was overtaken at the Big Black. Here he had stationed his main body on high land, but on the east of the stream the ground was low and wet, and on this spot the remainder of his command was held.

"We have got to dislodge Pemberton from his position," Ralph heard a comrade say. "He has a splendid view of all we are doing, and can make a stanch resistance. But we'll soon set him running again, and he'll have to find a better lookout than the one he now occupies."

"See!" shouted Ralph. "General Lawler is leading the attack on their right flank. They give way—they fall back! The General is in his shirt sleeves, and **PEMBERTON** looks as if he were in earnest!" **RETREATS.**

"Shouldn't wonder if he was. He's a hard one to tackle, and won't stand on ceremony. He don't go into battle in a full dress suit. Just look over there. Pemberton is retreating, skedaddling. His men have set fire to that bridge, and how is he going to cover the retreat of his rear guard down there in the bayou?"

"He's not trying to save them at all, but is looking after No. One. By George, he's off, and has left those poor fellows to be captured, or shot down, he don't care which."

It was true. He ran away in mad haste, making no effort to cover their retreat, but abandoned the panic-stricken men in the lowland to their fate. Wild with terror, with no leader to direct, many of them flung themselves into the river, only to sink beneath the waters, and those who were left were taken prisoners by the Federals.

CHAPTER XVIII.

CROSSING THE RIVER.

ENERAL GRANT set to work at once building bridges by which to cross the Big Black. General Sherman's corps were soon busy felling trees and laying planks. A raft bridge was now constructed, and a bridge was also hurried together, with cotton bales for pontoons. The next step was to cut trees on each side of the river in such a manner that their trunks were not severed, but clung to the stumps. In falling across the stream, their boughs met and grasped each other firmly, and the planks laid across them made a secure **BUILDING BRIDGES.** road, over which the troops passed, while the two Generals, Grant and Sherman, sat on a log and watched the living mass of blue-coats march over, with the smoky, ruddy light of pitch pine torches throwing their weird shadows over the scene. It was a wild and picturesque panorama. The vast body of human beings moving fearlessly across the swaying structure, the fitful gleams of light reflecting from their muskets, the two great generals sitting there as calmly as though watching a festive procession—the somber depths of the forest on either side, where danger lurked in many shapes—what heart could fail to be impressed by the solemn spectacle?

By the morning of the 18th that vast army had crossed to the west side of the river, but the rebel general had not waited to receive them, but flown, without attempting to give them battle. He hastened to the city of Vicksburg, behind whose walls he found shelter. He was speedily followed by Grant, who got his army in position, placing General Sherman on the right of the line, General McPherson on the left of Sherman, and McClernand next, his command touching the river below Vicksburg. Sharp resistance was offered, and the Confederates lost ground in a skirmish on the 19th, but made an onset which almost regained it for them, but the National troops checked their assault and moved to a more advantageous position. The Federal forces were nearly famished, for rations for five days had to do duty for three weeks, eked out by what they could confiscate from the people as they marched through the country, **SKIRMISHING GOES ON.** and one of General Grant's first steps was to make roads in the rear of his line, so that supplies could be obtained more easily. These roads ran through swamps and miry places, where no team could force its way.

GENERAL JAMES B. McPHERSON.

"We are expecting an attack from Johnston. He has been laid up with the wound he received at Seven Pines, and has all the Mississippi forces under him," Ralph's captain said to him.

"Our line of defences is thrown out six or seven miles, so I hear," answered Ralph. "We are well prepared for them."

"That is true, but we may look for an attack in our rear. McClernand reports that he has taken two forts, and is in imminent danger, and sends a request for reinforcements at once."

Ere he finished speaking, the ball was opened vigorously.

FORAGING IN EARLY TIMES.

197

The river heights were fortified strongly, earthworks rearing their heads for miles, bristling with guns, against which the Union

MAKING A MILITARY ROAD THROUGH SWAMP.

army hurled its strength in vain. Grant's purpose was to carry the works by storm, but though splendid courage was shown, and the color-bearers at many points reached the breastworks and planted flags upon them, they proved impregnable.

When Ralph saw their efforts, he could not repress his enthusiasm, but shouted—"Hurrah! Our flag is floating on the breeze. We shall soon be in the city!"

His excitement was contagious, and with a ringing shout the advancing men hurled themselves vigorously against the obstructions, only to be driven back slowly but surely.

"General Grant has just received a dispatch saying that

MAJOR-GENERAL WESLEY MERRITT.
MAJOR-GENERAL PHILIP A. SHERIDAN.   BRIGADIER-GENERAL THOMAS A. DEVIN.
BRIGADIER-GENERAL J. I. GRIGGS.   BREVET MAJOR-GENERAL GEORGE A. CUSTER.

McClernand has two forts of the enemy in his possession. A brigade has been sent to his aid, and firing has been resumed. Boys, at them with a will!"

As they entered a cut in the road, Ralph saw the color sergeant of one of the Illinois regiments, who could scarcely stand from fright. The balls were whistling by their ears, the leaves of the trees were falling in showers, scattered by the rifles' fire. The man was ashy pale, and his knees trembled so he could not stand erect. Ralph thought of what he had re-

A FRIGHTENED SERGEANT. lated to the boys months ago, about the French soldier, but this, he saw, was not a parallel case, for this man was clearly a coward, and as he watched him, he expected to see him fall down, and trail the colors after him. The man saw that he was observed, and he made one desperate effort to raise himself to his full height, but suddenly the pleas-ant-faced man who had taken interest in Ralph sprang forward, wrested the flag from the cowardly fellow, and carried it valiantly to the front.

Ralph looked for the sergeant. He had shrunk to the rear, and was busy hiding behind a huge tree which towered above the field.

"Thank heaven!" said Ralph, "our flag was saved." He felt sure that his new friend, who was corporal of the color guard, would be rewarded in some way, but the soldier who had rescued the flag, when summoned before the commanding officer, and offered promotion to color sergeant, promptly refused it, unless the one who had so belittled his trust were reduced to the ranks. This was not done, for some reason, but the man who had rescued the colors was made a sergeant—a deserved promotion.

The rumor proved false, for General McClernand, so far from taking the two forts, had been repulsed, and the men who were sent to help him were many of them killed; they were made the victims of a misstatement, to put it as mildly as possible. A short time after, General Grant relieved him of further respon-sibility, and General Ord succeeded him.

This assault was a costly one, for two thousand five hundred men were sacrificed, and Grant determined to

GRANT RESOLVES ON A SIEGE. besiege the city. He went to the rear, earth-works were thrown up, and mines were dug under the fortifications. By day and by night the big guns were booming across the space, which daily grew narrower, as the Union soldiers brought the trenches nearer to the line of defense. Those were days that tried their courage and patience, but not a murmur was heard.

One day a great commotion took place among the soldiers. Three objects were seen whirling through the air, and fell in the Union lines, within five feet of where Ralph was standing.

"What is it? Where did it come from?" was the query, as several hastened to the spot, to find three men, two white ones lying on the ground dead, and one negro nearly so.

A STRANGE VISITOR.

"Something struck some one that time," Corporal Calvin Strong said. "See—the colored man's coming to."

And so he was, and as he raised up, he began to rub his head, and look wildly about.

"Say, he's contraband of war, and we must confiscate him," the Corporal continued, laughingly.

"Whar—whar be I? Is dis yere de bottomless pit?" the black man asked.

"Yes, Sam, you've arrived at your proper destination, and now you've got to be flogged every day, until your sins are all paid for."

"Oh, massa, spare a poor cullered boy who neber did nuffing wuss den steal a chicken, or grab a few eggs. Neber did no mo'." And falling on his knees he began to jabber away in pure fright.

SAM CONFESSES HIS FAULT.

"Get up, you black rascal; you're in the Union lines now," Sergeant Harmon said, as he pulled the shaking darkey to his feet.

"Bress de Lawd! In de Union? I'se whar I'll git sumfin to eat, now, sure."

"How far did you come, Sam?"

"Bout free miles. I'se come to stay, too. I'll neber go back dar any mo'."

And Black Sam did stay, and made one of the most faithful of servants. He often referred to his first appearance among the soldiers. When the mine exploded at Fort Hill, it killed the two white men, but by some miracle Sam escaped, and when he recovered consciousness, and found himself surrounded by men black with powder and dust, he had really fancied that he had landed in a certain world where they tell us cold is unknown.

Day after day the noise of the great guns was heard. Shells were thrown into the beleaguered town, and much injury was inflicted. Vicksburg at this time might be called a city of caves, for they were dug in the banks wherever a street was cut through a clayey hill, and these caves were tenanted by entire families, who lived in comparative safety, while shells and balls were whizzing over their heads. Nor did the darkness bring a cessation of hostilities, the night proving no barrier to Grant's vigorous attack. As the two lines came nearer together, a mutual understanding was had, after this fashion:

"Well, Yank, how are you getting along?"

EXCHANGE OF COURTESIES. "Oh, fine. We'll soon be over there to see you. Have the ice-cream and cake all ready, for it's a hot day."

"Oh, that'll be all right. We'll freeze you out sure. Say, you come up on top where we can get a look at you."

"If you'll put your old guns away, and not pop at us, we'll come up."

"That's a bargain. We promise. But you must do the same by us."

"Agreed—that's fair enough." And true to their word, they would show themselves, and a running fire of jokes and ridicule would be launched at each other.

"Say, Johnnie, how are the hotels over there? Engage us rooms at the best one, for we want good accommodations when we get there."

"We have everything fine, and are waiting to receive you in first-class shape."

"Good eating?"

"The choicest cuts of mule-steaks, roasts, soups, any shape you order it. Say, Yank, what's the news your way?"

"Oh, we're having a jolly time. We've got everything we

want, save your town, and when we get that, the old mud stream will be open for a sail way down to the Gulf."

"Well, you won't take your sail very soon, then, for you'll never get Vicksburg. Say, have yer got any terbacker?"

"Lots of it. Want some?" Then the exchange would be made, and after this friendly pause, both sides would resume hostilities, as earnestly as ever.

Work in the trenches brought the prospect of subduing the almost invulnerable heights nearer and nearer. Famine

FAMINE IS AT HAND. threatened the besieged city, with its horrors. Forty-four days had been consumed in laying siege. Soldiers lay down in the same clothes which they had worn through all these weary weeks of bloodshed and resistance.

General Pemberton sent a flag of truce to General Grant, and negotiations were

.CAPTAIN CHARLES WILKE.

carried on, but the Federal commander was now prepared for a final grand assault. The Fourth of July was near, supplies had given out within the walls, and the Confederate general, who had held out bravely, surrendered without making any conditions.

FEEDING THE FOE. General Grant took possession in a most magnanimous manner. By his express command not a man of his army was permitted to cheer; not a single salute was fired, and silently, with dignity and generosity, the half-starved Confederates were fed bountifully, the Union soldiers emptying their own knapsacks, and giving their contents to them. All the prisoners taken at Vicksburg and those at Port Hudson were paroled, under the supposition that they would return to their homes, and await a proper exchange.

War has its humor as well as peace. The help afforded by Porter's fleet and Farragut's had been considerable during the siege. The Confederates had sunk the Indianola, one of Porter's boats, and were trying to raise it, when they saw a

HORACE GREELEY.

monitor coming down full upon them. Admiral Porter had fitted up an old flatboat with pork barrels for smoke stacks, and furnaces made from mud, in which a fire had been started. He sent it sailing down the river, with not a human being on board, to the evident terror of the Confederates, who were watching her and who fired point blank at her, without stopping the supposed monitor. Dreading lest they would lose their prize, they promptly blew up the Indianola, before they discovered that they were sold.

CHAPTER XIX.

THE PROCLAMATION.

LACKS were constantly coming into the Union lines, and though it was a hard problem to dispose of them, yet General Grant's care of them was most humane. Few among them were aware of the immortal proclamation of Abraham Lincoln, but believed themselves still subject to their old masters. The colored folks all through the war had shown very friendly feelings toward the Union army, as many an act of kindness at their hands had testified. Those who came into camp, as well as the white refugees, were put to various labors. Surely no race, save the African, ever produced

GENERAL WADE HAMPTON.

205

such a quantity of culinary artists, judging from the claims they set up. **PLENTY OF COOKS.** Whenever a darkey was queried as to his calling, whether he had been a field hand or a house servant, he always answered that he was "a fust-rate cook, massa; can gib yo' some fust-class dishes."

"Still more good news, boys; General Lee has been routed at Gettysburg, and several of his generals killed or wounded. Among the latter is General Wade Hampton. Lee's brilliant sortie has been checked by three of the hardest days' fighting ever witnessed in this war. Both armies fought like demons. But we have driven Lee and his followers off the soil of Virginia. General Meade, the master spirit, has given them a taste of his fine generalship."

"He's never jealous of his officers under him—that is another trait of his," spoke up a man who had fought under him.

"Yes, and Pickett, with his magnificent column, was there, and was nearly annihilated, for he lost nearly every officer he had."

"The fight was hottest, they say, at Round Top. The Confed sharpshooters held Devil's Den, and a ghostly place it is. I know every inch of the ground, for I was born three miles from there," said another man.

HARRIET BEECHER STOWE.

"How strange," said Ralph, "that two such glorious victories should follow each other—Gettysburg in the East, and Vicksburg in the Southwest. General Lee has been instructed that an invasion of the North is impossible, and we have cut the Confederacy in two by opening the Mississippi to navigation from Cairo to the Gulf. Surely, the God of battles is on our side," he reverently continued, for Ralph knew that without His overruling care, we are but naught.

PUNISHMENT IN THE ARMY.

The martyrs of Gettysburg, those who had laid down their lives for universal liberty, were not forgotten ¿: A National cemetery, in which the soldiers who fell in that campaign were to be buried, was laid out. The ground was dedicated on the **GREAT REJOICING OVER VICTORIES.** 19th of November, 1863, and here, with the wintry winds making music round their graves, the remains of 3,560 brave men were laid to rest, according to the order of their respective States. It was a fitting tribute to bravery, and the occasion was most impressive.

GENERAL MEADE'S HEADQUARTERS.

DEVIL'S DEN.

JENNIE WADE—THE ONLY WOMAN KILLED AT GETTYSBURG.

Edward Everett was chosen as the orator of the day. President Lincoln was invited to honor the event by his presence, and he received a gentle hint that his voice would be a welcome tribute.

He came, with no speech prepared, save a few fugitive thoughts which he scratched down on an old envelope, on his way to Gettysburg, and intended solely as references. When he was called on, he rose, and in his simple, unaffected way he gave to his hearers an immortal speech. A long time after its delivery, Mr. Lincoln, at the urgent request of friends, rewrote it and affixed his signature.

The copy gives an exact facsimile of his handwriting, and thus in a double sense it becomes a most valuable addition to one's reading matter.

14

GENERAL PICKETT.

Address delivered at the dedication of the Cemetery at Gettysburg.

Four score and seven years ago our fathers brought forth on this continent, a new nation, conceived in Liberty, and dedicated to the proposition that all men are created equal.

Now we are engaged in a great civil war, testing whether that nation, or any nation so conceived and so dedicated, can long endure. We are met on a great battle-field of that war. We have come to dedicate a portion of that field, as a final resting place for those who here gave their lives that that nation might live. It is altogether fitting and proper that we should do this.

But, in a larger sense, we can not dedicate—we can not consecrate—we can not hallow—this ground. The brave men, liv-

ing and dead, who struggled here, have consecrated it, far above our poor power to add or detract. The world will little note, nor long remember what we say here, but it can never forget what they did here. It is for us the living, rather, to be dedicated here to the unfinished work which they who fought here have thus far so nobly advanced. It is rather for us to be here dedicated to the great task remaining before us—that from these honored dead we take increased devotion to that cause for which they gave the last full measure of devotion—that we here highly resolve that these dead shall not have died in vain—that this nation, under God, shall have a new birth of freedom—and that government of the people, by the people, for the people, shall not perish from the earth.

Abraham Lincoln.

November 19, 1863.

COLONEL JOHN S. MOSBY AND A GROUP OF HIS RAIDERS.

211

The days of idleness had not come to them yet. Victory
did not mean inaction.   They were embarked on board a
steamer, bound for Natchez, Mississippi, which town was taken
with little resistance.   They also seized several pieces of artillery,
a large number of prisoners, and 5,000 head of cattle designed
                      for use in the Southern army. A quantity of
SKIRMISHING.   Government stores fell into their hands, also. At
                      Natchez they were detailed to do provost duty.
This was to Ralph a pleasant change from the awful scenes of

GETTYSBURG CEMETERY GATE.

carnage he had been a participant in.   The morning of September 1st the regiment was ordered out to attack a body of rebels
who were harassing the Union people at St. Catharine's Creek.
They found a small force stationed here who were levying contributions from the country around, but they promptly drove

GENERAL LONGSTREET WOUNDED BY HIS OWN MEN.

them back to their hiding-places. At Cross Bayou, Louisiana, they were again called into action, and suppressed the guerrilla bands who preyed on all alike.

Guerrilla warfare is most exasperating. The West was full of these vicious and irresponsible men, who, under a leader of courage and brains, would unite to prey on and murder rich and poor alike. They could skulk in the depths of the woods, and dash out upon their victims, and after gratifying their murderous designs, they would flee to their homes and lie in concealment till some new exploit would reveal their lurking place. Probably the best organized and most reckless of these bands was led by Colonel John S. Mosby, whose daring deeds made his name a terror. His raids were remarkable for their boldness and success. He never was captured, although his band was thinned often by the frequent efforts on the part of the Federals to bring him to justice.

COLONEL CHARLES W. LE GENDRE.

"We are ordered back to Vicksburg, to do provost duty there," the captain informed his **BACK TO VICKSBURG.** men, who heard it with variable feelings. Grumbling was heard from some of the younger ones, who were anxious to be "at the front," and to them acting as provost guards smacked too much of being kept in the background. The older ones heard the news with much satisfaction, however.

They returned to Vicksburg, with very different emotions to those they felt just after the surrender of General Pemberton, and even though they were not welcomed, their coming insured peace and protection from the

FALL OF GENERAL JAMES B. McPHERSON, NEAR ATLANTA.

215

JOHN M. MORGAN AND WIFE.

contentions without, and the rough element within. Doing post duty is quite as necessary as constant warfare, but few were the occasions for interference on the part of the soldiers.

Skirmishes were frequent, but the days of the rebellion were drawing to a close. The Confederates realized that the hours of the Confederacy were numbered, but still they struggled on. How ardently Ralph wished that peace would dawn. He abhorred the bloodshed that the protracted conflict entailed.

Time passed heavily, and he began to fret at the duty assigned. Events so brilliant that everything paled before them were transpiring elsewhere, and the boy's spirit burned to be in the fray.

Morgan, the Confederate guerrilla, had planned a bold raid across the Ohio, and had captured Columbia and Lebanon, Kentucky, seized two steamers, and, going into Indiana, had left a trail of ruin and destruction behind him, as he hastened toward Cincinnati, burning bridges and stores, tearing up railroad tracks, and plundering every one, irrespective of their views. How far his depredations would have been carried, cannot be judged, but at Buffington Ford he was pursued so closely that **A GUERRILLA AT WORK.** he was driven to make a stand and fight. Here he was defeated, and, fleeing up the stream, was again attacked at New Lisbon, where he surrendered, and was sent to the Ohio penitentiary, but a few months later he dug under the walls and fled.

July 18 the regiment was again aroused by receiving orders to move on to Grand Gulf, Mississippi, where a large force of

NATIONAL CEMETERY AT RICHMOND, VA.

217

CAPTAIN RAPHAEL SEMMES.

Confederates were posted. They found them waiting for them, and gave battle at once, taking a few prisoners, who were sent to the military post for future exchange.

The awful Battle of the Wilderness had gone down into history, with its record of unparalleled daring, and its list of 60,000 dead on the two sides, sending up a wail to Heaven. It was in this fatal battle that General Longstreet, of the Confederate army, received a severe wound on the same ground and under a similar mistake, as that which cost Stonewall Jackson his life, a year before The General was returning from the front, when he was seen by some of his own men, and fired upon, under the supposition that he belonged to the National cavalry.

The Atlanta campaign, which had added to General Sherman's everlasting renown, had lost to the Union cause one of its bravest generals—the brilliant McPherson, who lost his life by venturing into the woods almost alone, where he was shot by the Confederates, and his horse dashed into the Union lines bleeding, but riderless.

The Confederate vessel Alabama, commanded by Raphael Semmes, was at Cherbourg, France. She had been cruising round for two years, preying upon American commerce. The United States man of war, Kearsarge, Captain John A. Winslow, lay off the port, expecting Semmes to come out. The latter sent a polite request to Winslow, asking him not to leave those waters, as he intended to fight him. This was exactly Captain Winslow's wish. On Sunday, June 19, the Alabama went out of the harbor with flying colors, only to be lured off eight miles from the coast, by Captain Win-slow, who then turned and attacked the enemy. After the Kearsarge began the battle, the firing was terrific and her shots told heavily. Captain Winslow's shells cut the mizzenmast of the Alabama in two. The crew were half of them killed by a shell, and the gunners had been swept away. After an hour's battle, it was seen that the Alabama was sinking, her officers struck their colors, and threw the swords, that would no longer avail against their adversary, into the sea.

CAPTAIN JOHN A. WINSLOW.

Captain Winslow lowered boats from his vessel to save the remaining crew of the Alabama, when suddenly her stern went down, her bow was tossed into the air and the Alabama went to the bottom, carrying nearly all the men. Semmes was picked up by a yacht, with forty sailors, the Kearsarge rescued some, and all the rest were drowned.

The autumn had come. October had put on its gaudy dress, and the Seventy-second were still in Vicksburg. By their sedate and manly bearing and perfect discipline, they had won the friendly toleration of the very people who had dreaded their coming, but who now felt secure in the protection of their property. **STILL DOING PRO-VOST GUARD DUTY.** Business had been to a certain degree resumed, quiet had settled down over the city, and the great events of that year were had in the papers from the North, which came freely into the city.

"At last we are going to move again," said Ralph, as they gathered round headquarters. "We are to report to General Howard and go with Sherman on his 'March to the Sea.'"

"Well, it'll be a relief, for this sort of life is too much like playing soldier to suit me," a gray-haired private responded.

THEY LEAVE VICKSBURG. It was a light-hearted body of men who left Vicksburg that day, but when they reached Nashville, they were disappointed to learn that they were too late to join Sherman, but the Seventeenth Corps was cut off and assigned to General Schofield's command, then stationed at Columbia, Tennessee. It was approaching winter's rigors, and General Hood had harassed the Federal army at all points, and was trying to persuade Sherman away from Atlanta. When he found he could not do so, he massed his whole strength for the purpose of destroying General Thomas' forces. Turning his face in the direction of Nashville, he met a barrier in the heavy rains which had fallen, rendering the roads almost impassable, and it was well into November before he reached Duck River, forty miles south of Nashville.

GENERAL OLIVER O. HOWARD.

General Schofield expected him, but Hood flanked him by crossing to the other shore, which led the Union general to deem

CHARGE OF CONFEDERATE CAVALRY AT TREVILIAN STATION, VA.

221

BRIGADIER-GENERAL NEAL DOW.

it prudent to attempt to reach Nashville. Quickly he retired to Franklin, where he succeeded in getting across the river, throwing up earthworks, and placing his artillery. The scene was a stirring one. General Hood forced his men up against the strong breastworks with a recklessness that was appalling. They were doomed, for the terrific onslaught of musketry and artillery cut them down so fast that they were piled up in heaps, dying and dead, the entire length of the line. The struggle at the breastworks was so fierce that it became a hot, mad encounter between the two armies, who fought literally, hand to hand, while their fire flashed in each other's faces. Officers dismounted, and fought beside their men. The contest became so close that the standards of both armies were upon the earthworks at the same time.

A ditch ran outside the works, which was filled with the Confederates, who could not cross it under such a blinding fire. Here they met their heaviest losses. The smoke from the National side was so dense, and kept so near to the earth, that it added to the horror of the scene by bringing on almost complete

THE BREAST-WORKS THE SCENE OF DEFEAT.

darkness. It was one of the hardest fought battles of the war, and not until midnight did General Schofield order a retreat to Nashville, a wise move, for had he been content to remain at Franklin, the fortunes of the day would have been changed very essentially,

WALTER Q. GRESHAM.

for Hood planted all his artillery there that night, and thus, aided by General Forrest's cavalry, the victory of the day before would surely have been turned into a defeat.

They were worn out — unable to fight longer, and so completely exhausted by lack of sleep that many of the men in this retreat stumbled and fell on their faces, and only the vigorous pricking of the bayonet by their companions aroused them to a sense of the danger they were in of being captured, — thus they were hurried along.

The whole strength of the army was now concentrated on the defeat of Hood. On the fifteenth of December General Thomas, who had been grumbled at and called "slow," delivered a crushing blow by moving upon Hood's front and flank with such force that he fled precipitately toward Franklin, with Wilson's famous cavalry in hot pursuit. General Thomas made a clean sweep of

SHERIDAN RECONNITERING AT FIVE FORKS.

228

the artillery, capturing every piece, and taking forty-five hundred prisoners.

The morning of February 9 was cold and frosty, and as the soldiers huddled round the crackling fires built in the open air, they recounted tales of the incidents they had seen, or fought again the battles of the past four years.

"I enlisted to the end of the war," said Ralph.   "'When this cruel was is over,' I shall go home and try to be content." Some of his companions shared his feelings; to these the prospect of returning home was a delightful one, but others had grown so fond of this life of danger and peril that a return to the peaceful pursuits of home-life seemed tame and dull. War hardens and blunts the finer feelings, making men callous and indifferent to the gentler ministrations of home.

It was with mixed feelings of joy and regret that the regiment embarked on the steamer for New Orleans. The voyage was a break in the daily life, but when land soldiers **VARIOUS OPINIONS.** are penned up on board a boat there is not much to break the monotony. At noon of the fourth day they laid up at a little landing to "wood up." Not a house was to be seen, the tall trees stood up black and gloomy, and the dull gray sky lowered ominously over them. Glad to feel the earth beneath their feet, a few of the more venturesome leaped ashore for a "run in the timber," as they expressed it, though they prudently kept near the boat.

Ralph was sitting on the deck when he heard the report of a rifle, and jumping up, he called out, "Our men are attacked!"

Instantly every man's weapon was pointed in the direction from whence came the sound. A poor fellow had roamed a few steps farther from his comrades than caution would have dictated, and had been fired upon by guerrillas, who were skulking behind the trees in the leafy depths of the forest. Another man staggered to the edge of the bank, and would have fallen overboard, were it not for Ralph's quick leap. He had been wounded in the arm, and as he was helped on board he said: "There is a band of them up there in the woods."

"Fire!" came the word of command, and the bullets whistled after the fleeing band, who did not return the shots, however. Whether they were hit, was not known. A detail was sent to bring in the body of the dead soldier who had **A MAN SHOT.** fallen just at the edge of the woods. This incident checked the gay spirits of the men, but, after all, it was one of the possibilities of war, and might have befallen any one there.

They reached the city of New Orleans on the evening of February 21st, and encamped at a beautiful little village about eight miles below that city. But their stay was brief, and again they were transported across the Gulf to Dauphine Island, Alabama. The March weather was health-inspiring, but they had

MAJOR-GENERAL PHILIP H. SHERIDAN.

APPOMATTOX COURT HOUSE

no leisure for admiring nature's lovely face, for there was more fighting ahead.

Mobile Bay was now the destined point. Crossing over to the mainland, they spent several days in skirmishing, it being General Grant's design to divert the enemy's attention from his real intention, which was to attack and subdue Spanish Fort, before whose walls they were arrayed on the dawn of March 27. Bombardment began early. A dense curtain of smoke hung over the fort, like a pall, and after four days of vigorous assault, their guns were silenced, and just before the midnight hour, the works were carried, amid wild cheers and exultation.

GENERAL CUSTER.

Great events were taking place while the Western army was busy. Sheridan and his cavalry had not been idle in the Shenandoah Valley, and at Waynesboro' General Custer, the intrepid, who commanded his Third Division, routed General Early, and took 1,500 prisoners, and every gun and train he had. Sheridan was not content with this victory, but he ruined the locks in the James River Canal, destroyed parts of the railroad, thus cutting off supplies, and then joined General Grant's army, and passed through Dinwiddie Court House with his splendid body of cavalry, and attacking the right flank of the Confederates at Five Forks, found no difficulty in dislodging their cavalry, when a strong force of infantry came to their rescue, who in their turn routed Sheridan most unexpectedly. At once Grant hurried the **GRANT'S PLAN.** Fifth Corps forward to his assistance, but it was noon of the first of April before he could get them into position.

COLONEL JOHN B. GORDON.

Bringing up his mounted force in front, who dashed forward in gallant style, he led the Fifth Corps so as to completely

encircle the Confederates.   This manœuver was an unpleasant
surprise to the enemy, and a victory for the Federal side.   Five
Forks was held by them, and 5,000 prisoners fell into the hands
of the Union army.

Following up his advantage, General Grant leveled two
more forts, whose defenders still resolutely held out—Forts Gregg

JEFFERSON DAVIS.

and Whitworth, at the latter of which the Confederate General
Hill was shot.

General Lee's flight was a sad ending to his earnest hopes
and faithful espousal of the cause which he believed right.   He
was pursued closely by General Grant, who attacked him when-

ever the two armies approached each other. These conflicts were severe and destructive, as it presented the strange fact of two bodies of soldiers, both skilled and brave, moving along over the open country, unprotected by any entrenchments, and con-

GENERAL GRANT.

tinually falling upon each other with desperation. To add to the gloom of Lee's situation, his men were half-famished and nearly worn out.

Arriving at Appomattox Court House, a week after leaving Petersburg, he was again checked by Sheridan's dismounted

cavalry, who were massed in a solid line across his path, but this
gave him no uneasiness. He advanced with confidence that he

McLEAN HOUSE.

could easily break their ranks, when to his dismay they drew off
to the right, and his progress was barred by a
**LEE DEFEATED
AT ALL POINTS.** heavy force of blue-coats, with their glittering
weapons. A halt was made, and as Sheridan's

men were about to charge upon them, a flag of truce was sent out, which caused a cessation of hostilities.

General Lee's hopes had suddenly been destroyed. He had bravely held out, even in the face of adverse fate, and even in March had summoned General Gordon, who had command of Stonewall Jackson's old corps, to a conference, and that general had frankly told him the hopelessness of a further struggle. His own admission was that his army were almost starving, he could not furnish men, or food, or horses, and after visiting the Confederate Congress at Richmond the next day, he came back almost heart-broken, but with no power to stay the tide of blood. The desperate attack on Fort Steadman and the failure of the Confederate troops to cover their retreat followed.

General Grant's liberal terms which he dictated to the defeated men were a marvel of generosity. He merely asked that they lay down their arms and return to their homes, where he promised them fullest protection in all their rights, so long as they did not again take up arms against the government. He also permitted them to take their horses with them, as they "would need them for plowing," so sure he was that the end of the terrible war had come, and that men would be glad to resume the peaceful pursuits of life.

The two great commanders, Ulysses S. Grant and Robert E. Lee, had exchanged several notes relative to the surrender, and on the 9th of April **MEETING OF THE TWO COMMANDERS.** they met at the McLean House, where the terms were made known, and the next day General Lee issued a farewell address to his army, whose love and devotion to him had proven itself in many a hard-fought field.

CHAPTER XX.

THE SURRENDER.

ICHMOND has surrendered! The army of Lee has retreated! From every little village, and in every vast city the glad cry rang forth on that bright April morning, early in 1865, till the echoes bore the joyful tidings to every camp and bivouac in the Union army, "Shout the glad tidings!" The words rang out, and the streets of the cities were filled with excited crowds of men and women, who were frantic with joy. Even the little children seemed to have become inspired with the enthusiasm, and laughed and danced, they knew not why.

Flags were run up in haste, men and boys ran wildly around, singing and cheering, strangers clasped each others' hands gladly, while women wept with joy.

The "good news," however, had been received at first by the army to which Ralph belonged, with incredulity, and such expressions as "We've heard that before!" "My feet are pretty sore tramping!" "I'm going right on to Richmond now!" and it chagrined the officer in charge so deeply to think that they could not accept it as a truth, that he had the men drawn up in line, some 6,000 strong, in the pine woods through which they were marching, and appointed officers to ride up and down the line and announce it officially. And then what a roar and thundering of cheers aroused the echoes in those old trees! No more weariness then, no more stumbling and grumbling, but they made all haste to the town to which they were nearest, and set up a playful bombardment with blank charges, to celebrate the event, much to the rejoicing of the citizens there, who were as glad as they.

To the worn-out, sunburned soldiers it was good news, and

as they gathered in groups loud rejoicing and eager discussion was heard among them. To Ralph it brought the grateful thought that the dawn of peace was near, and the Union would once again be restored, and his heart was full of a quiet thankfulness that words could not express.

But alas, for the jubilant people—for those who were rejoicing, and to whom a feeling of relief had come, because there was no more war. Those who had so bitterly opposed each other on fields of battle, whose differences had received a "baptism of blood," met daily, more like brothers than late enemies. True, bitterness and disappointment rankled in some hearts, but it is also true that all over our broad **A GREAT SHADOW.** land, both North and South, men rejoiced together that they could return to the homes they had been so long exiles from, and once more take up the thread of social and business life, with a surety that it would be no more severed

But even while the North was trembling with excess of happiness, a terrible shadow darkened the brilliancy of the victory —the four years of struggle and bloodshed were obliterated, so it seemed, by a wave of sorrow that swept over the heart of the North, paralyzing its throb of ecstasy. Abraham Lincoln, the friend of all mankind, whose life was free from petty vindictiveness, and whose whole aim was the restoration of the republic on a fair and just basis, a grand and unselfish man, was struck down by the hand of an assassin—J. Wilkes Booth.

The President was shot while sitting with his wife and other friends, in a box at Ford's **LINCOLN IS ASSASSINATED.** Theater, Washington, April 14, 1865, and he died the next morning. The entire nation was dumb with grief and consternation. On the heels of sweet and gentle peace came the dread question—What will be the outcome? A nation had been plunged into mourning by the mad act of a fanatic.

At once the War Department issued a poster, offering a large reward for the capture of the murderer, and on April 26 he was tracked to an old barn on Garrett's farm, twenty miles from Fredericksburg, with a shattered leg. He refused to sur-

ABRAHAM LINCOLN.

render, and the building was set on fire, and he was shot in attempting to escape, and captured. He had received a mortal wound, from which he died.

The surrender of General Lee was followed by that of all the principal armies of the Confederacy; the last to throw down their arms being the command of General Kirby Smith, on the 26th of May. Thus very little **RECONSTRUCTION GOES ON.** was left for the Government to do, save to reconstruct the shattered portions of our land, to repress wandering bands of outlaws, and to maintain order.

JOHN WILKES BOOTH.

The close of the war was welcomed by North and South alike —it was as if a hideous nightmare had been banished, and now the waking dreams of desolated homes, reunited, could be realized.

To the boys in blue who had fought valiantly and untiringly, the news that the opposing armies had surrendered was a relief, although they sorrowfully turned their faces homeward, at the remembrance of those who came not with them; still a deep joy filled their souls as they thought of those who were waiting to receive them.

The same scenes **GOING HOME.** were transpiring at the South, where patient wives, mothers, sisters and daughters were waiting and watching for those who had been so strangely preserved to them, and happy voices and beaming smiles made their home-coming glad.

The two armies—the Army of the Potomac and Sherman's Army—were sent to Washington late in May for review, before being mustered out of service. The scene was inspiring. The

War Department, Washington, April 20, 1865.

$100,000 REWARD!

THE MURDERER

Of our late beloved President, ABRAHAM LINCOLN,

IS STILL AT LARGE.

$50,000 REWARD!

will be paid by this Department for his apprehension, in addition to any reward offered by Municipal Authorities or State Executives.

$25,000 REWARD!

will be paid for the apprehension of JOHN H. SURRATT, one of Booth's accomplices.

$25,000 REWARD!

will be paid for the apprehension of DANIEL C. HARROLD, another of Booth's accomplices.

LIBERAL REWARDS will be paid for any information that shall conduce to the arrest of either of the above-named criminals, or their accomplices.

All persons harboring or secreting the said persons, or either of them, or aiding or assisting their concealment or escape, will be treated as accomplices in the murder of the President and the attempted assassination of the Secretary of State, and shall be subject to trial before a Military Commission and the punishment of DEATH.

Let the stain of innocent blood be removed from the land by the arrest and punishment of the murderers.

All good citizens are exhorted to aid public justice on this occasion. Every man should consider his own conscience charged with this solemn duty, and rest neither night nor day until it be accomplished.

EDWIN M. STANTON, Secretary of War.

DESCRIPTIONS.—BOOTH is 5 feet 7 or 8 inches high, slender build, high forehead, black hair, black eyes, and wears a heavy black moustache.

JOHN H. SURRATT is about 5 feet 9 inches. Hair rather thin and dark; eyes rather light; no beard. Would weigh 145 or 150 pounds. Complexion rather pale and clear, with color in the cheeks. Wore light clothes of fine quality. Shoulders square; cheek bones rather prominent; chin narrow; ears projecting at the top; forehead rather low and square, but broad. Parts his hair on the right side; neck rather long. His lips are firmly set. A slim man.

DANIEL C. HARROLD is 22 years of age, 5 feet 6 or 7 inches high, rather lopod shouldered, otherwise light build; dark hair; dark eyes, eyebrows; weighs about 140 pounds.

GEO. F. NESBITT & CO., Printers and Stationers, cor. Pearl and Pine Streets, N. Y.

streets were packed with a surging mass of people, proud to shout and cheer for the brown-faced men who fought for the upholding of their beloved government. Banners, garlands of flowers, tumultuous cheering, marked the marching divisions of the Army of the Potomac, as they wheeled into line, and arriving

THE SURRENDER OF GENERAL LEE.

243

at the grand stand at the White House, where President Johnson and his cabinet reviewed them, the officers gave a royal salute with their swords, while the commanders of the divisions sprang from their horses, and went upon the stand as their commands filed by.

The following day, May 24, Sherman's noble army of bronzed and weather-beaten men were reviewed in the same manner, and as the marching columns kept step to the music of their bands, the enthusiasm was intense, and broke into cheer after cheer, while the houses, sidewalks, and every spot where human beings could find a foothold, was one mass of waving flags, handkerchiefs and streamers.

THE SOLDIERS BEING REVIEWED.

As Ralph, in far-away Montgomery, where the regiment was to remain but a day or so, read the account of the monster ovation, his bosom swelled with pride, and life seemed to take on a rosier color. Every cheer that was uttered, every look of welcome to those who passed through the streets of Washington that day, he considered a tribute to every soldier in the land; for had they not all done their duty and stood by their colors? He claimed a share in that rejoicing, even though he could not be there, and he vaguely wondered if those who had died to save this glorious Union did not also rejoice at the dawn of peace, and the new birth of a nation, whose proudest boast should ever be that "All men are born free and equal."

RALPH SHARES THE GLORY.

His soul went out in peace and love to all—to those who had fallen in battle or died of wounds on either side; to the dear comrades whom he remembered long; to that grand martyr —the type of freedom, justice and love for all—Abraham Lincoln!

"Dreaming, are you?" a cheery voice broke in upon his musings.

RALPH RECOUNTS HIS EXPERIENCE.

"Yes, Steve, I am dreaming—dreaming of the time when I can go to my mother, and tell her how grateful I am that I have been saved through all the sad scenes the past four years have shown me."

REVIEW OF THE SOLDIERS AT CLOSE OF WAR.

"Well, it won't be very long before you can go. I have no mother to welcome me; you're a lucky boy, Ralph. But we are ordered to Union Springs, about forty miles or so from here, to do post duty. They are having lively times down there between

HOUSE WHERE LEE SURRENDERED.

the darkeys and their former owners, and they need us to adjust matters. The boys are being disbanded as fast as possible, and it will be our turn soon."

"I shall not be sorry, but I have had many instructive and useful experiences. Life in the army has been to me the best school I ever knew. It has taught me the beauty of discipline, the value of freedom, and an insight into military affairs which I never could have had. It has left me, too, with a warmer admiration for the blessings of a wise, just and stable government,"

"Well, I never gave these things a thought, but I believe you are right, and I don't know but I'm better prepared to take up the business of life than I should have been without this training. But to the case in hand. We leave here in a day or two, and shall be compelled to say good-bye forever to some very nice people we have met."

"That's true, Steve, and I am sorry it must be so."

Two days later, and while the daily papers were full of the descriptions of the gorgeous spectacle the review furnished, they moved on to Union Springs. Here they found a turbulent element which only the presence of soldiers could quell. Remaining here until the middle of July, they had orders to proceed to Vicksburg, where they were to be mustered out of the service of the United States.

It was August before they reached Vicksburg, where they were discharged from further service. When Ralph stepped on board the steamer which was to convey them to Cairo, he was overjoyed. His spirits bubbled over like a schoolboy's, and he mingled with the gay crowd of passengers, with a light heart. The water was low, and as they sailed between the banks, the sounds of industry were plainly to be heard, as the blacks worked in the fields.

As they glided along, the merry throngs were amusing themselves, some in the cabin, dancing to the music of the piano, some chatting as pleasantly with the soldiers as if their acquaintance had extended over years, and all light-hearted and careless. A sudden commotion was heard, and the quick, sharp voice of the captain giving orders. Too late—a sudden jar, a trembling of the boat, and a crash, over **A WRECK.** all of which were heard shrieks of terror and the hoarse shouting of the officers, as the boat, with her hull completely torn away, began to settle into the muddy bottom.

A huge snag, floating down stream, had caught the boat's hull, and completely destroyed it, and the steamer was sinking like lead.

The river was alive with frightened human beings, some of

whom had jumped at the first shock, while others had been hurled into the water. Ralph was among the latter, and his terror was intense, as he wondered, with lightning-like rapidity, whether he had passed through so much danger, only to perish miserably just when he felt that he was safe. He was overcome but a moment, however, and seeing the gang plank floating a few yards away, he swam toward it, and seizing one end, he raised himself upon it and began to plan what he should do next. The cries of some were growing feebler. He saw men on the bank putting boats out from shore, and as he floated along he called loudly to those within sound of **RALPH SAVES MANY.** his voice, trying to encourage them. He caught a lady by her dress and placed her on his raft, then a child floated by, whose light form he grasped firmly, as he laid her on the planks. Thus Ralph managed, by courage and strength, to save fifteen persons on his clumsy but exceedingly useful craft.

He paddled them to shore, and on his way he saw a young black girl who had been on board with her mistress. She was being drawn at a rapid pace through the water, by hanging to the tail of a mule, who was swimming vigorously to land. One moment her head would be under the water, as the mule went along, and the next she would come up to the surface, sputtering and shaking it from her streaming head, but never for an instant relaxing her hold of the frightened animal, who must have wondered a little why he was being used for a tow boat. Ralph's love of fun and the queer spectacle overcame him, even in the midst of danger, and as she went by, he asked her how she was getting along.

"Fust rate, massa. We'll make de passage, I 'low, sooner dan yo' crew will."

All the passengers were saved, and those who owed their rescue to Ralph's courage, would have made him the hero of the hour, but he modestly disclaimed any praise, for it was by mere luck, he said, that the gang-plank came his way, and any one would have done as much, or even more.

THE BLUE AND THE GRAY—"THEY DRUNK FROM THE SAME CANTEEN"

245

A gunboat was sent to take them up the river, and soon
the placid scenery of the Mississippi was exchanged for the ripe
fields, the well-tilled farms of Illinois, as they were whirled on
the train toward Chicago. The sun poured down his hottest
beams, the skies were sultry, and the pavements hot and dusty,
THE BOYS REACH CHICAGO. when they reached that city, but a reception
awaited them, which made the heat and dust
seem trifles, as they marched through the lines
of people who greeted them on their return from the war. And
as the battle flags were borne aloft, some mere tattered rags,
some with blood dyed folds, carried by maimed and scarred
veterans, whose eagle eyes scanned the throngs to find some one
whom they knew and who would clasp them by the hand as in
the olden time, there was not a man in those thinned ranks but
thanked his heavenly Father that once more he trod the soil of
a clime where peace folded her snowy wings, and the sounds of
war and discord were heard no more.

When the train rolled into the depot, Ralph heard the
shouts and cheers going up for the boys in blue, and a six-
pounder was fired off, giving them a salute of thirty-six guns.
He felt proud to belong to that stalwart band of men who had
borne the brunt of the battle, and whose hands had helped to
rear the massive structure of a reunited nation upon an enduring
base—freedom for all. And then cheers broke forth from
thousands of throats, women's faces grew brighter, children caught
the contagion of joy, and men shouted and hurrahed until they
were hoarse. The boys had come home from the war, and their
toil and privations were past. Never again, it was to be hoped,
should the wave of dissension sweep across the land, but the
banner of liberty should float from every tower and dome, for
all nations to honor.

A REUNITED PEOPLE. The soldiers had caught the glad spirit of welcome, and as they wheeled into line and kept step
to the music of their bands, every nerve tingled
and burned, and their hearts beat tumultuously. They were
to be shown still farther attention, for they were escorted to a

hall, where, when they had " stacked arms," they clasped hands with old friends, and after a half hour passed in renewing old friendships and making new, they were invited to an elegant banquet, to which they all did justice.

To Ralph the scene was a revelation—the brightly lit hall, the perfume of countless flowers, the kind attentions of beautiful women, and the eloquent speeches—all in turn charmed him, and the home-coming seemed, indeed, a delightful fairy vision.

But there were yet three weary days of waiting ere the final forms were gone through with, the regiment paid off, the Board of Trade having assumed the payment, so as to permit the men to return home more speedily, and to Ralph they were the longest and most tedious he ever remembered. But at last his face was turned homeward, and as he sprang from the car, and hurried along the one short mile that divided the dear mother from him, his sunburned and speaking face, the erect form and swinging, elastic step, bore no resemblance to the boy who had come home to die, two years before.

His mother and sisters stood in the doorway, and as they threw their arms around him, and pressed him to their hearts, he knew at last the sweet and tender bliss those two simple words conveyed—"Home again!"

And when, in the years that followed, the simple army boy rose to position and fame in the field he chose for a life-calling, his dearest memories were of the toil and pain and sacrifice of the days he spent in the army. His proudest boast was that, humble as were his services, obscure as he was, he gave all he had, youth, energy, enthusiasm and endurance, to the cause of universal freedom, and dearly as he loved his mother and home, he still more dearly loved the land of his birth.

THE SANITARY COMMISSION.

I want to tell the boys and girls who have followed Ralph's simple story to the end of the war, about a grand body of men and women who worked valiantly for the soldiers while they were fighting in the field. Indeed, it would be unjust to the wives, mothers and sisters of the boys of the days of the war, did I not say something about this noble enterprise.

It has been said that women cannot fight, but even that assertion is not strictly true, for the records of history have furnished many cases of women going to the front with their husbands, disguised as men. But though they did not help swell the quota of soldiers, they did noble deeds—they cheered and comforted the boys in the field, and took tender care of them when sick or hungry. And one of the most powerful outgrowths of this humane and womanly sympathy was the Sanitary Commission.

When the war broke out, in 1861, the women of the North met at once in many places to confer with each other as to the best means for taking proper care of the sick and wounded. They commenced to form societies, and chief among **WOMEN TO THE RESCUE.** their objects was the wise one of bringing the sick home wherever it was possible, purchasing warm clothes, provisions and little additions to their comfort which the Government could not supply, the sending of books and papers to the camps, and keeping informed as to the condition and needs of the soldiers, by corresponding with officers of regiments, thus learning all they could about individuals.

Such efforts were lofty and patriotic, and coming to the notice of Dr. Henry Bellows and Dr. Elisha Harris, they talked the matter over, and proposed to call a meeting, to get things into shape. They saw the value of the aid which women could give, so selecting Cooper Union, New York City, for a gathering-place, they invited all the societies of women whose aims were similar to meet with them, and this hall, one of the largest at that time, could scarce contain those who came, so earnest was the interest taken in the matter. A permanent association was formed, and a constitution was framed by Dr. Bellows.

The next step they took was to send a **FORMATION OF THE COMMISSION.** committee to Washington, offering the Government their services. General Scott received it kindly, but did not see that it was right to give the

INTERIOR OF HOSPITAL—CONSTRUCTED BY THE SANITARY COMMISSION

249

members any authority. But they were not discouraged, though it is sad to say that the first days of the Commission were very dark, for they found army officials full of jealousy, for they could not see that anything which could be practical and useful could exist outside of the regulations.

The Government itself had just gone through the hard task of making matters straight between the regular army and the volunteer, and very naturally dreaded any further agitation, or the opening up of any new topic. But after trying so hard to accomplish something, they were glad of even the permission given them to form a commission, which should consult with the government as to the sanitary condition of the people. This was a small concession, but it was the beginning of an immense undertaking.

Still, they were distrusted and suspected, and at this unfor-
DISTRUST AND SUSPICION. tunate juncture, their friend, Surgeon-General Lawson, died, and was succeeded by Dr. Clement Finley, who was bitterly opposed to the move-ment. Another long struggle ensued, which was ended by permission being given them to form a commission that should act only in connection with officers of the volunteer army, and have no authority whatever. This was permitting them to do good only on their own responsibility. Even Mr. Lincoln, whose heart was ever in the right place, seemed to consider their plans and aims as of small account, but he, with Secretary of War Simon Cameron, yielded, and the association was, on June 13, 1861, made real.

One of its first steps was to obtain the discharge of boys (of whom there were a large number in the army) who were too young for hard service, and sickly men who had been mustered in through careless and hasty examinations.

From this time the Commission grew, until it had so many avenues of usefulness that it became too vast to attempt to carry out its designs under one head, and so women everywhere were called upon to help in the great work by forming local societies, to carry on their labors. More than 7,000 such sprang into existence, all of whom raised supplies of food and clothes and money to bestow on the brave boys in hospital and field. It is estimated that in the course of the war the Sanitary Commission provided 4,500,000 meals for sick and hungry soldiers. They also had ambulances, and were often found on the field with supplies, and at the very front, rescuing those who were wounded. It had hospitals and depots for the objects of its care. It had camps for soldiers who were convalescent, and not only looked after the physical needs of the boys in blue, but in connection with the Young Men's Christian Association measures were taken looking to their souls' needs, also, and religious reading matter was given them, prayers and addresses were had at the recruiting offices, and a hymn book was compiled, which seemed to be exactly what a soldier needed.

The Sanitary Commission had a ready assistant in the Christian Commission, which came into existence as a working body on November 14, 1861. These two organizations worked harmoniously together, and it can never be told how much good they did.

Among the many women who gave their whole strength with sincerity, we have space for but a few names, although the list might lengthen out indefinitely, **HOW THE COMMISSION GREW.** for to woman is due the credit of unselfishness

and patriotism and earnestness in whatever project she engages. She never gives her efforts grudgingly, but puts her whole soul forth. The women of the North and of the South gave all they had —their dear ones whose going away clouded the light of home, their services in ministering to the sick, their patient skill in furnishing articles for their personal use. All these things women did for the cause, and much more.

Miss Taylor was born in New York, but lived at the breaking out of the war

MISS NELLIE M. TAYLOR.

in New Orleans. She was ever ready to work in the hospitals, and gave liberally of her means to the boys in the army.

It is told of her that it was well known that she loved the old flag, and this caused bitter feelings, a mob once even surrounding her house, and demanding to know her sentiments. She was watching her dying husband. They gave her five minutes to say whether she was for the North or South, and threatened her that if she was for the North,

MISS TAYLOR'S COURAGE. they would tear down her house. Her brave answer was, that she was and ever should be, for the Union. "Tear my house down if you choose!" she said to the leader. To their honor, be it said, although very angry with her, they dispersed without doing her any injury.

A young lady who volunteered as a nurse just after the first battle of Bull Run was Miss Hattie A. Dada, also of New York. She worked incessantly through the entire war, part of the time in the Eastern and part in the Western armies. She was taken prisoner by the Confederates after the retreat of General Banks in the Shenandoah Valley, and was held three months. After her release she spent two years in the hospitals at Murfreesboro, a very arduous field of labor.

Philadelphia was a point which received

MISS HATTIE A. DADA.

MRS. MARY B. WADE.

a large number of soldiers who passed through that city, either going to the front or going home on furlough—often disabled. Several ladies established an eating-house for their benefit, where they could obtain meals free. One of the most tireless workers in this direction was Mrs. Mary B. Wade, who, in spite of her being over seventy years of age, never left her post

MISS CLARA BARTON.

save for necessary sleep, but waited on them night and day, during the four years of the conflict.

There were many other opportunities for women to work in the cause. Bazars were held, materials were solicited and manufactured for sale, speeches were made, arousing patriotic sentiments, and societies were

HOW WOMEN CAN WORK. formed to assist the families of soldiers. There was no end to the calls for kindly offices. Among the foremost of those who turned their talents to this use, was Mrs. Mary A.

MRS. MARY LIVERMORE.

Livermore, of Boston, the celebrated pulpit orator. Her efforts were given freely to making the Northwestern Sanitary Fair, held at Chicago, an immense success.

Perhaps no woman's name is so widely known, after Florence Nightingale's, of the Old World, as having labored long and unceasingly in the cause of humanity, as is that of Clara Barton. Her arduous services in field and hospital, her untiring devotion to the welfare of the soldier, her efforts to find the dead and missing, so as to send word to their kindred, her weary search in Southern prisons for news of the absent, and her formation of a corps of nurses to work for the helpless in the present war, have endeared her to every humane heart in our land. She knows no distinction—all are alike the objects of her bounteous care. And when the names of those who love their kind go down into history, Clara Barton's will be honored and revered among the first.

FLORENCE NIGHTINGALE.

MISS MARGARET E. BRECKENRIDGE.

Margaret E. Breckenridge, a relative of the celebrated Breckenridge family of Kentucky, served constantly in the hospitals, until she was prostrated by illness. Her pure face and lovely manners made the boys regard and call her "The Angel." She was very ill, but determined to continue her "labor of love," when the death of her brother-in-law, Colonel Porter, who was killed at Cold Harbor, unnerved her so that her own death followed soon, and on the 27th of July, 1864, she passed away to a heavenly shore.

The famous author, Louisa M. Alcott, whose "Little Women" almost every girl in the land has read, was a most devoted nurse in the hospitals, and afterward embodied her experiences in a book entitled "Hospital Sketches."

There were women on both sides of the contest

MISS LOUISA M. ALCOTT.

who did effective work as spies, for the cause they espoused. Among the most noted of these was Pauline Cushman, a Union spy, who was wounded twice while in the service, and was made a major by General Garfield, and Belle Boyd, who was famous throughout the war as one of the most daring and successful spies the Confederacy had.

BELLE BOYD.

The life of spies is one of incessant danger, and demands rare qualities of mind to carry out their designs. Whatever opinion may be formed of their vocation, it is a historic truth that spies are absolutely necessary in time of war.

The scars of the great Civil War we know are healed. We have given our dearest and best, and as one great and united people, we are marching on to a grander future than even the most hopeful could have foretold.

Peace had come to our land, but the man whose splendid generalship had won it for us, was seized with a painful affection of the throat, which soon developed into cancer. The heart of the nation went out to him in sympathy, but human aid could avail nothing.

He was an agonized but patient and uncomplaining sufferer, and during all his illness he worked laboriously at his "Memoirs," which he had undertaken to write for publication, and finished them but four days before he died. He had passed through a long year of pain and anguish, ended only by his death, which took place at Mt. McGregor, near Saratoga, New York, July 23, 1885.

His funeral was probably the most imposing ever accorded

17

to a citizen of our great Republic. Although twice called to
the Presidential chair as a tribute of the love of a grateful

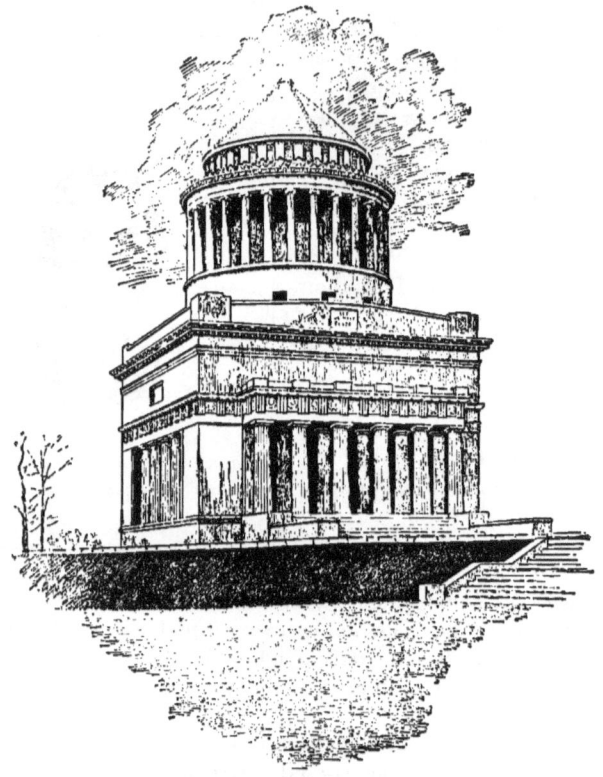

GRANT'S TOMB, NEW YORK.

people, yet his highest title when death came was that he was
a simple American citizen.

His admirers at once set to work to raise a fund to build
a tomb worthy of the hero; it was completed, and General Grant's
remains were removed to it, and the structure given up to the

CONFEDERATE SOLDIERS' MONUMENT, RICHMOND, VA.

259

city of New York, on the 27th of April, 1897, with magnificent ceremonies. The celebration occurred on the recurrence of his birthday, he having been born at Point Pleasant, Ohio, on April 27, 1822. His tomb stands on a height of land at the north end of Riverside Park, New York City, where a fine view of the beautiful Hudson is had, and is a just tribute to a truly great man.

PROPOSED MONUMENT TO JEFFERSON DAVIS, RICHMOND, VA.

Our dead are not forgotten. The custom of strewing flowers on the graves of the dead soldiers, in the cemeteries of the North and South, has taken a deep hold upon the hearts of the people, and yearly the beautiful ceremony is faithfully observed. Thousands wend their way to the resting-places of the dead and cover the green mounds with those sweet emblems of re membrance and love.

It is a blessed thought that, though they have gone hence, and their battle cry sweeps no more like a whirlwind in the faces of the enemy, yet the sacred anniversary brings back the memory of their heroic deeds, and as the bands of music peal out in solemn strains, and the tongues of orators are heard, recounting the story that will never grow old, the heart is stirred by a tender love for them, and goes out to the dead of the army who wore the gray as well. They were dear to their friends, among their most precious possessions, who mourn them deeply yet. The boys in gray laid down their lives with a complete renunciation of self, and their graves should be honored and remembered.

Memorial Day has become what its name signifies—a mingling of the friends of the Blue and the Gray, and a cordial exchange of mutual courtesies. The graves of both are decked in unison in many of the resting-places of the nation's soldier dead.

The thought of decorating the graves of their dead comrades originated with the Grand Army men, and they inaugurated the custom on May 30, 1868.

Let this hallowed duty· be observed in every graveyard of our land. And when the blossoms of beauty are borne to their resting-places, scatter them with lavish hands over the men who wore the Blue and the Gray, alike. They are slumbering peacefully under the green sward, and the sounds of conflict will disturb them no more. As we stand at their graves, let gentle thoughts of love and sympathy drive forever away all harsh or bitter memories. Let us think of them as having finished the battle—it is over, and they have gone to their reward.

The sun shines kindly down upon them; may its beams brighten and bless every living soul on whom they fall.

When the veil fell upon the drama of the Civil War, it was believed that the throes of battle would never again convulse our land. Peace was welcomed and hopes were indulged that it would be perpetual. Brothers met brothers again in the walks of social and business life, the scars of discord were healed and the rude sounds of dissension were banished.

DECORATION DAY, GETTYSBURG, A TRIBUTE TO THE MEMORY OF THE BLUE AND THE GRAY.

262

TWO VOICES.

A SOUTHERN VOLUNTEER.

Yes, sir, I fought with Stonewall,
　And faced the fight with Lee;
But if this here Union goes to war,
　Make one more gun for me!
I didn't shrink from Sherman
　As he galloped to the sea;
But if this here Union goes to war,
　Make one more gun for me!

I was with 'em at Manassas—
　The bully boys in gray;
I heard the thunderers roarin'
　Round Stonewall Jackson's way,
And many a time this sword of mine
　Has blazed the route for Lee;
But if this old nation goes to war,
　Make one more sword for me!

I'm not so full o' fightin',
　Nor half so full o' fun,
As I was back in the sixties
　When I shouldered my old gun;
It may be that my hair is white—
　Sich things, you know, must be—
But if this old Union's in for war,
　Make one more gun for me!

I hain't forgot my raisin'—
　Nor how, in sixty-two
Or thereabouts, with battle shouts
　I charged the boys in blue;
And I say I fought with Stonewall,
　And blazed the way for Lee;
But if this old Union's in for war,
　Make one more gun for me!

HIS NORTHERN BROTHER.

Just make it two, old fellow!
    I want to stand once more
Beneath the old flag with you,
    As in the days of yore
Our fathers stood together,
    And fought on land and sea
The battles fierce that made us
    A nation of the free.

I whipped you down at Vicksburg,
    You licked me at Bull Run;
On many a field we struggled,
    When neither victory won.
You wore the gray of Southland,
    I wore the Northern blue;
Like men we did our duty
    When screaming bullets flew.

Four years we fought like devils,
    But when the war was done,
Your hand met mine in friendly clasp,
    Our two hearts beat as one.
And now when danger threatens,
    No North, no South, we know,
Once more we stand together
    To fight the common foe.

My head, like yours, is frosty—
    Old age is creeping on;
Life's sun is lower sinking,
    My day will soon be gone;
But if our country's honor
    Needs once again her son,
I'm ready, too, old fellow—
    So get another gun.

A REMINISCENCE.

THE night had fallen slowly and softly. The stars had stolen out, now dancing gaily in one corner of the heavens, and now a cluster of them marched forth in stately fashion. The air was quiet; even the leaves had quit whispering, the breeze had died away, and they nodded sleepily on their stems.

Pretty Alice Whiting sat on the porch of the one-story, old style plantation house, and lazily wished the tea-table, whose disorder showed it had been attacked by hungry mouths, would vanish bodily. But it didn't, and she ruefully contemplated the prospect of clearing it up herself, with much chagrin, for such lovely nights, she declared, were not made to work in.

She had come to Memphis from the North with her husband and brother, who had "settled" in that hospitable city. Frank and Will had gone to the lodge, and she had been dreaming of her far Northern home. As she sat there her head rested against the vines which covered the porch, turning it into a perfect bower of beauty. Her dark brown hair waved and curled around a broad, full forehead; her features were far from regular, but the piquant nose and smiling mouth redeemed them, and gave a saucy charm which was more pleasing than set beauty. And as the moon rose in the sky, until her pale beams lit up the darkened porch, flooding every corner, she made as pretty a picture as one would wish to look upon. Something of this thought evidently passed through the mind of the man who had stolen noiselessly through the garden until he stood by her side, for he looked earnestly upon her as if loth to disturb her, and then longingly at the table, which had abundance, even after the appetites of the household had been appeased.

With a start she sprang to her feet. Her heart beat loud

and rapid with fear, as she looked at the stranger. Visions of burglars, guerrillas and all the clan, flitted through her brain, and held her dumb, unable to utter a sound, from pure terror.

Certainly the man before her was not one to reassure her, for he was wild-eyed and dirty, and his ragged clothes had fallen away from his thin frame.

"Don't be afraid, ma'am," he said, in a voice intended to be gentle and assuring; "all I ask is a bite to eat. I'd never hurt a woman."

She drew a quick breath of relief.

"Are you hungry?" she asked.

"Hungry? Look at me, ma'am. Do you see any signs of the gourmand about me?" pointing to his pinched face.

"I'll give you something to eat—for Eddie's dear sake," she added, in a faint whisper.

Bringing clean dishes, she poured out a cup of coffee, and bade him sit down and help himself.

"Can I have a wash fust?" he asked.

"Yes, and welcome." Bringing him a basin of clear cold water and a towel, she had the pleasure of seeing some of the tawny hue disappear, and he seated himself and began to eat most heartily.

It was just after the war, and the city was full of homeless men, who roamed its streets, unable to find work, and actually living on charity. Some of them had no home to go to, and others could not raise the means to take them there.

"Pears like we wus whipped bad," he said, between the mouthfuls.

She nodded an affirmative.

"I 'lowed General Forrest would help me to get back to Georgy. There's whar I belong."

"Did you ask him?" The General was a resident of Memphis at that time.

"I went to see him about it, and he couldn't do nothing—said he had no money," which was a fact, no doubt.

"I tell you, them cussed Yanks fit well. They had good pluck, after all."

"I think they proved that," she said faintly, her terror returning, for she saw he thought her a Southerner as well as himself, and she had misty visions of being strangled, the silly girl. "Oh," she thought, "will Frank never come?"

The man ate as if he had not seen food for many a day, and all the time his discourse was about the Yanks and what he'd like to do to them. At last his hunger seemed satisfied, and rising, with his ragged, faded soldier cap in hand, he began to thank her profusely for her kindness. Something in her face arrested his attention, for he suddenly paused, and coming a step nearer to her, he said:

"I didn't like to beg, but I was nigh dead. If those Northern cusses hadn't beaten us into poverty, I'd have been home with my old mother now. I don't 'low they'd ever give a crust to a dog to keep life in his body!"

Her face flushed, and a sudden courage came to her. She answered, defiantly—

"Indeed, you do not do us justice. You do not know us."

"Know you? Ain't you one of our people, ma'am?"

"I am one of those people you despise—a Yankee," she answered, looking him steadily in the face.

"A Yankee? And you have fed *me*. Fed a man who has been abusing you right along, and you must hate him?"

"I do not hate you. Oh, no, I could not hate a single human being. You are one of God's children, and so am I."

The scowl of doubt and distrust fled from the man's troubled face. He towered above her, tall, gaunt, but powerfully built.

"But it seems strange you'd be so willing to help me out, when you knew that I was agin your kind. Why did you do it?"

"You were hungry, and asked me for food. I have a better reason than that, even. I am but a girl, but I had a little brother younger than I, the idol of our home, who went to war, as a bugler. He was so frail and boyish that they wouldn't enlist him as an able-bodied soldier, but he would go. He was wounded and taken prisoner in the Battle of the Wilderness, carried to Andersonville, where he died. I made a solemn promise to my own heart that never, while life lasted, would a human being ask me for food in vain, even though I took the food from my own lips to give him. I will keep my word. You are welcome to all I have given you. May you never want."

The man looked down at her, and in a choked voice said: "Ma'am, may I take you by the hand?"

She held out both hands toward him, and as he grasped them and reverently bent over them, a tear dropped on their whiteness, and he walked quickly away into the silence and darkness of the night.

THE LITTLE BLACK COW.

AN INCIDENT OF THE WAR.

T was the autumn of 1864, and the supplies for the boys in blue were being hurried forward. The Government purchased cattle in the North and West, and sent them to its soldiers, for they must be fed or they could not fight. The Southern army had not fared so well—they were destitute of nearly everything. Foraging had been kept up by the troops on both sides, until the land was almost devastated. Families were suffering from hunger, for most of the able-bodied men were at the front, and only old men and pretended farmers remained to till the land. These latter belonged to the roving bands of guerrillas who pretended to work the farm lands. Want stared women and children in the face. Little ones who could not understand the dreadful fever of hate and blood that was abroad in the land looked into the faces of their elders, and asked for food.

Thomas Grant was a young fellow of nineteen who had seen some service in the Missouri militia, and was full of life and youth. His early days had been spent on a farm in Northern New York, where his reckless courage and fine horsemanship had made him a leader among his boy comrades. When he entered the Government service it was for the purpose of driving cattle to the army for its use.

The position was one of great danger. Their steps were watched by guerrillas by night and by day, and many a stray shot picked off a cattle driver or one of the soldiers who accompanied them as guards. Hurrying them over hill and dale, now in dense woods, and now over country roads, sometimes struggling and sticking in the clayey beds, it was a common event to have many of the tired animals, worn and footsore, fall down in their tracks, to be abandoned. These animals were a rich harvest for the guerrillas who hovered in their wake, like birds of prey, for they would capture the weary beasts, and convert them into food. It was the pride of a cattle driver when he could bring the bulk of his drove to the destined point, and deliver them to the quartermaster.

It was sultry, and the dust lay in heaps along the highway. The news had come that a large body of Confederate cavalry were about to attack Stevenson, Alabama, which was held by the Union forces, and the cattle were hurried out of the town as soon as the first beams of the morning sun lighted up the earth. The boom of cannon and the rattle of musketry lent wings to their going.

"The rebs are after us, and we'll lose every steer we have," the foreman said to Tom Grant, who rode beside him.

The morning breeze brought the scent of the wild flowers on its wings, and as the soldiers guarding the train marched with easy, swinging step, it seemed more like a lively walk taken for pleasure than a dangerous undertaking. The hills ahead were clothed in a beautiful green, sprinkled thickly with the white clover so dear to the bovine tongue.

"We'll get away all right, Tom," said the foreman, Jim Morrison. "But we must make quicker time than this. Our usual twelve miles a day ain't going to bring us out of the reach of the Johnnies, and before we get far they'd overtake us, and then good-bye to the steers, and to our own liberty as well."

"There's trouble ahead already," Tom replied. He was active and lithe, and ever on the alert, showing much skill in managing cattle.

"Blast that long-horned steer," Cleary, the assistant foreman, cried. "They're on the stampede. Boys, go after them, lively."

A score of drivers set spurs to their horses, while the frightened animals, with tremendous leaps, thundered across an open field, and made straightway for a gully just beyond the field. The scene was one of wild confusion. The shouts and oaths of the drivers, the trampling and crowding of the maddened creatures, as they tore over the grassy field, and the sounds of the firing behind them, in the beleaguered town, were indescribable.

John Morrison and Tom Grant spurred their horses toward the flying cattle, intending to head them off, but Tom's horse was fleet, and coming up to the leading steer, he threw the whole force of his horse's breast against the steer's neck, and vigorously plying the whip to its nose, he checked its headlong career, and drew him into a circle. At once the remainder of the drove followed their leader, and quiet was restored. The unreasoning animals, governed only by instinct, were soon started on their original course.

The lieutenant in charge of the drove complimented young Tom in the warmest terms, stating that he had accomplished more than any ten men.

The journey was finished without any further incident. They made such good time that they escaped capture at the hands of the Confederates, and on arriving at Chattanooga, Lieutenant Reed was promoted to the charge of a drove of 3,000. This honor he knew was due principally to the ability and quickness of manœuvre which Tom Grant had exhibited, and to show his gratitude he had the boy appointed to the superintendence of the drove, a position which many an older man coveted.

Days passed slowly by; the cattle, many of them, grew restive and footsore. Often one or two would lie down, and then it was impossible to get them up again.

"Where did that little black cow come from?" one of the men asked, pointing to a cow walking sedately along in the drove.

"I suppose she's wandered in from some farm place we've passed on the way," Tom Grant said. "But anyhow she's a godsend, for we'll have fresh milk now."

"Can you milk?" the Lieutenant asked.

"Can I? What was I brought up on a farm for, I wonder!" Tom responded.

"You're a regular encyclopædia, Tom," the officer laughed. "But, of course, the cream comes to headquarters."

"Certainly—but what shall I raise it in, my hat?"

"We'll fix that. On second thoughts, think I'll take the cream with the milk—just whenever I can get it."

The little creature was as smooth as satin, and quite plump. To Tom's charge she fell, and he milked her each day as he promised he would, and she soon became known as "Tom's cow." She seemed quite at home.

One hot and sultry day, when they had traveled with considerable speed, Tom's prize showed signs of exhaustion. At last she could go no farther, but lay down, hot, tired and footsore, at a cross roads.

"We'd better let her rest and then we'll come back after her," Jim Cleary said.

"That's the best thing we can do, I believe." So the animal was left where she had dropped, and the drove kept on till they found a place where they could feed and rest for the night.

As soon as it began to grow dark Tom and his companion started back to where they had left the cow. She was not there, but a woman sitting outside of quite a pretentious, two-story house, informed them that a man who lived "down the cross road a piece" had driven her to his own home.

"We'll have to get her back, Tom, for she's quite an acquisition to our larder."

It was quite dark when they reached the place to which they had been directed. It was a weather-beaten old log house, with one room down stairs to serve the family, and an attic or loft above. Rapping at the door, they heard a gruff voice bid them enter. By the dim light of a sputtering candle they saw a rough, poorly dressed man and a woman sitting at a table which had no cloth, on which was some corn bread and sorghum. The mother held a puny, sickly little girl in her arms, whose big eyes roved restlessly around, as if wondering who the strangers were. A tin cup stood by her plate, full of milk.

"Strangers, what ar' yer business?" The man's threatening countenance seemed to demand an instant reply.

"We are looking for a cow we've lost."

"Wall, what's that to me? Yer didn't expect to find it here in this cabin, did ye?"

"Not exactly in the cabin, but we heard it was down here."

"Wall, that's about so, but I found the critter lying down in the bottoms. and I concluded she was as much mine as any one's."

"That ain't so, for we own the cow; that is to say, she joined our drove of cattle we are taking to the army, and so we have the first claim on her." ·

The man seemed to be listening. He paused a moment, and looked furtively around, and then at the two armed men. He went on:

"I'd not have troubled it, only for the sake of my little un there. She's sick, and can't eat a thing. She'll die soon without some nourishment," and he pointed toward the child, who was the picture of starvation.

Tom's heart was tender. He saw the man had not overstated the case, and he rose to go.

"Come, Jim," he said, "You can see the child needs that milk bad—worse than we do. Mister," he said, turning to the man, "you are welcome to the cow, on one condition; and that is, that you promise on your word as a father that the little girl may have all the milk she can drink, every day."

The woman had not spoken till now, but with a glad look she started to her feet, and pressing the child into its father's arms, she said—"Jack, that's a fair bargain. And you're a fair man, sir, after all."

The man looked at Tom, then out of the window, and said—

"Look here, young fellow, you've shown you've got a heart, and I won't be beat in doing the fair thing, by any one. This neighborhood is full of fellows who wouldn't mind giving you a

chance shot. The woman up at the big house has given them
the word that you're here, and before you know it, there'll be
a committee sent to wait upon you. Don't go back the same
road you came, but strike for that piece of woods, and then cut
across the fields, and you may get away. Hurry—you haven't
much time before you—you know the rest."

Into their saddles the two men vaulted, after thanking the
man for his caution, and away they dashed. The stars were
out in full force, and the darkness of an hour before had lifted,
for the moon was rising, and as they entered the woods their
shade hid them from sight. They rode fast through them, and
struck a corduroy road, a rarity in that part of the country, and
as they left it behind them, and were going to take the field,
Jim whispered—

"Don't stir a step. Pull your horse into that thicket.
Over there I hear them after us."

They could hear the horses galloping down the road they
had just left, and by the faint light could see that there was a
dozen or more men.

"A narrow escape for us," said Tom.

"We haven't escaped yet. They'll not let us get off without scouring these woods."

"Which way shall we go?"

"Why, away from this vicinity as quick as we can."

"My Kentucky thoroughbred will carry me out of danger—
she can outrun anything they've got."

"But I've only got a long, lank, rangy old mule, and half-
blind at that. I'm destined to be captured," ruefully answered Jim.

"No, we're not—they are turning off into the left hand road;
no, there's three or four taking the other one. Some have dismounted, and are talking with the man we've just left. He's
true blue; he's pointing away in another direction."

"Well, he's not so bad after all, even if he is a guerrilla."

"Why, do you believe he's one of that band?"

"Sure as preaching he belongs to the gang who are bothering
the whole country round here, and all that saved us was your

generosity in making him welcome to the little black cow. He's got a heart hid away somewhere, and you just touched it."

Tom's eyes opened wide. "I couldn't see that little creature starving there, and not offer them something to help her out. Why, she was nothing but skin and bones."

"We mustn't loiter here. It is a good three miles to camp, and we must make it quick, or they'll head us off before we reach the road."

Touching their animals lightly with their spurs, they dashed across the open field toward another road, and were almost ready to congratulate themselves on their escape, when they heard a yell, and looking back they saw one of the guerrillas who had sighted them and was almost standing in his stirrups in his excitement, and shouting wildly to his companions, who were coming after him at full gallop. Tom and Jim did not need any further hint, but led the way, at a rattling pace. Tom was mounted on a racer, but Jim's army mule proved that he could run, for he kept pace with the horse, almost neck and neck. Whether he dreaded capture and being set to work, or feared being converted into mule meat, we are not able to say, but he held his own.

With shouts and oaths that were heard by the two men with distinctness, the guerrillas dashed after them, while they kept on with break-neck speed, now through a gully, then over a broken fence, and sinking in the furrows of fields that had been plowed in the long ago, now past a ruined building that rose up black and forbidding in the weird moonbeams, and then the lights gleamed friendly from one that was occupied. What the end of this John Gilpin ride would have been, it is hard to say, for the guerrillas were gaining on them, but at a turn in the road a dozen blue-coats were seen coming toward them. The pursuing foe fired a few wild shots, which were returned with a will, when they wheeled about and fled across the field, and were soon in hiding in the woods.

"Tom's cow came near getting me into trouble," Jim Cleary said, when he finished telling the story to the lieutenant.

A few weeks later, when they had reached Knoxville and gone into camp, an old, feeble-looking farmer came into the lines looking for Tom Grant. His hair was grizzled, and his beard uncut, and as Tom came toward him, he was surprised to see the wrinkled brown hand extended as if to clasp that of an old friend.

"You don't seem to recognize me," the man said awkwardly. "You haven't forgotten the little sick gal and her mammy down in the country a hundred miles or so?"

"You're not the man who showed us so much kindness when you knew the guerrillas were on our track?" Tom asked.

"The very same. You see a gray wig and a butternut suit make quite a farmer outen me. I'll never forget you, stranger, nor how you saved my baby. She was the only gal we had left—we'd lost three, and when she took to that milk so, and you told me to keep the cow, why, I couldn't hold still. I'd had it in my heart to kill you both, that night. I had only to whistle and I'd have brought the whole band about your ears. The little gal—Eda, we call her—began to pick right up on that milk, and now she's as peart as any child you ever saw. My woman says to me—'Martin, go and tell that young fellow the good turn he has done us.' I've followed your trail for nearly a hundred mile to tell you that you will never be forgotten in our home, and I'll never raise a gun against a Yank again."

THE SISTERS BIDDING EACH OTHER GOOD-BYE

A WAR STORY.

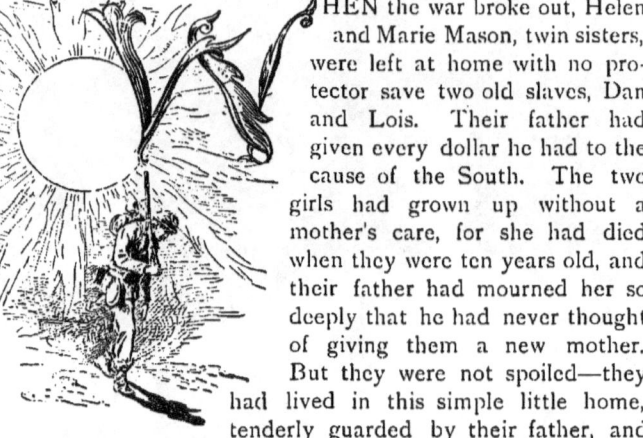

HEN the war broke out, Helen and Marie Mason, twin sisters, were left at home with no protector save two old slaves, Dan and Lois. Their father had given every dollar he had to the cause of the South. The two girls had grown up without a mother's care, for she had died when they were ten years old, and their father had mourned her so deeply that he had never thought of giving them a new mother. But they were not spoiled—they had lived in this simple little home, tenderly guarded by their father, and all their needs had been carefully looked after by the two old slaves, who would have laid down their lives for them.

But when in the second year of the war, Mr. Mason went into the army, their hearts were nearly broken. They declared they could not spare him, the "old darling." Were there not plenty of younger and stronger men? and besides, they were half Union at heart, and did not share their father's sentiments of fidelity to the Southern cause.

They showed no signs of their sorrow at the parting, but, with Spartan endurance, bade him a long farewell, and he set off, followed by the prayers of his beautiful daughters. Letters and messages came often to the little home by the Mississippi, and time did not hang quite as heavily as they had feared it would; but their father's letters were filled with bitter rancor, and he sought earnestly to impress upon their minds the enmity which they should cultivate as daughters of the sunny South, against the soldiers of the North.

But there was one chapter in their life which he had not fully conned. Marie would sigh deeply over her father's messages, but Helen, who had more independence and self-reliance, found words of consolation for her.

In the days before the war, their home had been the scene of many a pleasant gathering, and among their guests were several young men of Northern birth, whom business or pleasure had brought to the South, and who had found great attractions within their charmed circle. Marie did not know why she took such pleasure in the coming of Walter Ryder, or why she felt so lonely when he was away. Her father had liked the young man for his manly, straightforward bearing and honest principles, but he could not tolerate his becoming a Union soldier, and when he learned of his intention, he forbade his gentle Marie ever to see him again.

In vain Walter had striven to see her, if only for an instant, so that he might say good-bye to her. She would not disobey her father, and yet it was with a bitter pang that she refused to meet him once more before his departure.

Old Aunt Lois saw how her lily drooped, but she had great faith in her master's judgment, and she didn't "like Northerners nohow," and yet she wiped many a tear away with the corner of her blue-checked apron, as she lamented about "dis wah dat upset eberybody's 'pinions so."

Walter had gone without a word to cheer him. He had gone from the place which had grown so dear, and while pretty Marie wept, Helen chided her for her lack of fortitude.

The months went by, and they often heard through returned soldiers of Walter Ryder. Then came news that he was wounded, and then that he had died of his wound. The whole world seemed to have stopped then for poor Marie. She grew thin and white, and she reproached herself incessantly because she had so cruelly refused to see Walter. The house grew strangely still, for there were no more social meetings, and Helen shared the gloom that enveloped Marie.

"Pears to me dat eberyting goes wrong," Aunt Lois said, as she stopped in her mixing bread, and gazed out upon the landscape, which was beautiful to look upon.

But Aunt Lois was no poet or artist, only the colored cook in this lovely home. "Fust de wah cum—den Massa Mason brung home to die, and pretty Missie Helen sitting dar in her bodoor all alone all day, neber speaking a word to po' Miss Marie, who lubed her father dearly. Don't I know dat po' little gal is breaking her heart 'tween losing dat foolish man and her dear father?"

"Lois—Aunt Lois!" a sweet and girlish voice called.

"What is it, honey—Ise coming!"

Before she could take her hands from the dough a slender young girl, whose pure face would have made the veriest stranger admire it, burst into the kitchen, and sank in a heap at the feet of the old negress, who, now actually alarmed, seized her by the arm, and with a look of anxiety on her black face, asked the girl what had happened.

"I've seen him—seen Walter. They said he was dead. Oh, Aunt Lois, he looked so brave, so happy. I never thought he *could* look happy again," and the tears streamed down her face.

"Now cum here, chile, and sit in yo' old auntie's lap as yo' used to when yo' was a tiny gal, and I used to tell yo' stories and sing de old plantation melodies. Come, and you'll forgit all about yo' trubbles."

Lois had cleared her hands by this time of the dough, and as she took the girl by the hand, a loud rap sounded on the outside door.

"Oh, look, there's a whole lot of soldiers on the lawn, but he ain't with them!" Marie added, as she peered from the window.

"Ise not afraid of sogers! What do you want?" Aunt Lois said, boldly advancing to the door, where a tall soldier in blue stood, with a dozen men, all armed. "Hello!" he said rather roughly, but catching sight of Marie, whose face was blanched with terror, he spoke more courteously: "I beg pardon, Miss, but we are in search of a spy who goes by the name of Walter Ryder. We have tracked him to this place, and have orders to arrest him."

"My—" she choked the telltale words, and with dignity answered: "Walter Ryder is not a spy, neither is he here."

"I regret the necessity, Miss, but I must search the house."

"You can," she said, haughtily.

Leaving the soldiers posted around the house, the sergeant and two of the men entered the dwelling, and commenced the search, but it was useless, for no trace of Walter was found. When they came to the door of Helen's room, they found it locked, and yet they heard voices.

"I thought you were dead," some one was saying. "My sister has mourned you constantly."

They struck the butts of their guns against the panels of the door, and demanded admission, but no one answered. They pushed it open, and the girl who sat there sprang to her feet, thoroughly frightened, but no one else was in the room.

The three men looked at each other with a puzzled look. There was but one window in the apartment, and that was covered with a mass of clinging vines so dense and thick that they formed a complete mat. They pushed their bayonets through the tangled mass, but no one was there.

Helen gazed at them as if half stupefied. The sergeant courteously raised his cap, and said: "Miss, we are in search of a man whom we think is a spy—he certainly was seen in these grounds."

"We do not harbor spies, sir."

"I do not think you do—but he may have used your premises for a hiding-place. I beg your pardon for intruding. Right about face!" to his men. A still more prolonged search of the grounds revealed nothing, and after placing a guard, the remainder left.

But where was Marie? As soon as the soldiers had left the room she went back to Helen, who sat with bowed head, and touching her gently on the arm, she whispered—"Sister."

A tender light shone in Helen's face, but she answered—
"Marie, if you only knew how I have injured you—I have not
been a sister to you."

"Not a sister to me, dear Helen? Why, you are the dearest
of sisters. What do you mean?"

"Marie, could you dream that your sister, who loves you
so dearly, would willingly have wronged you so that you never
can forgive me?"

"I cannot believe you, Helen. Explain, will you?"

"I poisoned our father's mind against you. I wrote him
that you were receiving Walter Ryder's attentions, and that I
had prevented an elopement by my watchfulness."

"Helen! How could you? And that is the reason that he
would not see me when they brought him home wounded. How
cruel! Father, you cannot hear me, but you must know the
truth now."

"I dare not ask your forgiveness, nor dare I tell you why
I did it."

The girl stood before her sister, and in low and pleading
tones she urged—"Tell me all, Helen. I *will* call you sister,"
as the other put up her hand with a gesture of pain.. "You
know how fond you were of Walter once."

A frown contracted the brow of the girl who listened, and
she buried her face in Marie's lap, as she continued—

"I am ashamed to tell you, my unselfish sister, that I have
done such a grievous wrong. I, too, loved Walter Ryder. Do
not start. I was infatuated, and when he asked our dear father's
permission to address you, I hated him, and from that hour I
lost no chance of ruining him in his estimation. He went into
the Northern army, and that helped my cause. Father swore
that no daughter of his should marry a man who would take
up arms against the South. I played a double part. I told
Walter of our father's objections, and also persuaded him that
you were half promised to a colonel in our army. He went

away, and was killed at Chattanooga." And the stately Helen broke into a passion of weeping.

"Sister, who told you that he was killed?"

"I have letters from cousin Will, telling me so, and lamenting his death, for he was much attached to him."

"Did you not hear the soldier to-day charge Walter with being a spy?"

"I did not hear the name of the man they were looking for—it surely was not Walter?"

The rosy flush that rose to her cheeks made Marie turn faint. Could it be that her sister cared for him yet?

"Do not look at me as if you doubted me. That foolish passion has burned itself out. My only hope is that he lives, so that I may repair, in a measure, the wrong I have done you both. When I have seen you pining, my heart has ached for you."

"Oh, Helen dear, how good you are!"

The twilight deepened, as they sat there, and a shot was heard, which brought them both to their feet. Another rang out, and with a wild cry of alarm the girls fled from the house, toward the spot from whence they came. Marie saw a form fleeing into the darkening woods, and heard the command "Halt!" It never paused, and as the soldiers raised their rifles to fire, she sprang almost in front of their weapons, and cried—

"Do not fire again. You have killed him."

"We have not fired at all. It was not our shot that struck him, but we were about to fire on the man who wounded him, and whom you saw running away," Sergeant Hughes said, respectfully.

At a short distance they found Walter Ryder, who was wounded in the side, and as they carried him back to camp, he said—

"Take me to the Lieutenant. I can prove my innocence."

Marie and Helen threw themselves into each other's arms. Old Lois wrung her hands in despair.

"I tole you no good wud cum outen dat man's comin' round here," she said to old Dan.

"I doant know why not," he said. "Wat you got agin him?"

"He ain't our sort," she said, contemptuously. Nordern men am diffunt from Soudern—doan yo' sense it?"

"Dat's not for me to explaticate. But who was it gib'd us our freedom but dem same Nordern men; and isn't it worf sumfing to own yo'self? Dat's wat de Nordern 'trash,' as you call 'em, has done for you and me."

"I neber could talk wif you, old man, for youse always on de contrary side," and she left the partner of her joys and sorrows with what was intended for a very lofty step.

"De old gal doant like my plain speaking," Dan chuckled. "But Ise on de right side always."

Next morning dawned brightly. As the birds sang their welcome to early day, a young girl left the house and walked rapidly toward the camp, a quarter of a mile distant. No one would have recognized the elegant Helen in her disguise. She wore a calico dress, much faded and too large for her, pinned in folds about her form. A sunbonnet hid her lovely face, and an old black cape completed the outfit. She carried a basket of fruit, and to all appearances was a country lassie seeking a market for her goods.

No challenge was given her. The customary "Halt!" was replaced by a gracious smile from the guard, and permission was given her to enter.

"I want to see the General who has charge here," she said.

A broad smile was on the soldier's face. "The General is out on business just now, Miss. Indeed, I haven't seen him for some time. Won't the Lieutenant do as well?"

The haughty look she gave him brought the flippant fellow to his senses.

"Miss," he stammered, in an apologetic tone, "if you've got anything to sell, why you'd do better to see the cook. He buys all our provender, and will take your fruit, I'm certain."

"I wish to see the officer who is in command here," she continued.

"Bob," the guard said, "go tell the officer of the day that a lady wishes to see him."

"The Lieutenant will see the lady at once," the man said, on his return. Conducting her to a tent, she entered, and saw a very handsome young man, "far handsomer," she thought, "than Walter." His brown eyes rested inquiringly upon her as he arose and politely handed her a camp stool. She seated herself, but remained silent. He kindly said—

"Did you wish to see me on any particular matter? I am at your service."

Helen's heart beat fast. She knew that she was placed in a strange position, but she felt she could endure any unjust comment, so that she could undo the wrong she had done her sister and Walter Ryder.

"Sir, I came to ask you if the young man who was shot yesterday, was killed?" and her voice faltered.

"Ah," Lieutenant Gordon thought, "she is no simple country girl. Why is she interested in a Union soldier?" The query gave his voice a tinge of bitterness as he made reply—

"He was not, though he deserved death, for he is a Confederate spy."

"Oh, sir, you are wrong. Believe me, he is no spy, and I will prove it to you, if you will only listen."

In her excitement she had risen to her feet, and her sunbonnet had fallen off, while her long dark hair rippled over her face, which was flushed and eager. Again that bitter feeling crossed the officer's mind as he gazed at her, half forgetting that she was waiting for his permission to explain.

"You will not shoot him as a spy—you cannot be so cruel!"

"Miss, it does not rest with me to decide the fate of the young man. He will be tried on the charge of being a spy, and if guilty—why, you know the rules of war."

She looked at him steadily, and as their gaze met he felt there was some powerful reason for the feeling she showed. He waited courteously for her to speak, but her lips trembled and her voice failed her.

"Have you any reason to give why he should not be punished?"

"I have—he is innocent, and I come to you to ask for his life. I must tell you the truth, and leave it to your honor to conceal as much of the facts as you can, consistent with his safety. My twin sister and I are deeply interested in him." "And so you are yet," he thought, with a jealous pang. "He asked my father's consent to address her, but was refused because he joined the Northern army. I did not like the thought of her marrying him, and I did all I could to prevent it. He went away a long time ago, and we heard of him now and then, but at last we learned that he was killed at Chattanooga. Then my heart turned to fire, for I had driven him away without giving him a chance to hear my sister's promises of fidelity. I learned quite lately that he was not dead, but that his company was doing guard duty at this place. I was so thankful to know that he was alive, that I resolved to see him and tell him the truth. I wrote him, begging him to come to our house, and at a signal agreed upon I would see him and all would be made right. I signed my sister's name, for I wanted to be sure he would come. He was just outside my window, and I had begun to explain, when your soldiers burst into my room, and he hid in old Dan's quarters."

"I trust the men were not rude to you," Lieutenant Gordon said, alarmed.

"Oh, no, they treated us as all true soldiers will, with respect. But oh, if Walter is shot, I shall be a murderess!"

The look of distress upon her beautiful face made her still more lovely, so the Lieutenant thought.

"I believe your story, Miss," he said, "and will investigate at once. He had no right to be absent from his post without leave, but I suppose 'the end justifies the means,'" smiling into her inquiring face. "Meanwhile I will send a guard with you to insure your safety."

"Please do not. I came here disguised as a fruit peddler, so as to excite no remarks, and I can go back the same way.

But you have not told me what you have done with the young man?"

"He has been placed in the hospital. His wound is quite severe, but not fatal. The strangest part of the affair is, that not one of our men fired a shot. He was wounded by some one unknown to us."

"Who could have done it?"

"I have no idea—possibly he has some enemy; most of us have."

"I must hurry away. Breakfast will be ready, and my absence will make them wonder. Good-morning, sir, and many thanks for your kindness."

"Good-morning, Miss—"

"Mason. I live but a half mile away, and I hope, if you are ever near us, you will call and tell us how Walter is. Or, rather, I had better send old Dan, our servant, here every day to inquire."

"Do not trouble yourself to do that. I will do myself the honor of calling, to inform you how his wound progresses."

It was strange how long it took Walter to recover, or at least how many calls Lieutenant Gordon was compelled to make, ere he deemed Marie's nerves would endure the shock of seeing him. Helen always had a bright welcome for the Lieutenant, and when she requested him to allow Marie and herself to visit Walter, the officer shook his head wisely and promised to help the wounded soldier over at a very early day. The latter had been chafing at the delay. Lieutenant Gordon had long since received proofs of his innocence as a spy, and was satisfied that his punishment had been severe enough, but his own case perplexed him. Was he pleasing in her sight; could she care for him; and how dared he tell her his own feelings?"

Old Lois was always shaking her head in solemn disapproval. "What has dun got into dem two chillen?" she often asked old Dan. "Dey seems to be gitting 'witched wif dem couple Norvern men. Dey cahnt eider ob 'em hold a candle to Massa Colonel Allison, who's dun gone on Miss Marie. Why, he's de

man after my own mind. His big black eyes flash like diamonds,
and dat booful beard falls over his mouf like a willow tree.
Doan know what young gals is tinking of nowadays." Another
shake of the head and a puckering up of the thick lips. "But
here cums Dan; he never did like Massa Allison, so I won't
'spute wid him, for I 'spises family quarrels."

Old Dan walked slowly and as if thinking deeply, up the
path to the kitchen door, and stood there, looking in. Aunt
Lois at first thought she would ignore his presence entirely, but
curiosity triumphed, and as he showed no desire to talk, but
turned off into the woods, she unbent from her dignity, and
called loudly—"Dan—ole man!"

He turned impatiently, and said—"Let me alone. Ise engaged on particular business, dat wimmen don't know nuffin
about conducting."

Lois' nose went up into the air, or rather would have gone,
were it not so flat and heavy she could not elevate it.

"How high and mighty old niggers can be!" was her retort.

For a day or two there was an air of mystery about Dan
which offended Lois deeply, but she wouldn't ask any questions.
"If my ole man has any secrets from me now at his time of
life, well, I'll find 'em out," she said to herself. One forenoon
he astonished her by saying—

"Does yo' like Massa Allison?"

"I dus. He's de kind of a gemman dat I likes to see
'roun. Whar's Miss Marie's eyes when she cahnt see how far
s'perior he is to dose Norvern sogers who am jess libin' here
now."

"Yer wouldn't like him so well if yer knew he was a 'sassin,
would yer?"

The old negress was all attention. "A 'sassin, what's dat?"

"A wicked man what tries to murder anuder jess becase
he lubs de same gal dat he does."

"Whose de man? Whar am he?"

"I'll tell yer sumfing, but yer musn't tell. Ise had de secret
a long time, but I cahnt keep it any longer."

"Perceed, old man."

"Massa Allison lubs our sweet mistis."

"Which one?"

"Why, Miss Marie, ob course. I 'lows Miss Helen is all right, but she cahnt—"

"Dar yo' go, way off from de subjict. What did he do?"

Dan tiptoed nearer to his spouse. "Yer 'members de day Massa Walter was shot. I was in dem woods after rabbits, .when I seed Massa Allison wid a musket, lying flat on his face in some high bushes. I felt it was kind o' queer; yo' know he's home on leab ob absence, and so I watched him. Quick I heard de report, and saw Massa Walter fall right down, and Massa Allison rund away fast as a deer. I picked up his hankcher and his name is printed right on it, and I've kep' it in my bussum ever since."

"You telling de troof? If yo' is, my symperthies go right ober to dat ar wounded boy."

"Ise telling de troof, ole woman. And now yo' see why Ise got no lub for Massa Allison."

"Well, we'd best keep dis yere news to ourselves. Yo' know a nigger's word never'd go before a white man's down here, so we'll jess keep our moufs shut."

But Aunt Lois' prejudices were strong yet, and it took some little persuasion on the part of Dan before she would acknowledge that Massa Walter was as nice as one ob deir "own Soudern men were."

Lieutenant Gordon had at first, when the company was assigned to provost duty, chafed restlessly, for he preferred being at the front, but as the weeks rolled on he became wonderfully resigned to his orders, and so one day he assumed a fierce martial look, and stormed the fortress of Helen's affections. It was a singularly easy victory, for she capitulated at once.

Walter's recovery was slow. When he first met Marie, his joy was almost overshadowed by timidity. He could scarce credit the assurance that she loved him. He never alluded to her sister's part in their separation, and this delicacy won for him the gratitude of that young girl. The old slave, Dan, was jubilant. It had been arranged that Lois and he should accompany the two sisters to their Northern homes, where the parents of both the bridegrooms were awaiting them, eager to receive them. The dear old home was to be occupied by their cousin Will and his wife, a sweet-faced Southern girl, who assured them that it would ever be a home for them as well.

One fine morning in May a double solemn ceremony was performed which bound Marie and Walter and Helen and Lieutenant Harry Gordon together, for life. A few chosen friends were there, and Lois and Dan were decked out in all the colors of the rainbow. Dan chuckled audibly as he informed Lois that "dat ar Union was what de whole Souf and Norf ought to celebrate—a Union forever."

Walter's period of service had expired, and he was free to go. Lieutenant Gordon was to remain behind until the boys were discharged from the service.

"It will not be long before we shall be together again, dear sister," Helen said. "General Lee has surrendered, the armies of both sides are being disbanded, and the time will pass quickly." They sat on the veranda, where they had so often sat, and talked over their dreams and hopes.

The Colonel, whose shot came near ending a life, had disappeared after his murderous attempt. They never heard from him again, and in their luxurious homes the sisters dwell, loving and beloved.

ROBERT ANDERSON.

HIS brave and loyal officer was born at "Soldiers' Retreat," near Louisville, Kentucky, on June 14, 1805. His early days were pleasantly situated, his surroundings and companions being of the best. He was a graduate of West Point, leaving that school in 1825, when only twenty years of age. He was a very apt pupil. He entered the third Artillery, and saw considerable fighting in the Black Hawk War in 1832. He was appointed instructor of artillery tactics at West Point from 1835 to 1837, when he served in the Florida War, and in May, 1838, was made assistant adjutant-general to General Scott. He resigned this appointment upon being made captain, and accompanied Scott to Mexico in 1847.

He was wounded very severely at Molino del Rey, and for a time his life was despaired of. In 1857 he was lieutenant in the First Artillery; November 20, 1860, he assumed command of Charleston Harbor.

His loyalty to the old flag was proven at Forts Moultrie and Sumter. When he took command of the former he determined to place it in good condition, and he asked for money to make both forts more secure; large sums were allowed him for this purpose.

Fort Moultrie was far from being impregnable. Indeed, the land side was a good point for attack, so he concluded to remove to Fort Sumter, which was built on a rock at the entrance

to the bay, and could only be reached by boats. He made all
his preparations with such secrecy that no one suspected his
design, not even his second in command, Captain Abner Doubleday. The first intimation that the latter received was an order
to go to Fort Sumter in twenty minutes. The families of the
officers were sent to Fort Johnson, opposite Charleston, and
afterward taken North.

The clever manner in which Major Anderson deceived the

Confederates into believing that
the troops which silently marched
through the little village of Moul-
trieville that cold December eve,
just after sunset, were only laborers going to Fort Sumter, is
worthy of the cool and resolute
commander. When they reached
Sumter, the laborers who were
at work in the interests of the
Confederates, putting it in shape
for their occupancy, opposed the
landing of the Union soldiers,
but were driven into the fort at
the point of the bayonet. Major
Anderson afterward sent them
ashore, in the supply boats.

At noon of the next day,
Major Anderson celebrated his
possession of Fort Sumter by
raising the Stars and Stripes

GENERAL ROBERT ANDERSON.

and by prayer and military ceremonies.

His slender garrison, all told, comprised but sixty-one artil-
lerymen and thirteen musicians. After he had thus taken possession of Fort Sumter, they did not have a very enjoyable time,
for provisions were growing scarce, and the markets of Charleston
would sell them nothing. Fuel was scarce, and the cold was
severe. Besides, they had to resort to all sorts of stratagems

to keep up the appearance of being amply provided with ammunition and munitions of war, one of which was the filling of
barrels with broken stone, with a heavy charge of powder in
the center, which they would roll down to the water's edge, and
burst, giving their watchful enemies the impression that the fort

WEST POINT.

was filled with "infernal machines." The garrison were in no
very robust condition for fighting, for salt pork was nearly their
sum total in the meat line.

Meanwhile, arguing went on between the Confederates and
the garrison, to the effect that the United States government
had gone to pieces and they ought to evacuate the fort quietly.
But that was not the sort of material that Major Anderson was
made of. And when fire was opened upon him, he returned it
in kind, and fought valiantly. It was not till the 13th that he
had to surrender. Twice the wooden frame on the inside took
fire, and when the flag staff on the fort was shot away, a serv-

ant named Peter Hart made a staff of a spar, and nailed it to the gun carriages on the parapet under the hot fire of the enemy.

On the 14th Major Anderson and his garrison sadly left the fort after saluting the dear old flag, and went on board the *Baltic,* which bore them to New York.

In May, 1861, Robert Anderson was made brigadier-general in the United States army, commanding the Department of the Cumberland. His health failed so rapidly that he was shortly ·after relieved and brevetted major-general in the regular army, when he was retired from service. In 1868 his health had failed so rapidly that he went to Europe, hoping for relief. His translations from the French on military matters, have been accepted as valuable textbooks, and are used by the War Department. The health he sought eluded him, and his death took place at Nice, France, October 26, 1871.

GENERAL ROBERT E. LEE.

ENERAL ROBERT EDWARD LEE came from what is known in the South, as a good family. He was the son of Colonel Henry Lee, who was known in Revolutionary days as "Lighthorse Harry." Robert was born at Stafford, Virginia, January 19, 1807. He became a cadet at West Point in 1825, and graduated second in his class, composed of forty-six members, in 1829. He never received a mark of demerit or a reprimand during his four years at that institution, thus showing that he honored discipline—a fine trait in the young. He became a lieutenant in the corps of engineers, and superintending engineer in improvements of the harbor of St. Louis and the upper Mississippi. He also served with great distinction as chief engineer of the army under General Scott. His gallant conduct at Cerro Gordo, Contreras, Churubusco and Chapultepec, in the Mexican War, in the latter engagement receiving a severe wound, won him honors, and he was brevetted major, lieutenant-colonel and colonel.

He was appointed superintendent of the military academy at West Point from 1852 to 1855, when in the latter year two new regiments of cavalry were formed, in the second of which he secured an appointment as lieutenant-colonel, a most deserved honor. Two years were spent in Texas, but a leave of absence being granted him, he returned to Virginia. He had command of the forces sent to suppress old John Brown at Harper's Ferry, in October, 1859.

The year 1832 was an eventful one to him, for in that year he chose a fair daughter of his native State, for his bride. The lady whom he selected was Mary Custis, daughter of G. W. P. Custis; the latter was the grandson of Martha Custis, and the adopted son of George Washington. General Lee became heir to the estates of Arlington House on the Potomac, and the White House on the Pamunkey. The Arlington estate was confiscated by the Government during the war, and is now national property, and the site of a Union soldiers' cemetery.

GEN. LEE ON HIS FAVORITE HORSE.

When the ordinance of secession was passed in Virginia, April 17, 1861, he at once resigned his commission in the United States army, and wrote to General Scott these words—"Save in defence of my native State, I never desire again to draw my sword." He felt keenly that there was no need of revolution, and would gladly have asked for redress of whatever grievances his State felt that they suffered, but in vain, and he declared that although his devotion to the Union was sincere, and he knew what was demanded of the duty and loyalty of an American, yet he could not raise his hand against his friends, his children, and his home.

Virginia had seceded from the Union, but had not yet acknowledged the Confederacy. He was chosen major-general of the forces of the State, a trust which he honestly assumed, and for more than a year, although he was named as one of the five generals whom the State elected after it joined the Confederacy, in May, still he was merely superintendent of fortifications at Richmond, and a sort of military adviser to Jefferson Davis.

His military record, as commander of the Southern army, proves him to have been one of the ablest generals that history furnishes us any record of. When he met General Grant in that little Virginia village, to confer with him as to terms of surrender, it was the meeting of two great commanders, each worthy of a world's admiration.

After the war General Lee refused to attend any public gatherings, but lived a secluded life. His fortune had vanished, his hopes had been defeated, and he was compelled to accept the position of President of Washington College, Lexington, Va. This was in October of 1865. To the last he was in favor of reconstruction in the South, without recourse to arms.

On the evening of September 28, 1870, he was struck with paralysis, and lived but a fortnight, dying on October 12. Thus passed away a man of great nobility of character, brave and sincere.

His wife, Mary, followed him on November 6, 1873. The General had three sons and four daughters. All of his sons served in the civil war.

AFTER THE BATTLE.

T was just after the battle of Chancellorsville, and the storm of shot and shell had ceased to rain upon the wounded, who were pinioned in the blazing woods, when the sudden blow which Stonewall Jackson's army had struck, had left a trail of woe and blood. The dense forest had hidden the oncoming of Jackson's forces. They stole in noiselessly and fell upon the Union men under General Hooker, like an avalanche.

The pickets had not given the alarm, so swift and silent had been Jackson's advance. The battle was over. The musketry had ceased its rattle, and darkness had fallen, lit only by the red blaze which enwrapped the Confederate and Union wounded, without mercy. Some of them had tried to crawl away from the consuming fire, which played about them, and licked up leaves and underbrush, and now and then, as a gust of wind arose, sending the burning brands into the treetops to start a new conflagration.

The heat burned into their wounds, and as the shrieks of those who could not drag themselves away rose on the air, it seemed as if demons were calling to each other, so madly did they shout for help and mercy from the pitiless wall of fire.

Men were caught as if in a network, and held prisoners indeed. Choking with the smoke, blinded by the sparks whirling in every direction, there seemed no hope or chance for rescue.

BATTLE OF CHANCELLORSVILLE.
298

Here a dead man's face, caught by the flames, was scorched and disfigured so that his dearest friend could not have recognized him. Near him lay a living soldier with bloodshot eyes and aching wounds, terror written on his features—terror born, not from the fortunes of battle, not of the foe whom he has met face to face, but terror of the black night, the loneliness, the awful thought that the dead are all around him, a somber scene lit up by the fire that seizes some helpless one, never releasing him until he has lost the semblance of a man, and is only a charred fragment.

That night was a fearful reality to many. Its horrors can never be told, for those best able to repeat the story, perished where they lay. Details were sent out by the Federals after Jackson's advance had been checked, to save the victims in the burning forest, and heroically they worked, but alas, they could not reach half of the wounded.

At the foot of an oak whose lofty head towered above the scene, two soldiers fought valiantly for life. They were no longer arrayed against each other, but against their mutual enemy, the fire-fiend. One wore the blue, the other the gray. Both had gaping wounds, but their peril was the same, and as they struggled to their feet, weak from loss of blood, the bitterness died out of their hearts. They were once more friends, comrades, and together they labored to stamp out the destroyer. Their breath came quick and short, their voices sank to a whisper, but shoulder to shoulder as of old, they met as brothers— and nobly they battled with the flames, now smothering a burst of fire, now cheering each other with brave words, until, slowly and painfully they advanced, step by step, to a spot where the cool ground received them, as they fell, fainting, almost dying, where they were found by the boys who were sent to rescue, and whose work had been that of heroes.

And when, once more they struggled back to life, hand met hand in a friendly grasp, and heart beat joyously to heart, as they thanked their heavenly Father that they were saved from a fiery furnace.

A BOOTBLACK OF TENNESSEE.

SURELY Percy was a product of the war—one of those stray "chilluns" who drifted into camp with the refugees who were constantly coming under Uncle Sam's paternal care.

It was but a short time before he drifted out again and into our home. We (Allie and I) were in search of a boy "to run errands," and do odd jobs about the house, and this particular boy was sent to me by one of our soldier friends. When we saw his mirthful face (he had a perpetual grin) we thought he'd do very nicely for us. It was quite the fashion for boys to work in families in Memphis, washing dishes, preparing vegetables, and kindred labors, and though at first our Northern ideas were rudely disturbed by that fact, we soon became used to it, and enjoyed having a boy for such work. Indeed, it was rather a relief to Allie, for, as she said, if she hired a girl of the same age she would be in a measure responsible for her manners, and she would have to instruct her in the care of her wardrobe; but with a boy no such difficulties presented themselves. Like too many white boys of good families, it was supposed a boy could knock around and shift for himself; in other words he did not need any particular care, beyond providing him with enough to eat, drink and wear.

The boy informed us when he came to us that his name was Percy. Allie suggested that it would be much more ready to call him Jim or Sam. In an instant his family pride was up in arms.

A TENNESSEE BOOTBLACK

"'Scuse me, Missie, but I cahnt go back on my raising dat ar way. It wud be slighting my marsa's family. Percy it is, and I cahnt see my way clar to answer to no oder name."

We afterward learned that his name was Jerry, and that he had fallen deeply in love with the name Percy, it belonging to a colonel in the Southern army who used to visit at his master's house, and so he had appropriated it.

But Percy it remained, and if it was rather incongruous to see the high-born Percy scrubbing the kitchen floor or delving into the garbage box in search of a silver fork or spoon that he had thrown in with the remains of a meal, it couldn't be helped.

He had some odd ways about him, that rather startled Allie. He believed in Voodooism and when one day he informed her in a stage whisper that a very elegant old lady who called often, but who had lost one eye through some misfortune, was a witch, and was trying to "spell" him, she promptly ordered him out of the house till he could learn to keep his thoughts to himself. He despised winter, and one morning when he woke up and saw a light snowfall that had come down the night before, he expressed himself thus—

"Now, Missie, that's what you uns calls pretty. I jess tinks it's de debil whispering bad tings to de earth, and she's ashamed of 'em, and cobers up her face."

He never could be made to understand why certain articles in the china closet should have certain places. As for instance the closet in our house had shelves way down to the floor and he insisted on placing the silverware on the lowest shelf and then stepping into it. He had been talked to and threatened with punishment, and every time he'd promise to do better. One morning as usual the spoons, knives, etc., were found in the old place, and the look of perfect astonishment on his face would have immortalized a painter could he have caught it, as he threw up his hands and rolling up his eyes, said in the most tragic manner:

"I clar to goodness, Missie, I neber know how dey cum dar—dey must have walked down all by demselves!"

He went to market every day with his mistress, to show her how to select, as he confidentially informed his companions— "Yer see she's only a chile, not far frum my age (he was sixteen, she was nineteen) and isn't 'sperienced in de tricks of dem ar market folks, so I goes along and helps her."

We had been teasing for a dish of roast goose for a long time, so Percy and his mistress started just after breakfast and made a tour of the stalls. She selected a huge, but plump-looking white fowl, whose snowy feathers attracted her attention. She was quite ready to accept Percy's assurance that "dat ar fowl will make seberal good meals." The bird was purchased, and Percy slung it over his shoulder, while it squawked most horribly as mistress and boy went down the length of the market, greeted at every step by the grinning colored folks, who wished them "good luck wid dat ar young bird!" while some were anxious to know "whar yo' get dat snow bird, honey?" accompanied with many fervent hopes that it would "eat like cream." When the fowl reached the home of Percy's mistress, she nearly died with chagrin to find that what she preferred for its snowy plumage, thinking it an evidence of youth and beauty, proved to be a gander whose tough old skin Charlie assured her no amount of heat could penetrate. So when she slyly opened the gate, and bade him wander forth, he did so without delay.

Percy pretended much sympathy for her discomfiture, but she lost faith in all humanity after the goose episode, and deputed the marketing to her brother and the boy, who kindly relieved her.

But Percy was not entirely a trifler, as a few weeks after proved. One night when all were sleeping and the night was full of beauty, a little flame, so fine it was scarce observable, shot up into the room where the master and mistress reposed. It grew larger, as it danced across the floor, and curled up over the windows, drawn by the night breeze that played there. Now it seized the curtains of the bed, and still they knew nothing of the danger. And now the flames burst forth, lighting up the whole room. A feeling of suffocation, a frightened cry, and they awake, but the smoke is thick and lurid, they are blinded and dazed. Where is the window—how can they find the door? They are silent from fear, while the flames leap nearer and nearer.

"Ise here—doncher be feared! Percy's here to sabe you bof," and in the boy springs, and seizing Allie by the arm, he calls to her husband to follow close after him. He dashes to the window; he steps upon a ladder, and half-carrying her down, he shouts words of cheer to Charlie, who waits till they have reached the ground, when he takes to the ladder, and follows in safety.

Looking up, they see the room one mass of fire, and they know that they owe their lives to the watchful care of the black boy who had been only the subject for mirth and ridicule in their little home.

They were grieved indeed, when, a week later he came to the friend's house where they had found shelter, and after much scraping and bowing, he told them he wanted to "gage in anoder business—shining gemmen's shoes." They tried to persuade him that it was a precarious occupation, and rather uncertain of returns, but there was an independence about it that Percy craved. So they had to bid the boy good-bye, but the generous donation which Charlie and Harry gave him to "set him up in business," made his eyes shine and his teeth glisten, as he "fanked dem, and wished 'em luck."

CONFEDERATE CEMETERIES

MANY are the monuments that have been erected in Richmond, Virginia, through the liberality of her citizens. That city has paid particular attention to her brave boys who fell in battle, and her cemeteries are very beautifully laid out. The word cemetery is from the Greek, and means a "sleeping-place." There, indeed, do those who laid down their lives sleep in peace, and it is the pride and pleasure of the living to beautify their last home.

National cemeteries were first provided for by our government on July 17, 1862, and the noble provision has been carried out in all the States, both North and South.

Oakwood cemetery, Richmond, contains 16,000 dead Confederate soldiers. Libby Hill has a towering granite column, of great beauty, dedicated to all the soldier and sailor dead of the Confederacy—a beautiful memorial.

The cemetery of Hollywood is particularly distinguished for being the resting-places of Generals Stuart, Pickett, and Maury. Each grave has a tasty monument erected over it to tell who slumbers beneath. This cemetery has ninety-five acres, and was established in 1847. There are 12,000 Confederate soldiers in this picturesque burying-ground, and a granite pyramid has been raised to their memory.

All civilizations have respected and cared for their dead. Even the Indian decorates the graves of his people, and watches that they may lie undisturbed. He places the weapons of the chase in the grave that they may take them to the Happy Hunting Ground with them.

While Richmond has several cemeteries wherein her soldiers lie, it is noticeable for the statues of her heroes also. General William C. Wickham's statue adorns Monroe Park. One of the finest streets, Franklin, has a statue of General Robert E. Lee and General A. P. Hill, General "Jeb" Stuart, and President Jefferson Davis are also remembered.

In the eighty-three National cemeteries established by the United States, and containing 330,700 soldiers, 9,438 wore the gray.

> "There is a tear for all that die,
> A mourner o'er the humblest grave;
> But nations swell the funeral cry
> And freedom weeps above the brave."

In the cemetery at Beaufort, South Carolina, all feelings of distinction are swept away, and yearly, on Memorial Day, the noble-hearted women of that town direct their steps toward the graves and place flowers upon all—those who wore the blue and those who wore the gray, alike appealing to their womanly sympathy, and sharing alike their tender care.

On October 23, 1866, a fine and spacious cemetery was dedicated at Winchester, Virginia, with most imposing ceremonies. This abode of the dead is known as the Stonewall Jackson cemetery, in honor of that brave and true-hearted soldier.

PART II.

UNDER BOTH FLAGS.

NUMBER of years have gone by since the scenes told of in the first part of our book were enacted by the boy, whose interest has never wavered, and whose heart is as young as it was in that day. The scars of battle are tenderly smoothed away by the softening touch of time, and the blue and the gray are no more arrayed against each other, but stand shoulder to shoulder, eager to draw the sword, if need be, in defence of their beloved land and her institutions. The grassy mound and towering monument each tells its tale of the heroes who slumber beneath, and who are alike worthy of unstinted praise.

Our late war with a foreign power has proven the loyalty of Americans in every corner of our republic, and how earnestly the men of those days, from North and South, have come forward to fight the battles of their country—one, forevermore. Valuable services have been rendered by many of those who were the leaders of those days, in that sad conflict, and whose names have ever been renowned for courage, earnestness and bravery.

We are, as a nation, making history fast, and in a book

written for young people, it seemed proper to give them a few brief sketches of those whose names were prominently identified with the war of 1861. The boy who told his simple story is no longer a boy, but his pride and rejoicing are as hearty as if the "dew of youth" sat upon him yet, and in reviewing the lives of those who can truly be called great, and gone to their final reward, one of the first whose claims are strong is

ULYSSES S. GRANT.

General Grant's career was so extraordinarily brilliant, and was compressed into so short a time that it stands almost alone as one of the most astonishing succession of events.

His birthplace was Point Pleasant, Ohio. Here on the 27th of April, 1822, the future general was born. When he was but a year old his parents moved to Georgetown, where he grew into a sturdy, quiet lad, showing no particular smartness any more than the average boy. Indeed, he was rather dull, learning rather slowly, and with difficulty. There were no free schools when he was a boy. These institutions were supported by subscription, and one teacher had charge of all the pupils—from the primer class to the big boy or girl of eighteen.

General Grant never saw an algebra nor any mathematical work until he went to West Point.

He had a great fondness for horses, and was never so happy as when he could be with them. He was an excellent judge of them. When he was but seven he drove his father's horses, hauling all the wood used in the house and shops. When he was fifteen he made a horse trade with a Mr. Payne, at Flat Rock, Kentucky, where he was visiting. The brother of this gentleman was to accompany young Grant back to Georgetown. The boy was told that the horse had never had a collar on (it was a saddle horse), but he hitched it up, and started to drive the seventy miles with a strange animal. The horse ran and kicked, and made the companion horse frightened, and Ulysses stopped them right on the edge of an embankment twenty feet deep. Every time he would start, the new horse would kick and run, until Mr. Payne, who was thoroughly frightened, would not proceed any further in his company, but took passage in a freight wagon. The boy was left alone, but with that faculty for surmounting difficulties which distinguished him in after life, a happy thought struck him—he took out his bandana, a huge handkerchief much used then, and blindfolded the creature, driving him quietly to the house of his uncle in Maysville, where he borrowed another horse.

GENERAL GRANT'S BIRTHPLACE.

A laughable incident occurred when he was eight. He saw a colt which he very much coveted, and for which the owner demanded $25. General Grant's father said he would give $20. The boy was so anxious to possess the colt that his father yielded, giving him instructions how to make the bargain. Going to the owner the boy said: "Papa says I may offer you $20 for the colt, but if you won't take that I am to offer $22.50, and if you won't take that, to give you $25." It is needless to say what he had to pay for the colt.

The elder Grant was not poor in the usual sense of the term—on the contrary, he was quite well situated for the time and place.

Ulysses was sent to West Point at seventeen; he was quite apt in mathematics, but had no love for military tactics, and resolved not to stay in the army, even if he graduated. He was not brilliant in his class here, either—he says himself that had "the class been turned the other end foremost, I should have been near the head." He graduated four years after his entrance, No. 21 in a class of thirty-nine. It was feared at that time that he had the consumption, for he had a bad cough, but his outdoor life entirely removed it.

His real name was Hiram Ulysses Grant, but some one made a blunder in making out the document appointing him a cadet, and as U. S. Grant he will be known always.

On graduation he was brev-

GRANT PLOWING AT THE AGE OF 11. eted Second Lieutenant of Infantry, and placed in the Fourth Regiment, which was sent to the frontier. But two years went by, ere he was sent to Texas to join General Taylor's army, and here he became a full lieutenant. He was made quartermaster of his regiment early in 1847, after showing great valor in the battles of Palo Alto, Resaca, Monterey, and the siege of Vera Cruz. He participated in all of the engagements, and was promoted on the field of Molino del Rey for his bravery. A few days after an exhibition of the same quality won him special notice and praise from his brigade commander.

When the Mexican War was over, he was stationed at Sackett's Harbor, New York. He had long been attached to Miss Julia Dent, the sister of one of his classmates, and August 22, 1848, she became his wife. Four years later he went with

GRANT BREAKING A HORSE.

his regiment to California and Oregon, where he became captain. The summer of 1854 saw, apparently, an end to his military career, for he resigned his commission and tried to work a small farm near St. Louis, and attend to real estate in the city. He was not intended for either vocation. Greater things were in store for him, and, disheartened at his poor success, he went to work for his father, as clerk in his store—the leather trade, in Galena, Illinois.

At the first sound of war he offered his services to the government, and marched to Springfield at the head of a company. Governor Yates placed him on his staff, and made him mustering officer of all the volunteers from Illinois, but in June he was made colonel of the Twenty-first Regiment, which he had organized and drilled himself. Needing cars to transport it to a distant point, he was told they could not be furnished. So little a matter as that did not annoy him, but with that directness and energy which always marked his movements, he astonished the authorities by marching the entire regiment to the desired place.

In August he was promoted, becoming brigadier-general, and assuming command of all troops at Cairo. From this hour his successes were great, and have become matters of history. He was the idol of the army, and the surprise of the country, which gave him the popular name which seems to fit him so well— Unconditional Surrender Grant.

After the siege of Vicksburg and the defeat of General Bragg, it became plain to the government that one great mind should control all the forces, and General Grant was declared commander of the entire armies of the Union, early in 1864.

It was then that President Lincoln and General Grant met for the first time—a meeting between two great men. The commission of full general was bestowed upon Grant in July, 1866, this title being created especially for him. From August, 1867, to January, 1868, he was really Secretary of War, on account of the trouble between President Johnson and Secretary Stanton. He received the nomination for President, in May, 1868, at the hands of the Republican convention which met in Chicago, and was elected by an overwhelming majority. He was reëlected to a second term and at its close he made a tour of the world, with his wife. He was received with unbounded enthusiasm everywhere.

In 1881 he bought a house in New York City, which he made a home in the fullest sense, for his family and himself. On Christmas Eve, 1883, he slipped on the sidewalk, and injured himself so badly that he had to use crutches ever after. Becoming partner in a banking house, he was robbed of all he had by his associates in business and had to turn his attention to literary work, furnishing the *Century* with some articles. Being solicited to give his experiences, he wrote his "Memoirs," which he indited while suffering great anguish, and which he finished four days before his death. His wife received for the two volumes from his pen $400,000 as royalty.

The hero of many battles, the grand soldier, was doomed. In 1884 a trouble in his throat developed into a cancer, and for nearly a year he endured intense agony, never murmuring, but working on, that he might place those he so dearly loved beyond want.

On July 23, 1885, he died, in a cottage at Mt. McGregor, near Saratoga, New York—a man whom the world is better for having known.

JAMES ABRAM GARFIELD.

Few boys have risen from such humble surroundings to the highest gift of a great nation, as did the twentieth President of the United States, James A. Garfield. His boyhood's home was a simple cabin in the woods of Ohio, unbroken save by the few settlers who hewed the trees and made a clearing for a home. His father was one of these pioneers, and the future President of our great Republic was a genuine farmer's boy, and knew how to do all the hard work upon a farm. He chopped wood, and helped care for the few acres they called their farm. They did not live in luxury, for they had no means to squander. Living on the plainest fare, wild game and corn, or wheat cracked or pounded in a mortar, performing the hardest labor, the boy's strength grew, until he became a hardy, robust lad, the pride of his beloved parents.

GARFIELD LYING IN STATE.

He never had much schooling, as it was only three months each winter that his parents could send him to the district school, but most excellent use he made of his scant opportunities. At fourteen he was apprenticed to a carpenter, and three years later he worked on the canal. When he was a mere lad, he longed to be a sailor, but he fell sick, and after that he never seemed to long for the sea.

JAMES ABRAM GARFIELD.

The little village of Orange, Ohio, where he was born on the nineteenth of November, 1831, was soon to see him no more as a resident, for in March, 1849, he left home and entered Geauga Seminary at Chester, and soon was fitted to teach a district school. But he had to work at his trade (the carpenter's) to help pay his way, his mother not being able to assist him, save by a loan of $17.00 which she furnished him the first term that he was there. Every morning and evening, and Saturdays, as well as his entire summer vacation, he spent in labor at the bench. The next three years he passed in the Eclectic Institute at Hiram, and here his finances still continuing low, he willingly acted as student and janitor, and afterward as student and teacher. He was unable to earn enough to pay for his tuition at William's College, and although he practised the closest economy, when he graduated he owed that institution $500, a debt which he afterward faithfully discharged.

He accepted the Professorship of Ancient Languages and Literature in Hiram College, at twenty-six becoming its president, which he continued to be until he entered the army in 1861.

In 1858 he married Lucretia Rudolph, who was a teacher, and a very cultivated woman, who proved a valuable companion in his literary career. He had studied law while President of the college, and was admitted to practice in the Supreme Court of the United States in 1866.

His military services were large and valuable. He was an authority upon American finances. He held many important positions and was honored by all his colleagues. He was made

GARFIELD'S STRUGGLE WITH DEATH.

an honorary member of the celebrated Cobden Club of England. He made many able speeches in Congress, and was elected to the Thirty-eighth Congress in 1863, and reëlected successively to the Thirty-ninth, Fortieth, Forty-first, Forty-second, Forty-third, Forty-fourth, Forty-fifth and Forty-sixth Congresses.

The year 1880 was an important one to James A. Garfield, for in January he was elected by the Ohio Legislature Senator for the term beginning March 4, 1881, to succeed Allen G. Thurman. But on the 8th of June a still greater honor was shown him by the Chicago convention, which nominated him for president, and the November election showed him to be the choice of the people.

His public life was destined to be a short one, for on the morning of July 2, 1881, with bright expectations of a pleasant trip to New York and the White Mountains with his wife and several members of the Cabinet, he started from the White House for the Baltimore and Potomac station. As Secretary Blaine and he entered the station, arm in arm, they passed through the ladies' waiting-room. As they walked briskly on, two pistol shots were fired in quick succession, one of which took effect in the President's back. He sank to the floor, but was conscious. Dr. Bliss was summoned, and took charge of the case, but he named three other surgeons as assistants. Later two very celebrated physicians were added to the list of medical advisers. Their united opinion was that the ball had grazed the liver, and lodged in the front wall of the abdomen, but that it was not necessarily fatal. Still they did not deem it wise to extract it.

The assassin who struck down a good man, was Charles J. Guiteau, a crazy, disappointed office-seeker. After suffering for weeks, and fluctuating between hope of recovery and unfavorable symptoms, he died at Elberon Park, New Jersey, whither he had been removed on the 19th of September, 1881.

His life, with its early struggles, is a lesson to the boys of this age, to show them what great possibilities are within the reach of an American citizen.

THE ATLANTIC CABLE.

ARLY in October, 1851, the first effort at laying a cable for a submarine telegraph was begun by the United States brig Dolphin, which carried a line of soundings across the Atlantic. At that time there were but eighty-seven nautical miles of submarine cable laid, while now there are nearly 200,000 statute miles. Some of these cables merely connect islands with the main shore, others are thousands of miles long. A cable is laid so far below the surface that neither storms, tides or currents can disturb it. But the ends touching the shore are made much stronger and heavier, so that the waves will not impair them, and in some cases, near landings, they are heavily weighted to keep them in place—a thing it is not necessary to do in deep water.

In 1854 Cyrus W. Field obtained a charter for laying a cable, and when the first attempt was made at Kerry, Ireland, in 1857, the occasion was made a very brilliant affair. It was honored by the presence of a vast squadron of British and American ships of war. Representatives of many nations were there, as well as the directors of the Atlantic Telegraph Company, and most of the magnates of the English railroads. It was a momentous undertaking, but after laying 335 miles of cable, and causing the heart of its projectors to beat high with hope, the strands suddenly parted, and their hopes were crushed.

The next year another expedition was commenced, which ended in a similar failure. But nothing could dampen the ardor of its friends, and on the 16th of August of the same year another cable was successfully laid, and on the 17th Queen Victoria sent the President of the United States congratulations upon the successful termination of this great international work, to which Mr. Buchanan returned the courteous wish that the cable might "prove to be a bond of perpetual peace and friendship between the kindred nations." The two continents held great rejoicings, but disappointment was again their portion, for about the 1st of September the cable throbbed no more.

In 1865 a further attempt was made, and after 1,200 miles had been laid, the cable broke again. So grand an undertaking was not to be given up lightly. Mr. Field's perseverance was unconquerable. A strong, flexible cable was shipped on board the "Great Eastern," and on the 13th of July, 1866, this gigantic boat started from Valentia, Ireland, and two weeks later it "glided calmly into Heart's Content, Newfoundland, dropping her anchor in front of the telegraph house, having trailed behind her a chain of 2,000 miles, to bind the Old World to the New." It then went back to the mid-Atlantic, grappled the end of the broken cable of 1865, a splice was made, and the line was continued to Newfoundland by the side of the other. These lines have never failed to work. The cable having thus become a fact, the world was astonished and gratified. Mr. Field had worked heroically, and by our own land, by England and by France he was enthusiastically praised. The first message which passed over this line was a worthy one—the announcement of the treaty of peace between Prussia and Austria.

The charges for telegraphing were formerly very high, twenty pounds for a short message being asked, but as rival companies began to spring up, competition reduced the price considerably.

Marine cables have multiplied so fast that where there was originally but one or two, there are now eight, owned and op-

erated at a vast benefit to the entire world with which we are
in communication. The events occurring in the most distant
climes are brought to our doors through this medium so perfect
is the system. Cyrus W. Field received a gold medal from
Congress in recognition of his services, and the gratitude of the
world, as well.

ALASKA

Few can realize the magnitude of this far Northwest territory. To most boys and girls it seems a cold, barren, desolate
country, a perpetual scene of ice-bound rivers and frost and snow
the whole year round, with nothing growing. When Secretary

WILLIAM H. SEWARD, SECRETARY
OF STATE.

Seward accomplished the purchase of
this vast tract of land from Russia, he
showed great wisdom and foresight. No
wonder that, in view of its immense size
and valuable resources, he declared the
conclusion of this affair the crowning triumph of his life.

Russia had been anxious to sell for
a long time, but many feared that she
had drained all the value from the territory, and wanted to get rid of it.
There was bitter opposition in the United
States to the plan of buying what every
one considered would prove but "a field of ice and a sea of
mountains."

We want to tell the young folks how great a mistake these
sort of reasoners labored under, and how we came to be the
fortunate buyers of this vast stretch of land.

Many years ago a party of American explorers conceived
the idea of establishing a telegraph between our country and Asia,
and they went to Alaska for this purpose. Fancy their surprise
when they saw what they had supposed was a desert waste,
producing the largest pine and cedar trees in the whole world,
and the most extensive seal-fisheries, with here and there a town,

with its churches and buildings. They at once saw how rich it was in natural advantages, and they became very anxious that our government should confer with Russia as to its purchase. They presented good reasons for this desire to Congress, and Secretary Seward saw at once what an acquisition it would be to us, in many ways. So in March, 1867, the treaty between our country and Russia looking to its sale was ratified. It had at that time a native population of 60,000, and since we have come into possession of it, the United States Commissioner of Education has started schools and appointed teachers to care for the education of the young. There are now twenty-four of these schools in the different settlements, two of them in Sitka and a manual training school has been organized here also, where they receive instruction in the various trades. This school must be very popular, for it has a large attendance for a small city like Sitka, it numbering over 200 pupils on its list.

The chief city, or capital, is Sitka, very romantically situated on the shore, while high mountains rise behind it, forming a beautiful background for the streets and dwellings. It is an old-fashioned, quiet place, when compared with bustling American towns, but it boasts a lively weekly paper, and the Russo-Greek church has a good edifice there, showing that the religious education of its people has not been forgotten. The harbor is very beautiful, being deep, and affording safe shelter for vessels.

The purchase of this territory has extended our northern boundary from the 49th to the 71st parallel, and added to our growth westward by sixty degrees of longitude. It can boast of the highest mountain in America, Mt. St. Elias, which rises 14,000 feet above the sea. The magnificent Yukon river runs through the territory, and steamers of light draft can sail on its waters for 1,500 miles. We have gained 600,000 square miles, and this vast area really cost our government the trifling sum of two cents an acre, the sum paid Russia being $7,200,000. It would require thirteen of our States to equal its extent. As a writer jovially remarked, "It is a gilt-edged real estate investment."

The climate is quite endurable. The winters in the northern portion are excessively severe, but on the southwest coast it is warmer at that season than either Maine or Dakota.

The salmon are very plentiful, as well as mackerel, cod and herring. The streams are full of them. The salmon rival those of the Columbia and Fraser rivers, and immense canneries are daily in operation in the summer, preparing them for the markets of the world. The Chinese do this work principally, and they are brought up from San Francisco for this purpose and taken back there in the Fall. Fish are mostly caught in fish traps and nets, but the natives spear them.

The largest stamp-mill on this continent for reducing gold-bearing quartz is in operation near the town of Juneau.

Agriculture does not flourish on account of the shortness of the summers. Gardening on a small scale goes on, and plenty can be raised for home use. The region so long remaining almost unknown, has suddenly become the desired bourne for men and women of all classes. It has always been known that its mineral resources were fine, and gold has been found there in small quantities, but the hardships endured in getting it from the soil were too great in proportion to the amount, but a new impetus to the labors of the gold seeker has been given by the discovery of the precious metal in such large quantities that thousands have rushed to this field eager to dig for the yellow ore. Steamers are leaving Pacific ports weekly, laden with those who are willing to brave the terrors of the Chilkoot Pass. If the tales are true, it is surely a land of untold riches, as the entire region is gold-bearing, and for some years to come, that metal will be found by some, in paying quantities. One authority, Dr. Becker, states that the beach sand all along the Alaskan coast contains enormous quantities of gold. But even though there was not an ounce of it in the whole territory, Alaska has paid back to our commerce its price several times over.

CENTENNIAL EXPOSITION.

The United States, now in the midst of prosperity concluded to hold one of the most notable fairs any land has ever enjoyed. The first one was held in commemoration of the one hundredth birthday of our nation, and was projected on broad lines, and carried out in the same manner. It was opened May 10, 1876, and continued 159 days. It was a general invitation to all the world to bring their productions to our shores for admiration and instruction, and caused a unity and sympathy between the sev-

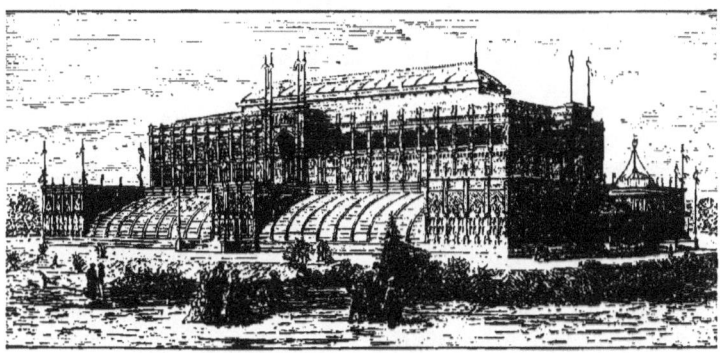

HORTICULTURAL HALL, PHILADELPHIA.

ered parts of our country such as no other event could have succeeded in doing. People flocked to Philadelphia from every land, and the North and South met in a friendly rivalry as to which section should be most fully represented. Over 61,000 visitors attended each day of the Fair, and at the close of the Fair the receipts were, in admissions, concessions and royalties, in round numbers, $4,307,749.75.

It had been the desire of many patriotic people for ten years to make a showing of our resources, and to invite, as it were, the whole world to see us at home. The hope had never met with favor, but by repeated representations as to the importance of the idea, the people of the United States were at last aroused, and worked so faithfully and rapidly to carry it out, as to surprise the world.

President Grant, on behalf of the United States, asked the nations to take part in our rejoicing, and they responded promptly, by sending commissioners to attend to the details. Congress appropriated large sums, and all the States entered into the undertaking with hearty good-will.

City governments and private individuals also contributed freely. A site was chosen, Fairmount Park, Philadelphia, one of the most charming locations which could have been found. Five large buildings were constructed, covering an area of twenty acres.

Each State erected a building, as did many foreign nations, within which to exhibit the products and manufactures of that particular State.

The exposition was opened by President Grant, with Dom Pedro, Emperor of Brazil, and his empress, by his side. Theodore Thomas' orchestra furnished the music, playing eighteen airs at the opening, the last of which, Hail Columbia, met with tumultuous applause. A cantata came next, a prayer by Bishop Simpson, and a hymn followed written by Whittier, the Quaker poet. General Hawley presented the buildings and their contents to the President, who accepted them in a few words, announcing that the exhibition was open. The two ponderous Corliss engines which were to put the whole machinery going, were set in motion by the President and the Emperor.

The exhibition was formally closed November 10, 1876, after a season of unexampled prosperity, in the simplest manner. Addresses were made by General Hawley and several others, the entire audience sang "America," and President Grant declared the International Exhibition closed. But it had taught foreign powers a lesson of respect for our republic, and caused wider intercourse between the Old World and the New.

EDISON, THE GENIUS OF THE AGE.

To-day the old system of illumination is giving way to the splendors of electric glow. With man's progress came the much

THOMAS A. EDISON.

needed question of artificial light. Electric lights not only adorn the streets of our cities, but grace our parlors, furnishing a stronger, a cleaner and more healthful light than any other known.   To Thomas A. Edison, who was born in Milan, Ohio,

in 1847, belongs the glory of bringing electricity for lighting
purposes to a successful basis.   Other scientists before him had

experimented, but to Edison remained the work of removing the final difficulties. Electricity is to-day furnishing the motive power for street cars, railroads, engines, etc., and it is predicted that before the dawn of a new century more wonderful still will be the achievements of this untutored and remarkable man.

With no less possibilities in scientific research comes the Kinetoscope, his latest invention, which by a thousand instantaneous pictures one is enabled to see the lifelike motions of "a child at play," "a distant battle," or the varied scenes of a "County Fair."

CHICAGO FIRE.

The terror which fire excites exceeds all other causes for fear. It is a subtle power that the average person cannot cope with. Its exhibitions are so terrible, so changeable, and so unmanageable, that it temporarily unnerves or unbalances the calmest brain. Great conflagrations have raged in many lands, and in all ages, doing exceeding great damage, but it is yet to be recorded that a fire ever swept over so wide a territory, and swallowed up so large an amount of wealth and products, sacrificing so much life as did the great Chicago Fire.

The history of the prominent events of the times would be incomplete were not the attention of the boys and girls of to-day directed to an occurrence so startling as to arouse the sympathies of the entire world.

The fire started on the night of October 8, 1871. The previous summer had been especially dry and hot, and was prolific of fires, many cities and towns having suffered in this respect, and the lumber districts of Minnesota, Wisconsin, Michigan, and the forests of New York State, having been visited by the destroying element. Many causes have been assigned for this fire, but its origin will probably remain forever unknown. It burned with unabated fierceness for two days, and three-fourths of the city were literally reduced to ashes.

On the evening of Saturday, the 7th, a fire had broken out

in a portion of the West Division of the city, and consumed property to the value of a million of dollars.   This was thought a terrible fire, and was heralded in all the Sabbath morning papers; thousands visited the spot on that day, and commented on and shuddered at the loss.   Little did they apprehend that

BURNING OF CHICAGO.

the same evening, Sunday, October 8, a fire would take place which would do the most deadly work, ruining business, licking up homes and property, destroying human life, and almost wiping out a whole city, whose prosperity and energy had become famous. Nothing escaped.   Private homes, public buildings, churches, banks, theaters, the postoffice, courthouse, newspaper edifices, hotels, all fell before it, and not until General Sheridan ordered the blowing up of buildings, was its progress stayed.

At half-past three in the morning, while a strong southwest wind was blowing, the anxious citizens were informed that the North Side was attacked by the fire fiend, and one of the first victims to its wrath was the engine house of the waterworks, thus cutting off the supply of water for use in fighting the flames, and driving the terrified people to despair. From here it leaped northward, taking in the elevators on the river banks, with their millions of bushels of grain, setting fire to vessels lying at anchor, then to the cemetery nearest the city, and to the beautiful park known as Lincoln, in short, to every conceivable object which could furnish food for the monster of destruction.

The tramp of hundreds of people fleeing from the fire, the shrieks of terror, the noise of the engines, the hoarse shouts and calls of those who searched in vain for their dear ones separated from them in the mad chase for life, the thunderous fall of stately structures, the roaring, crackling, howling flames, made a wild scene that Pandemonium was silence compared with. The fire burned the North Side until there was no trace of a building left standing save one, the residence of Mahlon D. Ogden, which stood in a large plat of ground, entirely detached. On the site of this house has since been erected a fine building of stone, devoted to a public library, and called the Newberry. The northern city limits and the lake were the only barriers to the further encroachments of the fire.

Blazing brands were seen sailing through the air, and, falling in some spot as yet untouched, they would kindle a new fire. The heat was intense, the very air one breathed almost scorched the throat. One vast sea of flame melted marble and stone till it crumbled and fell. But oh, blessed relief! The thousands who camped out on the prairie that night welcomed the torrents of rain that fell, even though it chilled them through. People went nearly mad with terror on that dreadful night. Robbers and thieves were busy plying their trade, taking everything they could carry away. Some of these perished with their ill-gotten gains. The lake was a welcome refuge, and hundreds waded out as far into its waters as they dared, to escape the heat that lay behind them. It was said that many were drowned through their temerity.

The 10th of October rose upon a waste, whose dwellers were clothed in the apathy of despair. For eight days after the fire, the city was without water, and the dread of a second outbreak hung like a pall over them. The city came under military rule, citizens patroled the streets, and every stranger was looked upon with suspicion, lest he be an incendiary. General Sheridan, by virtue of the fact that he was commander of the Military Division of the Missouri, took charge of the city, to protect it from the thieves and incendiaries who were at work. He ordered two companies of regulars from Omaha, three from Fort Leavenworth, and one from Fort Scott, here. General Halleck also furnished him with four companies from Kentucky.

A hundred men were put to work on the engines of the waterworks, and in a week the mains were filled by pumping water into them from the river. Some sickness resulted from drinking this water. But eight days' labor resulted in forcing water from the pure lake into the pipes, and once more Chicago could drink its fill. Meanwhile peddlers had dipped water from the lake and sold it from house to house at a shilling a pail. Mayor R. B. Mason, on the 10th, forbade any fires kindled for cooking, and "cold victuals," and in many cases no victuals at all, for a day or so, until the Relief Committee could distribute the stores pouring into the desolated city, were the order of the day.

And then the great heart of the world beat with noble generosity. From every city, and town, and village, and from foreign lands, the beneficent gifts flowed in, and food and clothing. From New York, Boston, Cincinnati, St. Louis, London, England, and all over the world, generous contributions of money were poured into Chicago, to feed the starving—not the "starving poor," but the starving people, for all were made beggars by

the calamity. Banks were destroyed, local fire insurance companies were wiped out of existence, and for months our fair city
was kept alive by the noble and unstinted liberality of the world.

The loss in property was over $290,000,000, at the lowest
estimate. How many lives were laid down no statistics have
ever been positively given, as there was such a large floating
population, of whom no account could be made, but accepting
the lowest computation, at least 250 people perished on that
fearful night, and over 100,000 were left homeless, and without
a shelter.

A writer, speaking of the great loss of the fire of 1871 says
that $1,000,000 of property was consumed every five minutes,
and 125 acres of buildings every hour.

THE TELEPHONE AND PHONOGRAPH.

No invention of modern times equals in interest the Telephone. It has remained for an American to solve the problem
of communication between persons at a distance from each other.
Scientists, by means of electricity and sound, have devised an
apparatus for transmitting the voice to a distance of hundreds
of miles. To Alexander Graham Bell, of Massachusetts, and to
Elisha P. Gray, of Chicago, is due the honor of originating this
wonderful invention.

Closely following the telephone is the Phonograph, an invention based on the same principle of science, but brought about
by different means. The phonograph is made to talk and sing,
thus enabling one to read by the ear instead of the eye.

THE JOHNSTOWN FLOOD.

"Fly for your lives! The dam is going!" Such was the
warning the inhabitants of the towns received from the lips of
a man who rode madly through the valley, warning every one
he saw, on that sad afternoon of May 31, 1889. It was five in
the afternoon. The people were beginning to think of leaving

their work and going to their peaceful homes, when this dread
news broke upon their ears. They could not credit it, and as
they heard the news, they looked doubtingly at each other. To
most of them, it seemed impossible. The dam was away up in
the mountains, on private grounds, and few had ever seen it or
dreamed how vast it was. Besides, they reasoned, it had broken
once or twice before, and no great harm was done. All these

WARNING THE INHABITANTS.

causes served to lull their fears. But even when they were
warned, it was too late, so impetuous was its course. Nothing
could have stayed the mad waters in their descent into the
doomed valley.

The Johnstown flood followed a long rain storm in the
Alleghanies—a storm of several days' duration. All the rivers
running east were swollen, and the immense dam of the huge
Conemaugh valley burst with a thunderous report. The reser-
voir was a large one, four miles long by one broad, and over
seventy feet deep. This vast body of water swept a wave
twenty feet high at the rate of twenty miles an hour, right down

into the narrow and deep valley, where were eight villages boasting a population of 58,000. Johnstown, Pennsylvania, the largest of the towns in the valley, lay at the junction of Stony Creek and the Conemaugh river, and had extensive iron works, banks, and many business houses. This and all the villages were swept out of being in two hours, so rapid and vehement was the coming of the torrent. Thousands were drowned, and nearly two thousand people were burned to death by means of a mass of wreckage which was caught and held at a new bridge near the town. The houses were all made of wood, timber had floated down the current and stacked up, and hundreds of trees were piled up at this bridge for a space of sixty acres. It is presumed that some furnaces set fire to this mass, and the poor creatures whose helpless forms had been entangled in the débris, met an awful death by fire. There was no chance for escape; the raging torrent was ready to engulf them, while the fierce flames were eager to lap up all that the waters spared.

Railroad tracks were swept away, telegraph poles leveled, and though Philadelphia and other cities sent help and food at once, it was impossible to reach the helpless victims for forty-eight hours, and when at last soldiers and navvies on rescue trains reached the scene, there was nothing to be done but to feed the living and bury the dead.

Nearly 10,000 perished, and all who had escaped with their lives tried to succor the sufferers, save a few Hungarian Slavs and Italians, who plundered the dead, but who were shot at once as a reward for their greediness.

It is not possible to picture the condition of the Valley after the waters receded. In many places the whole town was swept as bare as though a gigantic broom had passed over it, nothing but sand and gravel being left. Where a house chanced to be left standing, it was filled with mud and slime to the third story, while trees, broken timbers and débris was piled up to the second story. Not a house was fit for occupancy. Dead bodies were found in cellars, and in some dwellings horses had been forced into the rooms by the rushing waters, and lay there putrefying. They all fared alike. A few citizens were held prisoners in their frame houses, and floated over two miles to a place of safety, but these fortunate ones were the exception.

Medicines, clothing, money and food were liberally poured into the unfortunate region. Men and women from all over the country offered their services to care for the living and the dead.

The dam whose bursting caused this awful loss of life was very carelessly constructed, and had no stone work in its make-up. Indeed, it might well be called a vast embankment of earth.

EARTHQUAKE AT CHARLESTON.

Charleston, South Carolina, seems to have more than her

EARTHQUAKE AT CHARLESTON.

share of misfortunes. This thought occurred to me when the papers all over the country on the morning of September 1st,

1886, gave to the world an account of that dreaded convulsion known as an earthquake, which had taken place the night previous, just as the hour for retiring had come. The first intimation that the Signal Service Bureau at Washington city had of this catastrophe was only a surmise. They knew that something was wrong, for communication was not to be had. All the telegraph wires were suddenly cut off. Without a moment's warning the city had been shocked and rent to its very foundation. Hardly a building escaped injury and almost a third of the city was in half or total ruins. The whole Atlantic coast was more or less affected, and for leagues from the shore the ocean was thrown in a turmoil.

People fled from the tottering houses to the parks and public squares, where they erected tents and remained for weeks, afraid to return to their own homes. It was soon discovered that these shocks were only the dying away of great convulsions and that further alarm was unnecessary, so they returned home.

With true American energy the débris was in a few months cleared away, business was resumed and to-day were it not for a few cracks and fissures in buildings we would never know that anything had happened there to disturb their peace.

ATING from the time of the discovery of our continent there have been disturbances between the whites and the Indians. The first Indian war was between the colonists and the natives, and dates back to 1622.

At the beginning of the nineteenth century the Sioux Indians held all the lands between the Mississippi and the Rocky Mountains, north of the 40th parallel of latitude. These lands were grassy, rolling prairies, with a plentiful supply of timber growing along the rivers and creeks which abounded. The government established reservations thirty-two years ago for the purpose of keeping those Indians who are hostile, separated from the peaceably disposed ones, who only went upon the hunt for game for food and sale. When buffalo and large game grew scarce, the United States furnished them with food and clothing, and placed the means within their power, to support themselves.

The Indian question is full of interest, and comes forward constantly to perplex our government, which regards them as its wards. Articles by the hundred have been written about the red man, his possibilities and capabilities set forth; plans have been proposed to subdue, or rather civilize him, and still the fact remains that the savage nature, save in exceptional instances, is as untamed as the first day he came upon the scene.

ATTACK ON THE MAIL.

337

The first mail to California from the East was carried by
the overland route, in stages, and lucky was the party that made
the lonesome journey across the plains unmolested by the Indians, who swarmed about them and sent showers of arrows into
the coach which was carrying its bag of mail and the trembling
passengers. The stage was always guarded by United States
soldiers, but in spite of this the half-naked savages would press
closer and closer, hurling their sharp arrows with unerring aim,
as the stage went plunging along, the horses half-mad with fear,

A STOLEN CHILD.

but straining every nerve to outrun the screaming foe. The
settlers of those early days were brave men and women, or they
would not have risked falling into the hands of the roving bands
who were always on the war-path on some pretext. Many a
brave man has died defending the mail which the government
intrusted to him.

While our land was torn with dissension, the Indians cun-
ningly planned a general uprising. This was in 1862. The
Indians in Minnesota and Dakota massacred the settlers everywhere. In Minnesota the Sioux attacked outlying towns, com·

mitting terrible atrocities. They pounced upon New Ulm, a small but thriving village, and killed 100 of its people. They turned their attention to two other villages, but were driven

INDIAN DANCE.

away.   Colonel Sibley was sent after them, and met several
bodies of Indians, whom he defeated.   They fear cannon greatly,
and two were turned upon them, much to their terror.

CAPTURE OF A WHITE CHILD.

The garrison at Fort Kearney was surprised by Indians
December 21, 1866, and 100 soldiers were slaughtered.

The Indians have many peculiar customs.   One of them is,
their habit of daubing on the war paint and indulging in a war
dance whenever they resolve to attack the whites.   Once seen

they can never be forgotten, for their lithe forms, hideously painted faces, and demoniac yells would startle the bravest.

September of 1867 the Indians on the North Platte called a council to confer with General Sherman. They demanded that the building of several roads should be stopped, and particularly the work on the Southern Pacific, as it interfered with their hunting. The General would not accede to these demands, but promised that any loss they suffered should be made good to them.

September 18, 1868, the Indians attacked our troops at Republican River, and Lieutenant Beecher and several other officers were murdered. In 1871 the Apaches killed over 200 white settlers, not in battle, but skulking in ambush, and shooting them wherever they met them.

BUFFALO BILL, A FOE OF THE INDANS.

The whites met the Indians at Washita River, and defeated them, November 27, 1868.

Thus the continual outbreaks of the Indians, have been a source of trouble and anxiety to the government, which has sought to adjust the claims of the red men in a fair and just manner. That the latter have often been cheated and robbed by unscrupulous agents and traders, no one can deny, but the fact still remains that the Indian nature is peculiarly hard to subdue, and their natural instincts are cruel. There are, fortunately, many bright examples among several

DEATH OF SITTING BULL.

tribes, of the beauty of civilization, and its beneficial influence upon them.

The Modoc massacre was a cruel return for intended kindness. This tribe had for its chief Captain Jack, a very intelligent man of fine abilities. Their removal to another reservation was violently resisted by them, and they retreated to the Lava Beds, where trouble was anticipated. At last a peace council was arranged for, and although Colonel Meacham, the peace commissioner, urged the whites not to attend it, they paid no attention to his warning, but went. The Indians had concealed weapons, and they rose in a body, and attempted to massacre every white man present. General Canby and Dr. Thomas were killed, and Colonel Meacham received a dozen wounds, but survived them. Three months afterward the band surrendered, and Captain Jack and some of the other leaders were executed at Fort Klamath, Oregon, October 3. Among the men who had distinguished themselves in the Indian Wars was

GEORGE A. CUSTER.

A the close of the war of 1861 most of the boys in blue went back to their homes—but not so with General Custer. He was one of the most brilliant soldiers of the war, and had the distinction of being the youngest general in the army. His graduation from West Point took place just about the first year of the conflict, and he was made lieutenant, but before the close of the last year he had attained the rank of major-general, and assisted in some of the most remarkable victories.

He was not allowed time to visit his home in Michigan, but was ordered to lead a cavalry command through Texas, to teach the people there that the war was over, and to check the ravages of the "bushwhackers" who still infested that beautiful State. On his return home he accepted the lieutenant-colonelcy of the Seventh United States Cavalry, and nine years were passed in service at the frontier posts of Kansas and Dakota.

His wife lived with him through those scenes of interest.

She had the gift of transmitting to paper the vivid pictures of this wild and daring life. She passed four months in an army wagon, and rode the long marches which her brave husband was forced to make. He was a hero, she also was a heroine, for the hardships and privations which she endured so uncomplainingly, were worthy of so grand a spirit.

The Sioux (Soo) is the most powerful tribe of red men on our continent. They preyed upon all alike—with the defenceless settlements of our Minnesota frontier, with the Pawnees, the Cheyennes, the Arapahoes, and the Shoshones and, indeed, with all the other tribes, far and near.

They spared no one. At the end of the war of 1861 our army was called on to protect the peaceable settlers of the far West, for the Sioux were more hostile and bloodthirsty than ever. For ten years the cavalry regiments knew no rest. The Indians were on the war-path continually. They were always rash fighters, but when in 1874 they obtained breech-loaders and rifles, they became a foe more to be dreaded than ever. They burned our forts and massacred the small garrisons in a most atrocious manner.

Our government used every method to subdue them, feeding, clothing and coaxing them. Agencies and reservations were placed at good points, but this care for their comfort had no effect. The old worn-out Indians, women and children lived on these reservations, partaking of the government's bounty, while the young and vigorous warriors sallied out to murder and pilfer the whites wherever they could find them. The soldiers of the United States were not permitted to attack them on their reservations, and so they kept out of their way, and escaped punishment.

An Indian in his wild state has no respect for another of his race who has no scalps to show. There were, however, some who made treaties with the whites, and kept them. But among the many who never made any promise to behave was a powerful medicine chief known as "Sitting Bull."

In March, 1876, General George Crook was sent against

this renowned warrior, who had entrenched himself in the hills
with 6,000 "bad Indians" around him. From the south General Terry was sent with a strong body of cavalry and infantry,
and General Gibbon with a small but brave band of frontier
soldiers. They approached the stronghold of the chief. Major
Reno left camp to reconnoiter, and was readily convinced how
rash it would be to attack Sitting Bull, who was daily receiving
accessions to his numbers.

General Terry thought, however, it was time to start an
expedition to discover and dislodge the enemy, and he gave the
command to the brave and fearless soldier, General Custer. He
named the 26th of June as the day when he and Gibbon would
be there to assist Custer, but the latter, impatient to open the
conflict, had urged his horses and men to their utmost so as to
reach the scene. He started on the trail with the Seventh
Cavalry, riding sixty miles in twenty-four hours. His aim was
to have a bout with the Indians and defeat them single-handed.
Coming within sight of the village on the left bank of the Little
Big Horn River where Sitting Bull was encamped, he observed
such tokens of excitement and hurrying away of ponies as to
him had but one explanation—that the chief and his warriors
were running away. Dashing forward with panting chest and
the fire of courage flaming in his face, he placed himself at the
head of his men, plunged hastily into the valley, and the last
that General Reno, who followed him closely, ever saw of the
brave Custer and his three hundred, was the cloud of dust their
trail had left behind.

The valiant Custer had gone to his death! Expecting Reno
would make a dash such as his own, he had gallantly ridden
forward, to be met by a perfect storm of flame and lead. In
an instant he saw how vain was his attempt, and giving orders
to mount he sought a way out, but the red men swarmed around
his followers. Boys and even old squaws were firing at him
and his band most viciously. Vainly they tried to remount—
they cut their horses loose, and on a little mound, General
Custer, with scarcely a dozen men, all who were left, made his

CUSTER'S LAST CHARGE

last rally. In a few moments all was over. Of the twelve
troops of the Seventh Cavalry, but one thing escaped alive—
Myles Keogh's sorrel horse, Comanche, who came back into the
lines a few days later, a most pitiable object. Thus perished
General Custer, as brave and noble a soldier as ever lived!

The Utes gave a great amount of trouble in 1879, in Colorado, pouncing upon a wagon train and slaying Major Thorn-
burgh and eleven of his men. They next murdered Agent
Meeker, and carried many women into captivity.

The Apache Indians fell upon the settlers of Silver City, New
Mexico, October 19, 1879, killing twenty-one men and women,
and seventeen children. The men were shot and scalped, and
the women tortured. Troops were sent to protect the remainder, but it was some time before they could be reached.

The year 1890 witnessed one of the most serious outbreaks
of the red men of the Dakota reservations. The Ghost Dance
was indulged in, and the feeling of dread and fear spread all
over the Western country. This dance was instigated by Sitting
Bull, who had returned to the reservation eleven years previous.
It has always been a superstition among all the Indians that
the Messiah would come to them some day, bring all their dead
to life, and drive the whites out of the land. Sitting Bull
encouraged the Sioux in Dakota to believe this.

At once the War Department was given full control of the
Indians by the Interior Department. At the different agencies
it was found that the Indians were stealing cattle and horses
and running them off into the Bad Lands, where they designed
starting a camp. It was well known that if Sitting Bull reached
that stronghold he would be safe, so the Indian police at the
Pine Ridge Agency were told to arrest him, which they did, and
started back to the Agency, knowing a body of cavalry and
infantry were following in their wake to assist them. But Sitting
Bull's friends rushed to his assistance and a fierce hand-to-hand
encounter took place. They all fought like fiends, and lost
several of their numbers. But the police held the old chief

captive, and two of them shot him—Bullhead and Red Toma-
hawk. A son of the chief, Crow Foot, was slain also.

BATTLE OF WOUNDED KNEE CREEK.

In the annals of American history there cannot be found a
battle so fierce, bloody and decisive as the fight at Wounded
Knee Creek between the Seventh
Cavalry and Big Foot's band of
Sioux. It was a stand-up fight of
the most desperate kind, in which
nearly the entire band was annihilated, and although the soldiers
outnumbered their opponents
nearly three to one, the victory
was won by two troops, about one
hundred strong.

INDIAN CHIEF.

The night before the Indians
had agreed to submit, and the
troops were up bright and early
in readiness to move by eight
o'clock. At that hour the cavalry
and dismounted troops were gathered about the Indian village, the
Hotchkiss guns overlooking the
camp not fifty yards away. The
Indians were ordered to come forward, away from their tents, and
when the band, under the leader-
ship of Big Foot, walked out of
their lodges and formed a semi-
circle in front of the soldiers' tents,
there was nothing to indicate that
they would not submit. Colonel Forsyth, an Indian fighter of
tried worth, never gave a thought to the chance of a fight.
When it was made plain to the band that their arms must

INDIAN SCOUT.

be given up, the murmur of discontent was unanimous. When the soldiers proceeded to disarm them and search their tents the medicine man jumped up, uttered a loud incantation and fired at a trooper standing guard over the captured guns. That was the signal for fight, and in a second every buck in the party rose to his feet, cast aside the blanket which covered his winchester, and, taking aim, fired directly at the troop in front. It was a terrible onslaught, and so sudden that all were stunned but, quickly recovering, they opened fire on the enemy. The position of troops B and K would not allow their fellow-cavalrymen to fire, lest they shoot through the Indians and kill their own men. Thus the terrible duel raged for thirty minutes. Someone ordered "Spare the women," but the squaws fought like demons and could not be distinguished from the men. The entire band was practically slaughtered, and those who escaped to the ravine were followed by the cavalry and shot down wherever found. The chief medicine man, whose incantations had caused the band to act with such murderous treachery, fell with a dozen bullets in his body. It is claimed that of the Indians there were but two survivors, one of which was a baby girl about three months old, who has since been adopted by a wealthy lady in Washington.

After the defeat of the Indians at Wounded Knee Creek, they were ready to close the conflict and make the best terms possible with General Miles. On the 22d of January there was a grand military review in honor of the victory over the redskins. Ten thousand Sioux had a good opportunity to see the strength and discipline of the United States Army, the end of the ghost-dance rebellion being marked by a review of all the soldiers who had taken part in crushing the Indians. Thus passed into history probably not only the most remarkable of our Indian wars, but the last one there will ever be.

CHRISTOPHER CARSON.

BREVET BRIGADIER-GENERAL CHRISTOPHER CARSON.

The subject of our sketch was one of the most noted mountaineers, trappers and hunters that ever lived. He was no less renowned as a guide and a soldier. He was a native of Madison County, Kentucky, where he was born December 24, 1809. When he was a babe his father removed his family to Howard County, Missouri. Here he spent many happy days in hunting wild game, and making himself familiar with nature. The schoolroom had not very many charms for him, and at fifteen he was apprenticed to a saddler, with whom he remained two years. But this employment was irksome to him, and he soon freed himself, and we next hear of him as a trapper, which was more congenial to his taste, as he remained one for eight years. He next engaged as hunter to Bent's Fort, and eight more years glided by. Few men understood the nature of the Indians more thoroughly than did he. He dealt with them in a truthful, straightforward way, which won their regard, and the government appointed him Indian agent in New Mexico, where he was singularly successful in making treaties with the red men, which were religiously kept.

His services during the Civil War were inestimable in New Mexico, Colorado and the Indian Territory, for which he was promoted to colonel, and was brevetted brigadier-general.

He died from a rupture of an artery in the neck, at Fort Lynn, Colorado, on the 23d of May, 1868.

THE WORLD'S COLUMBIAN EXPOSITION.

The next great fair which our country saw, was planned on a huge scale. It was also an invitation to the peoples of all lands, who liberally responded. This was the World's Fair, and it was rightly named, for it proved a gathering of all nations. It was opened in May, 1893, and closed October 30. The features of the Fair were varied, and its inception and fulfillment were on a gigantic scale. Nearly every country on earth sent some representation to the Fair, and during its existence millions of strangers visited the city.

There was a long and earnest contest as to what city should have the honor of being selected to hold the great World's Fair, St. Louis, Cincinnati, New York, Washington and Chicago, each presenting powerful reasons why the choice should fall upon it. But Congress settled the question by giving to Chicago the coveted honor, and without delay commissioners were chosen,

THE ART PALACE, WORLD'S FAIR. CHICAGO

and officials and citizens went busily to work, hand in hand, to make the fair the grandest ever projected.

The grounds selected were at Jackson Park, Chicago, and comprised 640 acres. Magnificent buildings were erected, costing from $10,000 to $300,000 each, and every State engaged with the others in a friendly rivalry. There were forty-seven State and Territorial buildings, each one noted for a style of architecture dissimilar to any of the rest, and yet all remarkably beautiful.

It was well represented by foreign peoples, fifty-one nations and thirty-nine colonies participating. The edifices erected by the directors, such as Transportation, Machinery Hall, Electrical Building, etc., were numerous and costly. The beauties of the Art Gallery were a revelation to the busy, pushing American, and the man or woman who spent but a few days among the wonders of the great World's Fair of 1893 found food for reflection and pleasant memories to last a lifetime. Nature was not overlooked and the horticultural show was a marvel of beauty. The Fisheries Building was deemed among the handsomest on the grounds, costing $225,000, but where all were so fine and so well adapted to their intended use, it is impossible to particularize.

The fair, it was expected, would be opened by President Cleveland in person, but State reasons forbidding his presence, it was arranged that he should touch an electric button in Washington which should start the machinery here, which was done. The fair was dedicated on the 20th of October, 1892, with imposing and lengthy ceremonies, and opened to the world in May, 1893.

Figures do not appeal to the youthful mind, but still they are necessary for comparison, and when I tell my young readers that the Vienna exposition in 1873 expended $7,850,000, while Chicago's outlay was $17,000,000, it will easily be seen that the World's Fair of 1893, held at Chicago, was carried out with a magnificence never before equaled.

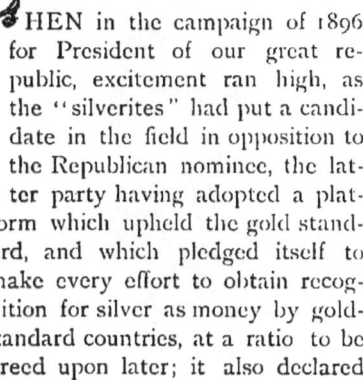

HEN in the campaign of 1896 for President of our great republic, excitement ran high, as the "silverites" had put a candidate in the field in opposition to the Republican nominee, the latter party having adopted a platform which upheld the gold standard, and which pledged itself to make every effort to obtain recognition for silver as money by gold-standard countries, at a ratio to be agreed upon later; it also declared in favor of a protective tariff.

The year of 1893 had brought a terrible panic, which caused more suffering in its train, than any that had preceded it. Business was not to be had, labor was not sought, and failures were of everyday occurrence. People began to ask why this state of affairs existed. The advocates of silver answered that it was because that metal was legislated against, while the protective tariff people asserted that the troubles were due to the fact that the tariff was faulty—it neither provided money for governmental uses, nor work for the toilers.

At once a fierce contest of words and arguments began. The silver men formed clubs, papers presenting their arguments were scattered all over the land, able speakers were employed, and nothing was heard but the all-absorbing currency question.

The Democrats held a convention at Chicago in July with the silver men in the majority. William J. Bryan of Nebraska proved so convincing a speaker in the debates, that he held the attention of vast and enthusiastic audiences. In return for his

PRESIDENT WILLIAM MKINLEY.

efforts he was nominated for President, and Arthur Sewall of Maine for Vice, as William McKinley of Ohio, had been named in the Republican body that met at St. Louis, in June, with Garrett A. Hobart of New Jersey as Vice-President. The platform sanctioned by the party was the free coinage of silver at the ratio of "sixteen to one," and that the tariff was to remain unchanged. The watch-word of the party became "sixteen to one."

When the Populists held their convention they chose Mr. Bryan for the Presidential chair, and Thomas Watson of Georgia for the position of Vice-President. The Silver party indorsed the choice of Bryan, and the whole country became engaged in the conflict. The excitement was intense, and party spirit ran high. The States seemed equally divided, the Eastern and Central coming out for gold, while the Western and Southern espoused the claims of the white metal.

Still another party arose, called the Gold Democrats, who convened at Indianapolis in September, and selected John M. Palmer of Illinois for their Presidential leader, and Simon B. Buckner of Kentucky for Vice. This party came out squarely for the gold standard only.

Mr. Bryan took the stump and addressed the people of the country at large. Mr. McKinley remained quietly in his own home at Canton, and received delegations. It seemed

WILLIAM J. BRYAN.

as though every man, woman and child took sides in the great question at stake, and each was equally sure of success. Debates noticeable for their bitter intensity were heard, meetings were held day and night, and each party felt certain that in an acceptance of its particular views alone rested the safety and perpetuity of our country.

The battle culminated on November 5, 1896, when William McKinley was elected by a large majority. The rancor and bitterness died out, all parties accepted the people's choice, and he was inaugurated President March 4, 1897, amid a scene of splendor.

Of his patriotism, his clear-sightedness, his wisdom, his administration is daily giving proof, and his conduct of our late war with Spain is the best vindication of the calm, unbiased, just and grand character of our chief executive.

FRANCES WILLAR'

"HOME, SWEET HOME."

FRANCES E. WILLARD.

In the spring of 1863 two great armies were encampled on either side of the Rappahannock River, one dressed in blue and the other dressed in gray. As twilight fell, the bands of music on the Union side began to play the martial music, "The Star Spangled Banner," and "Rally Round the Flag;" and that challenge of music was taken up by those upon the other side, and they responded with "The Bonnie Blue Flag," and "Away Down South in Dixie." It was borne in upon the soul of a single soldier in one of those bands of music to begin a sweeter and a more tender air, and slowly as he played it they joined in a sort of chorus of all the instruments upon the Union side, until finally a great and mighty chorus swelled up and down our army—"Home, Sweet Home." When they had finished there was no challenge yonder, for every band upon that farther shore had taken up the lovely air so attuned to all that is holiest and dearest, and one great chorus of the two great hosts went up to God; and when they had finished the sweet and holy melody, from the boys in gray there came a challenge, "Three cheers for home!" and as they went reverberating through the skies from both sides of the river, "something upon the soldiers' cheeks washed off the stains of powder."

War and Peace.

THE REV. O. H. TIFFANY, D. D.

HOW solemn a thing is death!—and yet, how wonderful a thing is life! God appoints it, man develops it, death seals its destiny, eternity unfolds its ultimate issues. Each human soul in which this power of life is has "its secrets and histories and marvels of destiny, heaven's splendors are over its dead, hell's terrors are under its feet, tragedies and poetries are in it, and a history for eternity." Every social organism, every grand national aggregation of lives but generalizes the history of the individual, and thus the history of all life and of all living, whether in individuals, families, societies or nations, is one history, and that history the record of its conflicts, its defeats, its victories. The dawn of this life is a struggle for being, its growth a constant warfare with antagonisms, its maintenance is by continued defenses. And each and all of these create crises of destiny which may retard or advance, destroy or establish the whole.

Our national birth was a contest with physical difficulties, our establishment a victory over political antagonisms; the last desperate struggle was a conflict of ideas, a contest of moral principles; and we may hope that its issue shall be one of prosperity and peace.

Mountains are rock-ribbed and enduring because the earthquake has settled them on their foundations; the pines that crest them like a coronet withstand the rudest blasts, because they have been rooted by the storms which toss their giant branches. So universal freedom has been made sure by the passing turbulence of rebellion, and our national prosperity established by the rude blast of war.

It was a war such as the world never before witnessed; it was fought by such armies as never before were marshaled on the field. But the end has come. These great armies have returned covered with honor and laureled with renown. They are merged again in the business and activities of life; they have disappeared from view like the snow in springtime, or the dew of the morning in the summer's sun; now and then the halting step upon the sidewalk, here and there an empty sleeve, remind us in our daily walks of the stern realities of war.

After war, peace!

Peace to the dead. Peace through their labors to the living. These "have fought their last fight," the salvos of artillery which soon shall sound from the guns they loved so well shall not awake them. The grass shall grow green in springtime, the birds of summer shall sing their sweetest notes, the bright glories of autumn shall tint the foliage above them, and the white snow of winter shall lie unbroken on their graves, but these shall sleep on in peace.

Peace, white-robed and olive-crowned, has come to us who linger. Peace, with its cares and toils, peace, with its plenty and prosperity, peace, with its duties for to-day and its destinies for to-morrow. Let us welcome it and become worthy of it. Let there be in all our lives, thoughts, hopes, endeavors, such devotion to duty as called and sent these brave men to the battlefield and sustained them there; and then we may safely leave our future to the care of those who, coming after us, shall pause, amid the ruins time may make, to trace upon the marble in our cemeteries the names of the heroic dead.

> God gives us peace! Not such as lulls to sleep,
> But sword on thigh and brows with purpose knit.
> And let our Ship of State to harbor sweep,
> Her ports all up! Her battle lanterns lit!
> And her leashed thunders gathered for their leap.

The Union Soldier.

ROBERT G. INGERSOLL.

THE past rises before me like a dream. Again we are in the great struggle for national life. We hear the sounds of preparation, the music of the boisterous drum, the silver voices of heroic bugles. We see thousands of assemblages, and hear the appeals of orators; we see the pale cheeks of women and

the flushed faces of men; and in those assemblages we see all the
dead whose dust we have covered with flowers. We lose sight of
them no more. We are with them when they enlist in the great
army of freedom. We see them part with those they love. Some
are walking for the last time in quiet, woody places with the maid-
ens they adore. We hear the whisperings and the sweet vows of
eternal love as they lingeringly part forever. Others are bending
over cradles, kissing babies that are asleep; some are receiving
the blessings of old men; some are parting with mothers who hold
them and press them to their hearts again and again, and say
nothing, and some are talking with wives, and endeavoring with
brave words spoken in the old tones to drive from their hearts the
awful fear. We see them part. We see the wife standing in the
door, with the babe in her arms—standing in the sunlight sob-
bing—at the turn of the road a hand waves—she answers by holding
high in her loving hands the child. He is gone, and forever.
We see them all as they march proudly away under the flaunting
flags, keeping time to the wild, grand music of war, marching down
the streets of the great cities, through the towns and across the
prairies, down to the fields of glory, to do and to die for the
eternal right. We go with them, one and all. We are by their
side on all the gory fields, in the hospitals, on all the weary
marches. We stand guard with them in the wild storm, and under
the quiet stars. We are with them in ravines running with blood,
in the furrows of old fields; we are with them between contesting
hosts unable to move, wild with thirst, the life ebbing slowly
away among the withered leaves. We see them pierced by balls
and torn with shells in the trenches by forts, and in the whirlwind
of the charge, where men become iron, with nerves of steel.

We are with them in the prisons of hatred and famine; but
human speech can never tell what they endured. We are at
home when the news comes that they are dead. We see
the maiden in the shadow of her first sorrow. We see the sil-
vered head of the old man bowed with the first grief.

The past rises before us, and we see four millions of human
beings governed by the lash; we see them bound hand and foot;
we hear the strokes of cruel whips; we see the hounds tracking

women through the tangled swamps; we see babes sold from the breasts of mothers. Cruelty unspeakable! Outrage infinite! Four million bodies in chains—four million souls in fetters. All the sacred relations of wife, mother, father and child trampled beneath the brutal feet of might. All this was done under our own beautiful banner of the free. The past rises before us; we hear the roar and shriek of the bursting shell; the broken fetters fall; these heroes died. We look—instead of slaves we see men, women and children. The wand of progress touches the auction block, the slave pen, the whipping post, and we see homes and firesides, and schoolhouses and books, and where all was want and crime and cruelty and fetters, we see the faces of the free. These heroes are dead; they died for liberty; they died for us; they are at rest; they sleep in the land they made free under the flag they rendered stainless, under the solemn pines, the sad hemlocks, the tearful willows and the embracing vines; they sleep beneath the shadows of the clouds, careless alike of sunshine or storm, each in the windowless palace of rest. Earth may run red with other wars, they are at peace. In the midst of battle they found the severity of death. I have one sentiment for the soldiers, living and dead—cheers for the living, and tears for the dead.

Our Noble, Heroic and Self=Sacrificing Women.

EMORY A. STORRS.

BRIGHT and shining on our resplendent annals shall appear the names of those thousands of noble, heroic and self-sacrificing women, who organized and carried forward to triumphant success a colossal sanitary and charitable scheme, the like of which, in nobility of conception and perfectness of execution, the world had never before witnessed, and which carried all around the globe the fame and the name of the women of America.

From camp to camp, from battlefield to battlefield, through the long and toilsome march, by day and by night, these sacred charities followed, and the prayers of the devoted and the true were ceaselessly with you through all dangers.

Leagues and leagues separated you from home, but the blessings there invoked upon you hovered over and around you, and sweetened your sleep like angels' visits.

While the boy soldier slept by his camp fire at night and dreaming of home, and what his valor would achieve for his country, uttered even in his dreams prayers for the loved ones who had made that home so dear to him, the mother dreaming of her son breathed at the same time prayers for his safety, and for the triumph of his cause. The prayers and blessings of mother and son, borne heavenward, met in the bosom of their common God and Father.

Antietam.

I'VE wandered to Antietam, John,
   And stood where foe met foe
Upon the fields of Maryland
   So many years ago.
The circling hills rise just the same
   As they did on that day,
When you were fighting blue, old boy,
   And I was fighting gray.

The winding stream runs 'neath the bridge
   Where Burnside won his fame;
The locust trees upon the ridge
   Beyond are there the same.
The birds were singing 'mid the trees—
   'Twas bullets on that day,
When you were fighting blue, old boy,
   And I was fighting gray.
I saw again the Dunker Church
   That stood beside the wood,
Where Hooker made the famous charge
   That Hill so well withstood.

'Tis scarred and marred by war and time,
   As we are, John, to-day;
For you were fighting blue, old boy,
   As I was fighting gray.

I stood beneath the signal tree
   Where I that day was laid,
And 'twas your arms, old boy, that brought
   Me to this friendly shade.
Tho' leaves are gone and limbs are bare,
   Its heart is true to-day
As yours was then, tho' fighting blue,
   To me, the fighting gray.

I marked the spot where Mansfield fell,
   Where Richardson was slain,
With Stark and Douglas 'mid the corn,
   And Brant amid the grain.
The names are sacred to us, John;
   They led us in the fray, [blue
When you were fighting Northern
   And I the Southern gray.

I thought of Burnside, Hooker,
Meade,
Of Sedgwick, old and grave;
Of Stonewall Jackson, tried and true,
That tried the day to save.
I bared my head—they rest in peace—
Each one has passed away;
Death musters those who wore the
blue
With those who wore the gray.

The old Pry mansion rears its walls
Beside Antietam's stream,
And far away along the South
I saw the tombstones gleam.

They mark each place where "Little
Mac"
And Robert Lee that day
Made proud the South, tho' wearing
blue,
The North, tho' wearing gray.

Yes, John, it gave me joy to stand
. Where we once fiercely fought.
The nation now is one again—
The lesson has been taught.
Sweet peace doth fair Antietam crown,
And we can say to-day   [blue
We're friends, tho' one was fighting
And one was fighting gray,

THE SWORDS OF GRANT AND LEE.

"Fame Hath Crowned with Laurel the Swords of Grant and Lee."

METHINKS to-night I catch a gleam of steel among the pines,
And yonder by the lilied stream repose the foemen's lines;
The ghostly guards who pace the ground a moment stop to see
If all is safe and still around the tents of Grant and Lee.

'Tis but a dream; no armies camp where once their bay'nets
shone;
And Hesper's calm and lovely lamp shines on the dead alone;
A cricket chirps on yonder rise beneath a cedar tree
Where glinted 'neath the summer skies the swords of Grant and Lee.

Forever sheathed those famous blades that led the eager van!
They shine no more among the glades that fringe the Rapidan;
To-day their battle work is done, go draw them forth and see
That not a stain appears upon the swords of Grant and Lee.

The gallant men who saw them flash in comradeship to-day
Recall the wild, impetuous dash of val'rous blue and gray;
And 'neath the flag that proudly waves above a Nation free,
They oft recall the missing braves who fought with Grant and Lee.

They sleep among the tender grass, they slumber 'neath the pines,
They're camping in the mountain pass where crouched the serried lines;

They rest where loud the tempests blow, destructive in their glee—
The men who followed long ago the swords of Grant and Lee.

Their graves are lying side by side where once they met as foes,
And where they in the wildwood died springs up a blood-red rose;
O'er them the bee on golden wing doth flit, and in yon tree
A gentle robin seems to sing to them of Grant and Lee.

To-day no strifes of sections rise, to-day no shadows fall
Upon our land, and 'neath the skies one flag waves over all;
The Blue and Gray as comrades stand, as comrades bend the knee,
And ask God's blessings on the land that gave us Grant and Lee.

So long as southward, wide and clear, Potomac's river runs,
Their deeds will live because they were Columbia's hero sons;
So long as bend the Northern pines, and blooms the orange tree,
The swords will shine that led the lines of valiant Grant and Lee.

Methinks I hear a bugle blow, methinks I hear a drum;
And there, with martial step and slow, two ghostly armies come;
They are the men who met as foes, for 'tis the dead I see,
And side by side in peace repose the swords of Grant and Lee.

Above them let Old Glory wave, and let each deathless star
Forever shine upon the brave who lead the ranks of war;
Their fame resounds from coast to coast, from mountain top to sea;
No other land than ours can boast the swords of Grant and Lee!

WAR WITH SPAIN.

NLY those who know the power of peace can realize the dread of war. For four centuries Spain has borne down upon her colonies, with a heavy hand. The brightest of them, Cuba, "the Pearl of the Antilles," has been the victim of two cruel and mercilesswars at her hands, waged with relentless barbarity. We could not, as a Christian nation, help protesting against her inhumanity to a people whose home was so near our shores.

For thirty years the sounds of war had been silent in our domain, but justice demanded that we interfere in behalf of a people who are struggling against oppression, and in the noble cause of humanity. Spain's cruelty and Spain's greed are matters of history.

THE MAINE DISASTER.

On the 25th of January the Maine, an American battleship, entered the harbor of Havana, Cuba, and anchored in her waters at a spot indicated by the harbor-master. The usual exchange of salutes and formal visits expected between two powers, took place, and there was no apparent unfriendliness shown. Just three weeks from that day, in the evening of the 15th of February, an explosion took place, which tore the boat to atoms, killing 266 of her crew and two officers. At once treachery was suspected, but the American people was asked to suspend its judgment until the long and searching investigation which was conducted by the naval board of inquiry was ended, when every evidence was produced proving that the awful calamity was due wholly to Spanish treachery.

This led to a severing of all diplomatic relations, which was ended by the Spanish minister's request for his passport. Spain declared war upon the United States on April 24, 1898, and it took the House of Representatives one minute and forty-one seconds to pass a declaration of war in reply to Spain, and the Senate acted with equal promptness.

Events of such vast importance have rarely followed each other with such rapidity a shave those of our late war with Spain. In less than three months a nation which deemed itself invincible, threw down the gauntlet which was as speedily picked up, and engagements and battles trod almost upon each other's heels, until its boast was proved a vain one, and victory was ours.

Our people were ready to accept the challenge. From North and South came the glad response. Once more the blue and the gray fought side by side, as brothers.

THE FIRST GUN FIRED.

Our history would be incomplete if I did not tell my young readers who fired the first shot in our war with Spain. The United States cruiser, Nashville, of the North Atlantic squadron at Key West, can lay proud claim to that honor.

It was a clear and beautiful morning in April when the American fleet left Key West, and proceeding southward across the straits of Florida, first saw the city of Havana and the battlements of the famous Morro Castle, on the afternoon of the same day. The fleet presented a gallant sight, and when at three in the morning Admiral Sampson's flagship, the New York, flashed forth her signal lights, the answering signals were given from all the ships of the fleet, black smoke began to pour from the smokestacks, and the crews needed no further hint that they had work before them.

REV. FATHER CHIDWICK, THE "MAINE'S" CHAPLAIN, DELIVERING A PRAYER AT THE BURIAL OF THE "MAINE'S" VICTIMS. GENERAL LEE, CAPTAIN SIGSBEE AND LIEUTENANT WAINWRIGHT IN THE FOREGROUND

A HEROIC DASH OF VOLUNTEERS

A NATIVE CUBAN HOME

After the Nashville returned to Key West, the rest of the squadron proceeded to the Cuban coast. Coming within fifteen miles of Morro Castle, the fleet scattered so as to form a complete blockade of the port. Every day brought new prizes to our squadron, and the blockade of Havana proved effectual.

It is well to call the attention of the boys to a few of the changes in phraseology between the old sea terms and the new. Once in the English navy (and ours was modeled after it) the term admiral was unknown—the word constable or justice was used. So with the title of captain, which is in reality a military one. In the earlier times this personage was called a master. The term commodore we have borrowed from that very nation with whom we have just measured arms—the Spanish, and comes from their word *comendador*. Cadets were not known by that name, but were called volunteers. Another item which furnishes food for reflection, is the origin of the United States navy. On October 13, 1775, the continental congress voted to fit out two vessels, one to carry ten guns, the other fourteen, for the purpose of taking English supply vessels. The same month it added two more vessels to its extensive equipment. On March 27, 1794, after our troubles with the Algerine pirates, six frigates were ordered, each to carry thirty-two guns. Congress appropriated $700,000 for the purpose of organizing a navy. Compare this feeble beginning with our splendid navy of to-day.

It is proper to explain here what the practice of nations is with regard to prize money. It is a strict rule of war that neutral powers must not interfere nor give help to either party that is engaged in a war. To furnish ships, ammunition, or supplies is a grave offence, and all such goods are termed "contraband of war."

Any boat at sea suspected of carrying "contraband" articles can be searched, but properly commissioned vessels only can perform this duty. Another thing which will subject a vessel to being seized or confiscated is an attempt at blockade running, or trying to pass the line established by the war vessels stationed in an entrance to a harbor or along the coast. These

TROOP TRANSPORTS LEAVING SAN FRANCISCO FOR MANILA

are rules of war common to all nations, and must be rigidly observed.

All neutral governments are notified that such blockade exists, and exactly how far it extends. But "paper blockades," or the mere declaration that a blockade is in force, are of no account. At the treaty of Paris, in 1856, the powers declared that "blockades, in order to be binding, must be effective," or in plainer words, a force must actually be stationed on the blockaded ground strong enough to make it dangerous to attempt to pass it.

"Prize money" sounds very tempting, and its meaning will be given. When a war is in progress properly commissioned ships are empowered to capture not only the armed vessels of the enemy, but its merchantmen as well. These vessels are taken to the country of their captors, the courts pass judgment upon their value, and if it is proven to be a lawful prize, it is sold, and the proceeds is called "prize money," and is awarded to the captors, the officers and crew, in proportion to their rank.

The prize money adjudged to them is thus given out in the following manner:

"1. The commander of a fleet or squadron, one-twentieth part prize money awarded to any vessel or vessels under his immediate command.

"2. To the commander of a division of a fleet or squadron, a sum equal to one-fiftieth of any prize money awarded to a vessel of the division under his command, to be paid from the moiety due the United States, if there be such moiety; if not, from the amount awarded the captors.

"3. To the fleet captain, one-hundredth part of all prize money awarded to any vessel of the fleet in which he is serving, in which case he shall share in proportion to his pay, with the other officers and men on board such vessel.

"4. To the commander of a single vessel, one-tenth of all the prize money awarded to the vessel.

"5. After the foregoing deductions, the residue is distributed among the others doing duty on board, and borne upon

THE ADVANCE OF A CUBAN CAVALRY SURPRISING AND CAPTURING A SPANISH CAMP

(Drawn by an eye-witness)

the books of the ship, in proportion to their respective rates of pay.

"All vessels of the navy within signal distance of the vessel making the capture, and in such condition as to be able to render effective aid if required, will share in the prize. Any person temporarily absent from his vessel may share in the captures made during his absence. The prize court determines what vessel shall share in a prize, and also whether a prize was superior or inferior to the vessel or vessels making the capture.

"The share of prize money awarded to the United States is set apart forever as a fund for the payment of pensions to naval officers, seamen and marines entitled to pensions."

On April 27 our forces bombarded the important city of Matanzas, a rich and flourishing point, the outlet of the agricultural districts. April 29 the city of Cienfuegos yielded to our shells, and on the 30th of April the frowning batteries of Cabanas were attacked.

DEWEY'S VICTORY AT MANILA.

The first great naval battle of the war took place on the 1st of May. Those whose opinion was considered valuable, declared that on this battle depended the result of the war—some even prophesying that a victory here would practically end it.

Another matter which engrossed the attention of the governments abroad, was the fact that this encounter would serve as a test of the merits of the modern fighting machine. Should it prove all that was claimed for it, then in truth, a new departure in naval warfare had come.

The eyes of the world were upon the fleet, which, under the command of Commodore George Dewey, was hastening toward Manila, the capital of the Philippines. Just after daylight, Sunday morning of May 1, Manila time, 6 P.M. Saturday, Chicago time, the Olympia opened fire, when two miles away from the enemy. As she drew nearer, she trained every battery upon the Spanish fleet, with deadly effect. When the battle was almost decided, the Reina Christina came out to engage our flagship.

A SUGAR FACTORY IN MANILA

One of the chief productions of the Philippine Islands is sugar. This illustration shows an extensive sugar factory. The square patches are sugar in its raw state, which has been carried from the factory in pelones, or earthenware jars, and deposited in patches in an open space, where it is left to dry under the sun's rays, after the manner of freshly molded bricks in a brick-yard.

She advanced with great bravery, but to no purpose. The big guns on the Olympia struck her fore and aft, totally wrecking her and setting fire to her magazine. The Spanish Admiral, Montejo, was standing on the bridge of his boat, when it was shot from under him. The Spanish sailors escaped into their boats, fleeing from the burning ship. Montejo carried his pennant to the Castilla, but five minutes after that ship was set on fire by the shells.

After two hours' hard fighting, a rest was taken, when the attack was renewed, and at the expiration of a half hour the long-dreaded and much-boasted of Spanish fleet was a name only—nothing was left to tell the tale of her greatness save the transport Manila.

This battle was fought off Cavite, ten miles to the southwest of Manila. The Spanish fleet, of which so much was predicted by Spain, and which met with such a crushing defeat, consisted of the following vessels: Reina Mercedes, cruiser; Reina Christina, cruiser; Isla de Cuba, cruiser; Isla de Luzon, cruiser; Castilla, cruiser; Don Antonio De Ulloa, cruiser; Don Juan de Austria, cruiser; Velasco, cruiser; Elcano, gunboat; General Lezo, gunboat; Marquis del Duero, gunboat; Quiros, gunboat; Villalobos, torpedo gunboat; General Alava, transport; Cebu, transport; Manila, transport; Isla de Mindanao, converted cruiser.

The United States fleet was composed of the Olympia, (flagship), first-class cruiser, Captain C. N. Gridley; Baltimore, protected cruiser, Captain N. M. Dyer; Boston, protected cruiser, Captain Frank Wildes; Raleigh, protected cruiser, Captain J. B. Coghlan; Concord, gunboat, Commander Asa Walker; Petrel, gunboat, Commander E. P. Wood; McCulloch, dispatch boat; Nanshan, collier; Zafiro, collier. The magnificent victory of the American Admiral has made his name famous. His achievement is unparalleled in naval annals, and entitles him to the proud rank of being the greatest of fleet commanders, a worthy pupil of his invincible teacher, David G. Farragut.

The gratitude and admiration of the nation are his. Pres-

REAR ADMIRAL GEORGE DEWEY
Commanding Asiatic Squadron

REAR ADMIRAL
Wm. T. SAMPSON
Commanding North Atlantic
Squadron

CAPTAIN R. D. EVANS
Of the Battleship Iowa

COMMODORE W. S. SCHLEY
Commanding Flying Squadron

CAPTAIN C. V. GRIDLEY
Of the Cruiser Olympia

ident McKinley, as a fitting acknowledgment of his splendid deed, at once appointed him Rear Admiral in the United States Navy, with access of pay.

When the Stars and Stripes were hoisted over the Philippine capital, the rejoicings at home were unbounded. But when the news reached Spain, it produced a contrary effect; the indignation of that power was profound. An uprising of the people was feared, and the governors of all provinces were ordered to place them under martial law at the first serious outbreak. The cable at Manila was cut by orders of Admiral Dewey, and thus the court at Madrid was kept in uncertainty as to what was actually transpiring.

The victory so bravely won was but the predecessor of others which gave every true American a thrill of pride. Admiral Sampson, commander of the North Atlantic squadron, arrived at San Juan de Puerto Rico on the 12th of May, making an early call, as he commenced operations before sunrise, bombarding the fortifications. The first shot was fired from the Iowa, captained by Bob Evans ("Fighting Bob"), and it was followed by the Indiana.

From the halyards of the flagship New York the signal flashed forth—"Remember the Maine!" The big guns pealed forth seven shots, and the works felt their force. Fort Morro was left full of gaps, where the shells had struck it, and torn away the masonry. The frightened populace fled to the interior, beyond the range of the guns. Word had been sent ahead by the commander of the American squadron that the works were to be attacked, thus giving the non-combatants a chance to seek safety.

The first blood on our side was shed at Cardenas, May 12. After a short encounter of thirty-five minutes between the torpedo boat Winslow, the tug Hudson and the gunboat Wilmington on the American side, and the batteries at Cardenas and four Spanish gunboats, our arms were again victorious. Five Americans fell in this engagement. Ensign Worth Bagley of the Winslow, a brave North Carolinian, was the first officer to yield

ADMIRAL PASCUAL DE CERVERA

up his life. It is stated that even after the Winslow's starboard engine and steering gear were useless, the crew kept hurling shot at the Spaniards on shore, until she was totally disabled.

On the next day, May 13, the Flying Squadron left Hampton Roads, and made Key West on the 18th. Santiago was the intended point of attack, and on the 18th also Admiral Sampson thought it time to turn his attention to that place. The second squadron sent out by Spain, under Cervera, lay at that time in the harbor of Santiago, in fancied security.

ROOSEVELT'S ROUGH RIDERS.

On Friday, June 24, a desperate engagement took place between four troops of the First Cavalry, four of the Tenth and eight of Roosevelt's "Rough Riders," who attacked a force of 2,000 Spanish soldiers, twice their number, and sixteen men were killed, among whom were Captain Allyn M. Capron and Hamilton Fish, Jr., belonging to the Rough Riders.

The Rough Riders followed the trail over steep hills that towered many hundred feet high. The weather was intensely warm, and each man carried 200 rounds of ammunition and his heavy camp equipment. On they toiled up the narrow path, often so narrow that they could only go in single file, while the sharp thorns of the prickly cactus tore and scratched them as they passed through the thick underbrush.

As the day grew hotter they threw away blankets and tent rolls, and even emptied their canteens. Soon they heard a call like a cuckoo. Every man was on the alert. They knew now that Spaniards were near, for that was their cry. A charge was ordered, and they dashed into the thicket. The rush was so sudden and bold that a panic ensued among the Spanish soldiers, and after fighting about an hour, they fled, firing as they ran, leaving fifty dead upon the field.

The crack of the Mauser rifles was heard, and the leaves flew from the trees and chips from the fence post were showered over the heads of the Rough Riders. The fire was a heavy one. Sergeant Fish was the first man to fall on our side—shot through

LIEUTENANT HOBSON AND THE SCENES OF HIS HEROIC EXPLOITS

the heart. Although the enemy was but 200 yards away, yet they were so securely hidden in the brush that only a glimpse of them now and then could be seen. Colonel Wood showed remarkable coolness, walking along the lines as he gave orders. Lieutenant Roosevelt rushed into the thicket cheering his men on, who were as anxious as he to reach the hidden foe. Captain Capron held his revolver in hand, and sent several of the Spaniards to the ground. Suddenly his weapon dropped from his hands and he fell, shot through the body. With his dying breath he cried—"Don't mind me, boys, go on and fight." After fifteen minutes more of hot fighting Lieutenant Roosevelt ordered his men back, and just missed a bullet which buried itself in a tree alongside his head. The Spaniards fell back, and ran down one hill and up another to the blockhouse, it was supposed with the intention of making a stand there. Instantly the Americans followed them closely, and poured a storm of bullets into the blockhouse; the Spaniards fled in haste, and the battle was over. This was the first battle which the Rough Riders had taken part in, and they proved their valor and bravery in a brilliant manner.

HOBSON MADE FAMOUS.

One of the most brilliant exhibitions of pure, unselfish courage ever exhibited was the act of Lieutenant Richmond P. Hobson. That officer, who was assistant naval constructor, had succeeded in convincing Admiral Sampson that there was but one way to prevent Admiral Cervera's escape. His daring scheme gave the fleet of the Spanish admiral its death blow. Under the direction of Admiral Sampson he volunteered to take the collier Merrimac into the channel leading into the harbor, and sink it, so as to prevent his escape with his ships. In other words, he literally "bottled" the unlucky Admiral up.

He needed but six men to help him accomplish his purpose. Admiral Sampson explained to the brave sailors that it was a desperate mission, that death was almost certain, and yet when only six volunteers were asked for, over 1,000 responded, anxious,

DESTRUCTION OF CERVERA'S FLEET.
JULY 3, 1898.

MANEUVER OF SHIPS DURING THE FIGHT

glad to be of service to the cause. Tears filled their eyes as they begged for the honor of going with the brave commander who had been chosen for the perilous undertaking, and dying, if need be. It was a gallant deed, and as the Merrimac steamed into the channel, a furious cannonading from the Spanish forts greeted their coming, but on they went into the "very jaws of death," and amid shot and shell Lieutenant Hobson went to the point indicated by Admiral Sampson, anchored, and swung across the channel. Then a hole was blown in the ship's bottom, and a dash was made for a boat. They were loudly cheered by the Spaniards, who were lost in admiration of their heroism, and Cervera himself, although he took them prisoners, sent a flag of truce to Admiral Sampson, by his chief of staff, Captain Oviedo, in honor of their bravery, offering to exchange them without delay for Spanish prisoners in the hands of the United States.

The names of the gallant men who offered their lives so freely were—Daniel Montague, George Charette, J. E. Murphy, Oscar Deignan, John P. Phillips, and John Kelly.

After being kept prisoners from June 2 until July 6, Lieutenant Hobson and the six men who were made prisoners with him, were surrendered by the Spanish military authorities in exchange for prisoners which we held. Captain Chadwick, of the New York, escorted them through our lines. The soldiers were wild with joy, and paid no attention to discipline or order, so anxious were they to see the heroes of the Merrimac, whom they wildly cheered. Lieutenant Hobson talked very little about his experiences, but said the Spanish authorities had treated them well, and their health was excellent.

The bombardment of Santiago's forts was vigorously kept up. On the 22d and 23d General Shafter landed at Baiquiri, and moved toward Santiago. He attacked the Spanish outposts July 1, and a fierce fight raged all day. He demanded the surrender of the latter place. General Lawton carried the heights of San Juan, after a determined charge.

DESTRUCTION OF CERVERA'S FLEET.

Another notable victory, and one of the greatest naval battles ever recorded, was the total destruction of Cervera's proud fleet, which was accomplished by Commodore Schley, on the 3d of July. The American fleet's commander, Sampson, was absent conferring with General Shafter regarding future movements. Meantime the government at Madrid realized that the city must fall sooner or later, and it had ordered Cervera to make one bold dash out of the harbor. This he attempted to do, but was received so warmly by Schley that in two hours the "invincible" fleet of the Spanish admiral was a series of wrecks, strewn along the beach for fifty miles, with a loss of 600 killed, and 1,100 prisoners taken by our forces, among whom was Cervera himself. The attempted escape was made with great courage on the part of the Spaniards, who fought to the last, and when hope was gone, threw themselves upon the mercy of their captors, who accorded them protection from the Cuban insurgents who had watched the battle in all its terrible earnestness.

SURRENDER OF SANTIAGO.

Santiago had not yet yielded, however, and on the 10th of July bombardment of that town was resumed.

The 14th of July saw the long-expected surrender of Santiago to General Shafter, and at 12 o'clock noon, the glorious Stars and Stripes were hoisted over the Governor's palace, and we held the situation. The American general rode into the city escorted by the Second Cavalry. The people were very quiet, many of them even showing satisfaction at the event. Courtesies were exchanged between the Spanish and American officers, and General Shafter returned to General Toral his sword. The Spanish flag was displaced by the American—the eternal symbol of liberty.

On the 26th of July the Spanish government made overtures for peace, through the French ambassador, M. Cambon, who called on our President and by proper authority stated that

Spain was willing to treat with the United States, and would like to consider terms. After discussing the proposal with the Cabinet, President McKinley notified the French ambassador of his ultimatum. The terms of the protocol were these:

"1. That Spain will relinquish all claims of sovereignty over or title to Cuba.

"2. That Puerto Rico and other Spanish islands in the West Indies, and an island in the Ladrones, to be selected by the United States, shall be ceded to the latter.

"3. That the United States will occupy and hold the city, bay, and harbor of Manila pending the conclusion of a treaty of peace which shall determine the control, disposition and government of the Philippines.

"4. That Cuba, Puerto Rico, and other Spanish islands in the West Indies shall be immediately evacuated, and that commissioners to be appointed within ten days shall, within thirty days from the signing of the protocol, meet at Havana and San Juan, respectively, to arrange and execute the details of the evacuation.

"5. That the United States and Spain will each appoint not more than five commissioners to negotiate and conclude a treaty of peace. The commissioners are to meet at Paris not later than the 1st of October.

"6. On the signing of the protocol hostilities will be suspended, and notice to that effect will be given as soon as possible by each government to the commanders of its military and naval forces." ·

The government of Spain sought to evade the payment of the Cuban debt, but President McKinley was firm, and declined to discuss the matter until Spain had accepted his ultimatum. Days passed before our government received notification through M. Cambon that the Spanish ministry had approved of his management of the negotiations, and he had been authorized to sign the protocol. At 4:33 of the same day the agreement was signed by Secretary of State Day on behalf of the United States, and M. Cambon, of France, on behalf of Spain.

MAIN BUSINESS STREET IN MANILA

Our President at once issued a proclamation stating that the United States and Spain had formally agreed upon terms for negotiations through which peace between the two countries should be established, and official orders were sent to the various commanders of the forces of the United States, that all military operations be suspended.

SURRENDER OF MANILA.

But the latter order did not reach Admiral Dewey in time to prevent his adding more luster to his name by uniting his naval forces with the land forces of General Merritt.

July 31 a battle was waged at Malate, a small town half way between Cavite and Manila. Here General Greene was posted with 4,000 men. Our troops were strengthening their position, when the Spaniards attempted to give the Americans a surprise. The rain was pouring down in sheets, the typhoon was raging furiously, and it seemed a most auspicious time for the attack. Three thousand Spaniards were massed in the vicinity. They forced the American pickets in, and assaulted the soldiers in the trenches. But they did not know the men they attacked. The Tenth Pennsylvania stood their ground, and were reinforced by the First California and two companies of the Third Artillery. The mud was up to the axles, the rain and wind raged wildly, and the enemy was on top of the trenches, while they sent a withering fire into the ranks of the Americans, who never wavered, but returned it with earnestness.

The Spaniards retreated in confusion, but were not pursued, as our infantry had exhausted its ammunition. The scene was a thrilling one. Darkness covered the earth, save when a flash of lightning lit up the faces of the dead and wounded, who lay side by side, in the trenches half filled with water which was red with their blood. Not a cry was heard from the lips of the wounded, but they spoke words of cheer to those who were still able to fight.

The fighting began again August 1, but the enemy kept at long range. The next night they made another attack, but were repulsed, with severe loss, 350 killed, 900 wounded, while we lost fourteen, and forty-four wounded.

August 8, Admiral Dewey and General Merritt notified the authorities in Manila that unless they surrendered the city to them in forty-eight hours a combined attack by the land and naval forces might be expected. When that time had expired the Spanish officials asked one day more so that they might remove the women and children, which request was granted.

When the foreign warships were appraised of the intended attack, they prudently got out of range. The English and Japanese warships joined our fleet at Cavite, while the French and German ships went to the north of the city, where they were safe. At 9:35 on Saturday, the 13th, a shell was fired from the Olympia and hissed dangerously near the fort at Malate. The other boats began a rapid fire upon the intrenchments. A few feeble replies came from the Spaniards.

The battle was short. In half an hour General Greene ordered an advance, and six companies of a colored regiment sprang over the breastworks and sought the shelter of some hedges about 300 yards from the Spanish lines. Then the remaining six companies moved along the shore, partly hid by a ridge of sand and at 11 o'clock were in the stronghold.

At this critical moment 2,000 Spanish soldiers came on the scene, but they did not engage the Americans. As soon as the white flag was seen, General Merritt, who had made the steamer Zafiro his headquarters, sent General Whittier, with flag lieutenant Brumby to meet the captain general and discuss a plan of capitulation. The terms were agreed to by Jaudenes, and were as follows:

"An agreement for the capitulation of the Philippines:

"A provision for disarming the men who remain organized under the command of their officers, no parole being exacted.

"Necessary supplies to be furnished from the captured treasury funds, any possible deficiency being made good by the Americans.

"The safety of life and property of the Spanish soldiers and citizens to be guaranteed as far as possible.

"The question of transporting the troops to Spain to be referred to decision of the Washington government, and that of returning their arms to the soldiers to be left to the discretion of General Merritt.

"Banks and similar institutions to continue operations under existing regulations, unless these are changed by the United States authorities."

At once Lieutenant Brumby hastened away to take down the Spanish flag. Two signal men accompanied him. At Fort Santiago, in the north part of the city, they were vigorously hissed when the flag of Spain was hauled down, and the flag of the free rose grandly in its place.

This day's battle resulted in a loss on the American side of eight killed and thirty-four wounded, while the Spanish had 150 killed and 300 wounded.

The Americans captured 11,000 prisoners, 7,000 of them being regulars; 20,000 Mauser rifles, 3,000 Remingtons, eighteen modern cannon, and many of the old pattern.

Thus ended a war which has covered us with glory—a war we did not invite, but which was forced upon us in the interests of humanity; a war which has taught European nations to respect us as a great power. May it be the last which our nation is drawn into. May the dawn of peace herald the day when wars shall be no more; when wise counsels and generous arbitration shall decide questions of moment between nations.

War has a terrible meaning; it means desolated homes, and bitter tears shed for those who come not; it means angry passions and cruel expressions of them; it means want and suffering and the humiliation of defeat for one side or the other. May the days of rancor end forever!

ANNEXATION OF HAWAII.

In connection with the war so recently concluded, we should mention the annexation of the Hawaiian Islands, a measure

NELSON A. MILES—GENERAL COMMANDING THE U. S. ARMY

which has been agitated for many years, and the conflict only increased the sentiment in favor of making them part and parcel of our Republic.

The islands comprise a group of eight, and were discovered by Captain Cook in 1788. They are important to us from their commercial value, and also from their strategic uses, and the necessity for a closer relation has been recognized by nearly every President and Secretary of State through all the successive administrations.

After many long and arduous debates, the vote for and against annexation was taken by Congress, and an overwhelming majority declared in favor of annexation, and Hayti with her vast commerce, her rich agricultural productions became a member of our great body politic, and on Friday, August 12, the American flag waved over Honolulu, the capital of the new "Territory of Hawaii."

PUERTO RICO.

The city of Santiago had not yet fallen. Bombarding had, however, long since ceased, and negotiations for the peaceful surrender of the city had been going on for several days, when General Miles arrived and assumed personal command of the army that was massed there. General Shafter of our forces and General Toral, of the Spanish, could not easily agree as to terms, but on the 16th the conditions of surrender were decided upon. By this agreement, about 5,000 square miles, the capital of the province and the entire army of Toral, fell to our share.

Santiago was ours. The ceremony sealing the surrender was impressive, though simple. Early as 9 o'clock the division and brigade commanders reported to General Shafter, and all took up the line of march toward the city. About halfway, under a lofty tree, General Toral with some of his officers awaited their coming. As General Shafter approached this tree the Spanish general raised his hat with dignified politeness, and the American general returned the bow. Quickly the soldiers of the Spanish side came through the hedge, preceded by the king's guard, 200

HEROIC DASH OF AMERICAN SOLDIERS NEAR SANTIAGO

strong, while two trumpeters and a color bearer led the column. Marching and countermarching they halted in front of our men, and only ten yards away.

Thus they stood, curiosity and excitement plainly visible in their faces, although they were motionless as statues. The trumpets then rang out, a Spanish officer gave a word of command; their colors were lowered to salute ours, they presented arms and their officers removed their hats. Captain Brett gave the word, "Present sabers," and downward flashed our sabers. General Shafter removed his hat, as did his staff. The stillness of the morning air was broken by the command of the officer in charge of the king's guard, they filed past our soldiers, who presented arms until the last man of the guard had gone by. Then the Spaniards marched toward Santiago, stacked their rifles which were of the Mauser pattern, and then, with neither arms nor flags, went back to their camp. Thus ended hostilities around Santiago.

Early in July the yellow fever began to attack the men of Shafter's army, but it was of a mild type, but it would have done incalculable injury had not the officers of the Fifth Army Corps addressed a protest to General Shafter who sent it to the War Department at Washington. The officials there hastened to transport the troops as fast as they could back to the United States and sent "immunes" to Santiago to do garrison duty.

An expedition commanded by Major General Nelson A. Miles left the bay of Guantanamo July 21, and sailed for Puerto Rico, reaching the port of Guanica July 25. This move was intended as a surprise, and a complete one it was to the Spaniards, who did not dream of an army of invasion attacking them. The naval part of the expedition comprised the Columbia, Gloucester, Dixie and Yale, and was in charge of Captain F. J. Higginson. General Miles was on board the Yale. The troops were carried by the transports, of which there were eight. The Gloucester, with the expectation that the harbor was full of mines, went pluckily in, and found five fathoms of water very near shore. The first hint of an invading army at their door, was the boom of a gun, demanding that the Spanish flag come down, from a blockhouse east of the village.

Tney took aim with the next two shots at the hills on either side of the bay, so as not to injure the women and children. The Gloucester then laid to, and sent a launch on shore, without being molested.

Quartermaster Beck sent Yeoman Lacy to haul down the obnoxious flag, and up went our glorious Stars and Stripes, the first that ever floated over the soil of Puerto Rico.

But the Spaniards, though apparently making no resistance, suddenly opened fire with thirty Mauser rifles. Lieutenant Huse and his men, who had gone ashore in the launch, returned the fire with telling effect, their Colt gun being equal to the occasion.

Without waiting, the Gloucester opened fire with all her armament and shelled the town. Lieutenant Huse put up a small fort, calling it Fort Wainwright, and laid down barbed wire so as to repel the cavalry attack, which he expected. A few of the cavalrymen joined those who were fighting, but reinforcements had come for the Americans, and after some more vigorous fighting, at 9:45, with the exception of a few scattering shots, the town was won, and silence succeeded the din of battle.

The plans of General Miles had been faithfully carried out, and he went ashore at noon. He next turned his eyes toward Ponce, determined to shell that town if necessary. While he had given the inhabitants of Puerto Rico a surprise, he received one in return at the hands of the people of Ponce, for when the Wasp steamed up to the shore, instead of a force of soldiers arrayed against them, they found everybody in town had turned out, and was waiting to receive them with open arms. Ensign Curtin stepped nimbly on the beach, as though he did not doubt their sincerity, and was surrounded by people forcing presents upon him and his men, and saluting them with shouts of welcome.

A message was sent to the Spanish commander demanding that the town surrender, and Colonel San Martin acceded at once upon General Miles' assurance that the garrison should be allowed to leave, that the civil government be permitted to continue its functions, that the police and fire brigade patrolled without weapons, and that the captain of the post should not be held a prisoner.

These conditions were reasonable enough, and were acceded to, and the rejoicings of the populace were enthusiastic. It was a genuine ovation, and more like a grand festive occasion than the surrender of a town to a foe.

When General Wilson landed, the local band played ''The Star Spangled Banner.'' The celebration went on, even after the United States troops landed. The people dressed in their finest garments as though it were a holiday, and kept open house.

General Miles issued a proclamation to the effect that our army came not to devastate the land or to interfere with existing laws or customs, and all that he required was obedience and order. He told them that the military forces were brought there to overthrow the arms of Spain and to give them the fullest amount of liberty consistent with the military occupation of their island.

An invitation from the city officials at the city hall was given him, and when he entered the park which surrounded it, the local band played ''See, the Conquering Hero Comes,'' to which he responded by taking off his hat, and saluting the vast crowd. The band then played several of our national airs.

The news that peace was near was a disappointment to General Miles, as he had planned a masterly movement with great care, and had it been carried out it would have taught the Spaniards an invaluable lesson. Puerto Rico was occupied with a very small loss—two killed and thirty-seven wounded.

GENERAL FITZHUGH LEE.

When a successor to the Cuban consul-generalship was needed, President Cleveland selected Fitzhugh Lee for this important post. The health of Ramon Williams, former consul-general, had failed so visibly that he could no longer attend to its

GENERAL FITZHUGH LEE—EX-CONSUL-GENERAL TO HAVANA

arduous demands, and so in the spring of 1896 the choice of the president fell upon Mr. Lee, as the most suitable man for the place.

Fitzhugh Lee was born in Stafford County, Virginia, in 1835, and came of an illustrious family. His grandfather had served in the Revolutionary war, being the famous "Lighthorse Harry," and he himself was the nephew of General Robert E. Lee—both of which facts insure the existence of courage and tact in the subject of our present sketch. His wise and patriotic administration of the duties of his office as consul won for him in a very brief time the confidence and admiration of the entire country, and the judgment of Mr. Cleveland was long since indorsed by it.

His father was an officer in the navy, but the young boy had no taste for a sea-life—his leaning was toward the army. So to West Point he went, from which he graduated in 1856 with a high record, and became a lieutenant of cavalry on the frontier, for five years, repelling the attacks of the Comanche Indians. He received an arrow in his lungs, in one of these engagements, but youth and a good constitution prevailed, and he recovered. He became an instructor in cavalry tactics at West Point, when only twenty-six years of age. But when the civil war broke out, he resigned his commission, and joined the fortunes of the confederacy, where his record as a brave and dashing soldier is well known. It is said of him that he always showed great coolness and composure, in times of battle, never seeming to have any anxiety as to the result. His resolute and daring demeanor was contagious, and he was much beloved by the men whom he commanded.

He is a magnificent horseman. During the war of 1861 he owned a fine mare, Nellie, a graceful creature, to whom he was much attached. She was struck by a shell at the battle of Winchester, and a fragment of the same shell tore her master's leg badly.

All through the war he was a fearless, honest adversary, and when peace came he retired to his native county, where he

GENERAL WESLEY MERRITT

GENERAL JOSEPH C. WHEELER

GENERAL WM. R. SHAFTER

THEODORE ROOSEVELT

GENERAL JOHN R. BROOKE

led the quiet, unpretending life of a farmer and miller.   He was married in 1871, and was peculiarly happy in his home, devoted to his wife and children.

In 1875 he was persuaded to engage in political matters, and was sent to the national convention of 1876 as a delegate. Ten years later he was elected governor of Virginia and served to the complete satisfaction of his people.   His political record is as worthy of the man as was his military, and no finer example of both can be found.   When Mr. Cleveland entered upon his second term he made Fitzhugh Lee collector of internal revenue, at Lynchburg, Virginia.   His official position at Havana remained unchanged, when Mr. McKinley entered the executive chair, the latter being well aware that no better example of what a brave, cultivated and level-headed American gentleman should be, was afforded than by General Lee.   He was respected by the Spanish officials for his firmness in looking after the interests of his countrymen, and his unvarying courtesy to every one with whom he came in contact.

He was, however, treated with great rudeness on his farewell visit to the Spanish Captain-General Blanco, that person refusing to see him, on the pretext of being too busy.   And when he entered the boat which was to bear him to the steamer, the Spanish rabble at the docks showered insulting epithets upon him, but with that dignity which is native to him, he paid no attention to them, but made the remark that he would be back with troops before long, to uphold him.

All honor to General Lee.   He has proven himself capable of self-control, and the man who can govern himself, can govern others successfully.   And we trust that at some future day this gallant and chivalrous soldier may receive some gift at the hands of the nation worthy of his ability.

ADMIRAL GEORGE DEWEY.

To speak of this brave sailor as a hero, is to utter but faint praise.   He was born in Montpelier, Vermont, sixty-one years ago, and was the youngest of three boys.   Not one of his elders could have foreseen, when he was a boy, how proud they would become at a future day, of their young townsman. As a boy he was full of mischief, loving adventure and ever ready for anything that came along. In fact this great man was just like all other boys —he felt the world was his, and all that was in it, to enjoy! At school he proved himself an apt student, quick to comprehend his lessons, and a ringleader in all kinds of sport, but hating anything small or mean in his associates. He was also a great favorite with older people.

He came of a prominent family, his father being a doctor, and two of his name, both nephews, are said to inherit much of the Dewey talent. When he was a lad, the town of Montpelief was very small, but it had great pretensions, as it was the capital of the State, and naturally attracted the best elements of society, men and women of education and character, the former of whom had been chosen to represent the people of the State in her legislative halls. In such an atmosphere of culture young Dewey grew into manhood, and to his early advantages (his parents holding high social standing) he owes that polish of manner which he is said to possess in a remarkable degree.

He was much of a reader when he was a youth, and the books he read were upon naval matters. Sea stories and tales of travel were his delight. It is told of him about this time, to show how little he waited for events to shape themselves, that he planned to go on a fishing excursion with two schoolmates. The hour was to be four in the morning, but he was not to be found, and so they started for the river without him. When they reached the fishing grounds he had been there two hours, and had an enormous string of trout which he had caught. At the time the boys called it unfair, but in telling it now, the narrator calls it a good evidence of his habit of doing for himself, and not waiting for anyone's prompting. As he expressed it,—"You see he didn't wait till next morning before going into Manila harbor."

His fondness for the water led him to spend his play hours on rafts and on an old ferry which was not used by the town.

Once he thought he'd cross the ferry in an old leaky buggy of his father's. Not being able to get the horse into the water, he took the box off the running gear and tried to run it across as a boat. He came very near drowning, and would have perished but for timely assistance.

His birthplace has sent forth many notable people, lawyers, doctors, statesmen, but of all the renowned names she claims, her greatest boast is that Commodore Dewey was born within her limits.

He was sent to the military school at Norwich, Vermont, at the age of fifteen. Here he stayed two years, at the end of which he concluded that he would rather enter the navy than be a land soldier. His father was a man of influence, and easily got him appointed at Annapolis.

In the year 1858 he graduated, and passed three years of service aboard ship before the war of 1861 broke out. He received his commission as lieutenant on the 19th of April, 1861, a few days before Fort Sumter was fired upon. He was sent at once to the steam sloop Mississippi, which joined the West Gulf squadron, and he was with Admiral Farragut when that gallant sailor forced an entrance to the Mississippi River.

The boat had a hot fight in March, 1863, when it tried to pass the Confederate batteries at Port Hudson. A heavy fog prevailed, so dense not an object could be seen; they lost their bearings, and ran into shore right under the guns of one of their heaviest batteries. They were the recipients of 250 shots, which tore the boat from one end to the other, but the gloom of the fog proved a blessing, after all, as it enabled the crew to take to their boats and escape, after setting their sloop on fire.

In 1870 he was given his command, when he did good work on the Narragansett. Until 1876 he surveyed the Pacific coast, when he became inspector of lighthouses.

He commanded the Juniata in 1882-83, and was made a captain in September, 1884, when he took charge of the Dolphin. This boat was one of the four vessels comprising the original "White Squadron." Honors still flowed in upon him, for the

AMERICAN PEACE COMMISSIONERS

EX. SECT'Y OF STATE, WM. R. DAY

SENATOR CUSHMAN K. DAVIS,
of Minnesota

SENATOR W. P. FRYE,
of Maine

SENATOR GEORGE GRAY,
of Delaware

WHITELAW REID,
of New York

next year he took command of the Pensacola, belonging to the European squadron, on which he stayed till 1888, when he was made chief of the bureau of equipment and recruiting, as Commodore. This position he filled until 1893, when he became a member of the lighthouse board.

It was not until February 28, 1896, that he received the commission of Commodore, and in January, 1898, he was placed in command of the Asiatic squadron.

But it remained for him to eclipse all records in his daring fight at Manila, which is probably the greatest naval battle ever fought, and ranks its commander among those names that will never be forgotten. The action was so brilliant, so decisive, that President McKinley named him for a rear admiral in the United States Navy, and the Senate without a dissenting voice confirmed the nomination. He deserved it richly, and great as is the honor, still greater is the esteem, the love, the gratitude of the American nation for this grandest of naval commanders—George Dewey, the generous and manly conqueror on the sea.

ACTING REAR ADMIRAL SAMPSON.

This distinguished and gallant officer is a native of New York, he having been born at Palmyra, that State, fifty-eight years ago.

He was a boy of very industrious habits. Loving the sea with ardor, his sole ambition was to obtain a nautical education. But he was not rich in this world's goods, and he could not go to Annapolis unless he could earn the money in some way to pay for his training there. So he worked as farmer's boy, raking hay and splitting rails, or doing any labor that would bring him the coveted reward.

But though he was not rich, he had friends who admired his manly spirit, and among them was Congressman E. B. Morgan, of New York, who used his influence to get him appointed to the naval school toward which his eyes so longingly turned. Here he proved worthy of the privilege, and when he graduated in 1860, when just twenty years of age, he held the rank of Lieutenant, and was put on the frigate Potomac, where he became master, then executive officer of the Patapsco. This boat met a hard fate, being blown up in the harbor of Charleston in 1865.

His promotions came rapidly, first being made Lieutenant-Commander in the navy, then Captain, and finally Acting Rear Admiral.

But it is not alone as a sea commander that he has won renown. He has served as a member of the Board of Fortifications and Defences, Superintendent of the Naval Academy at Annapolis, Chief of the Bureau of Naval Ordinance, and he was also President of the Maine Board of Inquiry.

He does not enjoy the sweets of domestic life to any great extent, his time on shore being so limited; but he is very happily married, and passes all of his leisure with his wife, and sons and daughters, in his beautiful home in Glenridge, New Jersey.

COMMODORE W. S. SCHLEY.

Among the "boys" of 1861 may be mentioned Admiral Schley, whose deeds have given him a world-wide fame. He was of the class of 1860. Winfield Scott Schley was a midshipman in the early days of the civil war, and many are the comical stories told of his youthful days—among others, was that this now redoubtable commander was dubbed "Peggy," owing to the "trousers" he wore in those days, which were excessively peg-topped, or balloon-shaped. Another story is that he had a very small foot, No. 5 fitting it easily. Of this fact he was boyishly vain. He did duty on the Niagara at that period, and his pranks were numerous, for he had a great love of fun, and yet was a very orderly, well-disciplined sailor.

He graduated near the foot of his class, so he could not have been very studious, however, his after career has been one series of brilliant successes.

Commodore Schley was born near Frederick, Maryland, in

1839, and even as a baby came under military influence, for his
father, who had served in the navy in the war of 1812, was very
friendly with General Scott, and named the child after that
warrior. His early ancestors were stanch Huguenots, coming to
this country after the revocation of the Edict of Nantes, and
one of them was afterward a Governor of Georgia.

He entered the Naval Academy in 1856, remaining there
till 1861. He was given duty then, being assigned to the frigate
Potomac, and a year later received command of the Winona,
which belonged to the blockading squadron of the West Gulf.
He knew real war, for he was in many skirmishes on the Mississippi, and in July, 1862, became Lieutenant, serving with distinction from 1864 to 1866 as executive officer of the Wateree,
a steam gunboat, at the Pacific station.

He received a gold medal from Congress, and the position
of Chief of Bureau of Equipment from President Arthur, afterward being made Captain, for his bravery in rescuing Lieutenant
Greeley and six others at Cape Sabine, and carrying them
safely home.

He wedded a lovely young woman, Miss Nannie Franklin,
at that time the belle of Annapolis. He has two sons, one
Frank, an officer in the army, the other, Winfield Scott Schley,
Jr., is a physician of great repute in New York City. His
daughter, Virginia, is the wife of an Englishman of position.

ENSIGN WORTH BAGLEY.

Life is sweet to all—especially so to the young. And yet
it is sweeter to die for one's country; to know that the last
throb of the heart beat for the cause of liberty and humanity.
Such a fate was that of young Ensign Worth Bagley, the first
officer to fall in our late war with Spain. The life of this young
man was brief, to have achieved so much; he was only twenty-
four years old, having been born in Raleigh, North Carolina, on
the 6th of April, 1874. Yet he had known in that short time
all of life's experiences—pleasure, pain and honors—all compressed

into the few years of his existence. His father was an editor
and a lawyer, and enlisted in the first company raised on the
Confederate side in the county in which he lived. He fought
bravely, and never abandoned the fortunes of the Confederacy
until 1864, when he went home on parole, and was elected to
the Senate of his State.

His son, young Worth, a fitting name for the boy, had cause
to be proud of his ancestry, on both sides, his father's family
being well versed in law, politics and business, and his mother's
family being originally Quakers. She was the daughter of one
of the governors of Virginia.

But Worth Bagley's boyhood engages the attention of the
young, most. He grew up under good influences, and as a boy
was a model of courtesy and gentlemanly bearing; a favorite in
the schoolroom or playground, he loved his home, and was equally
beloved within its walls. Possessed of a noble and unselfish
nature, how could it be otherwise than that he met appreciation?
He was a very apt scholar, learning rapidly, and retaining it as
firmly.

His father died when he was twelve, and it is a beautiful
record that he became his mother's comfort. He was the oldest
son, and seemed to feel that she needed his counsel and protection.

When only ten he entered a classical school, with the intention of preparing for college. He loved the sea, and was
appointed a cadet at the naval academy at Annapolis, when he
was a little over fifteen, the youngest member of his class.
How happy he was when he received the appointment. He
was of a sunny temper, full of jests and laughter, writing the
most loving letters to his "dearest little mother," as he called
her. He despised anything that took on the character of tat-
tling. "Hazing" was strictly forbidden at the Academy, but he
was subjected to it, and when called before the commandant
and asked the names of the classmen who had participated
in it, he answered firmly that he meant no disrespect, but he
considered it dishonorable to tell on his classmates. He was
threatened with punishment, unless he would tell, but he still

refused, and was sent to a ship which was used as a place of
severe discipline for cadets who disobeyed any of the rules.
Here he was kept eighteen days in confinement, and possibly
he would have remained a good many days longer, had not the
cadets who had done the hazing confessed their share in it, and
begged for his release.

When the time came for his examination he fell below the
mark, and he wrote at once to his mother, giving her the reasons
for his failure, and saying that he hoped the Hon. B. H. Bunn,
Member of Congress whose influence had secured him the appointment, would use it in his behalf once more. Mrs. Bagley
took the letter to that gentleman, and he promptly made out
the papers for the grateful boy. All went smoothly after this,
and he graduated in the class of 1895, when he was put on the
receiving ship Vermont, and one month after he went to the
cruiser Montgomery. Again he was transferred to the Texas in
October. On the 20th of January, 1896, he was sent to the ill-
fated Maine, where he remained six months, then being sent
back to the Texas, which boat he remained with till he returned
to Annapolis to take his final examination, which was successful,
for he was made an ensign on the 1st of July, 1897.

He was quite a musician, and sang in the Naval Academy
choir. His letters home were gems of wit, breathing the most
sincere devotion to his friends.

His first service as ensign was on the Indiana, but three
months of 1897, from August 17 to November 19, were passed
on the Maine, as executive clerk to Captain Sigsbee. He was
then ordered to Baltimore as inspector of the Columbian Iron
Works, which firm was fitting out the torpedo boat Winslow.

When Lieutenant Bernadou was given command of this
boat he sought for the best junior officers, and among the names
presented Worth Bagley's stood high, but he was reluctant to
leave Captain Sigsbee, to whom he was much attached, and to
whom his services were almost invaluable. But he was persuaded
to accept the post offered, and on the 28th of December he
entered on his duties.

He was a hero. He went out in a lifeboat, with two sailors, and rescued two men who were adrift on a scow some fifty miles from New York, with a frightful storm raging, and brought them aboard. The Secretary of the Navy wrote a letter of approval to Lieutenant Bernadou, Ensign Bagley and the crew, commending the heroism of all on the Winslow.

Of the fatal engagement in Cardenas Bay, May 11, 1898, the whole world knows. He gave his life for his country on that day, without fear or flinching, his last words being as cheerful as though it was a holiday. There was some delay in heaving the towline and he called out cheerily—"Heave her. Let her come—it's getting pretty warm here." They were the last orders this brave and grand young officer ever gave. The next moment the bursting of one of the enemy's shells sent Ensign Bagley to his last home.

May his life be an incentive to the young, to do their duty in all situations and in all places as nobly and faithfully as did this brave boy.

OUR NAVY.

Nearly every one understands the terms used in the military branch of service, but since the war has had such extensive use for the naval forces, and so many engagements have taken place on the sea, it has been the source of much perplexity as to the various titles in use by the navy department.

When older and wiser heads are puzzled by the many terms, it is necessary that our young readers receive a little instruction as to their meaning. We therefore give them in full, knowing that the boys (and the girls also) will be pleased to learn that officers are divided into two classes—the line or navigating, and fighting officers, and the staff, or specialists, such as engineer, medical, pay, construction corps, the civil engineers and chaplains. The grades of the line officers are rear admiral, commodore, captain, commander, lieutenant-commander, lieutenant, lieutenant junior grade, ensign, naval cadet.

Of the staff officers the engineers have three grades—chief

engineer, passed assistant engineer and assistant engineer. The medical corps is divided into medical director, medical inspector, surgeon, passed assistant surgeon, assistant surgeon. The pay corps includes in order pay directors, pay inspectors, paymasters, passed assistant paymasters, assistant paymasters. The construction corps comprises naval constructor and assistant naval constructor. Then there are the chaplain, civil engineer and professor of mathematics. Before one comes to the enlisted men are the boatswain, gunner, sailmaker and carpenter; the enlisted men or crew are divided into three classes—seamen, artificers and *special* class.

The pay of the officers varies from $500 a year, which the naval cadets get, to $6,000 paid rear admirals. Each officer at sea is allowed thirty cents a day for rations. This thirty cents he may turn into cash and pocket, for officers pay for their food and uniforms out of their own salary. If he desires the officer may actually draw the rations instead, but most of them prefer their private larder.

The enlisted men in the navy are paid from $9 a month—apprentices of the third class—to $65 or $70 a month—chief machinists. The insignia of their rank worn by the multitude of officers great and small is quite bewildering and unintelligible to the uninstructed dweller on land, so many and different are the stars, crosses, bands, colors and chevrons.

CONCLUSION.

The author's labors are finished; but it is with almost a feeling of sadness that he parts company with those for whose pleasure he has told his experiences. In the pages of this volume the man has lived again his days of boyhood when his heart was aglow with the fire of youth and patriotism, as his country called him to the battlefield. Of the many painful scenes, of the tedious marches, privations and dangers, that war ever brings, he has told the boys and girls who have followed his transcript of those days. Another war has been forced upon us, and the man feels the same ardor burn within his breast, the same longing to join the ranks as he did in the far-away days of '61.

True, this war that has just ended was not so terrible in its aspect as was that one which roused his youthful energy, for that was a contest between brothers, the late one was between our forces and those of another clime, but none the less sad and gloomy were its accompaniments. But one glad ray of brightness cheered the gloom. The nation has joined hands and those who were once divided have together fought valiantly for one common cause—the honor of their country. From the far-off North and the sunny South, the boys in blue and gray have taken up arms and stood side by side, equally heroic, equally ready to defend the right. Is not this a cause for thankfulness?

Shall we not have still greater cause for joy when strife shall cease forever—the strife that brings bloodshed in its train? Will not the whole earth be purer and better were it to accept the grand invitation of the Czar of all the Russias, to consider a plan by which friendly relations shall be established all through the world? He proposes laying aside the weapons of war, and disbanding great armies—thus bringing about a time of universal peace, when questions of possession and precedence may be decided by arbitration. This noble plan is a step toward that brotherhood of nations which alone can make them truly great. No exigency could arise which could not be settled by an appeal to the calm judgment and love of fair play which would prevail.

This beautiful thought is possible, and we welcome the coming of that glad day when "wars and rumors of wars shall cease."